"It's quite impossible," Catherine said softly. "My father would never allow such a match."

"Then you have no objection to my approaching him?" Raven asked calmly.

"You intend to approach my father?" she repeated unbelievingly, incredulous that he didn't seem to understand the width of the gap that lay between them.

"Yes."

"With that proposition?"

"Not couched in precisely those terms," he said, amusement in his voice. "Simply as an offer for your hand."

"He'll have you thrown out," she warned.

"Will he?" he asked, sounding interested. "I wonder how."

"By the servants," she responded with deliberate bluntness, finally angered at his continual mockery of the reality of the world she lived in. Coal merchants, however wealthy, did *not* ask for the hand of the Duke of Montfort's daughter.

"I should like to see them try," Raven suggested softly, and found that he really would. He'd *damn* well like to see them try…!

Dear Reader,

When an American businessman and a British heiress agree to a marriage of convenience, both are in danger in *Raven's Vow*, a dark new Regency novel from former March Madness/Romance Writers of America RITA Award nominee Gayle Wilson, the author of *The Heart's Desire*. Don't miss this exciting new tale from this talented author.

Elizabeth Mayne, another March Madness/RITA Award nominee author, is also out this month. *Lord of the Isle* is a classic Elizabethan tale featuring an Irish nobleman who unwittingly falls in love with a rebel from an outlawed family. Ana Seymour's *Lucky Bride* is a sequel to *Gabriel's Lady*. Set in Wyoming Territory, it's a delightful story of a ranch hand who joins forces with his beautiful boss to save her land from a dangerous con man.

Our fourth title for the month, *The Return of Chase Cordell*, is a new Western from Linda Castle, who is fast becoming one of our most popular authors. It's a poignant love story about a war hero with amnesia who rediscovers a forgotten passion for his young bride.

Whatever your taste in reading, we hope you'll enjoy all four of these terrific stories. Please keep an eye out for them wherever Harlequin Historicals are sold.

Sincerely,

Tracy Farrell
Senior Editor

Please address questions and book requests to:
Harlequin Reader Service
U.S.: 3010 Walden Ave., P.O. Box 1325, Buffalo, NY 14269
Canadian: P.O. Box 609, Fort Erie, Ont. L2A 5X3

Gayle Wilson

Raven's Vow

Harlequin Books

TORONTO • NEW YORK • LONDON
AMSTERDAM • PARIS • SYDNEY • HAMBURG
STOCKHOLM • ATHENS • TOKYO • MILAN
MADRID • WARSAW • BUDAPEST • AUCKLAND

ISBN 0-373-28949-9

RAVEN'S VOW

Copyright © 1997 by Mona Gay Thomas

This edition published by arrangement with Harlequin Books S.A.

® and TM are trademarks of the publisher. Trademarks indicated with
® are registered in the United States Patent and Trademark Office, the
Canadian Trade Marks Office and in other countries.

Printed in U.S.A.

Books by Gayle Wilson

Harlequin Historicals

The Heart's Desire #211
The Heart's Wager #263
The Gambler's Heart #299
Raven's Vow #349

GAYLE WILSON

teaches English and history to gifted high school students. Her love of both subjects naturally resulted in a desire to write historical fiction. After several years as the wife of a military pilot, she returned with her husband to live in Alabama, where they had both grown up.

You can contact her at: P.O. Box 342, Birmingham, AL 35201-0342.

For my beloved sister Joy

Prologue

London, 1826

"What you need, Mr. Raven, is a wife."

The tall man at the window turned, a slight indentation deepening the corners of the hardest mouth Oliver Reynolds had seen in his seventy years. He had learned through experience that the look John Raven was now directing toward him was intended to indicate amusement.

"A wife?" the American repeated, that amusement now touching the rich tones of his voice as it had marked the stern lips.

"Unless, of course," the banker continued with the merest trace of sarcasm, "you have a duke hidden away somewhere in your family tree. Or an earl. Short of that, sir, I'm afraid..." The old man let the suggestion trail off. He had made his point, and he knew his client's ready intelligence needed no more prompting.

Oliver Reynolds had been paid, extremely *well* paid, to guide this American nabob through the perils of London society, and the solution he had just broached to John Raven was really the best advice he had to offer.

"Three of my grandparents fled Scotland after the '45, half a step ahead of Cumberland's butchers," John Raven confessed. The mockery lurking in those strange, crystalline blue eyes proved his very New World lack of embarrassment over the mode of his ancestors' departure from the

Old. He had been born on the edge of the American wilderness and had watched the influx of settlers move across the land, always westward toward the great river. His country was changing, the vast forest tracts gradually giving way to farms and communities, the conquest of its wildness the result of the hard work of people like his parents and his grandparents.

"In that case—" the banker began, only to be cut off by the sardonic voice.

"My paternal grandmother, however, was a princess."

"A princess?" Oliver Reynolds repeated carefully. "Royalty, Mr. Raven? And from what dynasty did this fortuitous ancestor spring? Despite its supposed sophistication, the British nobility still finds a certain fascination in foreign royalty."

"The Mauvilla, Mr. Reynolds."

"Mauvilla," the old man repeated, trying to think. "I don't believe I'm familiar with that particular family."

"They defied de Soto, virtually destroying themselves in the process. My grandmother was the last of the royal line."

"De Soto?" the banker questioned. He had heard the name, of course, in conjunction with the exploration of the American continent. Surely, Mr. Reynolds thought, those who had defied him would not be mentioned in the context of royal families.

"Indian?" He spoke his sudden realization aloud, his voice rising. But even as he did, he acknowledged that the heritage John Raven had just confessed would explain so much. The American's coloring, for example—the bronze skin that offered such a striking contrast to the clear blue eyes. And his hair, of course. "Indian," the old man said again, an affirmation that put so many pieces of the puzzle John Raven had represented into place.

Raven's dark head inclined slightly in agreement. The small upward tilt at the corners of his mouth increased minutely. "Indian," he agreed softly. "Do you think they'll be impressed?"

"I should think," the banker began, wondering how to warn him without being too offensive, "that you should be damnably certain this noble mob never finds out about your grandmother."

"Not royal enough for our purposes?" Raven suggested easily as he moved back to the chair he had earlier occupied.

Watching his client traverse the short distance, Oliver Reynolds inventoried his recent accomplishments. The American's shoulders were now shown to advantage by Weston's expert tailoring, the coat of navy superfine covering their broad width without a wrinkle. Underneath, a striped French silk waistcoat was discreetly visible. Fawn pantaloons stretched over the flat stomach and accented the firmness of long, muscular thighs. Tasseled Hessians fashioned by Hoby's master hand completed the picture of elegance that finally matched the vast wealth the American had brought from the East into the English capital.

On his arrival in London, John Raven had sought Reynolds's advice and had, surprisingly, followed it to the letter. Except for one thing, the banker thought with regret. The only concession he had been able to wrest from his client regarding the length of his hair was compromise satisfactory to neither. The American had agreed to secure the dark strands, their blue-black gleam rivaling the feathers of the bird whose name he bore, into a queue tied with a black silk ribbon. He had adamantly refused to cut it, and given, of course, the startling revelation he had just made, Reynolds at last understood.

"If words gets out about *that*, Mr. Raven, you won't need a wife. A fairy godmother, perhaps. Or a guardian angel."

"A fairy godmother who'd wave her wand to make me acceptable? An angel to ensure that my many faults are hidden under the splendor of her wings?" the American jeered quietly, not bothering to hide his frustration.

Damn them, John Raven thought bitterly. He'd come to England to build. Instead, he had found the doors to those gracefully proportioned drawing rooms and exclusive clubs where the real power resided closed to him because he was an outsider.

The arrogant, pompous bastards. He had visited their
tailors and their boot makers, and Raven knew—because he
was certainly no one's fool—that he was as well dressed as
any man in London. And as wealthy. Still they refused to
deal with him. Because he wasn't a member of their bloody
ton.

"I've told you before. You'll never find a more closed or
closed-minded circle in the world," Reynolds said. "They'll
back the outrageous schemes of the most profligate
bounder, drunkard or scoundrel of their own class, but an
outsider? You had as well have stayed in India and attempted to do business from there as to try to force your way
in. You can't make them invest."

"They won't even meet me. Polite refusals is all I've gotten. If only they'd listen, they would know that what I propose is not only advantageous to Britain, but profitable for
investors as well. Why the hell won't they listen?"

"Because you don't belong. Birth is the only membership in this society, and yours is unacceptable. You need a
wife whose place within the ton is so secure that she will be
able to win you a grudging entry by virtue of her own con-
nections."

"How do you propose that I convince this paragon to
marry me? Introduce her to my grandmother?" Raven
countered with savage politeness.

"The usual procedure is to offer enough money that her
family can't refuse."

"Buy her, do you mean?"

"It's done everyday. Not in those terms, of course.
However, that is the general idea. You certainly have the
funds. All we need to do is find some impoverished noble-
woman whose family is willing to marry her off in return for
a guarantee of financial security for themselves for the rest
of their lives."

"I thought slavery in Britain disappeared with the Sax-
ons," Raven commented bitterly. "I damn well don't intend to buy a wife. I wouldn't want a woman who'd be
willing to sell herself."

"I suppose," the banker said carefully, recognizing the truth in the American's argument, "that most of them aren't."

"I beg your pardon?"

"Willing," Oliver Reynolds explained regretfully.

"Good God," Raven said with a trace of horror. "And they would call my grandmother's people savage. I won't buy a wife, Mr. Reynolds, willing or unwilling. If the mines and railroads I came to Britain to build don't become a reality, then the bastards will have only themselves to blame."

Fighting to control his anger, John Raven descended the stairs that led from the old man's office. If buying a wife was what it would take to succeed in England, he would damn well find somewhere else to invest his energies.

Raven moved from the narrow flight of stairs onto the street with an unconscious grace, a smooth athleticism that had already attracted attention in the capital. More than one pair of female eyes, accustomed to the sometimes delicate fragility of the gentlemen who set the mode for London society, had on occasion during the last month followed that purposeful stride.

The feminine voice that attracted his attention now, despite the bustle of traffic that rushed past the bank, did so by the sharpness of its tone, and not because of Reynolds's suggestion.

"If you strike him again, I shall have my groom take that stick from you and apply it to *your* back."

The peddler paused in his determined attempts to move the pitiful creature fastened between the wooden tongues of his overloaded cart. Unable to pull the burden up the inclined street, the small donkey stood shivering and flinching under the blows from the rattan stick the man was using as encouragement.

The words had stopped the cruelty momentarily, but the face of the man who turned to confront the girl on horseback reflected neither embarrassment nor regret for her reprimand. Instead, the coarse features were reddened with anger.

The gleam of pure hatred that had shone briefly from the mud-colored eyes made John Raven take an automatic step closer to the scene. His forward progress was halted when the lady's groom swung down easily from his saddle. Although not up to Raven's size, he certainly appeared to be of a bulk sufficient to handle whatever threat the wizened driver represented.

"Lighten the load of your wagon," the girl ordered. "He can't possibly pull that heap." The truth of her statement was obvious to the onlookers, but until she had stopped the beating, none of them had considered the unfairness of the man's actions.

"I don't have time to be coddling him. Lazy is what he is, my lady," the peddler said, removing the shapeless felt that served as his hat. "He can pull the load. Always has. It's just temperament," the man assured her, his ingratiating smile revealing blackened teeth. "Nothing to concern your ladyship."

"If you beat your animal to death in the public street, it should be of concern to *someone*," the girl said, giving no quarter, and at the same time controlling the skittering side steps of her restive mare.

The thin lips of the American lifted slightly in admiration of that assessment, and the shrewd blue eyes took their own inventory. The black habit the girl wore was heavily frogged with silver, the darkness of its high collar and the matching cravat stark against the porcelain of her skin. Strands of dark auburn hair had escaped the modish hat and veil to curl around her heart-shaped face. Despite the perfection of her features, it was her eyes that held Raven's fascinated gaze. Clear russet, they were the exact color of leaves turning under the touch of autumn's chill. At this moment, they were fixed with determined concentration on the hawker, totally unaware of the interested bystanders.

"It be necessary 'times to prod him, ladyship. Animals don't feel the blows like we do. Don't trouble yourself about the beast. He'll pull it, I promise, 'ere I've done with him."

As an accompaniment to his last words, he turned back to the small animal, raising the stick high in the air to bring it down again in the whistling arc that had first attracted the girl's attention. This time its fall across the trembling back was arrested, the thin rattan captured by a slender gloved hand.

"I said no more. Unload the cart," she ordered. The fury in her eyes brooked no defiance.

"I've no time to be unloading. And who's to guard what I leave? You're thinking my goods will still be here when I return, are you? This ain't Mayfair, your highness."

At the taunting incivility, the girl's lips tightened. She gestured to the groom, who took the captured stick from the peddler's hand and broke it quickly across his knee.

"How much?" she asked.

The vendor paused, seeing his livelihood threatened, but at the same time greedily calculating what he could get from the lady. "For the donkey?"

"Donkey, cart, load. Whatever it takes to free the creature," the girl suggested. There was no trace of impatience in her voice now. She watched the man's devious expression impassively.

"If I sells my kit, I've no way to make me living."

"The donkey then."

"But without me donkey—" he began to argue.

"Get the constable," the girl ordered her groom, who turned almost before she had finished speaking, his intent too clear for the man to doubt that he would do exactly as she'd commanded.

"Two quid," the peddler suggested, a ridiculous amount.

"All right," she agreed. "Give my groom your name and lodging and he'll bring it round to you this afternoon. Get the donkey, Jem," Catherine Montfort ordered, turning her mare away from the scene, already late for her appointment in Hyde Park.

The peddler began to protest as the groom efficiently dealt with the traces. "You'll not be taking property without paying me. How do I know you'll send him with the money? How do I know this ain't a plot to steal a poor man's livelihood? I'm the one who'll be calling the constable, I think, if you take the beast. I knows me rights, nobs or no," he finished belligerently, pulling against the line the groom was using as a lead rope. "Here, you, give me back me donkey."

Catherine Montfort's lips tightened in frustration. She had no money with her, of course, and she doubted Jem would be able to come up with that much. Glancing at the groom, who was still in control of the exhausted donkey, she saw him shake his head in response to her unspoken question. She had no option but to send home for the amount and try to stop the hawker from leaving in the meantime.

"If I might be allowed to offer assistance," a deep, accented voice at her elbow suggested.

She glanced down into the bluest eyes she had ever encountered. The clear, rare color of a summer sky, they were set like jewels in the golden skin surrounding them, emphasized by small, white lines radiating around the crystal blue and the black sweep of lashes.

A man who'd lived a long time in a climate where the sun left its mark, she thought briefly. He was very tall, tall enough that she needn't look down far to be lost in those blue depths. She watched as his hand, lean, long fingered and remarkably graceful, automatically smoothed the sweating neck of her impatient mare. He whispered something, the words too softly spoken for Catherine to make sense of the soothing sibilants, and Storm's ears flickered with interest.

Amazingly, as he continued to whisper, Catherine could feel the tension caused by the street's commotion and the delay in the promised run leave her mount. Storm turned to nuzzle those strong fingers, and Catherine found herself watching their caress with something approaching fascination. "Two quid, I believe," the stranger said.

Still disconcerted, Catherine nodded. She watched him give Storm one last competent stroke and then walk to the waiting peddler. If Jem's intimidating size had affected the man, he had given no sign of it, but his response to the American seemed one almost of fear. His instinctive recoil when the tall man held out his hand brought a brief reactive movement to those thin lips. Raven waited patiently until the peddler had worked up his courage to take the money and restore his cap to his head.

Slipping between the wooden tongues in the donkey's place, the vendor awkwardly turned the heavily loaded cart so that it was now headed down the slight incline. The three watched as the wagon gathered momentum on the slope and the usual street sounds again intruded into the stage where the drama had been played out.

Raven turned back to the girl to find her eyes no longer watching the merchant's retreating figure, but on him. She was questioning the color of his skin, he supposed, or his hair. Making her fascinated distaste apparent. He didn't know why her frank appraisal bothered him. He had certainly grown accustomed to the stares he'd attracted in London in the last few months.

"Thank you," she said simply, her eyes meeting his. She held out the small gloved hand that had caught the peddler's stick. Not to be kissed, Raven realized, but to be shaken.

Her hand was almost lost in his, but her grip was pleasantly firm. He controlled the quick amusement at the sight of those slender fingers captured by his hard, dark ones.

"If you'll give Jem your address—" she began.

"Consider him a gift," he interrupted softly, and watched her eyes flick quickly to the animal he'd just bought. Head drooping, the donkey stood patiently waiting for the next blow to fall. In several places where the stick had cut, blood oozed.

The girl's lips tightened and she took a deep breath. For the first time an emotion besides anger tinged her voice. "Damned bastard," she whispered. Realizing that she'd spoken the epithet aloud, she glanced quickly at the American. The russet eyes swam with tears, but before they could overflow, she blinked, a fall of impossibly long, dark lashes concealing feelings Raven read quite clearly.

"Thank you," she said again, looking down into that strong-featured face. Something in the crystalline eyes had changed. And he made no response to her gratitude.

"For my gift," she explained softly, her lips lifting into the smile that had set masculine pulses hammering since she'd turned fourteen. Catherine Montfort thought of all the presents she had received from suitors in the last three years, not one of whom had, of course, thought to give her an abused donkey.

There was no response in the still, dark face. Not handsome, Catherine thought; it was too strongly constructed to be called handsome. But there was something, some indefinable something in the hawklike nose and high cheekbones that was very appealing. And in his eyes, she thought again. She had never seen eyes that shade of blue.

Raven became aware suddenly that she was talking to him, but he didn't have any idea what she had said. Something about a gift. Something... He took a deep breath, realizing that air was a necessity he had neglected in the last minute. The perfection of the heart-shaped face floated before him against the background of clouds and sky.

"Angel," he said softly in his grandmother's tongue, although the word's connotation there was not exactly the same. Oliver Reynolds had told him he'd need a guardian angel. The stern line of John Raven's lips tilted upward at the corners.

Catherine Montfort found that her hand was still resting in his and her throat had gone dry. The small movement of his mouth fascinated her until she recognized the expression for what it was—he was smiling at her.

Sensing her inattention, Storm sidestepped suddenly, and the pull against their joined hands broke the spell. Reluctantly, Catherine disentangled her fingers. She had thanked the man twice, and there was really nothing else she could say. She didn't even know his name. She might never know it. She'd never seen him before and would, in all probability, never see him again. He was certainly not a member of the select group, the London ton, with whom she associated, the only people with whom she had associated since her birth. What had happened today was simply a chance meeting with a stranger on a crowded London street.

Raven stepped back, clearing the way for her departure. Her boot heel touched Storm in command, and, her back flawlessly straight, Catherine Montfort directed her mount around the donkey and back on the course of her normal activities.

John Raven watched the slight figure until it was lost in the throng of riders and carriages. Realizing that he had been staring far too long for politeness, he turned back to find the groom carefully inspecting the animal's injuries.

"Shall I find him a home?" Raven asked, wondering what her ladyship would do with a donkey in Mayfair.

"You think she'll forget him?" the groom asked, not bothering to look up from his examination. "You think she bought him on impulse and will forget him before she gets home?" The rude sound that followed was indicative of his opinion of what Raven had suggested about the girl.

"Then she won't?" Raven asked, the slight smile again marking the hard mouth.

"If I don't have him back in the stables and these injuries tended to by the time she returns, she'll serve my head to the old man with his supper."

"The old man?" Fear stirred suddenly in Raven's gut.

"Montfort," the groom informed him, as if, that said, there was no other explanation needed. He moved to the other side of the donkey to run skilled hands over the protruding ribs and to pick up a trembling foreleg to examine an untreated cut.

"Montfort," Raven repeated, feeling like Echo.

"The Duke of Montfort," the groom said, glancing up at last to assess a man who was so ignorant as not to recognize *that* particular name. "The Devil Duke, they call him. Not out loud, of course," he said, remembering his employer's temper. The sobriquet was well earned and well deserved.

"Who is she?" the American asked, his gaze moving back to the street down which the girl had disappeared.

"The Devil's Daughter," Jem said, noticing for the first time the style of the foreign gentleman's hair. The groom's eyebrows climbed slightly, but it was not his place to ques-

tion his betters. "Lady Catherine Montfort. The Duke of
Montfort's only heir."

"Thank you," Raven said, and reaching into his waistcoat pocket, he flicked a coin to the groom. The man smiled
his thanks and then turned back to his careful survey of the
donkey.

John Raven crossed the street and, taking the narrow
stairs two at a time, retraced his path to Reynolds's office.
The old man looked up from his notations in a leather-
bound ledger.

"Lady Catherine Montfort," John Raven said, his wide
shoulders filling the doorway.

"Montfort?" the banker repeated, wondering again, as
he had when he'd first met the American, if he were more
than merely eccentric.

"Is Lady Catherine Montfort angelic enough for our
purposes?" Raven asked calmly.

The old man stared blankly for a moment, wondering
how his client had come up with that name.

"Is she?" Raven prompted, knowing that the banker's
reply really didn't matter. The die had been cast in the middle of a crowded London street, but at least Reynolds's approval would provide an acceptable excuse.

"Catherine Montfort is bloody well the entire seraphic
choir," the old man acknowledged truthfully. He watched
the smile that touched the American's mouth again deepen
the indentions at the corners. "But I'm afraid that the
Montforts—"

"You said one only had to offer enough money."

"Montfort's one of the few men in London even *you*
couldn't buy. And I must tell you..." The banker's voice
trailed off. He really hated to offend the man, but he knew
that the duke would never accept John Raven as a suitor for
his daughter's hand. His only daughter. His only surviving
child and heir. Reynolds's mind having dealt too long with
the prospects of profit, he briefly allowed himself to consider those combined fortunes being handled by his bank.
And why not? Was his not the oldest financial establishment in the city? The bank had financed the East India

Company's venture into the Russian market in the six-teenth century. He cleared the tempting visions from his mind and shook his head regretfully.

"He'll never allow you to even present your suit. Forget Catherine Montfort, John. You'll never convince her father, and I must warn you that it would be dangerous even to try. Montfort's as proud, cold-blooded and arrogant as any of the old aristocrats. His was a generation that made its own rules—whatever they wanted, whether legal or moral, they took, consequences be damned. There's nothing you can do to win Montfort's daughter. You have nothing to offer the girl that she doesn't already have."

The blue eyes rested on the seamed face of the old man a moment, their farseeing gaze untroubled by the obstacles Reynolds had just thrown in his path.

John Raven had believed he had come to London to make money. The call had been so strong that he had left India in the middle of an incredibly successful mining venture. His intuition had directed his journey to this city as surely as it had previously drawn him to Delhi, leaving the profitable exporting business he'd founded in New York to be run by his assistants. Wherever there was money to be made, John Raven could sense it. He could feel it moving in his hands as clearly as he had felt the reality of the rubies and sapphires he'd mined in India. He thought he had been drawn to England by the growth of the mining industry and the possibilities offered by the new developments in the loco-motive.

Now he knew that his arrival in London had had nothing whatsoever to do with that. *What you need is a wife,* Oliver Reynolds had told him, almost exactly the words his grandmother had said to him when he had last seen her more than five years ago. He wondered how many prayers had accompanied the sacred white cedar smoke directed to the All-Spirit in the intervening years. And with amusement Raven found himself wondering if, in one of her dream trances, his grandmother could possibly have envisioned anyone like Lady Catherine Montfort.

Chapter One

"I didn't come out to be pawed. I came for a breath of air that wasn't contaminated by a hundred perspiring bodies wearing too much perfume," Catherine Montfort said, wondering why the lovemaking of this extremely handsome and highly acceptable suitor left her so cold. She moved out of the attempted embrace of her escort, who released her with a small laugh.

The Viscount Amberton watched as Catherine leaned gracefully against the stone railing of the balcony. He knew she was as unmindful of the nearly priceless material of her gown as if she had been wearing sackcloth. Of course, none of the tedious hours of beading that had gone into its creation had been performed by her hands. She propped her chin on fingers covered in the finest kid and stared out into the darkness that hid the garden.

"Admit it, Cat. You're bored. Too many ballrooms. Too many dinner parties attended by the same people. Too many suitors declaiming their undying love. Why don't you name the lucky man and put them all out of their misery?" the viscount suggested.

Since Amberton was well aware that he held the inside track, with the duke, certainly, if not with the daughter, he was becoming increasingly impatient with Catherine's refusal to accept the necessity of matrimony. Especially when he considered all the diligent toadying to the old man it had taken to acquire that inside track. The viscount was not nearly so impatient as his creditors were, however. The only reason they had held both their tongues and his bills was that they, too, were well aware of how this game was played. The faintest hint that Lord Amberton needed Montfort's money, and he'd never see a guinea of it.

"All of *them?*" she questioned mockingly, slanting a quick smile at him over her shoulder.

"All of us, then," he conceded. "You know my heart's yours. It always has been. You are very well aware of that fact."

"But the problem is in *my* heart," Catherine said softly.

"Not being in love is not generally considered to be a hindrance to marriage," he assured her. Indeed, they both knew how rare a love match was in their circle.

"I keep thinking there must be a man who won't bore me to tears after the first month."

"You're such a wonderfully spoiled chit, my dear. There are worse things than boredom," Gerald suggested lightly, knowing she wouldn't understand just now the truth of his statement. But she would. One day soon she most certainly would. Then she might long for boredom, Gerald thought with a touch of malicious humor.

"I doubt it," she said, but she smiled again.

"You're eighteen, at the end of your second season. The Duke of Montfort's only child, and he wants a grandson. He's not going to wait much longer."

"I know." She'd heard the same arguments all too often, from both Amberton and her father. She had begun to be afraid the duke would brush aside the promise he'd made two years ago to consider her wishes in the selection of her husband.

There was no need to base that decision solely on the amount of the marriage settlements. And no one unsuitable by birth would be so absurd as to offer for Montfort's only daughter, so her father had seen no reason not to give her the assurance for which she had so charmingly begged. But now he was growing impatient. Her refusal to choose was becoming a source of discord in what had always been, despite the duke's notoriously volatile temperament, a loving relationship.

"Give in gracefully before you're left with no choice at all," Gerald suggested smoothly. *And before I'm clapped into Newgate,* he thought bitterly.

"Give in," she repeated, with her own touch of bitterness. "Always to be at someone else's command. Forever hemmed in by his wishes and desires. Governed by his—"

Amberton's laugh interrupted her litany of complaints. "And you, of course, believe that you should be the exception to those restrictions, allowed to make your own decisions."

"To a certain degree. Why not? I've not made so many errors in judgment that I must always be constrained to accept a husband's guidance in every decision," she argued.

"And if you *have* made errors, your father has been remarkably willing, and certainly more than able, to extricate you from situations that were, perhaps, not in your own best interests. Such as a certain clandestine journey to the Border."

Catherine had been only sixteen, and the fortune hunter who had arranged that elopement had been handsome and charming enough to turn older and wiser heads. However, his carefully selected target had been, almost from his arrival in London, the Duke of Montfort's daughter.

"Don't," she ordered softly, her humiliation over the incident still acutely painful. "I shouldn't have told you about that. And you promised never to repeat it."

"Your secrets are safe with me, my dear. Especially if you agree to favor my suit," he suggested truthfully, smiling at her. "Then I'd have a vested interest in protecting your reputation."

"Such as it is," she finished for him. "Blackmail, Gerald?"

"Not in the least. Simply another heartfelt avowal from quite your oldest suitor."

"Oldest?" she repeated, laughing, relieved to be back on the familiar ground of flirtation. "You've forgotten Ridgecourt."

"Then earliest, my love. I think you know that we'd rub along together very well. And I promise to permit a certain amount of freedom. Not, I'm afraid, that I'm willing to give you as long a tether as your father has allowed."

"Tether!" she echoed despairingly. "Oh, God, Gerald, that's just the sort of thing I'm talking about."

"Simply a figure of speech, my dear. There's really no need to pounce on every idiom as if I'm trying to imprison you."

"That's exactly how I *do* imagine marriage. I'm already surrounded by enough restrictions to enclose an army. Don't ride too fast. Don't dance with the same gentleman more than once. It's not seemly for unmarried females to wear that color or this style. God, I'm so sick of it all. Even my father has lately taken to issuing dark warnings about my being left languishing on the shelf, despite the fact that he's received at least three offers in the last week."

Eventually, the viscount knew, she would have to succumb. Everyone did. And Amberton intended to be prominently at hand, conveniently under her father's nose and eminently suitable, when she did. But she had damn well better hurry. He had heard the wolf howling at his door too often to have any peace of mind.

"There is a solution," Gerald reminded her.

"Marriage. To exchange one prison for another. To give *another* person the right to correct, criticize and chastise. Do you know, Gerald, that there are men who beat their wives if they don't obey them in every instance? How would I know—"

He held up his hand, palm out, and vowed, "I shall never beat you, Cat. There are better ways to achieve control over a recalcitrant wife than violence. Far more pleasant ways." There were methods that he'd be delighted to demonstrate to this girl, who was seriously endangering his plans with her stubbornness.

"Really?" she said with a touch of haughtiness, disliking the suggestive undertone of that declaration.

"Marry me, my sweet, and I shall be delighted to demonstrate the controlling power of love."

"No," she said simply, returning to the contemplation of the garden that stretched below her in the darkness. "I don't want to get married. To anyone."

"But eventually—" he began.

"Not tonight, please. I don't want to think about that tonight. Go away, Gerald. Let me just enjoy being alone. I have a feeling that the days when I control my own destiny are dwindling, which makes each more precious. My days of freedom may be numbered, but I'm not at your beck and call yet. Nor any man's. Not yet," she said with an almost fierce resignation.

Amberton watched the slight heave of the slender shoulders as she took a deep breath, but smiling still, he obeyed.

Let her enjoy the illusion that she had some choice in the matter as long as she was able, he thought. The Season was coming to an end, and her days of freedom *were* certainly numbered. Like it or not, Catherine Montfort would have to choose, forced to that decision by the demands of her father and of society. Amberton knew that there was not another of her suitors who enjoyed the rapport he had so carefully cultivated. Soon she, and more importantly her fortune, would be under his control, and there were a few lessons that he would delight in teaching Catherine Montfort, proud and stubborn as she was.

With Gerald's departure, only the calm of the night sounds and the drifting music from the ballroom surrounded her. Propping both elbows on the stone railing, she interlaced her fingers under her chin and sighed again.

Unbelievingly she heard behind her the sound of a pair of hands slowly clapping. She turned to see a tall figure standing in the shadows at the edge of the balcony.

"Bravo," the intruder said softly. "A remarkable declaration of independence. I applaud the sentiment, even if I doubt the possibility of your success in carrying it out."

"How long have you been there?" she demanded.

"I believe you were being pawed. And objecting to it."

"How dare you!"

"*I* didn't. That was Gerald."

"You were listening to a very private and personal conversation. You, sir, are obviously no gentleman."

"Obviously," he said agreeably.

Now that she was over her immediate shock, she had begun to notice details of his appearance. He was far taller than any of the men she knew—over six feet tall. Several inches over, she accurately guessed. And very broad shouldered. Massive, really.

As he moved into the light from the windows, she became aware of bronzed skin stretched tautly over high cheekbones and lean, smoothly shaved cheeks. Dear God, she thought in disbelief, it was the man who had bought the donkey. The man with the eyes—crystal blue and piercing, set like jewels among the uncompromisingly strong angles of his dark face.

She swallowed suddenly, fascinated again by his sheer foreignness. No fashionable cut scattered curls over the high forehead. His black hair was pulled straight back and tied at his nape, the severity of the style emphasizing the spare planes of his face and the strong nose.

She realized that she had been staring. Angry with her display of near country simplicity and still embarrassed at having been caught in such a compromising situation, she turned back to the railing, trying to regain her composure.

The silence stretched, only the muffled strains of the music invading the quietness. She had expected some reaction—an apology for his intrusion, a reminder that they'd met before and that she was in his debt, something. He was certainly not responding as Amberton or any of her other courtiers would have reacted to her very deliberate lack of attention.

Almost against her will, she turned back to face him. He was standing exactly as he had been before, watching her with those strangely luminescent eyes. Those damnably beautiful eyes. Even as she thought it, she wondered what was happening to her. She was surely sophisticated enough not to fall tongue-tied at the feet of a stranger because he had blue eyes.

"I'd like to talk to you," he said. The accent was marked, and she wondered why she hadn't been aware of it when he'd spoken from the shadows. Probably because she'd been too mortified by the idea that he'd witnessed Amberton's attempted lovemaking.

"If I don't want to talk to Gerald, who is a very old friend, it should be obvious that I don't wish to talk to you."

"I'm not Gerald," he said, unmoving.

"I beg your pardon?" She had gaped at him like the veriest schoolroom miss. Yet she didn't intend to be treated like one.

"I'm not Gerald," he repeated obligingly.

"I know what you said. I didn't mean that I didn't hear you. I meant . . ."

He waited politely for her explanation. His hands were relaxed at his sides; his face perfectly composed.

"I meant I don't know *why* you said that—that you're not Gerald. Obviously you're not Lord Amberton."

"My name is Raven," he said calmly.

"Mr. Raven," she said sweetly, acknowledging the information. Raven? What kind of name was Raven?

Raven inclined his head, not the least bit taken in by her politeness. She was certain by now to be wishing him in Hades.

"Go away," she responded, turning once more to the railing.

Behind her she heard his soft laughter. He was laughing at her. Whoever he was—whatever he was.

"I'm not accustomed to gentlemen who refuse to do as they've been requested," she said with frigid politeness.

"I didn't imagine you were," he said reasonably. "However, I have some business to discuss with you. I believe that this is an opportunity I may not be offered again."

She could still hear the amusement in the deep voice.

"Business?" she repeated, turning once more to face him. "I assure you that I do not discuss *business* with strange men."

"But I'm not a stranger. We've met before. I thought you might remember."

"Of course I remember. I believe that I *did* thank you for the donkey. And now, I really must insist that I be left alone. If you would be so kind." She didn't understand why she was trying to drive him away. She was honest enough to admit that his image had intruded frequently in her brain during the days since their first encounter. She had even envisioned meeting him again, but not while baring her soul on a dark and isolated balcony where no well-brought-up young lady should be found.

"I have a proposition to offer you," Raven said, completely unperturbed by her repeated attempts to dismiss him.

She turned back to face him, appalled beyond words, feeling her skin flush hotly. He had witnessed Gerald's very improper embrace and apparently believed that she would entertain...

"My father will have you horsewhipped," she threatened.

The line of his lips tilted upward at the corners. "Not *that* kind of proposition," Raven corrected. "And I'm shocked that a gently reared young woman would believe that I'm about to offer her carte blanche. I *am* surprised at you." He made a small *tsk*ing sound, shaking his head. The anger he'd felt watching the blond Englishman hold her was beginning to dissipate. She was obviously not the kind of flirt he'd feared when he'd followed the pair from the crowded ballroom.

"What do you want? Please state your *business* and then go away," Catherine ordered. "You have the manners of a barbarian."

"American," he admitted pleasantly, knowing that she was probably correct—at least by her standards.

"Ah," she said, giving him a mocking smile of agreement. "That explains so much." American. No wonder he was unusual.

"I hope so," Raven replied graciously, as if there had been no trace of sarcasm in her reply. "I'm not very familiar with the apparently intricate courtship rituals of your circle. So forgive me if I fail to say all that's proper. I'm a

man who believes in cutting to the heart. I'd like you to
marry me.''

Despite her genuine sophistication, Catherine's mouth
dropped open slightly. She made a small strangled sound
and then, controlling her shock, began to laugh, in honest
amusement that he should believe he could appear out of the
shadows—a stranger with all the panache of a red Indian
and the physical presence of a prizefighter—and offer her
marriage.

Raven made no outward reaction to her amusement. He
hadn't expected her to laugh, despite the fact that she knew
nothing about him. Few people ever laughed at John Raven.
If nothing else, his sheer size was too intimidating. But, he
remembered, Reynolds *had* tried to warn him.

The American waited with only a calm patience evident
in his features. Eventually her laughter began to sound a
little forced, even to her own ears, and she allowed it to die
away.

His lips lifted slightly in what she was beginning to recognize as his version of a smile. A mocking smile.

''I'm glad I've amused you. I imagine you haven't found
an occasion for such a prolonged bout of laughter in
months.''

''You *are* amusing,'' she taunted, knowing he'd seen
through her. Could he possibly realize how he'd affected her
at their first meeting? She forced sarcasm into her voice. ''I
can't tell you how deliciously ridiculous I find you. And
your suit. Quite the most unconventional suitor I've ever
had, I assure you.''

''At least I'm not boring you,'' he suggested softly.

She realized with surprise that he wasn't. She was not—
definitely not—bored and had not been for the last few
moments.

''There are worse things than boredom,'' she retorted
mockingly, unconscious that she was repeating Amberton's
statement, which John Raven, of course, had certainly
overheard.

''I doubt it,'' he responded, exactly as she had. ''At least
we agree on something.''

"I would imagine that's the only thing we are ever likely to agree on," she said, opening her fan and moving it gracefully.

His eyes watched the play of her hands a moment and then lifted to study her features. He'd never seen a woman as beautiful. Despite her coloring, there was no scattering of freckles across the small, elegant nose. The long lashes that surrounded the russet eyes were much darker than the auburn hair. Almost certainly artificially darkened, he realized in amusement.

Catherine was glad of the covering darkness that hid the slight flush she could feel suffusing her skin at his prolonged examination. Her acknowledged beauty, which had been her heritage from her mother, had attracted the usual masculine attention, but he was tracing each individual element of her face as if he were trying to memorize them.

"And I believe there are other, more important considerations about which we are in agreement," he said finally, the piercing crystal gaze moving back to meet her eyes.

"Such as?" she asked indifferently.

"Such as the idea that a woman need not be at the beck and call of her husband. That she should enjoy a great deal of personal freedom. With a few necessary limitations, of course."

You have nothing to offer the girl that she doesn't already have, Reynolds had told him, but Catherine Montfort herself had given him a key, an inducement that might tempt her to consider his proposal. She had said that she wanted freedom, and perhaps, if he promised her that . . .

"Of course." She smiled tauntingly. "But there are those limitations—those very *necessary* limitations."

"I'm offering you almost unlimited wealth. Enough money to become the most fashionably dressed woman in London. You'll have your own household, furnished and staffed exactly as you desire. An unlimited account for entertainment. And the more lavishly you entertain, the better it will suit me. Jewels, horses, carriages, travel—whatever appeals to you will be yours to command."

She smiled again, almost in sympathy at his naiveté. "And if I told you that I already enjoy all of those enticements? What do you have to offer that I don't already possess?"

He studied her upturned face a moment. "Freedom," he said again, and laughing, she simply shook her head. "Freedom from being courted by men you abhor," he continued, as if she'd made no response. "Freedom from society's restrictions. Freedom from your father's demands for a grandson."

"Ah," she said, mocking again, "but to achieve that particular freedom..." She let the indelicate suggestion fade.

"I don't need a mistress," Raven responded softly. "What I need is a hostess." She wanted his assurance that he didn't intend to make physical demands on her, and although her rejection of that aspect of his proposal had not occurred to him before, he knew that he would do whatever was necessary to ensure that Catherine Montfort would be his. Even if it meant restraining for a time his very natural inclinations to do exactly what Lord Amberton had been attempting moments ago.

A platonic marriage was definitely not what John Raven had in mind, but he was a very patient man. He had been carefully trained in that stoic patience since childhood. He could wait for what he wanted, for the kind of relationship he intended to have with this woman.

At his rejection of her taunt, Catherine was surprised to feel a tinge of regret. *Good God,* she thought, examining that emotion. *Why the deuce should it matter to me if he has a dozen mistresses? A hundred mistresses.*

"Then how should I answer my father's demand for a grandchild?" she asked. "Or will your mistress handle that, too?"

"Our marriage would answer for a time. And eventually—"

"Eventually?" she interrupted, smiling at the trap he had created for his own argument.

"He'll decide you're barren or unwilling to share my bed—whichever version you prefer to put about. I assure you I couldn't care less."

She hid her shock at his matter-of-fact assessment of her father's probable reaction. "You won't require an heir for this unlimited wealth you intend to put at my disposal?"

"Eventually," he said again, as calmly as before, the blue eyes meeting hers. "But you may take as long as you wish before satisfying that desire." The word hung between them, its sexual connotations implicit in the context of their discussion. "You will surely begin to feel maternal stirrings before I require you to carry on my family line," he continued. "After all, I believe you're only eighteen. Or was Amberton wrong about that, too?"

"And how old are you?" she wondered aloud.

"I'm thirty-four," he said.

Almost twice her age. Older by several years than most of the eligible suitors who had approached her father. Except, of course, for the highly unsuitable—like the Earl of Ridgecourt, on the lookout for his fourth wife, someone to preside over his shockingly full nursery, the production of its inhabitants having brought a swift and untimely end to his first three wives.

"Why do you need a hostess?" she asked. She didn't understand why she felt such freedom to delve into the intricacies of the patently ludicrous proposal he'd made. Maybe it was his willingness to discuss any aspect of his plan with her, despite its nature. He didn't seem to be shocked by her questions. On the contrary, he had treated them as legitimate attempts to solicit information necessary to make her choice.

"I've already made investments in British industry—"

"What kind of investments?" she interrupted.

"Coal," he said, thinking with pleasure of the mines that were already producing a far greater tonnage than he had thought possible when he'd bought them.

There was a spark of something in the crystalline depths of his eyes, and she could hear the same quality of possessiveness in his deep voice that one sometimes heard in the voices of women discussing their jewels or, more rarely, their children.

"I buy coalfields," he continued.

"Why?"

"So I can build railroads from them."

When Catherine shook her head slightly in confusion, he smiled that small, controlled smile. "Coal is going to fuel what's beginning to happen here, and the man who controls the coal . . ." His explanation faded away and he simply watched her face.

"You've made investments in coalfields and railroads?" she questioned carefully. Again she felt a sense of unreality that she was standing in the darkness with a stranger discussing coal.

"And foundries. To make iron. However, most of the men who will be instrumental in deciding on the direction British industry will take in the next few crucial years belong to the circle you frequent. I need to talk to them, to influence them in ways that will increase the value of my investments. But I have no access to those men. I need a wife who does."

"What men?" she asked, interested despite herself. There was some strange compulsion in listening to his deep voice.

"Men like your father. Men of power and influence. The men who control the House of Lords. Who control the land and property of this country."

"Men like that don't discuss business over the dinner table," she told him seriously, falling in with his fantasy.

"And after dinner? Over their port and cigars? With the ladies safely out of the way?" Raven questioned. It was what Reynolds had told him.

"Perhaps," she was forced to admit.

"But first . . ."

"First they must agree to *come* to dinner."

"Yes," he said simply.

She studied the lean, harshly defined planes of his face.

"I can't marry you," she said finally. She paused, thinking about all he'd offered. "Even if . . ." She carefully began again, wondering why she was making an explanation.

It was almost as if he had constrained her to consider his proposal seriously. "Even if I wanted to."

"Freedom," he invited softly.

"With limitations," she reminded him. And then, remembering, "I never heard the limitations." Almost against her will she responded to the small movement of his lips. Seeing his smile, her own was given with a warmth usually reserved for old friends.

"No lovers," he said. Raven wasn't exactly sure of the conventions of her society, but he'd seen little since he'd been in London to reassure him about the morality of the ton. And he knew that he wouldn't allow another man to touch her. No matter what he'd promised about freedom.

"What?" Catherine gasped in shock, her smile vanishing.

"No lovers," he repeated, trying to think of an excuse she'd believe, something other than the truth—that he couldn't endure the thought of any other man touching her. "I won't leave what I've worked so hard to acquire to some other man's—"

"How dare you?" she interrupted before he could finish.

"Other than that, I can't really think of any additional limitations," he continued smoothly. "You would be free to come and go as you will, to spend as much of my money as you possibly can, provided you bring to my house the men I need to meet to successfully carry out my investments."

"You're free to have a mistress, but I'm not allowed to have lovers. Is that the arrangement you're suggesting?"

"Unless you have some other plan for satisfying my physical needs," Raven said, wondering how he would manage to control those needs if, by some miracle, she did agree to marry him.

"And what about my needs?" she countered angrily. This was exactly the sort of thing she hated about the restraints imposed by society. It was perfectly acceptable for him to have a mistress, but she was to be bound by his "limitation."

"I hadn't intended to make that a requirement."

"What?" Catherine asked. She must have missed something.

"I would, of course, be delighted to satisfy your needs," Raven agreed, fighting to control his amusement. "However, I—"

"How dare you!" Catherine repeated scathingly. "I assure you that I don't want you to..." She couldn't believe where he'd led her, or what she had been about to say.

"I never assumed you did," he agreed, deliberately clearing any trace of humor from his voice. "What I'm offering is a simple business proposition. You have to marry. You'll be forced to do so, and you are very aware of that. You want freedom to do *exactly* as you please. I'm offering you that freedom, with one restriction. A very reasonable restriction. And in exchange, you provide me an introduction into this society I should never be allowed to enter without your help."

"Do you think you can discuss these arrangements—"

"You're very well aware of the considerations we've discussed tonight. The understanding of them is implicit in most marriages. You and I have simply put all the cards on the table, open and aboveboard. That's also a freedom you'll enjoy if you agree to marry me. I promise you I'm unshockable. You may say to me whatever you wish. You may ask whatever questions occur to you. About anything. I will endeavor to answer them honestly."

"However appealing that may be—" she began.

"Then you do find something in my proposal appealing?" he questioned softly, wondering if he dared hope.

"Freedom." She repeated the tantalizing word. "But..."

"But?" he urged at her hesitation.

"My father would never entertain the idea of you as a son-in-law. He would never consent."

His lips twitched again with that slight upward movement. "How much?" he asked.

"How much?" she repeated blankly.

"To convince your father that I'm a suitable suitor. Marriage settlements, I believe is the proper term."

"Are you proposing to *buy* me?" she asked incredulously. "Surely you don't believe that the Duke of Montfort would simply sell his daughter to a coal merchant? You really are incredibly ill informed." There was, she knew, some truth in his ideas about how such things were done. She wondered suddenly just how much it *would* take for her father to agree to what this man proposed.

"You don't have that much money," she said bitingly.

"You might be surprised," Raven suggested calmly. There was no challenge in the quiet avowal.

"My father is a very proud man. Of his name and heritage."

"I understand pride," he answered, his eyes still watching her reaction. "I, too, am proud of my heritage." He remembered the quiet strength of the loving family he'd left behind in the haze-shrouded mountains of Tennessee when he'd begun his long quest. "I assure you it wouldn't sully the purity of the Montfort stock. In horse breeding they make such matches to inject new blood, to add vigor to bloodlines that are outworn."

"Are you suggesting—"

"I'm suggesting that what has existed as the standard for judging a man's quality is about to change in England, as it has already changed in the New World and in France. I believe you are intelligent enough to grasp that concept, even if your father will not. A man's titles and the nobility of his lineage will soon matter less than his intelligence, his hard work and his ability to create, to forge new ideas and turn them into practical applications for the benefit of all. Your father's day is drawing to a close. As is his society's. The world is about to change, and it will never again be the same."

She blinked to clear the spell woven by the conviction in John Raven's voice. Whatever the validity of those views, he certainly believed them. There was no doubt he sincerely thought her world was about to disappear. But she, having known no other, was unprepared to accept that assessment.

"I'm sorry," she said softly. There was nothing else she could offer a man who had revealed to her a dream she could not accept. For in doing so, she would admit that this society, into which she fit as well as her slender fingers fit into the gloves that had been cut to their exact measurements, was doomed. In admitting the reality of *his* vision, she would be forced to deny all the security *she* had ever known.

She brushed by him, leaving John Raven, an alien in the world she understood so well, in the darkness of the balcony, choosing instead to return to the brilliant light of a dozen chandeliers and the elegant music and the endless restrictions.

Chapter Two

The enormous black was entirely suitable. On anything less magnificent, its rider might have appeared ridiculous, but the black *was* magnificent and, therefore, exactly right for John Raven's size. Catherine supposed she should not have been surprised, on the morning after the ball, to find the American approaching her out of the mist that had not yet been burned away by the sun. The vapor swirled around the gleaming forelegs of the black as the man cantered to where she had reined in her mare.

Raven slowed the stallion, controlling the powerful animal with sure horseman's hands. "May I join you?" he asked.

"I'm waiting for someone," she answered truthfully, her voice deliberately cool.

"A gentleman given to puce waistcoats and horses too long in the tooth and too short in the shank?" he asked.

Recognizing all too readily, from his very accurate description, her intended companion for this morning's exercise, Catherine laughed. She watched the corresponding upward tilt in the corners of that forbidding mouth. "Yes," she said, still smiling despite her earlier intent to keep her distance.

"He's not coming. Unavoidably detained, I should say."

"What have you done to Reginald?" she asked, fascinated.

"Reginald?" Raven repeated, allowing disbelief to creep into his deep voice. "Gerald and Reginald," he added, shaking his head. "My God," he said under his breath, and then clearing the derision from his voice and the mischief from the blue eyes, he shook his head again.

"I assure you I had nothing to do with it." Not exactly the truth, he admitted to himself, but all's fair in love and war. "He seemed to be having trouble with his animal, but I promise you, he won't be joining you this morning."

Although, through visible effort, Catherine had managed to control her lips, her eyes were still laughing. They were deep amber in the morning light, darkened with flecks of the same rich auburn that gleamed in her hair, which was almost hidden under the modish hat that matched the dark green habit she wore. The garment, although cut very fashionably, was relatively free of decoration, designed for riding, Raven was pleased to note, rather than parading.

His eyes answered the amusement in hers, and for a moment a decided jolt of power from their crystal depths curled upward inside her body, fluttering against her heart. Catherine swallowed suddenly, dropping her gaze to her gloved hands that were perfectly relaxed over the reins. There was a moment of silence, and then she once more directed her mare onto the bridle path she'd been following before she'd paused to admire the stallion. Long before she had recognized the rider.

Taking that for permission to join her, Raven guided the black alongside, and they rode without speaking for a while.

"He's magnificent," she said finally. Surely horses were a safe topic and apparently one they both appreciated.

"He's a brute with an iron mouth and a heart as black as his hide," Raven answered without a trace of annoyance, "but we're beginning to understand one another."

"Then you haven't had him long?" There was no evidence of anything but perfect understanding between horse and rider. If the black was a brute, he was keeping his temperament hidden.

"Since this morning," Raven said calmly.

"This morning?"

"Tattersall's, I believe, is the name of the establishment where I found him."

"But..." She paused, glancing at that dark face to see if he were teasing her.

Raven turned at her hesitation and met her eyes, his brows raised slightly, questioning her surprise.

"It must be...it's barely daybreak," she finally managed to say.

"I needed a horse," Raven said, as if that explained it all.

"They aren't open this early," she persisted.

"They are today," he assured her. Then, closing the subject of the power of his money, a subject he had never intended to open, but which had just been demonstrated, Raven asked, "Would you like a run? I haven't had a chance to see if he lives up to the promise of his looks or if he's all flash and no substance."

"Here?" she asked, looking at the narrow, tree-lined path.

"Is there a *rule* against it?" he questioned, almost mocking.

"Probably," she answered tartly, but even as she said it she touched the mare with her crop.

Catherine had caught him by surprise and was therefore able to maintain her lead for a short distance, but, of course, they both had known that the black had a decided advantage, by size if by nothing else. She was forced to admit that his rider also had an edge. Although she was widely acknowledged as one of the finest equestrians in the ton, John Raven seemed to be one with his horse, blending with the reaching effort of the black and almost adding energy to the stallion's powerful motion.

Recognizing defeat and feeling nothing but admiration for the pair who had beaten her, she slowed Storm until eventually they were moving again side by side, at a pace that almost demanded conversation.

"Is this where you always ride?" Raven asked, thinking with sympathy how constricted the area was for a horsewoman of her skills. He wished they could race over the vast lowlands along the great river called Mississippi, space and time unlimited.

Catherine wondered if the American was planning on joining her each morning. She had been forced in the past to give some sharp setdowns to suitors who believed she would welcome company on her early morning excursions. She did occasionally allow very old and trusted acquaintances like Reggie to join her, because she could be sure that they would fall in with any suggestion she made as to the speed or duration of the ride. But, except for her groom, following behind, this was a private time.

"It's the only place in London for a gallop."

"A gallop," Raven repeated derisively. "If that's what you call a gallop."

"No, it isn't, of course. But there's really nowhere else. This *is* a town, you understand—streets, houses, people."

"We have towns in America," he answered, and she knew he was laughing at her again. His face didn't reflect his amusement, of course, but he was laughing just the same.

"And in which one do you live?" she asked sweetly. She tried to dredge up the names of some of those distant cities. New York and Washington. Boston. And Baltimore, of course.

"I haven't been home in several years," Raven answered.

"I thought you'd only recently come to England."

"There are other parts of the world besides England."

"And in which parts were you?" she asked almost sharply. She didn't know how he could make her feel so provincial. He was the one who should be aware that he was lacking polish, and instead, when they were together, she ended up feeling very much out of control of the situation. That had never before happened to her where men were concerned.

"China and then India. For the last five years," he said.

Images of the East as she imagined it to be floated through her consciousness. The old lures of silks and spices. Jewels and precious metals. Ivory and drugs.

"Is that where—" She broke off, realizing the rudeness of her question.

"Where I acquired my money?" he finished easily. "I told you that you might ask me anything. There's no reason to guard your tongue with me. Most of it came from the East, but I have interests in America also."

"What kind of interests?"

"Shipping, which led naturally to my contacts in the Orient. I became fascinated by the cultures. And there, too, fortunes were to be made."

"Too?" she repeated.

"As there will be here."

"In coal and railroads?" she said, remembering.

"And in iron and steel. For the machines."

"What machines?"

"All of them," he said, his lips flickering upward. "Machines for everything," he offered, wondering if she could really be interested.

"I don't understand."

"The world is changing. What has been man-made is about to become the province of machines. To build machines, there must be iron. And to make iron…" He paused, glancing at her face.

"There must be coal," she repeated, as if it were a lesson she'd learned. As indeed, she had. "And the railroads?" she asked. "Why are you building railroads from your coalfields?"

"Because to make iron you must bring the coal and the ore together. The iron ore. So I buy the coalfields, employ the power of machinery to improve the mining techniques, and eventually I'll carry the coal to the foundries by rail," he explained patiently.

"But won't that take a long time? To build railroads from the mines?"

"Yes, but the process can be speeded up by the cooperation of the men who matter in this country. Or it can be slowed down by their refusal to cooperate."

"And that's why—"

"I need a wife. The kind of wife I described to you."

He waited for her response, but it seemed that she'd finally run out of questions. The only sounds that surrounded them were the brush of the wind through the leaves of the trees above and the soft impact of the horses' hooves over the loam of the bridle path. She had no more questions, and so he asked the one that remained unanswered between them.

"Have you decided about my proposal?"

"Mr. Raven, I'm sorry, but you must realize that I can't marry you. My father would never agree, and even if he did, we should not suit. Please, I beg you, don't mention it again."

"I think..." he began, and then stopped. He certainly couldn't tell her that he believed they'd suit extremely well. That he believed he had been deliberately led to her by the efforts of an old woman who was very far away. He'd been led to Catherine Montfort exactly *because* she was the woman who would best suit John Raven's needs. All his needs.

She looked up quickly at his hesitation. He had always seemed so sure of what he wanted.

"It doesn't matter if we suit," he continued, but she was aware that was not what he had begun to tell her. "If you'll remember, ours isn't to be that kind of marriage. I promise that I will leave you strictly alone, free to make your own decisions and to follow your own desires, with the one exception we discussed. Other than that, you need consider me no more than a business partner who happens to live in the same house."

"A *mariage de convenance.*" Smiling, she identified for him the term for the kind of arrangement he had described. One that was certainly not unheard of in the ton.

"In the truest sense of the word. At your convenience. I shall not interfere in your life."

"And you expect the same noninterference in yours?"

"Of course," he responded smoothly. "Nothing more than a business deal. No personal involvement whatsoever." *At least for the time being. At least until I've convinced you that you want to belong to me,* he promised silently. "Other than that involvement necessary to give the ton the opinion that we are united in our social contacts."

Catherine Montfort was unused to men who treated marriage to her as a business arrangement. She was more accustomed to men who made ardent vows of undying devotion. Raven, on the other hand, had in no way suggested that he was attracted to her—other than as one of his machines needed to perform a certain task.

"No," she said softly. She wondered at her sense of disappointment at his clarification of his original proposal. "It's quite impossible, and you might as well understand that now. My father would never allow such a match."

"Then you have no objection to my approaching him?"

"You intend to approach my father?" she repeated unbelievingly, incredulous that he didn't seem to understand the width of the gap that lay between them.

"Yes."

"With that proposition?"

"Not couched in precisely those terms," he said, the amusement back in his voice. "Simply as an offer for your hand."

"He'll have you thrown out," she warned.

"Will he?" he asked, sounding interested. "I wonder how."

"By the servants," she responded with deliberate bluntness, finally angered at his continual mockery of the reality of the world she lived in. Coal merchants, however wealthy, did not ask for the hand of the Duke of Montfort's daughter.

"I should like to see them try," Raven suggested softly, and found that he really would. He'd damn well like to see them try.

He inclined his head to her and turned the black away from the path, touching the animal's gleaming sides with his heels. Catherine wondered if that had been anger she'd read in his voice, but the statement had been too quietly and calmly made. It had sounded like a simple declaration of fact.

She watched horse and rider until they disappeared into the line of trees across the park, and then, disgusted with her attention to the American nabob, she once more touched

Storm's flank, breaking into what passed for a brisk gallop within the careful restraints of London. And she didn't even wonder why her morning's ride was so bitterly dissatisfying.

Two days later, returning from a particularly dull afternoon musicale, she was approached by the duke's butler as she entered the door, his agitation obvious.

"His grace requests that you join him, if you would, my lady. He's awaiting you in the salon."

"Thank you, Hartford. I'll only be a moment. Please convey that message to my father, and tell him—"

"I think..." the servant interrupted, and then paused, unaccustomed to denying her ladyship's requests. "If you would be so kind, my lady, I believe you should join him immediately."

Catherine considered the man before her. Hartford had never before shown her the slightest sign of disrespect, so she decided that whatever had distressed him enough to cause this small breech of his usually careful manner might really need her immediate attention.

"Thank you, Hartford," she said softly and walked to the wide doorway of the town house's formal salon.

Her father greeted her appearance with something that sounded like relief. He was dressed with his usual elegance, every white hair in place, but because she knew him so well she could sense his annoyance.

"This... gentleman," he said sardonically, the pause clearly deliberate, "insists he's an acquaintance of yours."

The duke's disbelief was patent. His thin hand moved to indicate the man standing at his ease before the straw-colored sofa. He had not, of course, been asked to sit down on it.

Catherine felt an absurd urge to smile at the picture John Raven presented. He, too, was perfectly dressed: his cravat, faintly edged with fine lace, flawlessly tied; his expertly tailored coat of Spanish blue stretched over wide shoulders; his silk waistcoat and pantaloons revealing the strong lines of his muscled body. And yet he looked as out of place in the genteel confines of this room full of priceless family heirlooms and fragile furniture as her father would look in a coalfield.

"Mr. Raven," she greeted him, her amusement at the image of the duke in the middle of a coalfield still showing in her eyes. There was a gleam of reaction to that amusement in John Raven's eyes, and then he inclined his head as regally as royalty was wont to do at an audience. If he felt any unease at being in the Duke of Montfort's elegant salon, he hid it very well indeed.

"You do know him?" her father asked, apparently finding it hard to believe his daughter was confirming Raven's claim.

"Of course," Catherine said easily, advancing across the floor to present her hand to Raven. He glanced down at her fingers, as if contemplating their cleanliness, and then, at the last second possible to avoid outright rudeness, he took them in his own and conveyed them to the line of those straight lips. She was briefly aware of the warmth of his breath above her skin for a second before he released them. His fingers had been hard against the softness of hers, their callused strength very unlike the well-cared-for hands of the men she knew.

"Lady Montfort," he said, controlling his anger at her amusement as impassively as he had at Montfort's rudeness.

"Mr. Raven," she answered, smiling. "How delightful you could visit today. No coalfields up for bid?"

An almost indiscernible reaction moved behind the crystal eyes, which were taking on the glint of ice. "No, I'm confining my bidding to other properties today," Raven mocked, his meaning apparent only to her.

Good God, she thought, *he* has *come to offer for my hand.*

"Coalfields?" Her father repeated the word as if he'd never before had occasion to use it. Or as if he couldn't quite believe he had just heard his daughter employ it.

"Mr. Raven is a coal merchant," Catherine said, reducing all he had taught her to an object of derision. How dare he embarrass her before her father? He had probably told the duke that they'd discussed marriage settlements. She had *told* Raven how impossible this was, but here he was, determined to humiliate them both and to anger her father in the bargain.

"A coal merchant?" Montfort repeated.

"I'm an investor," Raven said simply. He'd be damned if he'd let the two of them belittle honest labor. He certainly wasn't ashamed of what he did.

"In coal," Catherine interjected helpfully. "And railroads."

"In locomotions?" Montfort's voice rose.

"Locomotives," John Raven corrected quietly. He wondered if he could have been so wrong about what he had seen before in Catherine Montfort's eyes. She was deliberately trying to embarrass him before the duke, but there had been no derision in her voice when she'd asked him to explain his businesses to her.

"For carrying the coal," Catherine continued. "Or was it the ore? I'm afraid I've forgotten which. And I'm sure it was very useful information. I was thinking only today how I might work that into a conversation at some dinner party. I'm sure—"

"Are you serious?" the duke interrupted.

"Perfectly," she said. "I assure you I have it on the best authority, even if I'm a trifle unclear on the details. I'm certain Mr. Raven would be willing to explain it again. He seems to feel everyone else finds coal as interesting as he does."

"I find human progress interesting," Raven said simply. There was no trace of answering amusement in his voice.

"Indeed," Catherine said primly. "How...interesting."

"Is there a reason," the duke began, looking at his guest, "for your call today?"

Catherine could almost see her father mentally repeating the phrase she'd used, as if fixing it in his mind. *Coal merchant.* She could imagine the laughter at his club tomorrow when he told his cronies about it. And she, of course, was only making it worse. Humiliation was inherent in the situation; that was why she had tried to warn the American. But he had been so sure that what he'd suggested was as reasonable as he'd made it sound.

She glanced at Raven's face and found he was watching her instead of her father. A muscle tightened briefly beside his mouth, and then even that was controlled. His eyes moved back to the duke, and he said finally, despite her warning, what she had known he would say from the moment she had walked into the room.

"I've come to offer for your daughter's hand. I would like your permission to marry Catherine."

Her father's face quickly drained of color, and then, his eyes never leaving those of the man who had made that ludicrous suggestion, it suffused with blood, purpling with rage.

"You—you would *what?*" he sputtered.

Raven drew papers from the inside pocket of his coat and unfolded them as if he had all the time in the world. "One of these is a listing of my assets. The other is a marriage agreement that the man of business I employ here in London believed might be appropriate in such a merger. As you will see, the death settlements are extremely generous, and I require nothing from you except your permission for the match to take place. Not the usual contract in matters such as these, I'm aware, but my financial success has given me the liberty of not having to be a stickler for the conventional terms. Your daughter's hand is dowry enough, I assure you."

Raven had just uttered more words than Catherine had heard him put together in their previous conversations, except when he was talking about coal. The speech had had a rather endearing charm, if one thought about it—not that her father would.

"How dare you!" the duke said.

Although the old man certainly presented no physical threat to the American, his fury was rather awe inspiring—to Catherine at least. She couldn't remember seeing her father this enraged since she'd run off with the fortune hunter. Resolutely, she turned her mind away from that memory.

"Listed here also are the properties I am willing to settle on your daughter after our marriage," Raven added.

Catherine wondered if she were to be given a coalfield as an inducement to marriage. The words *with my worldly goods, I thee bestow* ran fleetingly through her mind.

"Get out," her father said ominously.

"Or a cash settlement if you prefer," Raven offered reasonably. Reynolds's warnings began to stir darkly in the back of his mind. Because the settlements were indeed extremely generous, he had believed that a man of the duke's intelligence would immediately see the advantages for his daughter. *Not of his class,* the banker had counseled. *Notorious for his temper,* the groom had suggested. And Catherine's own advice, given almost with regret, he'd believed: *My father would never allow such a match.* All the warnings Raven's pride had ignored were repeated in the old man's features.

The Duke of Montfort stalked across the room to ring the bell, which Hartford answered too quickly. The butler must have been standing in the hall in case of just such an occurrence.

"Get out of my house," the duke repeated.

"Your daughter has voiced no objection to the match," Raven averred calmly.

Not exactly the truth, Catherine thought, but he was certainly not easily discouraged.

Her father, however, had apparently had enough. "Throw him out," he said, gesturing to Hartford.

The butler walked up to John Raven, who turned those remarkable eyes from the contemplation of her father's face to the servant's. As the duke's had, Hartford's features lost color, but for a different reason altogether. The American's controlled smile appeared briefly at the man's hesitation, and then he turned and walked around him.

There would be no advantage to Raven in a meaningless confrontation with Montfort's butler. Fighting with the servants would only make him appear more ridiculous than he already had.

However, he didn't resist the impulse to issue his own warning. He turned back in the doorway to speak to the duke.

"I intend to marry your daughter, your grace. Nothing that has been said today has changed that. I have never done business this way in the past, and I believe it was a mistake on this occasion, but because I'm a stranger here, I allowed others to influence my actions. You may name your price, but I mean to have Catherine. You can be certain of that."

The duke's shock held him motionless a moment. Raven's eyes moved back to meet Catherine's. He nodded to her and finally, mercifully, he turned to leave.

Something in that last challenge to his authority, his pride or his honor had broken Montfort's control, never particularly reliable under the best of circumstances. He rushed after the departing American, almost shouting in his fury. "You'll marry Catherine over my dead body. You'll not bring your sweat-stained lucre into my family. You're another damned fortune hunter, and you're not fit to *speak* my daughter's name. I'll see you in hell before you insult her with your proposal again. You stink of sweat, and your stench offends my nose!"

Raven turned back to face the duke, and for once the warrior Scot in his heritage overcame the hard-learned Indian stoicism.

"If my money's stained, it's with my own sweat, your grace. Not that of the peasants your family robbed for hundreds of years. Mine's a far cleaner stench than yours, sir," he said bitterly. "And as for being a fortune hunter, I assure you I'm not interested in your money. It's Catherine I want, and I intend to have her. I assure you I meant no insult to your daughter. I have made her the most honorable offer she's likely to receive. Even if you're both too insular to understand that."

"Insular?" Montfort shouted. "You colonial jackanapes, don't you dare call me insular."

His gaze found the crop Catherine had left on the hall table that morning after her ride. It was not her custom, but she had apparently forgotten it when she had stopped to examine the calling cards in the salver that rested there. The crop's position proved far too convenient for her father's fury.

In his fit of blood lust, he grasped the whip, flying across the narrow space that separated him from his unwanted guest, to slash a blow across the mouth that had spoken those insults.

Raven wrenched the crop from the duke's fist, but a slim, feminine hand caught his wrist, just as it had caught the rattan stick. Although he could have easily freed himself from the grip of Catherine's fingers, Raven hesitated, another emotion interfering with his anger. She had touched him, slender fingers resting on the bare skin of his wrist, and he could feel the results of that realization beginning to move through his body, replacing the involuntary flood of adrenaline with a different, but just as uncontrollable, response.

"He's an old man," she begged. "Please don't hurt him."

Raven's eyes, filled with a fury that matched her father's, moved down to meet hers. Somehow, at the sight of russet eyes full of regret and apprehension, he found control.

She took a deep breath as she felt the rigidity gradually leave the upraised arm. "Just go away," she whispered. "I tried to tell you this would happen. Please, just go away."

Catherine's fingers slipped across the back of Raven's hand, and he allowed her to take the crop he could never have used against the old man. The welt her father had raised across his face was beginning to change from livid white to angry red. He raised his own fingers, which to his disgust trembled slightly, to explore it. The upper end was the most heavily damaged, a crimson thread there beginning to overflow and spill across his high cheekbone. He brushed his hand over the welling blood, feeling the fighting fury of his ancestors build again.

Catherine could hear the harshness of Raven's breathing. She was close enough even to smell him. There was no cloying perfume, but rather a pleasant aroma composed of the starch that had been used in his cravat, the fine leather of his boots and the warmly inviting, totally masculine scent of his body.

She lowered the hand that now controlled the whip and found, surprisingly, that she was fighting an urge to touch the brutal stripe her father had laid across his face. She knew that the duke's rage was not really directed against John Raven. This blow had been struck in revenge for another insult to his daughter, for another man who *had* been exactly what Montfort had accused the American of being. What had happened here this morning was not what she had wanted, but she knew very well her mockery had played a role in what had occurred. Raven would never know how deeply she regretted that.

"I'm sorry," she offered softly.

It seemed almost as if he didn't hear her. Finally the blue flame of his gaze focused again on what was in her face. His lips were white with the pressure he was exerting. The small, throbbing muscle jumped again in his jaw.

"Tell him," Raven ordered, reading the look in her eyes— the look he had seen there before. He had *not* been mistaken.

"Tell him what?" she asked, truly not understanding what message she was supposed to give.

"That you're mine. And that he might as well get accustomed to that reality."

John Raven had disappeared into the street, slamming the door behind him, before she could think of an answer.

Chapter Three

In the ensuing days, her father said little about the confrontation with John Raven. He had grudgingly admitted, knowledge assuredly gained from his friends at White's, that the "coal merchant" was exactly what he had claimed to be.

"Rich as Croesus," the duke acknowledged. "They're calling him the American nabob, but I am led to understand that most of his wealth was accumulated in the East."

"China and India," Catherine agreed, remembering their ride.

The old man's eyebrow lifted. "God's teeth, Catherine, exactly how well do you know this damned miner? Surely you must realize what you're doing by this ridiculous delay—making it appear you *desire* the attentions of men like this American. Choose a man of your own class, suitable for your birth and position, and do it damned quickly. I'll not be accosted by any more importunate jackanapes with coal dust under their fingernails." The duke's slender, elegantly erect frame shuddered dramatically, illustrating his distaste.

"Importunate?" Catherine repeated. "I should think that would be one adjective that wouldn't apply in this case. He's hardly the fortune hunter you called him." Recalling her father's fury over the disastrous incident of two years ago, she added, "I should think you'd be glad you don't have to worry about that with Mr. Raven's proposal. Actually..." she began, savoring the rather exciting bluntness of that proposal.

"Don't press me, Catherine. You think to wind me around your finger as you've always done, but I warn you, girl, this is no trifling matter. Pick a husband, or I shall do it for you. And be damned sure that I will, Cat. Damned sure."

The problem was that she knew very well his temper might cause him to do exactly that, regardless of his promise to her. Despite her father's warning, she had found herself reliving that last encounter with John Raven more times than she wished, mentally watching her crop descend across the high cheekbone. The memory that was most clear and, to her disgust, most often repeated in her mind, was what he had said just before he'd departed.

Tell him, John Raven had said, *that you belong to me.*

Once more in the midst of a crowded ballroom, Catherine forced her thoughts away from the remembrance of whatever, besides anger, had been in Raven's eyes that afternoon. She was still not certain of the emotion that had called forth his declaration. Fury at being denied what he wanted, certainly. And at her father's treatment of his suit. But she had begun to believe that she had seen something else stirring in that blue flame.

Resolutely she broke off her fruitless attempt to identify that fleetingly glimpsed emotion and tried to focus on what her partner was saying. She wished he'd simply let her enjoy the waltz, but he seemed to think that *he* must entertain her rather than allowing the flowing movements of the dance and the pulse of the music to do so. She allowed her lids to close over eyes that were beginning to glaze with boredom, and there appeared before her, in her mind's eye, John Raven's face. That had happened far too frequently lately, and she had found herself at too many social engagements unconsciously seeking that dark head which she knew would tower above those of the room's other inhabitants.

Guilt, she had finally decided. Guilt over the role she'd played in her father's brutality that day. By her mockery she had thrown Raven to the wolves when, she knew, she could have handled the situation differently, perhaps even have mitigated the duke's fury. Apparently she wasn't going to be given a chance to explain or apologize. John Raven seemed to have disappeared from London as quickly as he had appeared. Unconsciously, she sighed.

"Bored, my dear?" Gerald asked solicitously.

Good God, she thought, shocked at that familiar voice. She had changed partners in such a perfect fog that she'd been unaware until that very moment that she was floating across the floor in Amberton's very capable arms.

"Tired," she offered, wondering what she'd said to him before, while she was thinking of the American's strong features.

"It's nearly over. The Season is winding down and—"

"Don't," she ordered with something of her old spirit. "Don't tell me what's going to happen after that. I assure you I don't intend to repeat the argument we had two weeks ago."

She began to take her hand from his, resolving, since he seemed determined to remind her, to move away from him. But his fingers tightened over hers, controlling.

"You really are too accustomed to having your own way. I don't think public humiliation, my dear, is on tonight's agenda."

She turned in surprise at his unexpected masterfulness. Smiling smugly, he ruthlessly swept her back into the rhythm of the waltz, holding her far closer than was acceptable.

"Let me go," she demanded imperiously.

"Quit behaving like the spoiled chit I called you. We're in the middle of the dance floor, for God's sake. Don't you dare try to walk away from me."

Furious, she struggled again, and his fingers ground into hers more strongly, hard enough to bruise.

"You've had your own way too long, my pet. But I think you'll not find me so easy to deal with as your ever-indulgent parent. You really have no option here, and you must know it."

Catherine was forced to realize the unpleasant truth of his assertion. She could literally fight him for her freedom, here under the eyes of the gossiping old tabbies of the ton, or she could give in gracefully and finish the set. She couldn't imagine what had come over Gerald, but in this instance she recognized the validity of what he had said. As much as she hated the admission, she really had no choice.

Finally the music ended, and with what she hoped was an icy dignity, she allowed him to lead her from the floor. Still furious, she had said nothing after his unconscionable behavior. She was relieved to find that her next partner was an old and trusted childhood friend, Lord Anthony Dellwood. Gerald released her with what appeared to be satisfaction with his mastery, and she nodded coldly before he turned away.

"I'm sorry," she said as soon as Amberton had moved out of earshot, "but I'm feeling a trifle unwell. Do you suppose you might find my father, Tony? I really would like to go home."

She dealt charmingly with his expressions of concern and was infinitely relieved when he left her alone in the small sheltered alcove to which he had taken her to wait while he saw to the arrangements. It was not just Gerald's bizarre behavior, it was everything. The Season *was* coming to an end, and with its conclusion, her father's repeated ultimatums for her decision had increased. And the only man with whom she could imagine...

The thought impacted like fireworks in her brain. The only man with whom she could imagine spending the rest of her life was not Gerald, nor any of the other perfumed and pompous members of her set, but... Surely she couldn't be contemplating marriage to the coal merchant. The words *you belong to me* echoed again in her brain, causing their own small explosion of sensation. My God, she wondered, could he possibly be right about that? "The bride was conveyed to her wedding by locomotive," the *Morning Post* would say.

Catherine's lips slanted suddenly as she remembered Raven correcting her father. She doubted whether anyone else in his very long and noble life had had the gall to point out the duke's obvious errors to him. No wonder her father had been so furious that day. John Raven certainly did not play by the rules that had been set down for members of this society to follow.

"I'm sorry, my dear, but your father seems to have been called away. Some unexpected emergency. I'm sure a very minor one, but I've ordered your coach brought round and will very gladly escort you home," Dellwood offered gallantly.

"There's no need for that, Tony. You know how short the distance is. And Tom's perfectly reliable. He's been in my father's service for years."

"I insist. I'm sure your father would much prefer that I come with you. He probably already made arrangements for you to be conveyed home, and I've inadvertently countermanded them. I would never forgive myself if anything were to happen."

"And what do you imagine might happen to me between here and home? This is London, you know, not the wilds of America."

He laughed cooperatively at her feeble attempt at humor, while she wondered why that particular analogy had leapt into her mind. Obsessed with things American, perhaps? she questioned herself mockingly.

"I really insist on being allowed—" her escort began, and was quickly interrupted.

"And I must insist that I'm better off alone. Please. I really am not well, and I'm afraid this pointless argument..." As an added inducement, she pulled her small lace handkerchief from her glove and pressed it delicately against her lips.

Although still worried about the impropriety of allowing her to depart without escort, Dellwood was forced to agree. As Catherine had logically pointed out, this *was* London. What could possibly happen to the Duke of Montfort's daughter while being transported to her home by her father's own coachman?

The rain that had been a shower at the beginning of the evening had turned into a deluge, but through the solicitude of Lady Barrington's servants, Catherine was put into the coach, suffering no more than a drop or two spotting the emerald silk. She sat morosely in the darkness of the swaying carriage, listening to the pounding fury of the storm against its roof. She was angered and bewildered by Gerald's attempt at domination tonight. And, she was honest enough to admit, to herself at least, she was again disappointed that she had not at some point in the evening found two piercing blue eyes meeting hers with unusual directness. She missed the excitement her encounters with the American had added to her existence, and if she were completely honest, she knew that she also missed the man himself. Her lips moved into a slight smile, again remembering.

The small jolt of the carriage as it drew up to its destination pulled her attention from those memories, and she gathered her skirt in preparation for the descent into the driving rain. The door was opened and an enormous black umbrella held over her to shelter her from the deluge. Hurrying down the steps the coachman had dropped, she ran, head lowered against the force of the blowing rain, toward the welcoming glow that shone into the dark street from the door of the town house.

She heard it close behind her as she was shaking raindrops from her ball gown. She turned to hand her gloves and reticule to Hartford and found she was standing in the foyer alone.

In a foyer she had never seen before in her life. It took a moment for the reality of that to sink in. She was not in her father's town house. There had been some terrible mistake.

"Good evening," a deep voice intoned from the shadows at the end of the enormous hallway. She glanced up to find John Raven standing there, quietly watching her. His voice had echoed slightly across the empty expanse of softly gleaming black and gray squares of Italian marble that stretched between them.

She swallowed against the fear that constricted her throat. He had brought her here to avenge himself on her for what her father had done. She turned to the door behind her and began struggling to open it, her fingers trembling uncontrollably.

Before she could manage the intricacies of the unfamiliar lock, his beautifully shaped hand, which she had admired caressing Storm that day, gently closed over hers and removed them from the door. He turned the key that was in the lock and, removing it, placed it in his waistcoat pocket.

Catherine's fear was reflected in the strained face she raised to his, so he smiled at her before he spoke. "I'm not going to hurt you," Raven promised softly. He hated making her afraid, especially afraid of him.

"What do you want?" she whispered past the unfamiliar tightness that threatened to block her throat.

His mouth moved slightly, the corners deepening. "I *thought* I had made that perfectly clear. Even your father finally managed to understand what I want," he answered, and she was allowed to read his amusement.

Catherine was beginning to calm down, Raven's quiet humor making her believe that he really didn't intend her harm. There was no anger in his tone or posture. Apparently he didn't intend to seek revenge for the father's insult by ravaging the daughter, but she could still see the mark the crop had made that day faintly lined on his cheek.

Raven let her study his face a moment, and then he said, "There's nothing to be frightened of here."

Somehow, she found herself believing him. But he must know—surely he must know, even stranger that he was— what being found in such a situation would do to her reputation.

"Why did you bring me here?" she asked, and then wondered for the first time how that had been accomplished. "And how? That was my father's coachman. I saw him quite clearly before, at Lady Barrington's. He would never—"

"He has an invalid wife and a multitude of children."

"You *bribed* him?" she asked, unable to believe that Tom would betray her for money.

"He was very concerned about you. But I gave him my word that you would come to no harm at my hands."

"And he believed you?"

"Of course. He seems to be an excellent judge of character. He likes you very much, but he thinks your father's a bastard."

"You and the coachman discussed my father?" she asked. This must be some sort of nightmare. Soon she'd wake up, and she would still be on the dance floor, safely waltzing through another evening of deadly sameness. *Safe,* she thought longingly.

"Not at length. But we found ourselves in perfect agreement, I assure you."

"Why did you bring me here?" She was beginning to be able to control her fear. To be able to think.

"I wanted to show you something. Two things, really. Both of which I thought you should see."

"You abducted me to *show* me something?" she repeated carefully. "And when I've seen whatever it is?"

"Then I'll arrange to have you taken home. If you decide that's what you want."

"If I decide...?" Her voice rose. "What else do you imagine I would want?" She paused and took a breath, again seeking control. "Of course I shall want to be taken home."

"Perhaps not. We won't know until we've completed our business."

Business, she echoed mentally, wondering with irritation if that was all John Raven ever thought about. Apparently he had kidnapped her to discuss business. She felt a spurt of fury. She'd been abducted by a man whom, she admitted, she was fascinated by, and all he wanted to do was to talk business. As if she were some solicitor or shopkeeper instead of what she was—the acknowledged toast of the last two London seasons. The final thought was reassuring in light of his disinterest.

She glanced up and realized he knew exactly what she was thinking. His amusement was obvious in that dark face. His eyes, which were warmer than she had ever seen them, displayed a clear understanding of her disappointment.

"Then why don't you show me whatever you've brought me here to see and let me go home? The sooner the better, I assure you," she said decisively.

Raven inclined his head in agreement and gestured with his hand, urging her ahead of him down the wide hall. She hesitated a moment and then swept up her damply clinging skirt and proceeded in the direction he'd indicated.

On her left was a vast salon, perfectly proportioned from the sweep of its tall Palladian windows that lined the wall to the graceful Adam fireplace and the finely executed plaster medallions overhead. And perfectly empty. Catherine wandered in, wondering what she was supposed to do. She turned, allowing a small sarcastic lift of one beautifully shaped auburn brow.

"And?" she said.

"This way," he commanded and, shrugging, she followed.

It was exactly the same over the entire lower level of the mansion: elegant rooms of stately design and size, completely unfurnished. Raven didn't comment as he led her through the vast dimness, their footsteps echoing over the bare floors. He took her finally into a small study, sparsely furnished with a huge desk and chair, another chair facing the desk, and a tall cabinet. The surface of the desk was cluttered with ledgers and papers.

"I had thought, if you didn't mind, that I would leave this as it is. To serve as my office. And there's a small bedroom that I've left as I found it, simply for convenience. However, if you have any objections, I assure you I won't stand in your way in redecorating those. I myself have little interest in such things. A chair and a bed and I'm perfectly happy."

"This is your house?" Catherine asked, beginning to make some sense of this mysterious tour. "You're living here."

"A rather Spartan existence at present. But soon, I hope—"

"In *my* redecorating?" she interrupted, having just registered the gist of his explanation. "You expect *me* to redecorate?"

"I promised a house you might furnish as you pleased."

"This... You intend that I... That you and I..." Despite several attempts, she couldn't seem to complete the suggestion he once again appeared to be making. Apparently her father had not convinced him that he couldn't have what he had decided he wanted. "Mr. Raven, you must realize—"

"They tell me it's rare that such a property becomes available in Mayfair. That such houses as this seldom change hands. It was the first one they showed me, and I must confess, I felt it to be perfect. However, you know far more about such matters than I. If you think—"

"Mr. Raven..." She broke in again and then found herself at a loss. Nothing she said seemed to make an impression. Nothing her father had said or done seemed to matter at all. John Raven was without a doubt the most obstinate man she'd ever met.

"Then it won't do?" he asked in the sudden silence.

"It's not the house. It's wonderful. You must know that."

"The original furnishings are in storage, until you've had the opportunity to choose any of them you wish to keep. Or you may discard them all and begin anew. My solicitor assured me there are some very fine pieces among them, however. I'll make arrangements for you to see everything as soon as—"

"Mr. Raven," she interrupted, more strongly than before.

He stopped. The small depression at the corner of his lips deepened, but his expression was otherwise under perfect control, the blue eyes resting on her face with polite interest.

"I can't marry you," she said softly.

He glanced down briefly at the toe of his evening shoe, which gleamed softly at the bottom of his impeccably cut formal trousers, and she saw the breath he took before he spoke.

"Then perhaps I should show you the second thing I brought you here to see," Raven said.

"Perhaps that would be wise," Catherine agreed. "And then you promised to have me returned to my father's house. I can only hope that he hasn't already found that I'm not there."

"Your father won't be home for at least another hour."

"How can you possibly..." The realization was as startling as the idea that he could simply bribe her father's trusted servant to do whatever he wished. "You arranged for my father to be called away. So you could bring me here."

"If things don't turn out tonight as I hope they will, it seemed the safest way for you. No one will know that you've been here. Tom will take you home, and nothing will ever be said about your visit. If you decide that's what you want."

"*If* I decide?" she questioned.

"After you've seen what I would like to show you now."

There seemed to be nothing to do but let him play out this fantasy, whatever else he had in mind. Whatever else he had to show her. Jewelry? she wondered, trying to think what he had mentioned in the original offer.

Turning, he chose a paper from the clutter on the desk and held it out to her.

Catherine had hesitated in the doorway, somehow reluctant to enter the suddenly too small confines of the room, which he seemed to dominate simply by standing, completely unmoving, waiting for her to take the paper he offered. In the dimness, his eyes shone in the spare, rugged beauty of his face.

Beauty? She repeated that incredible thought, wondering at her own description.

Shaking her head slightly to break the spell he always cast over her senses, she walked forward, laid her gloves and reticule on the desk and took the proffered sheet. She looked down at what she held, expecting a deed or some bill of sale, some added inducement to all that he had already offered. Something to sweeten the pot. And yet... he had never offered her the one thing she was beginning to realize she really wanted from him, the one thing that she knew would affect her decision.

She started to read, scanning what was written on the paper. One more obstacle to be overcome, and then he had promised to have her conveyed home.... She stopped suddenly, some sense of what she held finally dawning, and her eyes flew back to the top of the page to carefully peruse what she had only glanced at before: "...His Grace, the seventh Duke of Montfort, is pleased to announce the forthcoming marriage of his daughter, Lady Catherine Montfort, to Gerald Blaine, third Viscount Amberton."

"That's to appear in the *Post* and the *Gazette* tomorrow," Raven said.

"How did you get this?"

"Most things are for sale—given enough money. I was afraid your father might try something like this, so I took precautions against it." Raven had offered her freedom, the only thing she did not have, and he could only pray that she would desire it enough to escape the trap they had devised for her.

Catherine felt the sickness growing in the pit of her stomach. Her father had broken a promise to her for the first time in her life. He was going to give her to Amberton without in any way considering her own wishes. And then, even more disturbing than that betrayal, came the remembrance of Gerald's behavior on the dance floor. As if he were already certain of his control over her. As, of course, he had been, she realized—assured of that control through her father's treachery.

Unconsciously she flexed the bruised fingers the viscount had gripped so painfully earlier tonight. "But he promised," she whispered, fighting the urge to give in to the tears that she so seldom shed. Her own father had forsaken her.

"I'm sorry. I believe my proposal probably played a part in his decision, at least in the timing. You *did* try to warn me."

She looked up at the unexpected confession, surprised to find what appeared to be a look of concern on his face. It was almost immediately replaced by the controlled expression John Raven's features always bore. So quickly did the change occur that she was forced to doubt her identification of the emotion she had seen. How could he possibly know what she was feeling—this sense of betrayal and despair over the fate her father had arranged?

"It's not your fault," she admitted, because in all fairness it wasn't. "I suppose I've always known this was inevitable. And Gerald..." she began, again remembering his actions tonight. She had held to the illusion that if she were forced to choose from the men she knew, Gerald at least offered some possibility of rapport. Until tonight. Tonight he had seemed almost a stranger, determined to force her to his will.

"There *is* another option," Raven said, interrupting her despondency.

She glanced up from the announcement her father had had composed. An option. Freedom and wealth. *Rich as Croesus.* At least she would never have to wonder if John Raven had wanted her for her father's money. No, she remembered suddenly, he wanted her for a far different reason. His promise of noninterference in her life was to be in exchange for her becoming his hostess, for arranging his entry into the ton. A business arrangement. If only he had offered...

She banished that ridiculous thought, trying to decide if accepting Raven's proposal could possibly provide a way out of the trap Amberton and her father had so blithely created. A marriage trap—weighed against the promise of freedom.

"Freedom?" she questioned aloud. And as if he had been following the convoluted path of her reasoning, he nodded.

"You have my word. Within the constraints of our contract. You invite to this house those men who would certainly not come otherwise, entertain them so well that the invitations to dine here become the most fashionable in London, and you refrain from taking lovers. Other than those responsibilities, you may do entirely as you wish. I promise that I will never censure you," he vowed, and again she found herself believing him.

"You must know my father will disinherit me," she warned.

"The fewer ties you have with your father, the better pleased I shall be," Raven admitted. His gut twisted at the remembrance of what the old man had said. That insult had cut far more deeply than the gash across his face.

Catherine hoped that, like her father's coachman, she was a good judge of character. "All right," she agreed softly.

Raven said nothing, relief and exultation blocking his throat, a reaction as automatic and uncontrollable as that which tightened his stomach muscles and stirred painfully in his groin. She had just agreed to become his wife. Against everyone's assurance that she never would.

Because he didn't respond, Catherine was unsure that he had heard her whisper. She looked up and said it again. "All right, Mr. Raven. I accept. And now, how do you intend to bring this off, in light of the announcement tomorrow of my betrothal to Lord Amberton?" Somehow she had no doubt he had already devised a plan to handle the practical aspects of their wedding.

"I had thought..." Raven paused, trying to gauge her mood. There had been too much pain in those beautiful eyes. Pain quickly hidden beneath her pride.

She met his searching gaze with her face deliberately cleared of emotion and her chin unconsciously raised. Once committed, she was prepared to burn her bridges spectacularly.

"You intend to let my father find us together?" she guessed, realizing that he certainly didn't know the duke as well as she. "Hoping that he'll then consent to our marriage?"

"Would that work?" Raven asked, amused at the scenario she'd suggested. Far more melodramatic than what he'd planned, but when he considered the possibilities it offered...

"I'm afraid not. He'd shoot you, or hire someone to do it, and then cover it up. He also has a great deal of money."

His lips moved slightly, and she knew she'd amused him.

"Then do you suggest I tell him that you've agreed to become my wife?"

"He'll shoot you, or hire someone to do it, and then—"

"I see." He interrupted her repetition of the outcome. And he was still amused. "Then perhaps you have a suggestion."

"Gretna Green," she said decisively, fighting memories of another run for the Border. Another man, very different from this. "Shocking, I know," she forced herself to continue, "but it's really the only way."

"And your reputation?" Raven could imagine how their elopement would be viewed by the ton. He hadn't intended to ruin her life, to cut her off from everyone she'd ever known.

"Oh, dear Lord," she said, chiding his ignorance. "A scandal of the proportion *this* one is going to be? The love story they'll imagine is at the root of *this* runaway marriage? Your wealth? And your appearance?" she added unthinkingly, and saw again the small, upward quirk of his lips. "Give the gossip two months to ferment, and we'll be able to charge admission to the first dinner party." She glanced down at the paper he had handed her. They really had given her no choice.

"Let me worry about the ton, Mr. Raven. You worry about what horses you have in your stables that can beat my father's best in a race to the Border. I'll take care of the rest. It's what I was born to do," she asserted confidently. Having been bred and reared in the world he desired to enter, she was secure in her membership. She was already thinking of the best way to handle the necessary explanations when the time was right.

"I don't think that's what you were born for at all," Raven said, knowing exactly for whom Catherine Montfort had been created. His angel. His wife.

At that surprising comment, she looked up from the hated announcement. John Raven, however, was already striding through the door to make those arrangements that she had suggested were his responsibility in this merger they had undertaken.

Only a business arrangement, she reminded herself, her eyes resting again on the evidence of her father's treachery, which had driven her to this contract and to this man.

Chapter Four

Once the flight up the Great North Road had begun, they did not stop except to change horses. It seemed to Catherine that they flew through the darkness, the coach rocketing along the well-maintained thoroughfare. The horses Raven had arranged to be waiting at the various posting inns were not only fresh, but bred for stamina and speed. They finally reached their destination in less than thirty hours, without having seen any evidence of what she had been sure would be a determined pursuit.

Despite the inducements of the professional "witnesses," Raven sought out a real blacksmith shop. The ceremony over the anvil was quickly completed, an exchange of vows as stripped of pageantry as even, she believed, the American might wish.

Raven then took time to discuss with the smith the quality of the metal he had been using, before they'd interrupted him, to shape the products that came from his forge. Even the taciturn Scot responded to his well-informed comments.

"Aye, well, you're right enough about that, my lord," the smith said in answer to Raven's observation that nowhere in Scotland was wrought iron produced, which would be free from the impurities that often ruined an object of some hours' work.

"My name is Raven," the American had corrected, offering his hand, "and I'm no lord."

"Your pardon, then, Mr. Raven. I meant no offense," the smith said, smiling, his pale eyes twinkling at his joke.

"Offense?" Catherine Montfort Raven questioned.

Her husband turned, smiling, to answer her slightly affronted inquiry. "There are men," he explained, "who believe that to be accused of being English nobility is a deadly insult."

"Why?" she asked, never having encountered such a ridiculous prejudice. But then, of course, she had never before talked to a Scots blacksmith as he worked his forge.

"Because it implies uselessness, perhaps," Raven answered hesitantly. He had known instinctively what the smith implied, but he didn't intend to explain the insult to Catherine.

"Like my father, you mean," she suggested.

Without answering, Raven took her elbow to guide her back to the waiting carriage, scarcely able to believe that this incredibly beautiful girl, serenely elegant even after their long journey, was now his wife. His to care for and protect. And her comment had brought him back to the still-precarious situation in which they found themselves. The Duke of Montfort, when crossed, could be a very dangerous man. Despite the Scots' friendliness, Raven doubted they'd be willing to fight the duke's hirelings to defend a stranger who happened to know something of their trade.

He helped Catherine into the coach and walked back to the forge to wait for the mulled wine the smith's daughter had been dispatched to fetch.

"That girl's too delicate for marriage to the likes of you, Mr. Raven," the blacksmith offered, eyeing the foreigner's broad shoulders, which looked more than capable of handling the heavy hammers that were a part of his own trade. "She'll be whining and denying you after the first child. You'd best hope she gets you a son on her first swelling. Though, come to that, she don't look sturdy enough to bear a babe. Not up to your riding weight, if you get my meaning," he suggested, slapping his blushing daughter on her ample rump as she passed. "You need a fine Scots lass who'll welcome your lovemaking and bear you a houseful of strong sons. You'll soon be regretting this day's work," he said, becoming more daring in response to the hooting enjoyment of the men who had gathered to watch as he plied his bellows.

Even hidden from sight in the isolation of the waiting coach, Catherine was well able to hear the smith's comments. She felt the hot blood flowing upward into her cheeks, not only at the crudity with which he was discussing the consummation of her marriage, but at the contempt in which he obviously held her and her class.

"You may know a great deal about iron," her husband said, his voice coming to her as clearly as had the Scotsman's, although he had not raised it to entertain the listening crowd. "But I'm forced to tell you, sir, that you know nothing about women. My wife is, I assure you, the purest cast steel. You need have no doubts about her quality. Or," Raven added, "about anything else you've called into question."

At the burst of laughter and the catcalls that greeted his response—all made, surprisingly, at the expense of the smith and not the American who had so eloquently defended his choice of woman—Raven touched his hat, planted a quick kiss on the cheek of the smith's daughter as he took the stone bottle from her hand, and walked back to the waiting carriage.

Catherine's blush made it obvious, she was afraid, that she'd overheard the entire conversation. "They don't think much of the English, do they?" she commented, with what she hoped was a convincing display of nonchalance. "Or of me," she added almost bitterly, spoiling the effect.

"I told them they were mistaken," Raven said, smiling. When her lips moved slightly into a reluctant realignment, almost an answering smile, he finished, "About you at least."

Finally, she did smile. There was really no need to argue with him about the smith's assessment of the English nobility, an assessment she realized she had at times even shared.

She was also beginning to realize that she was no longer just a part of the world she'd always inhabited; she was, by virtue of the vows she had spoken, simple though they were, a part of Raven's. A world which, apparently, included vulgar Scots blacksmiths. She shivered slightly, whether from the cold of the morning air or from her acknowledgment that she belonged not only to Raven's world, but also, of course, to John Raven himself.

"Would you like some wine?" he asked into the uncomfortable silence that had fallen between them. "I can't vouch for its quality, but at least it's warm." He had wrapped his ungloved hands, their golden color reddened slightly with the cold, around the bottle, using it as a warming stone.

She tried to block the image of those strong hands moving over her body, one she was sure the Scotsmen whom they were leaving behind at the smithy were also picturing. She knew her life would never be the same. She had committed herself to this man who had promised her freedom, but now, in the swaying confines of his coach, she acknowledged that that was no longer the thing she most desired from him.

Raven watched the slender fingers smooth tremblingly over her arms. Somehow the sophisticated surety that had characterized Catherine Montfort since he'd met her had softened, had lessened in this unfamiliar environment. He could only imagine what she must be feeling now. She had committed herself to him without any certainty that he would honor their agreement. And if he broke his word, she would have no legal recourse. By virtue of the vows they had just spoken, she had given herself into his control. Because, he reminded himself grimly, he had promised her freedom.

"Here," he offered softly.

She looked up from the tangled emotions of the last few minutes, to find Raven holding out a steaming cup of the mulled wine. She took the tin mug, her fingers gratefully encircling its heat. As she sipped the comforting beverage, her frame still racked by occasional shivers, her husband's arm came around her shoulders. He pulled her, unresisting, to lean against the pleasant heat of his body.

At least he could hold her, Raven thought, as frustrating as he was finding the restraint imposed by the terms of their contract to be. For the time being he must be satisfied with the relationship he'd promised. A vow, his grandmother had taught him, was sacred and must be kept, no matter the cost.

Eventually he felt Catherine's breathing deepen, and he knew that she slept. Asleep in his arms. Her small frame sheltered by his. He would give his life, without hesitation, to guard and protect this woman who now belonged to him. At least in name, he acknowledged bitterly.

Catherine Montfort Raven, he thought again, feeling the pleasure of that stir hotly in his groin. Slowly and carefully he shifted his weight, trying not to waken her, but needing to find a more comfortable position for the painful hardness of desire. John Raven knew, of course, there was really only one position that would ever offer true relief for that particular ache, and he wondered how long it would be before he might be allowed to savor its sweet release.

Two months later

Catherine sat, nibbling the end of her pen, once again remembering that flying journey home from the Border. She had slept, exhausted, through most of the trip, and whenever she'd awakened it had been to the comfort of Raven's steady heartbeat, just under the hard muscles against which her cheek had rested. That was, however, the last time her husband had touched her, and in the months since their marriage, his apparent lack of interest had become almost unbearable.

He had promised her freedom from his interference, and it was a promise he had certainly kept. He had made a contract with her for certain services and then, surprisingly, he had scrupulously kept to its terms—terms that she had never believed he would be able to adhere to. She had expected to be courted, and instead he virtually ignored her existence.

She had occupied her time and energy during those weeks in staffing and furnishing the elegant mansion he'd purchased. Although her instructions had been carried out to the letter, the task of seeing that they were had been left to Mr. Reynolds, Raven's very efficient man of business, and his staff.

Her husband had taken no part in choosing the nearly priceless items she'd retained from the original furnishings, which she'd found stored, as he'd promised, in a vast warehouse near the East India docks. She had discovered that the warehouse was one of many London properties he owned, most of its space devoted to the temporary storage of goods that he imported from the Orient for the insatiable English market.

She had also been allowed to choose the finest of those imports for her new home. She had spent hours wandering among the bolts of newly arrived silks, the porcelains still in their straw-packed crates. Her skirts brushing against the Holland covers, she had examined countless pieces of furniture, paintings and objets d'art that had been purchased with the mansion, and which Mr. Reynolds's clerks uncomplainingly uncovered for her inspection.

She was conscientiously trailed by one of the banker's staff, and almost by magic, the pieces she had chosen from the warehouse, plus the additional ones she purchased from the manufacturers on Bond or Oxford Streets, arrived at the Mayfair residence and were set up in the rooms they were intended to grace.

And grace them they did, she thought with satisfaction, glancing around the small salon in which she was sitting. It was almost certainly the finest house in the capital. As it should be, considering the sums she had spent. But if she had been hoping for some comment on that almost deliberate extravagance from the man who paid the bills, she had been disappointed.

Now that the first task he had set for her was almost completed, she knew it was time to move on to the second—the introduction of her husband into the closed circle of the ton. She had carefully chosen the occasion at which they would make their first appearance together.

She had begun, of course, immediately on their return from Scotland, to mingle again with her closest friends. Catherine often attended the small, private entertainments that comprised the limited summer activities for those who were unfortunate enough to remain in the city. Her father might choose to treat her as an outcast, but her own clique's acceptance of her runaway marriage had been automatic. It had, however, been surprisingly tinged with curiosity and, she had come to recognize, a certain unspoken envy. Apparently she was not the only woman who had noticed John Raven's physical attributes.

"But an American, my dear?" Charlene Rainsford had questioned.

"An extremely rich American, if only half of what we've heard is true," suggested Amelia Bentwood.

"Well, Cat?" Charlene prodded with a graceful laugh. *"You should certainly be in a position to verify the depth of your husband's pockets."*

"I don't know," Catherine said, her own smile a mocking one. *"I, for one, never listen to gossip."*

They had been forced to accept her refusal to discuss her husband's financial status, but the questions about her marriage hadn't ended with that exchange.

"I have never thought men of that size attractive. So primitive, don't you think? All that vulgar brawn," Anne Aston said, her thin frame shuddering as she recalled the breadth of John Raven's chest and shoulders.

There was a distinct, though ladylike, sound of derision from someone in the group of women who had been sitting in Charlene's music room, languidly at their ease, long after the Italian soprano had provided the afternoon's entertainment. The response to that unspoken comment was a burst of extremely unladylike laughter.

"I don't suppose you would like to remark on your husband's size, either, my dear," suggested Lady Rainsford, with an air of resignation. *"Something else you would certainly be in a position to discuss."* Most of the ladies were

aware of the obvious double entendre Charlene had thrown into their midst.

With what she'd hoped was an enigmatic smile, Catherine had discreetly lowered her eyes, as if that particular memory were too private to share.

But she had admitted to herself, as the talk had finally moved on to other topics when she didn't rise to the bait, she could readily testify to the breadth of Raven's shoulders, having slept on the return from Scotland closely sheltered against them for hours. But nothing else.

With the exception of the Honorable Anne, who was still a spinster and who, considering her unfortunate tendency both to squint and to throw out spots, was likely to remain one, everyone present had known what information Charlene had tried to elicit. Information Catherine could not have shared, had she had any desire to, simply because she did not know.

"Forgive my intrusion," Raven said from the doorway. Catherine had appeared so deep in thought he'd hesitated to interrupt, but he wanted to see her. He had thought of nothing but seeing her since he'd left London. He wondered if she were unhappy, if the brown study in which he'd caught her was as melancholy as it appeared.

She looked up in surprise. Her husband had seldom sought her out in the weeks of their marriage, and it was obvious from his apparel that he had just returned from the business trip to the north of England on which he had been engaged for the past week.

"I didn't know you were back," she said, straightening the papers on the secretary to cover her momentary confusion.

She didn't know why simply seeing him again could throw her emotions into such disarray. He was dressed for traveling, his coat of Forester's green molding his upper body. The tight pantaloons that fashion demanded did more to delineate than to hide the muscles of his thighs. His Hessians were lightly covered with dust, and knowing by now his custom, she assumed he'd been traveling since dawn.

"I hated to interrupt. You appeared so deep in thought."

Her eyes lifted quickly to his face, and she smiled involuntarily at the thought of the memories he'd interrupted. She hoped he'd never know that she had been daydreaming about him and the interest he'd aroused in the sisterhood of the ton.

"I'm working on the seating arrangement of the small dinner party you're hosting next week," she lied. She offered for his inspection the table chart she had quite truthfully been considering before her thoughts had strayed, as they did frequently, to the other member of this marriage of convenience.

"Good God," Raven said, refusing the offered paper with a shake of his head. "I hope you don't believe that I have any expertise or interest in that. Simply tell me where to sit and whom to talk to, and I shall attempt not to embarrass you."

"As long as you promise to refrain from talking to the ladies about coal," she advised, smiling.

"I assure you there's only one lady to whom I've ever mentioned coal," Raven said, his lips lifting in response.

"Then I suppose I should be flattered," she suggested. "Or insulted. I can't quite decide which."

"Well, I'll leave you to work that out."

Raven wondered what she'd do if he kissed her. Surely that was acceptable for a husband returning from a week-long trip. But even as he thought it, he knew it was not acceptable, of course, in their marriage. He was no more her husband than he had been before those simple vows over the smith's anvil. Controlling his desire—something he'd had a bloody damned lot of practice at in the last few weeks, Raven thought—he turned to leave.

"But," Catherine said rather forcefully, reluctant to let him go, "there *are* matters that require your personal attention."

He hesitated in the doorway and then turned back, an expression of resignation masking his feelings.

"This *is* what you said you wanted," Catherine reminded him.

"My apologies. What must I do? I assure you I'm your willing victim."

"My great aunt Agatha is giving a rout, a celebration of another niece's birthday. She courageously sent an invitation, despite my father's refusal to acknowledge this marriage."

"And?" Raven asked, propping his shoulder casually against the frame of the doorway.

"She's also agreed to introduce us to her guests." Obviously the information meant less to him than Catherine had hoped. Seeing his puzzlement, she continued, "To introduce us as man and wife. Our first foray into the ton as man and wife."

"And what exactly will that involve?" he questioned, naturally suspicious of what would be expected of him.

"For one thing, leading out the first waltz. Along with my cousin and her father, of course," she explained, watching the lift of one midnight brow. "You do dance, don't you?"

"The reel," he admitted, beginning to enumerate. "And a passable Highland fling, which my grandfather taught me. I know a score of rather more exotic Eastern dances that I don't believe have ever before been seen in a London ballroom."

He paused, and the small movement at the corners of his lips should have warned her, but Catherine was concentrating instead on how much of the doorway his shoulders filled. And remembering again what they had felt like under the softness of her cheek.

"Then you must learn," she said decisively when it appeared he had finished his list of accomplishments. His inexperience was only what she had feared, and she was glad she had thought to plan for this eventuality. At least, now that she knew the worst, she could see to it that he was properly instructed.

"Very well," he agreed, fighting to control his amusement.

"I can have a dancing master here tomorrow," Catherine said.

"A dancing master?" he repeated. He hadn't considered that she might hire someone to teach him. "And will I be waltzing with the dancing master at your aunt's shindy?" he asked pointedly.

"I beg your pardon?"

"At the ball or whatever. Who will I be dancing with?"

"With me, of course. I thought you understood. We're to lead the dancing."

"Then you teach me," Raven suggested, his anticipation at holding her so great that he wondered how she could be unaware of what he was feeling. "I don't intend to prance around at the instruction of some hired popinjay."

"I don't know how to teach you to waltz," she argued, but the image of slowly circling the floor, closely held in Raven's hard, extremely masculine arms, was very enticing.

"Who taught you?"

"A dancing master my father employed."

"Then just show me whatever he showed you. It can't be that difficult. You'll find I'm an apt pupil," Raven said, the corners of his mouth again marked by his amusement.

"But I don't know if I'm an apt teacher," she reiterated hesitantly, her stomach fluttering with anticipation.

"I'll take my chances. And besides, it's that or nothing. I'm terribly afraid I shall have unbreakable appointments at whatever time you arrange for the dancing master to visit."

"Do you always get your own way?" she asked, smiling.

"If I can manage it," he admitted. "When shall we begin?"

"After dinner tonight?" she suggested. Surely that would give her long enough to get her emotions under some control.

"Are you dining in? Cook will certainly be in for a shock if that's the case," Raven said. "And Edwards. He'll be delighted. I keep talking to him while they serve my dinner. He never answers beyond 'Yes, Mr. Raven' or 'I don't believe so, Mr. Raven,' but I can tell it's a strain. I don't suppose he's ever had an employer who's tried to carry on a conversation before."

"You're not supposed to talk to the butler," Catherine said, but against her will, her smile was again pushing at the corners of her mouth. "It confuses the servants if you're too familiar."

"Are you trying to tell me that Edwards is ever confused? I've never met a more self-assured individual in my life."

"He is rather intimidating," she admitted, and watched Raven's blue eyes flick up to meet hers.

"I'm surprised he consented to lower himself to be our butler," he offered, matching her teasing tone.

"Well," she said, "you *are* paying him an enormous amount of money. Enough, I suppose, that he decided to condescend."

"Ah, that explains it. He probably refuses to speak to me because he's richer than I am."

Laughing, she watched him turn toward the door, and this time, having obtained his promise, she let him go.

It was not until she was gathering up her guest list and the seating arrangement she'd been working on that Catherine realized the significance of what he'd said. Raven had definitely indicated that he preferred not to eat alone, and more tellingly, that he'd noticed her many absences from their dinner table, absences occasioned by her deliberate attempt to accept as many social invitations as she possibly could. She had been carrying out her own redemption and reemergence into the folds of the nobility, a redemption she must complete before she brought her husband into that select world, given the shocking circumstances of her marriage. But, she decided suddenly, she would refuse any further invitations that would require her absence from her own dinner table, an absence her husband had just indicated he'd noticed.

"I understand, Edwards, that we're to be hosting a small dinner party next week," Raven said as the butler oversaw the removal of the final course.

"So madam has informed me," Edwards answered stolidly.

"I'm sure you'll be delighted to have something to do besides hover over my solitary dinners."

"Indeed, Mr. Raven, I have been very pleased to serve you," he said, a small flush creeping across his smoothly shaved jowls.

"And you've done so with remarkable skill. I don't believe I've told you how glad I am that you decided to work for us."

"I thank you, sir," the butler said, his spine rigid with embarrassment.

Raven had not been considering the effect of his teasing on the dignified Edwards. He had instead been watching Catherine across the table, wondering if his words were causing her to remember their meeting this morning and if she might be anticipating, as he had been all day, the promised dancing lesson.

"Edwards," Catherine interrupted the exchange, her russet eyes meeting her husband's, "if you would, please, fetch my shawl from the salon. There's a distinct draft in here."

Raven watched the butler's retreat without comment.

"I told you you shouldn't carry on a conversation with the servants. You would probably enjoy teasing the lions in the menagerie," Catherine said when he was safely out of earshot.

"I probably would—except for the fact that they are unfortunate captives. Are you attempting to compare Edwards to the lions?"

"I'm attempting to compare you to a small boy who would pull the wings off flies. You embarrassed the poor man to tears."

"That was never my intent. Do you suggest I apologize?" Raven asked, sincere contrition in his deep voice. He certainly hadn't intended to show the butler any disrespect. The man had treated him with none, despite the fact that they both were well aware Raven had no idea how to get on with servants.

"Apologize to your butler? I shouldn't think so."

"Not done?" he questioned mockingly. "The under classes are undeserving of an apology?"

"No." She tried to explain. "Your apology would simply further the embarrassment. You would be acknowledging that you'd noticed his discomfort. Edwards would then feel he'd made a terrible faux pas by allowing you to read his emotions."

"It must be very frustrating to have an employer who has no idea of how these things should be done."

"I shouldn't be surprised if he decides to leave us," Catherine warned, watching her husband play with the fragile stem of the Venetian goblet. His fingers were not at all blunt as one would expect, considering his size, she thought. They were long and tapered, the nails very clean and closely trimmed, the skin darkly tanned. She remembered with pleasure their callused warmth holding her hand to bring it almost to his lips.

"I would," he said, replacing the glass on the table. "I checked on what you're paying him."

"He's worth every shilling. He adds to your consequence."

"I hope in proportion to what he subtracts from my bank balance," he countered, smiling at her.

"Cheeseparing already," she chided, returning his smile.

"I don't believe you can accuse me of that."

"No," she answered with some seriousness, "but I do realize that furnishing this house has been a very expensive undertaking. If you wish me to economize, I shall certainly understand."

"The house is perfect," Raven said, the first compliment he'd allowed himself to pay her. Fascinated, he watched its effect, the soft, becoming spread of color under the translucent skin of her cheeks. "And I'm not yet in dun territory."

"Despite my dressmaker's bill?" she asked, teasing him now.

"That I *haven't* seen," he said. "Perhaps I spoke too soon."

His hand had again found the stem of the elegant crystal, and her eyes unconsciously rested once more on the lean fingers.

"I hope you know," he continued, "that you've not yet strained my resources. You have simply carried out your part of our bargain exactly as I'd hoped. I am not quibbling over the cost of your success."

"Thank you," she said simply.

"But I *am* wondering if I passed?"

"I beg your pardon?" she asked, raising her gaze from the contemplation of that dark, graceful hand, so fascinating to her.

"I assumed your attention to my table manners was to ferret out any unacceptable habits before I fall under the less-kind scrutiny of the ton."

"My attention to..." she began, and then realized that he must have noticed her watching his hands. He was far too observant, and she, apparently, far too obvious in her fascination. Luckily he was attributing her near compulsion to look at him to some other cause entirely.

"Your manners are excellent," she said, "as you must know."

"I should have asked Edwards," Raven said consideringly. "His standards are certain to be higher than yours."

"You place your hand here," Catherine instructed, feeling the warmth of his palm against her back with a decided frisson of reaction. Her gaze rose to his face, to see if he had felt the energy that had leapt between them at the touch. She licked her lips, which were, for some reason, suddenly dry, and continued, "And take my hand."

The tall body moved into too-close proximity to hers, the hard muscles of his chest brushing against the softness of her breasts.

"Not too close," she cautioned breathlessly, and he obediently moved back a few inches.

"The music is in three," she began.

"What music?"

"To the waltz."

"Then we seem to be lacking something. Unless I am badly mistaken, there *is* no music." Raven made a pretense of looking around the vast, empty ballroom and even cocked his dark head as if listening for some faint strain.

"But there will be that night."

"Then wouldn't it be better to practice with music?"

"I don't believe we are at that point," she said rather briskly, fighting an inclination to laugh.

"You could hire an orchestra. Or a small string ensemble."

"Not tonight," she said sternly. "I believe that you are simply trying to postpone the inevitable. You *did* promise."

"I must have been thinking of something else. Are you sure this is necessary?"

"In three," she said, ignoring his delaying tactics.

"Why don't you hum?"

"All right," she agreed patiently, her palms beginning to perspire slightly at being this close to him. Unconsciously she took a deep breath, enjoying once again the pleasant masculine aromas that surrounded him. "I shall hum."

"Something I know," he suggested.

"I don't know what you know," she said reasonably.

"That's true. Then something they'll play that night. Could you tell them what to play? So I'd be familiar with it?"

"No, I could not," she said. "In three," she insisted again and began to move as she counted. "One, two, three. One, two, three."

"That's all?" he asked, following her steps as if in deep concentration, a little uncertainly.

"Except you turn, so you're not dancing in a line. Turn as you move. Surely you must have seen the dancing that night."

"The night you danced with Amberton and everyone else?"

"Not everyone. I didn't dance with you," she said, relaxing with the increasing surety of his movements.

"No," he agreed. "But you should have," he said, sweeping her suddenly in ever-widening circles across the polished floor.

Her eyes locked with his, and he smiled at her, mocking her surprise at his expertise. Eventually her lids drifted closed, and she savored the pleasure of moving in the embrace of a partner who knew exactly how to hold her and whose steps, despite his size, matched perfectly with her own. She could almost hear the music he obviously felt. They were one. At least here.

This was as near to heaven as he was likely to get, Raven thought—holding Catherine, who floated gracefully in his arms as if she belonged there. As if she enjoyed being there.

God, he wanted her. She was his, legally and morally, and he wanted her more than he'd ever wanted anything in his life. More than the money that, in his impoverished youth, he'd thought was so important. More than success or power. More even than the desire to create structures and industries that would exist long after he was dead and gone. Even after his children were gone. At the thought of a child of Catherine's, his body betrayed his iron control again. Like a damn schoolboy, he mocked himself.

He released her finally, knowing that if he didn't leave soon, he'd not be able to. She swayed slightly against his chest, as if reluctant to have it end.

"Will you save me another waltz?" he asked softly, and she opened her eyes to find him regarding her with something that looked very much like possessiveness. "Besides the one we'll be forced to share under the inspection of your friends."

"Yes," she promised, mesmerized again by being this close to him, in his arms for the first time in so long.

"Somewhere between the Reginalds and the Geralds?"

"You can tell me when the musicians play something you know," she teased, stepping back from the circle of his arms, before she betrayed herself by revealing how pleasant she had found having them hold her to be. "I wouldn't want you to be embarrassed."

Having chided him for making her go through this farce of a lesson, which had almost turned into something else, she curtsied as carefully as if they really were partners at a ball and then catching up the skirt of her gown, made her graceful way across the echoing emptiness of the ballroom.

She forced herself not to hurry, but when she was safely in the hallway and away from the steady scrutiny of that knowing gaze, she closed the door and leaned against it a moment.

Playing with fire, she warned herself honestly, wondering how much longer she was going to be able to endure the very inconvenient restrictions of this marriage of convenience.

Chapter Five

"**D**eserted already?"

Catherine looked up from her contemplation of the crowded floor of her aunt's ballroom to find Lord Amberton at her elbow. Since she had been wondering the same thing, she knew at once what he was suggesting about her husband's absence.

Raven had danced with her after her aunt's rather tremulous announcement of their marriage. He had not led her in the sweeping circles that they had made across the empty dance floor of their town house, but had guided her sedately over this floor's far smaller expanse, his performance polished enough, but without the flash that would have invited comment. The ton had been forced to watch without being given any additional reason to question the couple's inclusion at the small entertainment for family and old friends.

Catherine's husband had said and done everything that was required, and after he had completed the tasks she'd carefully laid out for him during the short ride to their destination tonight, he had disappeared, allowing her freedom to slip back into the flirtatious camaraderie she shared with several former beaus who were in attendance. Until now, however, she had not been called upon to talk to the Viscount Amberton.

"I doubt it," she answered, her tone sharper than she'd intended. She had not yet forgiven Gerald for his behavior the night Raven had abducted her. Intellectually she knew the viscount's lapse had been far more her father's fault for allowing Amberton to believe that she already belonged to him. But it still hurt that he'd so readily destroyed the friendship they had enjoyed, simply to prove his dominance. His comment had been apt, however. Her gaze *had* been moving around the room, unconsciously looking for the dark, towering head of her husband.

"He's in the card room," Gerald offered. "Apparently dancing isn't something our American visitor enjoys."

"He's hardly a visitor," she said, a trace of ice in her tone.

"Because he has a house in Mayfair and an entrée here tonight due to your aunt's senility? I assure you, my dear, he will *always* be a visitor," Amberton replied sardonically.

"And what does that make me?"

"Sorry?" he suggested softly.

"Hardly," she denied. "He's a very interesting man."

"He's probably told you all about his coal mines."

And seeing her expression, he laughed. "By God, I believe he has. Probably nothing else to talk about."

"A successful marriage is not dependent on conversation alone," she said unthinkingly, and then, at his shout of laughter, blushed scarlet to the roots of her hair.

"I was sure there was some secret to his success. Not that I guessed *that,* of course. Somehow he doesn't appear to be—"

"If you'll excuse me," she interrupted, moving away.

He caught her wrist, continuing to hold her even when she looked down rather pointedly at his fingers, whitened with the pressure they were exerting against the kid of her glove.

"I think you should remove your hand."

"Such the proper matron," Amberton said, obeying. "So he's tamed you to the bit already."

"Tamed me?" she repeated, feeling a surge of anger.

"You weren't once so concerned about the conventions."

"And what makes you believe I am now?"

"You've not danced the last two sets, and you appeared to be trying to locate your husband. Hardly the behavior I should have expected from someone who was always the merriest hoyden of the Season. It's hard to picture you subdued and settled."

"Hardly *settled* because I am wondering where my husband is. Most women like to have an idea of their spouse's whereabouts. Raven doesn't have many acquaintances in this gathering."

"Wives who are concerned about their husband's whereabouts are usually up to mischief and don't wish to be discovered. But I hardly believe that to be your case. You seem far too enamored of your 'Raven,' as you call him. That's not a title, my dear."

"It fits him," she said truthfully. Perhaps because of the darkness of his midnight hair, she mused. And he *should* have a title. If anyone were arrogant enough to deserve a title, it was he.

"Shall I fetch him so you can play the dutiful little wife?"

"*That* title, however, doesn't fit," she responded tartly. She allowed her gaze to travel around the room, hoping Gerald would go away. Somehow she knew he'd had the better of this encounter.

"Then perhaps I might offer a different diversion."

She turned back to meet his eyes. He was laughing at her, and she wondered what he had guessed about her marriage.

"Give me a game," he suggested. "You always loved a hand of cards. And since your lord and master is engaged elsewhere—"

"He is *not* my lord and master."

"Then if you are allowed such freedom, play with me."

"I'm sorry, but I'm not interested in cards. The room is always so crowded. Half of Aunt's cronies come for the whist."

"I wasn't suggesting the card room, but then I suppose a private hand is far too daring for the sedate Mrs. Raven," he taunted. "Why don't you ask him if it's all right to accept my invitation to a hand of cards? Maybe you can talk him into giving you permission to play."

"If I wanted to play cards with you, Gerald—"

"Oh, I understand completely, my dear," he agreed, his mockery clear. "I wouldn't want you to get into trouble."

"My husband and I don't have that kind of marriage," she assured him, realizing belatedly that she had made things worse.

He cocked his head, studying her face. "Then what kind of marriage *do* you have, I wonder? This is becoming more interesting by the moment."

"Raven doesn't attempt to restrict my activities."

"Is that why you married him? A very impetuous marriage, I might add." *And damn the bitch, bloody disastrous for me,* Amberton thought bitterly.

"I married him because my father had promised I should choose my husband, and then you and he decided to do it for me."

"What *are* you talking about?" Amberton asked with what he hoped would appear to be genuine puzzlement.

"I saw the announcement intended for the *Post,*" she said, but something in his tone had been very convincing. Gerald had sounded as if he really *had* no idea what she was talking about.

"I must seem slow, but I'm afraid I'll have to ask what announcement." It was so easy to manipulate Cat, he thought. She was too honest herself to doubt the motives of others.

"It doesn't matter," she said, wondering for the first time if she had been gulled. *You belong to me,* Raven had said. Had he then set out to trick her, using the overheard conversation with Amberton to bait the trap? If so, he must have congratulated himself on how easily she'd been fooled.

No wonder there had been no pursuit in their journey to the Border, she realized suddenly. Her father had never intended to announce her betrothal and so, when she'd disappeared, he'd had no idea of why she'd run away or of where to search for her. No idea that she might have eloped to escape the marriage trap she believed he'd arranged. Instead, Raven had apparently tricked her into creating another trap, one of her own making.

"Then if you intend to stand beside the other matrons all evening, I believe I shall be forced to leave you, Cat, my heart," Gerald commented, interrupting her humiliating realization of how she'd been duped. "Boredom overtakes one so easily in the summer. It must be this oppressive dampness."

"I thought you mentioned something about cards?" Catherine asked, raising her chin. Damn Raven, she thought. How dare he trick her? She would never forgive him for that.

"I thought you'd decided to play the good wife."

"It's still a woman's prerogative to change her mind, I believe," she said, smiling at him with a warmth that caused his brows to raise slightly.

"Now there's my Cat. I'm afraid, my sweet, I really was beginning to believe he'd turned you into a tame tabby."

"Set your mind at ease. That's something no one will ever do. Not even Raven." Especially not Raven, she vowed silently.

"Do you suppose anyone else has discovered your aunt's solarium? Such a delightfully secluded room."

For the first time since she'd accepted his challenge, Catherine felt a small flutter of unease. This was certainly not what she'd intended. She had only wanted to show Gerald that she was still as daring as she had always been. And as for Raven . . .

She wasn't exactly sure what she wanted to show Raven, but she had a feeling, despite his promise not to censure her, that he wouldn't like her to be with Gerald in any "delightfully secluded room."

"I make that sixty points, my dear, and my game, I think. Your luck seems to have run out tonight."

Catherine took a deep breath, knowing that it was not her luck that was at fault. She couldn't seem to keep her mind on the cards. Her decisions regarding her discards had bordered on the absurd. She kept visualizing the ballroom below and a pair of crystal blue eyes searching the throng for her. Thankfully this was the last hand, and she would be free to escape.

"I'm really rather glad we decided on piquet. So much more challenging. And I believe, my dear, that your wager was..."

She met Amberton's look and knew again that he was making fun of her. Her lips tightened slightly, but she slipped the narrow diamond-and-ruby bangle, which Gerald had suggested would be an appropriate stake, off her wrist. When Raven had admired it earlier tonight, she'd thought with embarrassed amusement that he had probably not yet received the bill for it. She wondered if he would notice the loss of such a recent purchase, a purchase he had commented on. The first time, now that she thought about it, that he'd remarked on anything she'd worn.

"Unless..." Gerald began, and then hesitated.

"Unless what?" she asked, watching his face.

"I've just realized that the loss of a bracelet might be awkward for you. If Mr. Raven begins asking questions."

Since she had had the same thought, her betraying fingers hesitated in the act of placing the jeweled circlet on his side of the small gaming table at which they were seated.

"It's what I wagered," she said, seeing no way out.

"Well, I'm amenable to an alternate suggestion," Gerald said pleasantly. "I'd hate for you to get into trouble."

She flicked the bracelet angrily onto the gleaming wood of the table, and it bounced twice, the gems catching the light.

"I won't 'get into trouble.' It *is* my bracelet."

"And you may redeem it for a kiss," he said smiling at her. "One kiss between old friends."

"No."

"Well broken to the bit," he mocked. Come on, Cat, he urged silently. Get that famous Montfort temper up.

"That's not—"

"Afraid your dolt of a husband might object? Frankly, my dear, he doesn't seem to give a damn what you do. Rather a laissez-faire attitude. But he *is* a businessman, with what rumor suggests is a decided flare with money. He'll never miss the kiss, but I wouldn't be so certain about the jewels.''

"All right," she agreed, fearing Gerald was correct. Anything to get this over and done. After all, it was not as if she'd never before been in Amberton's arms. But, her conscience reminded her, she'd never been there as a married woman.

How had she gotten herself into this? she wondered bitterly. She'd been married two months, had never even been kissed by her own husband, and she was about to allow another man that privilege. How could she have been so stupid?

"I'll send you word," Gerald said, rising and looking down at her. So easy. And now if the rest went as well, he'd be back where he'd been before the American had interfered.

"What do you mean?" Catherine asked, not understanding.

"You'll be hearing from me. When I want to collect." Smiling, he slid the bracelet back across the table. "I enjoyed the game, my dear. A very pleasant evening altogether, I must say."

Still smiling, he strolled to the door and, her eyes on the wagered jewelry, Catherine heard it close behind him.

When she was sure he was gone, she took the narrow bangle from the table and slipped it over her wrist. The beauty of the gems seemed to mock her as he had.

You'll be hearing from me, Gerald had said. And she had no doubt that she would.

"Did you enjoy yourself?" Raven asked on the way home.

Perhaps if he gave her the opportunity to tell him where she'd disappeared to, she would. By the terms of their contract, he had no right to ask. He had promised her freedom, he reminded himself bitterly, and noninterference in her activities.

Catherine knew she had been too silent, thinking about what had happened tonight instead of discussing the evening as he seemed to expect.

"Of course," she lied, trying to clear her mind of the circling recriminations. Why had she let Gerald convince her to go upstairs with him? She wondered for the hundredth time if anyone had seen them. And if so, had it been mentioned to Raven? Her husband had seemed exactly the same when, having made her furtive way down the servants' stairs, she had, upon reentering the ballroom, spotted him almost immediately.

Seeing his tall form, she had surprisingly lost all her anger about whatever tricks he'd employed to get her to marry him and had felt instead a sense of relief and of safety. He'd been talking to a group of gentlemen who appeared interested in whatever views he was sharing, but he'd turned his attention to her at once when she'd appeared at his side. At her whispered suggestion, he had immediately arranged for their departure.

"I looked for you for the waltz you'd promised," Raven said, hoping she'd relieve the pain eating his gut at the thought that she might again have been on some dark balcony in the arms of one of her former beaus, who had swarmed around her all night.

Catherine found that her hands were twisting the kid gloves she'd removed upon entering the coach, and she forced them to lie still in her lap. Guilt, she thought.

"Someone told me you were playing cards," she answered, turning to watch through the window the sweep of the elegant facades of the town houses they were passing, revealed by the brilliance of the moonlight.

"For a while. Some of the men I wanted to meet were playing. I managed to lose and then returned to the ballroom."

"Managed to lose?" she repeated, thinking of her own losses tonight.

"They really aren't very good card players."

"And you are?" she asked, smiling.

"Reasonably. It's all numbers. I'm good with numbers."

"I would have said it's mostly luck and intuition."

"And you probably lose more than you win," he answered, that small smile playing again over the stern line of his lips.

"You might be surprised."

"I might at that. Did you play tonight?" he asked casually, and she felt her heart stop.

"No," she managed to say, but even to her own ears, the whispered response sounded unconvincing.

"That's probably just as well. If you *really* believe it's all a matter of luck."

She waited through the remainder of the ride for the question she had expected and for which she still had no answer. *Where were you? Where were you when I looked for you to fulfill the promise of a second, more private waltz?* And she found herself regretting having missed the pleasure of that dance.

But he never asked. And, because she had thought he might care, she was perversely disappointed that she was *not* going to be called upon to explain her absence from the ballroom.

The days preceding the first small dinner she'd planned were crammed with last-minute preparations. Catherine resolutely put from her mind the events of her great aunt's party. She didn't allow herself to think about the threat of having to redeem her wager or about Gerald's seemingly genuine puzzlement about the announcement of their betrothal for the *Morning Post*.

She had found, on reflection, that it was rather flattering if Raven *had* taken the trouble to arrange that ruse. It must mean that he had really intended to marry her from the beginning and was willing to do almost anything to accomplish that. No woman could be very unhappy with that thought, whatever her husband's reasons for desiring the marriage. Especially, she was honest enough to admit, if that woman had fallen in love with the man who had gone to all that trouble.

She couldn't pinpoint the exact moment when it had happened, or even when she'd first acknowledged that it had. But there was no longer any doubt in her mind that she was, very unfashionably, in love with her own husband. She now knew how much she wanted their relationship to move into other directions, while he, it seemed, was content to allow their original agreement to stand. Of course, he didn't yet know a great deal about Catherine Montfort Raven. He had likened her to steel, and in the face of her determined decision to enchant him, it seemed an apt description.

Every night she faced Raven over the dinner table, listening with what had become truly fascinated attention to his quiet discussion, made in response to her encouragement, of his various business dealings and of the men whom she needed to win over in order to carry out those activities.

She found herself watching his hands or his mouth as he talked or enjoying the laughter in his eyes as he answered some perfectly ridiculous question she'd asked. Or as he teased her about why she might possibly want to understand the process by which steel was cast. But he answered her, patiently explaining and even reexplaining whatever she questioned. And if in those few days their time at table, under the watchful eye of Edwards, stretched far beyond the proscribed dinner hour, she was pleased to think neither of them minded.

The afternoon before the long-awaited dinner party had finally arrived and, carefully reviewing her arrangements, Catherine believed there was nothing else that needed her attention. She looked forward to a long bath and several hours in the skillful hands of her hairdresser and her maid. Her dress had arrived the day before and, made up in blush taffeta overlain with cream lace, it was far more becoming than she had hoped. For the first time, she allowed herself to relax. She knew enough about her husband now that she had ceased to worry about how he would be accepted. His manners were as polished and his conversation as interesting, to her mind at least, as anyone she'd encountered in her long familiarity with the haut monde.

One of the maids tiptoed in, apologizing for interrupting her solitude. Catherine, seated at the small secretary in her bedroom, raised her eyes from the list she was checking off. She was still in her silk wrapper, having seen no reason to dress. Edwards would take care of everything downstairs, and she had thought he'd appreciate her being out of the staff's way as they made the arrangements she'd carefully gone over with him.

"What is it, Maggie?" she asked, wondering what could possibly have gone wrong with her meticulous planning.

"It's a letter, madam. They said it was urgent."

Catherine wondered if her father had changed his mind and decided to attend after all. His refusal had been expected and his response had obviously been composed by his secretary, but at least it had been polite.

"Thank you," she said, taking the proffered envelope.

She waited until the maid had left before breaking the wax seal, which she had recognized at once.

The words, after the first, began to run together, and with a growing sense of unreality, she was forced to reread what Gerald had written, the salient part of the message coming after the usual vows of friendship couched in rather flowery terms in the first paragraph.

...I now find myself strapped for funds for a minor undertaking. With my heartfelt apologies for any inconvenience it might cause, I thought it fair to tell you I intend to apply to your husband for the repayment of the debt you incurred on Thursday last. He has agreed to a six o'clock appointment today. If, however, this arrangement presents a problem for you, I will, as a gentleman, be forced to accept the forfeiture we previously agreed upon. I look forward to hearing from you.

Yours faithfully,
Amberton

Faithfully, she reread with bitterness. The scoundrel. To think that she had been so foolish as to place herself in his power like this. And then, knowing that there was nothing to be gained by useless recriminations, she glanced at the clock. It was already past four, and the first guests were to arrive at eight. Apparently Gerald had planned his revenge with precision. And with some knowledge of her arrangements.

She wondered suddenly if it were a trick. Would Amberton be brazen enough to apply to her husband for payment of a wager he had won in their very clandestine and improper game? But, of course, the chance that he really didn't intend to meet with Raven was not one she could afford to take.

Reacting as decisively as she ever had in her life, she swiftly rang for her abigail, and before five she was in Raven's town coach heading to Gerald's apartment.

She had worked herself into a froth of rage by the time she arrived, and it wasn't in the least mitigated by the almost contemptuous fulsomeness of Amberton's greeting.

"My dear, what a delightful surprise," he enthused as he held open the door for her furtive entry. She could imagine what the wagging tongues of the ton would say if anyone saw her entering the apartment of an old beau less than three months after her runaway marriage. There would be a great many *I-told-you-so*'s exchanged across the ton's dinner tables if her visit today became public knowledge.

"How dare you approach my husband about a very private wager? Have you no honor at all, Gerald?"

"But you were quite insistent that your Mr. Raven didn't attempt to censure your behavior. And my financial need is, I'm sorry to say, quite pressing."

"How much?" she asked, opening her reticule, into which she'd stuffed every pound left out of this quarter's pin money. She knew that her useless anger was only playing into his hands and making this entire episode even more distasteful. Her temper had gotten her into this situation, and she must control it until she had gotten herself out. Whatever value he put on the bracelet she'd gladly pay, just to have done with this farce. In her head, a clock ticked ominously, measuring the brief hours before she would be expected to be at home, poised, assured and beautifully turned out, to play hostess to the beau monde. And the even briefer time until Raven's threatened arrival here.

"You surely didn't believe this to be a matter of money?" Gerald asked silkily.

Glancing up, Catherine was surprised to see a very smug expression on his handsome features. "Your letter indicated that you were strapped for cash."

"I assure you my pockets are not quite empty, my love. Though not, of course, as deeply lined as they would have been had you gone along with the plans for our nuptials. That really was too bad of you, Cat. I had such hopes for our union, an opportunity to see you really tamed. You always were such a hellcat. I wonder how your Mr. Raven is enjoying all that fire and passion."

Gerald paused, considering the effect of his comment. Because he did know her very well, he believed he could read the answer in her blush. What he'd begun to suspect about this very strange marriage was apparently true. It was a marriage of convenience, and not at all the love match the ton had proclaimed it.

"You never did anything by half measures," he continued smoothly. "And because of that, I don't believe anyone will be surprised that you've managed to become bored with your marriage to that barbarian after only a few short weeks."

"Leave my marriage out of this," she said coldly. "And he's not a barbarian."

"Oh, of course he is. That, and his unlimited funds, of course, are probably why you were attracted to him. He's rich enough that you didn't have to worry about whether he wanted you or your father's money, and you were always attracted to the bizarre. Your American husband certainly is that. Does he beat you, my sweet, when you make him angry?"

"*He's* never given me occasion to make him angry," she answered sarcastically, and was rewarded by the rush of furious color into the viscount's pale cheeks.

"Damn you," he said softly.

"If not money, what do you want? I have guests coming."

She hoped her cold display of rigidly controlled impatience was successfully masking her fear. Somehow Catherine knew that Gerald wanted to make her afraid. That it was part of the revenge he had planned to take on her for marrying Raven instead of him. He wanted her to be afraid of her husband finding out about the card game and afraid of what his own intentions were during this highly improper meeting, here in the privacy of his home.

"I think, my darling, you owe me what you promised. A kiss. If you're not giving those delightful embraces to that dolt of a husband, you might at least give the one you promised to me."

It was indeed what she had so foolishly agreed to. She found it hard to believe Gerald had gone to all this trouble simply for a kiss, but she couldn't take the chance of refusing him. Unrequited love? Could that be motive enough for all this elaborate plotting? He had never seemed that passionate before, so it didn't really fit.

But whatever his reasons, she knew she had little choice. A kiss and then make her escape. She would still have time to dress and meet her guests with some modicum of composure.

"All right," she whispered. Seeing his smile at that small revelation of her distress, she said more loudly, "Let's get it over and be done with this business."

Business. Raven's word for their agreement. Here she was, again kissing Amberton, when all she really wanted was her husband's love. And that, of course, Raven had never offered. Only business.

"Such an eager lover," Gerald said chidingly. His smile was too smug, altogether too satisfied with his attempt to embarrass her. She wondered again if something else was going on, but her temper quickly overcame that whisper of suspicion.

"Never *your* lover," she answered mockingly.

She had gone too far, she knew, as he ruthlessly caught her wrists. She fought, realizing suddenly that he was not going to be satisfied with the chaste kiss she had intended to bestow. But he soon had her arms twisted behind her back, her wrists securely held in one of his hands.

He bent her uncomfortably over the back of the high sofa, pushing his body familiarly into hers. She struggled fiercely, even trying to kick at his legs. Her thin slippers made negligible impact against the leather of his high boots, and he ignored her. With that effort, however, she lost her footing and slipped farther back, her body totally in his hold now, only the tip of one foot still making desperate contact with the floor.

His lips descended with determination, but she turned her head away. He caught her chin with his free hand, his fingers brutal, gripping hard enough to leave bruises, she thought in panic, remembering the very observant people she would have to confront tonight. He turned her face until his wet mouth fastened over hers. He pushed his tongue past her lips, moving it against hers until she thought she might be physically ill with disgust.

Some inarticulate sound apparently made her nauseated response clear to him, for suddenly his mouth was removed from hers, and he lifted his head to look down on her in fury.

At least she was free from the subjection of that revolting kiss. But before her relief had fully registered, his fingers were digging into the bodice of her gown. His hand slipped under the globe of her left breast and lifted. For the first time, she felt terror replacing her fury. The cool air touched her exposed flesh, and then, unbelievingly, his mouth fastened over her nipple, biting and sucking.

At that painful contact, she twisted, bringing her knees up automatically in a protective gesture, and felt the right one connect sharply with Gerald's body. His reaction to that unintentional blow was startling. He released her with a howl, and, unbalanced, she slid backward onto the seat of the sofa and then down in an unladylike heap onto the Turkish carpet.

She never even looked at Amberton or tried to guess the cause of the keening noises that were coming from his huddled figure. She scrambled to her feet, stumbling awkwardly over the skirt of her gown, which had caught under her knees. She heard the material rip, but nothing mattered except getting out of here. She was up and running, trying with trembling fingers to pull the material of her dress up over her breast, thankful that in his wrath Gerald hadn't torn the delicate muslin bodice.

She reached for the handle of the door, only to watch in dismay as it swung away from her searching fingers. She looked up to find her husband standing in the doorway of Gerald's small salon.

"Hello," Raven said simply.

She closed her eyes, hoping that when she opened them, the hallucination would have disappeared. Raven could not—oh dear God, she thought despairingly, he could *not*—be standing in the door of this room where Lord Amberton had just attacked her. But when she opened her eyes, her husband was still there, his slight smile touching his lips.

"You're leaving it very late, my dear," he said, his tone as relaxed as his greeting had been. "You have little more than two hours until our guests arrive. And I don't believe you're dressed for dinner."

With something approaching horror, her gaze fell, following the slow appraisal of his blue eyes. She found what had attracted that calm survey—her gown so disarrayed that the dusky rose areola that surrounded her left nipple was still exposed.

There seemed nothing she could say, and so she yielded to the impulse she had had since she had looked up to find him there. She threw herself against his chest and with unbelievable relief felt Raven's hard arms close securely around her.

Chapter Six

"May I see you home?" Raven asked.

Thank God she was safe, he thought. He had arrived in time to prevent whatever Amberton had been attempting. Catherine was trembling in his arms, but she was safe. That had been his only concern when he'd gotten the anonymous note inviting him to this address to witness his wife's indiscretion. Despite the terms of their agreement, he had been certain she had not come here to cuckold him, that something else had brought her to Amberton's apartment.

Unable to force a reply past the lump in her throat, Catherine nodded, her curls brushing against his shirt-front.

Raven's thumb and forefinger touched her chin and he raised her face to meet his gaze. His fingers were determined, but there was no painful pressure. He studied the tear-washed eyes, surrounded by the wet tangle of lashes. "You *were* ready to leave?" he inquired, and at the small, sobbing intake of breath that accompanied her nod, his lips lifted again in that slight smile. He had promised her freedom, and so he was honor bound to ask.

"I tried to leave," she whispered, wanting him to know that it was not by her choice that he had found her in this situation.

"Are you saying that he wouldn't let you go?" Raven asked, fighting his fury. He knew the bastard had somehow forced her to come here, and now she was telling him that Amberton wouldn't let her leave.

Something had replaced the calm with which he had greeted her, but, as always with Raven, Catherine was unsure about whatever emotion colored his tone. The adrenaline that had been sustaining her was draining away, and she felt almost faint in reaction to the security Raven's presence provided. Gerald was no match for her husband's strength, and she knew she was safe. But even as she thought that, she remembered with revulsion how Amberton's wet, loose mouth had closed over her breast. She retched softly, pressing her fingers tightly against her lips.

"Are you hurt?" Raven asked.

Controlling her nausea with the strongest effort, she looked up to reassure him. There was something very strange in the clear blue depths of his eyes. Fury, she thought, trying to imagine what he was feeling. He had every right to be angry.

"No," she said. "I managed to get away from him before—"

"Will you forgive me, Catherine, if I send you home with Tom?" Raven interrupted her to ask softly, knowing he was about to lose what tenuous control he had. "I believe I still have some business to conduct with Lord Amberton."

"He's had his kiss," she said unthinkingly. She didn't want him to give Gerald money. She'd paid for her foolish wager. She only wanted to go home and forget that Amberton had touched her. Whatever Raven wanted to do to her she deserved, and he was right about hurrying home. She wanted to be there, in the privacy of her own chamber, and to wash away, in the hottest water she could stand, the filth of what had happened this afternoon.

"I assure you I don't intend to give him another," Raven said. And when she glanced up, he was smiling at her—a real smile, the corners of his lips tilted farther upward than she'd ever seen them. "Go home and make yourself beautiful. I'll be there before the first guest arrives. I promise you."

At the quiet assurance in his deep voice, she nodded. He reached behind him and opened the door. On legs that continued to shake, she walked across the short expanse of

Gerald's foyer to place herself into the competent hands of her father's former coachman, who had so willingly come to work for her husband.

"My lady!" Tom said, and she could hear the shock in his pleasant, country-bred voice.

"I'm all right," she lied. "Just take me home, please, Tom. You can return for Mr. Raven. He said he had some business."

"I should imagine he has!" said the coachman, putting his hand under her elbow and practically lifting her into the coach. In its dim interior she gave rein to the tears she had denied in front of Raven, and for the first time in her life she didn't consider what such a bout of weeping would do to her complexion.

"My wife informs me that, despite her attempt to leave, Lord Amberton, you tried to detain her."

Although the American's voice was perfectly calm, Amberton felt a flicker of unease. What he had planned had not gone off exactly as expected due to Catherine's painfully effective resistance and John Raven's surprising lack of infuriated response. But Gerald believed he could still achieve his ends if only he could goad the American enough.

"I would never be so ungallant, Mr. Raven, as to dispute a lady's word," Amberton said mockingly, "but I would ask you to consider that I didn't abduct Catherine."

"My wife is free to visit whomever she wishes, but she should *also* be free to leave whenever she desires."

"You must know, Mr. Raven—"

"The only thing I *must* know, my lord, is why you chose to hold Mrs. Raven here against her will."

"*Mrs. Raven?*" Amberton repeated derisively. "I had almost forgotten. Poor Catherine always did have a penchant for eloping with unsuitable men. The first one, however, was both handsome and charming," he taunted, "and he swept Cat off her feet. But, of course, she was only sixteen. That time, I understand, the duke was more successful in saving Catherine from herself. You should be grateful Montfort didn't catch you. He tried to kill Henning, to whip him to death. Had to be forcibly restrained, I'm told. Rumor was Henning had managed to convince Cat her father wouldn't prevent their marriage if she already belonged to him in . . . some way," he suggested, allowing one eyebrow to rise and a small, salacious smile to touch his lips. "I'm sure you've already discovered the rather irreversible result—"

The mocking suggestion was abruptly cut off by the American's lightning-fast movement. Raven was across the space that had separated them almost before the viscount could raise the sword he had carefully concealed behind his right leg. He had taken the opportunity Catherine's greeting of her husband had offered to arm himself, the blade already prudently at hand.

God, the bastard was quick, Amberton thought, his body automatically executing the classic dueler's lunge that he'd practiced with his Italian fencing master for so many hours. The heavier blade affected his movement only slightly, but the American's reaction to the sword was as swift as his attack had been.

Raven couldn't avoid the point entirely; Amberton's lunge had been too well timed. The viscount had been waiting for his control to slip, and when the nobleman's taunting had achieved the result he'd wanted, he'd brought out the hidden weapon. Raven had time only to execute a small downward twist of his body to direct the shaft through the muscles of his shoulder rather than into his heart, which had been Amberton's target. He could feel the impact of the blow and even the slide of the blade into the muscle, its impetus driven by the viscount's graceful lunge.

There was no pain. Not yet, at least. And wouldn't be until he'd finished what he intended, Raven prayed. He blocked all thought of the sword and focused instead on the supple wrist of the man who held its hilt. "Release it," Raven ordered softly. His thumb found the vital nerve and exerted unbearable pressure. Without the viscount's volition, his fingers unclenched, surrendering control of the sword.

As soon as the hilt had been freed, Raven maneuvered the wrist he held, easily turning the Englishman's body and pinning his right arm behind his back. The position was so painful that an involuntary cry was wrenched from the viscount.

He could feel the American's breath on the back of his neck. More frightening than the steel of his grip was the fact that Amberton could see, out of the corner of his eye, the hilt of the sword that still impaled that massive shoulder resting on his own. Horrified, he realized he could even feel it move as Raven whispered, "Gossip, my lord, is for old women and cowards. If I ever hear that filthy lie on anyone's tongue, I'll come after *you*. And if I ever hear that you've touched Catherine again with your vile slander or with your viler hands, you may be very sure I'll kill you. Do you understand?"

Raven wanted to kill him now, had never been in a situation where he had wanted to kill a man more. The control he was exercising in not breaking this English bastard's neck would make his grandmother extremely proud, he thought. Almost without conscious intent, he jerked the arm he held upward as he released it. Although he hadn't anticipated it, the resulting snap of bone was somehow deeply satisfying. Uncaring of the damage he'd inflicted, he pushed the viscount away from him and stepped back. Fighting to control his murderous rage, Raven watched Amberton take a staggering step, trying to cradle the injured arm.

Allowing himself a small smile of satisfaction, Raven took another step backward, and with that movement was uncomfortably reminded of the viscount's sword. His eyes never leaving the ashen face of his adversary, Raven gripped the protruding hilt and pulled. Although the operation required more effort than he'd thought it would, he managed to prevent any expression of discomfort from touching his face. Nothing was allowed there other than a mocking smile as he held the Englishman's eyes.

When the sword was free, Raven threw it on the sofa, the dark blood marking the elegant cream satin. He allowed his gaze to rest on the viscount a moment more. Amberton huddled against the wall, his right arm held carefully by the slender, fashionably white fingers of his left hand, his mouth open in shock.

It was never wise to humiliate your opponent, Raven's grandfather had warned. Pride was something the Scots understood, and Raven knew he had damaged whatever pride Amberton had left. A dangerous enemy, Raven thought, but he didn't regret what he'd just done. Not when he remembered how Catherine had trembled and what the viscount had suggested. Turning, Raven let himself out, departing as calmly as he had entered.

Behind him, in the silence of the salon, Amberton shivered suddenly. He had never seen anything as cold-blooded as the American calmly removing that still-quivering sword from his own body, that damn strange smile playing over his lips. It was diabolical. Almost inhuman, he thought, shivering again.

"Bloody savage," he whispered bitterly.

Despite the heat of the bath water the servants brought up, Catherine found she couldn't stop shivering. Not only did she have to face thirty guests, but she had begun to think rather more clearly about Raven's actions this afternoon. She supposed he intended to knock Gerald down for what he had done, and he appeared capable of doing that with ease. But now she was far less worried about what he would have to say to her about her exploit and more worried about him. She knew that lesser offenses than the Viscount Amberton had committed today resulted in duels. The insult he'd offered her, even mitigated by the fact that she had gone to his apartment voluntarily, was certainly of a serious nature. Despite Raven's calm and his smile, she didn't believe he had taken Gerald's actions lightly.

He had, however, promised to return before the arrival of their guests, and not allowing herself to think about what possible explanation she could offer if he didn't, she permitted her body to be perfumed, groomed and gowned. When she found she was ready with a full five minutes to spare, she indulged in another finger of her husband's brandy. If she was unsteady in her movements tonight, she supposed that was to be preferred to giving in to a fit of vapors. That ridiculous performance was something she had never indulged in in her life, and despite all that had happened, she didn't intend to now. Fortified, she was able to sweep down the gracefully curving staircase seconds before Edwards opened the door to the first callers.

Catherine stood alone, automatically welcoming her guests with a practiced warmth and a deliberate sparkle in her eyes that was intended to enchant those gauche enough to wonder about her explanation that Raven had been temporarily detained. In the midst of that refrain, made this time to Lord Elliot, a friend of her father's and a cabinet member as well, she felt Raven's warm, callused palm rest on her shoulder and slip caressingly down her upper arm. She leaned briefly against his strength and then stepped away, looking up into his face with a teasing laugh.

"You will have to make your own excuses, my dear," she said truthfully. "I'm afraid they looked askance at mine."

"To be candid, gentleman, I have had an experience that you should be able to sympathize with."

At his words, her breath caught. She met Raven's eyes, wondering if he could possibly be angry enough to betray her before the elite of the world he professed to want to impress.

"My valet ruined every cravat he'd prepared. I had to wait until he had heated the irons and readied another. I threatened him with my wife's displeasure should he manage to ruin this one."

He lifted long, dark fingers to touch the snowy linen, tied in the intricate folds of the Trone d'amour. Because she had been looking for any sign of what he had done to Amberton, Catherine's eyes examined the knuckles of that hand. Seeing her gaze on his fingers, Raven allowed his hand to catch hers and bring it to his lips.

"Am I forgiven?" he asked formally, his blue eyes lifting over their joined hands to meet hers.

"If our guests will forgive you, then I suppose I must."

"Be kind, my dear," advised Elliot. "You really have no conception of the demands on a man's patience an inept valet can make. I'm surprised, Mr. Raven, that you were in any condition to join us after a disaster of that magnitude."

"As am I," Catherine said softly, and knew by the flicker of reaction in his eyes that her husband understood her comment.

"I'm generally a very even-tempered man," he said to Lord Elliot, still holding Catherine's fingers in the warm clasp of his. "It takes a remarkable event to unbalance my composure."

Aware that they had been playing their dangerous game of repartee for quite long enough, Catherine secured the freedom of her fingers and turned with a smile to the next guests. Her husband continued to talk easily to Lord Elliot for a moment, before he, too, turned to be introduced to the new arrivals.

Eventually the hardest part of the evening—the greetings and the introductions—were gotten through, and they were finally seated around the vast table, where the skill of Edwards's well-trained staff would carry some of the burden.

There were a few references made to her husband's interests in Durham and Tyneside, but he didn't dwell on those aspects of his business dealings. He might believe coal and the rails would be the key to whatever was going to happen in Britain, but he didn't seem inclined to talk about his commercial activities over his wife's dinner table.

He answered the inquiries politely and with the same serious attention with which he'd always responded to her questions, and then turned the topic to those more familiar to members of the quality. Racing and hunting, horses always being a safe subject, dominated for a while, as did the failures of the present government, which sparked a rather spirited debate between a gentleman with Whig leanings and Lord Elliot. When called on to offer his support, Raven presented a few well-informed remarks and again adroitly turned the talk in a less volatile direction.

When it was finally time to lead the ladies into the salon and leave the gentlemen to their port, Catherine knew that the evening had been a decided success and was relaxed enough to have stopped worrying about whatever would happen in the dining room when the feminine influence had been removed.

The gentlemen joined them in little more than an hour, the ladies not yet having exhausted their store of gossip nor their shared musical expertise. The guests eventually left in a pleasant babble of conversation, pledging to finish half-completed stories and interrupted *on-dits*.

When the door had closed on the last of them, Catherine found she didn't want to face her husband's censure tonight, however well deserved she knew it to be. She had dealt with enough for one evening, she thought, even though, she admitted, she had foolishly brought it all on herself.

When she turned, she found Raven leaning lazily against the door frame of the grand salon, watching her with those crystal eyes. Unwilling to meet what she was certain would be a rebuking stare, she made her way to the dining room, intending to congratulate Edwards on the success of the service and to ask him to pass on her compliments to the chef and, of course, to the staff, which had worked so hard to bring off tonight's triumph. She found the butler on his knees, a basin filled with soapy water on the floor beside him. Damp cloth in hand, he was scrubbing at a stain on the back of the chair her husband had occupied at dinner.

"What is it, Edwards?" she asked, and the dignified servant rose with an unaccustomed agitation, his body blocking her view of the chair, his smooth face flushing as it had when Raven had attempted to engage him in conversation.

"A stain, madam," he said, but he wouldn't meet her eyes. She wondered if he had spilled something on the imported silk.

"What sort of stain?" she asked, a delaying tactic while she tried to decide how to handle the situation. She knew he would expect her comment, but she was so genuinely grateful for the smoothness of the service tonight that she hated to spoil it by having to chastise him or some member of his staff for the careless destruction of what was a very costly piece of material.

"It appears to be . . . I believe, madam, although I might be mistaken—"

"I imagine it's blood," Raven interrupted matter-of-factly.

When she turned, Catherine found her husband standing in the doorway of this room, his right hand resting high on the frame.

"Blood?" she echoed. "But how would blood—"

"The usual way. Someone bled on it. And it's not the servants' fault. I'm only glad your guests are less observant than you and Edwards seem to be."

"It's not *their* embroidered silk," Catherine said, trying to think what he could be talking about. She stepped closer to get a better look at the dark stain, which almost covered the colorful peacock that had been painstakingly worked into the cream material. When the realization of what his words implied finally struck her, she turned back to find the doorway empty.

She found Raven halfway up the curving stair, which he was climbing much more slowly than his usual rapid, two-steps-at-a-time ascent. She hurried up beside him and caught his arm. She was afraid he might refuse to talk to her, but he stopped immediately, meeting her searching gaze without hesitation.

"What have you done?" she asked.

"Nothing to brag about, I promise you," he said, the blue eyes full of self-derision. "But I don't think you'll be bothered with Lord Amberton's attentions again."

He took a step past her, but her firm hold on his sleeve prevented him from moving farther up the staircase without rudely pulling his arm away.

"Did you kill him?" she asked, knowing very well the consequences of that to his business activities if he had.

"Did you expect me to?" Raven asked. "You led me to believe . . ." he began, and then stopped, his eyes resting on her face, wondering if he could have misinterpreted what had been happening this afternoon. "You know, I hope, that if you hadn't told me he'd tried to prevent your leaving, I'd never have touched him. Our agreement was that you might do as you please, up to a point. And I trust you to keep your word. Beyond that restriction, I recognize your right to entertain as many gallants as you wish. But I *thought* you implied that Amberton went beyond the boundary you'd set for him. Or was I wrong?"

"Of course, he went beyond those bounds!" she declared, hearing the doubt in his voice. "I would never have allowed the liberties he took. He..." Her voice faltered, because she thought she couldn't bear the humiliation of having to tell him.

"Then put him out of your mind. He'll never bother you again. And I didn't kill him." I should have, Raven thought, trying not to imagine what Amberton had done to make her look like that. I should have broken his bloody neck.

Controlling his renewed fury, he gently removed her fingers from the material of his sleeve and, once free, proceeded up the grand staircase before he said all the things he wanted to say to her, things he knew he had no right to say.

Catherine stood a moment, feeling distinctly deserted and wondering what she should do. Then, remembering with sudden fear the vivid stain on the Chinese-style chair in her dining room below, she followed the path the tall, dark figure had taken to his small bedroom on the second floor.

Raven never kept his valet waiting up to undress him. So despite the fact that his left arm hung rather awkwardly at his side, he was struggling to remove the dinner jacket. His back to the door, he didn't know that Catherine stood watching him.

"Let me get my scissors and cut the coat off," she said.

Raven paused in his efforts, and then, deciding that her suggestion made a great deal of sense, he nodded. He leaned against the high footboard of the bed, willing the ringing in his ears to cease. He hated his weakness. He hated being vulnerable. He hadn't wanted her to see him like this. He would never want anyone to see him like this, but especially not Catherine. She would surely despise his weakness, his inability to control the sensations the loss of blood was causing.

She ran to her room and rummaged among her embroidery silks for the small scissors. By the time she'd found them, her hands had begun to shake almost as much as they had after Gerald's assault.

When she reentered his room, her husband was standing exactly as she had left him. His slumped shoulders straightened slightly, however, as soon as she began to cut up the back of his jacket. When she had finally succeeded, having realized very quickly that the tiny scissors were not the ideal tool for the task she'd undertaken, she slipped the relatively unstained half of the coat off his right arm, allowing it to fall to the floor. She began to ease the blood-soaked left half off, but his right hand lifted and, gripping the ruined material, pulled it over his shoulder and down his arm. She was not pleased to notice that he didn't bend the left elbow, but held the entire arm as still as possible, given the nature of the operation.

The white, watered-silk waistcoat was far more revealing of the amount of blood he'd lost than the dark material of the coat had been. Resolutely forcing herself to grasp the bottom edge of the sodden garment, she quickly cut up the back seam and freed him of that, too, revealing the lawn shirt. It was covered with the same dark color that had marred the chair in which he'd sat tonight, casually exchanging pleasantries about horses and politics with people he barely knew, while his blood seeped through shirt and waistcoat and even through the heavy material of his jacket.

"I can manage the rest," he said. He had been so silent throughout the ordeal that she jumped at the authority in his voice.

"What happened?" she asked, ignoring his suggestion that she leave him and beginning the struggle to cut the material of the shirt with the now-dull sewing scissors.

"I must have had my mind on something else," he said, and she heard again the self-derision in his voice.

"Did he shoot you?" she asked, finding it difficult to conceive that even Gerald would shoot someone in the back.

"He had a sword. I didn't notice it."

"How could you not notice a sword?" she exclaimed, beginning to peel the soaked shirt off his back.

"I told you. My mind was on something else."

"And he stabbed you in the back?" she whispered. Having removed the shirt, she could see the wound, finally revealed, a dark slit in the muscled brown shoulder, nastily oozing blood.

"No, to give him credit, he was quite straightforward about it. He went in under the collarbone."

The import of what he'd said reached her brain. Catherine moved around him to find a wad of blood-soaked cloth covering what she guessed was a matching slit in the front of his body.

"He ran you through," she said, her stomach heaving once at the thought of the cold steel of Amberton's sword piercing the warm skin and cutting through the firm muscle of his chest.

"I believe that's the term. I confess I'm not very familiar with fencing. However, I suppose I must now admit to more than a nodding acquaintance with the art." Seeing the blanched features of his wife, Raven said, "It's all right, Catherine. I'm all right. A trifle embarrassed that I let the bastard stick me."

"But you weren't armed," she said, thinking how dastardly the honorable Lord Amberton had proved himself today.

"Not until I took his toy away from him," he agreed with a trace of amused satisfaction.

She glanced up and found that small smile again playing about his lips. But his face was too pale under the bronze skin, almost gray under the tan, and belatedly she realized she had forced him to stand while she cut away the ruined clothing.

"Sit down," she ordered, taking his right elbow, intending to help him to the small straight chair that stood near the bed.

He lifted his arm from her hand, smiling still.

"Feeling maternal, Catherine?" he asked softly, and she remembered his comment about the likelihood of that eventuality.

"Not about *you,*" she answered with more spirit than she felt, thinking only of how secure in his masculinity he was and how reassuring she found his strength.

"Good," Raven said, searching her eyes for any disgust that he'd let Amberton catch him off guard. Only when he had assured himself that there was nothing in the russet depths except a natural concern for his injury did he turn to the chair she'd indicated.

She followed, wondering what she intended to do about the wound. She had no experience with illness. Someone else always saw to those things. She supposed she should send for a surgeon.

"I'll have Edwards send for Dr. Stevenson. He's—"

"No," Raven interrupted. "Surely you realize what would happen if word of this got out."

"But I don't know what to do. I could ask Edwards—"

Again he cut her off. "Just bind it up. There's nothing else anyone can do. I couldn't reach the back, and it seemed to have clotted. I can only suppose the wound reopened when I moved my shoulder. I'm sorry I ruined your chair. I'll try to find a matching silk, or you can have the entire set redone."

"You can't really believe I care about the chair," she said hotly. "It's your house. You may bleed wherever you wish."

"Thank you, Catherine," he said, smiling. "I'm reassured by your consideration, but I don't believe I shall avail myself of the offer. At least, not if you'll bind this up. It's not so very bad. I haven't passed out on you yet."

"Don't you dare. Even Edwards couldn't get you up. You're too large," she said unthinkingly, tentatively touching the stiffened wad of padding that covered the entry wound.

"I'm sorry," he said. It was not the first time she'd referred to his size, so different, he knew, from the slim elegance of the London gentlemen she flirted with.

"What?" she asked, not even realizing he was answering her unthinking comment about his size.

"I should imagine," he suggested, "that you might begin with the other. It *is* still bleeding?" he asked.

"Yes," she whispered, feeling very foolish. The slit he had covered with a pad before he'd come down tonight had apparently closed. She put her hand against the hard warmth of his shoulder, forcing him to lean forward enough that she could see the one in his back, still welling blood.

"You'll need something to make a compress and strips of cloth to bind it around my chest," he advised.

She wondered if he could feel her fingers trembling against his skin as she studied the wound. "A sheet?" she asked.

"If you can find the linen press. I couldn't. I'm afraid I was forced to make do with something less appropriate."

She found it hard to believe that he could still mock himself, but the amusement was clear in his voice. "Of course I can find the linen press. This *is* my household," she said.

Curious despite the situation, she turned at the doorway to ask, "What did you use?"

"One of the cravats my valet had laid out. He was very puzzled as to why there was one less than he'd prepared." Raven was still leaning forward in the chair, apparently unwilling to take up her offer to bleed at will on her furnishings.

"He'll probably leave you. Disappearing cravats *and* not being allowed to help you undress. You are really a most unsatisfactory gentleman."

"I suppose Edwards will follow after the disaster tonight," he said. "You'll have your hands full keeping staff, but I promise I'll try, from now on, not to scandalize your servants."

"Concentrate on staying upright instead," she said. "I don't want to have to explain a husband who's bled to death."

"Then I suggest you hurry," Raven reminded her quietly, but again he was smiling.

* * *

He had endured her inept nursing with a calm patience. Catherine had first cleaned the blood off his back as well as she could with the cool water in his bedroom pitcher. She had decided to leave the wadding he'd pressed into the entry wound because she didn't want to start it bleeding again. He had lost quite enough blood as it was. She'd placed a thick square of cloth over the slit in his back and had bound it in place with long strips she'd torn from the remainder of the sheet. The white material she had wrapped under his arm and across his wide chest, covering both wounds, was stark against the dark skin. She had had to fight the urge to run her fingers caressingly over the reassuringly warm expanse of his chest as she'd worked.

Catherine had never before thought about touching a man's body. And she was surprised, given the events of the day and Gerald's behavior, that she should be attracted to the very masculine strength of Raven's. He could far more easily bend her to his will than Amberton, but she wasn't frightened by the latent power of Raven's body, strongly apparent despite the injury he'd suffered. Instead she was fascinated by the way the muscle shifted under the golden skin when, in response to her direction, he moved to allow her greater access to the wound.

"I think that's all," she said, stepping back to view her handiwork. The bandaging didn't look all that secure, and she hoped it wouldn't shift in the night. With that thought she realized that she should probably help him into his nightshirt.

"Do you want me to help you finish undressing?" she asked, not really thinking of what her offer implied. Since he was wearing only his trousers, that didn't leave much to remove.

"I don't think that's necessary," Raven said. He hadn't gotten up from the chair. He seemed to be waiting for her to leave before he disrobed for the night.

"Will you be all right?" she asked, feeling strangely reluctant to desert him. "I could ring for your man."

"No, Catherine. Go to bed. And thank you," he said, taking her hand in his. He pressed a warm kiss into her palm, then closed her fingers over the place he'd just touched.

Without her volition, her other hand was suddenly touching the raven gleam of his hair, smoothing back the dark strands. He didn't move as her fingers stroked his head, then under his ear and along the strong line of his jaw. She took his chin in her palm, her thumb sliding along the thin bottom lip. She thought he might react in some way, but he was perfectly still, unmoving under what was, she admitted, decidedly a caress.

She applied enough pressure under his chin to lift his face so that she was looking down into his eyes. Very slowly, giving him the opportunity, if he wished, to avoid her touch, her mouth lowered to meet his. He allowed the brush of her lips over his, but he didn't react in any way. He certainly didn't open his mouth and move his tongue, as Gerald had done today, and she found herself wondering what the hard line of his lips would feel like pressed closely over hers. What his tongue would be like, moving inside her mouth, against hers.

Finally, realizing that she had certainly broken the terms of their agreement, she lifted her head. His eyes had been closed, the long, dark lashes lying against the small network of lines beneath, and for some reason she was pleased. They opened at the desertion of her lips. Again there was something in the crystal depths that she couldn't read.

"I think you'd better go," Raven suggested softly.

Embarrassed by her display, Catherine nodded and turned to walk to the door, her knees again trembling, but for a very different reason from before. He didn't want her here, didn't want her kisses, she thought with a touch of bitterness. He had made very clear what he wanted from her, and it wasn't what she had just offered him. *I don't need a mistress,* he'd told her, and having been exposed to the beauty of his very masculine body, for the first time she was forced to think about what that declaration really meant.

The blue eyes of the man she had left in the small bedroom closed again, and he drew in a breath, so deep its force jolted agonizingly through the torn nerves and muscles of his shoulder.

It had been so difficult to let her go. She had kissed him, touched him, her fingers trailing across the darkness of his skin as if she found nothing to dislike in its color. And he had wanted to pull her down to him, to carry her to the narrow bed where he lay every night and dreamed of loving her, to finally make the temptations of those dreams a reality.

You made a promise, Raven, to give her freedom, his grandmother's voice reminded him through the dizzying light-headedness. *And no matter the consequences to yourself, you must keep it.*

Silently, in the dim solitude of his lonely bedroom that night, John Raven made another vow, as binding as the first. Only this time it was a promise he made to himself—that Catherine would be his in every way intended by the covenant they had made over the smith's anvil. Their souls would become one, the joining of the spirit as important in his heritage as the joining of the body. But with that thought, a harsh groan slipped past his control. He had ignored the pain, locking it away, during Catherine's tender and touchingly inept nursing. This whisper of sound was an acknowledgment of a far different agony, one that clawed his guts every time his fingers accidentally touched hers or their eyes met over the dinner table.

Tonight she had kissed him. He couldn't allow himself to hope that it had meant more than a recognition of the role he'd played in her rescue today from Amberton. But someday... Soon, my darling, Raven vowed again. Someday very soon.

Chapter Seven

For many reasons Catherine passed a nearly sleepless night. The longer she lay in her lonely bed, the more guilt she felt over the events of the previous day. She had allowed Amberton to put her in such a situation that her husband had been forced to defend her honor, suffering a serious wound for his efforts. And she had not even asked whether a challenge had been issued as a result of her foolish behavior.

She had reacted like a headstrong child to Gerald's taunts, but there had been nothing enjoyable about the outcome of her daring this time. She wanted to explain to her husband the convoluted path that had led to the predicament in which he had found her yesterday. Then if, in response to that explanation, Raven wanted to chastise her, she really couldn't blame him.

It was after eleven when she finally screwed up her courage enough to face him. She thought that discomfort from his injury might have prevented him from passing a restful night, just as her regret had interfered with her sleep, and so, she reasoned, he, too, might already be up. When she slipped through the partially opened door of his chamber, however, she found only his valet, who was straightening the room. He looked up in surprise at her entrance. She knew that nothing was ever hidden from the servants, and the knowledge that John Raven and his wife did not share a bed would certainly have been bandied about below stairs.

"Mr. Raven is in his office, madam," the valet offered.

She had enough presence of mind to take a quick inventory of the discarded clothing he'd gathered into a pile on the neatly made bed. There were no bloodstains visible on any of it, although the stack appeared to contain the requisite shirt and waistcoat and jacket along with the trousers. Raven must have gotten rid of the stained garments she'd cut off his body last night and replaced them with others from his wardrobe.

Apparently he intended to give the staff as little cause for comment as possible. Depending on Edwards's discretion, the ploy might have some chance of succeeding. After all, the butler might properly have required the maids to clean up the stain on the chair, and the fact that he hadn't seemed to indicate his concern that its origin not become common knowledge.

"Thank you," she said and closed the bedroom door.

Without allowing her guilty conscience time to find a reason not to confront her husband, she made her way resolutely to the room where Raven spent hours engaged in the unending correspondence necessary to maintain a financial empire the scope of his. Although he traveled extensively, she knew he still carried on a great deal of his business through the mails.

She stood a moment in the doorway, reluctant now that she was here. Raven seemed unaware of her presence, and it was not until he had finished whatever he was writing that he looked up.

"Come in, Catherine," he invited. "It's not often this environment is graced with your presence. I don't believe you've visited my office before."

"Not since you showed me Father's announcement of my betrothal to Gerald. Or perhaps I should say *your* announcement?"

She could hear the slight challenge in her voice, and from his puzzled expression, she knew he had heard it, too.

"*My* announcement?"

"Did you fabricate that entire scenario? Gerald indicated that he knew nothing about any plan to announce our engagement."

"Then Amberton is a liar," Raven said calmly. Whatever story the viscount had told her probably had something to do with her presence in his apartment yesterday. "Surely you aren't inclined to believe anything he asserts. Not after yesterday."

"But, you see, I *did* believe it. On the night of Aunt Agatha's party. He implied that you'd created that announcement to trick me into a runaway marriage."

"If you remember..." He stopped, allowing her to complete his thought.

She did remember. She had been the one who'd suggested that flight to the Border.

"The announcement *was* sent, to the *Post* and the *Gazette*. Reynolds was barely able to prevent its publication. And I don't believe it was sent without Amberton's knowledge," he said.

"No," she admitted, convinced by the quiet sincerity in Raven's voice as he reiterated what he'd said the last time they had been together in this room. "But I did believe him. That night. And since he'd already suggested that you'd managed to break me to the bit...I'm afraid I reacted very foolishly. He invited me to play cards. Not in the card room, but alone upstairs. And to prove that I wasn't under your thumb, as he'd said, I agreed."

There was no response, either verbally or in the blue eyes. Catherine had expected that by this time Raven would have chided her for her actions or have made his disgust over them apparent, but there was nothing but polite interest in the lucid blue depths.

He doesn't care, she thought, and that idea was remarkably painful. Or I've destroyed whatever feelings he might have had about the impropriety of his wife's playing cards alone with a man by my far-more-improper actions of yesterday.

"And I lost," she forced herself to continue, swallowing the tightness that had begun to gather in her throat.

"I told you it was all a matter of numbers," Raven said, the corners of his mouth deepening. He hadn't really expected this confession. By the terms of their agreement, he had no right to an explanation, yet she seemed to believe he was entitled to one.

"I couldn't keep my mind on the game," she continued. "He suggested I wager my bracelet—the ruby-and-diamond one you'd admired on the way to the party. But when I tried to give it to him, after the game, he said it was something you'd surely miss. And you wouldn't miss . . . the other."

"The other?"

The question was very quietly spoken, but there was still no censure in Raven's face when she glanced up to answer him.

"A kiss. That was to be the forfeiture. And I *was* afraid you'd notice I'd lost the bracelet. You'd hadn't even had time to receive the bill," she said, her voice faltering slightly.

Raven looked down at his fingers, which had found the silver letter opener on his desk. He traced the handle's design with his thumb, trying to control lips that seemed determined to smile. Catherine had believed he'd rather she give up a kiss to that bastard than a bracelet.

He wondered for the thousandth time why he'd made this agreement. *Because that was the only way you could win her and you knew it,* he reminded himself grimly. At that unpleasant thought, he lost the inclination to amusement her hesitant confession had evoked. She was his wife, and she knew nothing about him, nothing about the way he felt. Especially the way he felt about her.

"And I missed our waltz," she continued, the non sequitur revealing, perhaps, how painful her recital was. But when his gaze lifted to her face, Catherine realized by the slight movement of the stern line of his lips that Raven knew exactly what she was talking about.

She took a deep breath, determined to finish. "And then he sent me a message. Yesterday. Just before I should have begun dressing for the party. If I didn't come to pay the forfeiture, he'd tell you about the wager. He said he needed the money."

"And so you went."

His eyes were once more on the movement of his long fingers, their darkness a contrast to the palely gleaming silver of the opener they held.

"Yes," she whispered.

"And he demanded more than his kiss," he suggested.

"He put his tongue in my mouth," she admitted, shivering at the remembrance of the disgusting slackness of Gerald's lips over hers. She wished suddenly that she hadn't told Raven that, but it was too late to deny what had happened. And the other was even more repellent. "And then—he put his mouth on my body," Catherine finished, determined to tell him everything. But if, as they said, confession was good for the soul, she wondered why she felt so awful. Her husband's face was completely calm, and when he spoke again, he didn't say what she'd expected.

"I have only one question," Raven said. "In light of our agreement, I don't understand why you didn't tell Amberton to call due the bet and be damned. I *did* promise not to restrict your actions, and nothing you've told me seems serious enough to warrant a breach of our contract. You certainly weren't entertaining a lover yesterday afternoon. It appeared that I'd interrupted a brawl rather than a romantic interlude."

"I thought you'd be angry," she said truthfully.

"Then I'd have violated the freedom I promised you."

"I suppose I never thought you'd hold to those terms," she said almost hopefully.

"I always honor my contracts, Catherine," Raven said, "no matter how unfavorable to me they may eventually prove to be. It's the only way to have your word trusted. If you break one agreement, then the person you've cheated will never trust you to keep your promises the next time."

Catherine reflected disappointedly that she really didn't want to hear a dissertation on contracts. Nothing had gone as she'd expected. She'd made her painful confession, and Raven had treated the entire incident as if she had been making mountains out of molehills. All he could talk about, it seemed, were contracts and agreements. What she wanted, on the other hand, was the comfort of his arms about her as they had been yesterday after Gerald's attack. Why did he never react as she expected him to?

"What did you do to him?" she asked, thinking suddenly that he'd never told her what had happened between them after he'd sent her home with Tom. Beyond the fact that Amberton had had a sword and he'd taken it away from him.

"Not, apparently, as much as you did. I think that's why he had to resort to stabbing me. He didn't have much fight left in him after you got through with him."

She could hear the sudden amusement in his voice, but she didn't understand its cause. "What *I* did?"

"I only hope, Catherine, that if I ever manage to displease you to the extent the viscount did, you won't resort to such desperate measures against me."

"I don't understand," she admitted.

He smiled at her confusion, realizing that she really didn't. Confirmation, had he needed any, that the story Amberton had told him was a fabrication. At least the supposed ending of that story had been fabricated by the viscount's vicious tongue.

"For all your professed recklessness," Raven said, savoring that knowledge, "you're a remarkably innocent child."

"I am *not* a child," she denied, stung by his evaluation. She was aware again of the difference in their ages and experience. Raven had traveled all over the world, and she had never even left England. He was the only man who always made her feel childish.

"No," he admitted, "you aren't. You are, however, a very beautiful young woman who's been confronted for perhaps the first time with the bitter lesson that people are not always what they seem. I hope it doesn't make a cynic of you."

"I should never have trusted him." She had fallen into Gerald's trap as easily as she had into that set for her two years ago by Richard Henning's charm. Too trusting by far, she acknowledged bitterly, of the gentlemen of her circle, who had, in the end, proved themselves to be far less than chivalrous.

"You have to trust someone," Raven said easily. "Next time you'll be wiser in choosing the object of your confidence."

Next time, he thought, perhaps she'd confide in him. If he taught her that he could be trusted. Knowing it was time to leave, Raven pushed himself up from the desk, an awkward effort, made with his right hand flat against the cluttered papers.

For the first time since she'd begun her confession, Catherine remembered his injury—an injury she'd been the cause of. Her eyes traced over his left shoulder, looking for any indication of the bandage that she knew concealed the wound made by Amberton's blade. The morning coat, however, seemed to fit with its accustomed smoothness over his muscular frame. Her gaze lifted from her examination of his body to find his eyes on her face.

"Try not to grow up entirely while I'm gone. I should hate to miss any of your further adventures," he said, smiling at her.

"Where are you going?"

"Manchester, and then perhaps into Scotland. I haven't quite finalized my itinerary."

"But I should think..." She hesitated, knowing that she had no right to question his plans. She couldn't imagine, however, that a jarring carriage ride would be very comfortable.

"I shouldn't be gone more than a fortnight," he continued, the clear blue eyes still resting on her face. "Reynolds will keep you informed."

"And that?" she questioned, lifting her hand in the general direction of his broad left shoulder.

"Is nothing for you to be concerned about," he said quietly.

His denial of her right to worry over him hurt. "But what if it becomes inflamed? And you're away from home."

"Home?" He repeated the word questioningly, wondering if her concept of a home was this politely distant relationship they shared. So different from what he'd hoped for, from the warmth of the home and family he'd known all his life.

Catherine couldn't read whatever emotion was hidden in that word. "This *is* your home, Raven. And I am your wife. Even if we intend to keep our relationship on a business basis, I should think you must know that I'm concerned about your welfare."

"Are you, Catherine?" he asked. And at her slight nod, he smiled at her again.

Altogether, Raven had smiled at her more today than in the entire length of their previous encounters, she thought. And that was very strange, considering that she had expected quite the opposite reaction, given the events of yesterday.

"I don't suppose your business could be postponed?" she suggested hesitantly. "At least until your shoulder's had an opportunity to heal."

"I think not," he said. "I told you not to worry. I'm well accustomed to looking after myself."

Reluctantly, she was forced to admit defeat. "Then I'll see you when you return."

Raven had moved very close to her, and she realized she was blocking his access to the doorway leading to the front of the house. She stepped aside just as he moved to go around her. Once again she found herself in breathtaking proximity to his very masculine body. Her hand lifted to find something to help her regain her balance, and what it found, quite naturally somehow, was the wide expanse of a muscled chest. Surprisingly, his right hand came to rest warmly over her left, which was lying now against the fine material of his coat.

"Try not to bring London tumbling down about your ears while I'm gone," he said softly.

She nodded, but she was remembering her head resting against this same chest yesterday and his hard arms reassuringly locked around her body. And last night... Most of the night she had spent remembering the feel of his lips un-

der the caress of hers. And remembering his body, the width
of his shoulders and the muscled chest.

Raven didn't say anything else for a long time, but there
was no discomfort in the continued silence of their strange
tableau. Only his hand was touching hers, which rested on
the solid strength of his body. After a long time he lowered
his head, moving very slowly, perhaps as she had done last
night, giving her an opportunity to step back, to break the
delicate connection between them. His lips touched against
the smooth cream of the skin stretched over her collarbone, above the low neckline of her jonquil yellow morning dress. At the first electric jolt of sensation, her eyelids
fell, closing suddenly in response to what he was doing.

His mouth moved without any pressure along the fragile
bone that led to the slim column of her neck. The feeling of
his lips gliding over her flesh was like nothing she'd ever felt
before. There was no attempt at domination, no application of the unusual power of his body. Raven was touching
her exactly as his strong, dark fingers caressed the frail stems
of the imported crystal with which his table was set each
evening. The fingers she had watched every night with such
fascination.

She wondered what they would feel like against the
rounded globe of her breast, their callused strength pleasantly abrasive against her skin. She must have taken a breath
at that image, for she realized that she had forgotten to
breathe before, holding her body still so that she wouldn't
miss any of the sensations caused by the movement of his
mouth. His lips hesitated, lifting away from her throat at
that quick intake of breath, and desperate for their touch,
she heard herself whisper, "Please."

Raven waited a heartbeat, evaluating the meaning of that
request, but finally, hoping that he had rightly interpreted
what she wanted, his mouth began again its slow, relentless
journey. Up the slim column of her neck now, as she turned
her head to give him freedom to touch her there. The caress
slowed again when he reached the pulse under her jawline,
nuzzling against the increased flow of blood through her
veins caused by his nearness. She realized suddenly that he

was running his tongue gently over the fluttering beat. She could feel the heat and wetness, and she had never felt anything more sensual in her life than the warmth of his opened mouth on her body.

It was nothing like yesterday. Nothing like Gerald's touch. It was as different as day and night, as dusk and dawn. The dawn of her recognition of just how much she had hungered for this. She hadn't known what she had wanted those nights she'd watched Raven's hands moving over the fragility of the glass he held so securely. Those times she'd studied the slight movements of his firmly chiseled lips. But her body had known. And it was responding to his touch now as if in those weeks it had simply waited in blind anticipation of this moment.

Raven removed his hand from hers, and she felt his thumb and forefinger against her chin. She opened her eyes as he lifted up her face. The blue of his eyes was more clear than she'd ever seen it, dazzling in the sharp brightness of his gaze. His mouth was not smiling, its hard line stern and set. And she wanted it. Over hers. Involuntarily, she moistened her lips with her tongue. His eyes followed its movement, and then his eyelids closed, hiding the blue flame. And in response to the unspoken invitation, his dark head lowered to find the moisture her tongue had left on her lips.

His mouth wasn't hard, as she'd expected from the thin, forbidding line in which it was too frequently set. Instead it was warm and gentle. Firm and knowing. He knew exactly how to touch her—not domineeringly, but with none of the disgusting slackness of Amberton's kiss. His lips settled over hers, moving, almost taunting her with their power to make her respond. Suggesting that there was more that she wanted, and now needed.

The expression of her need was running in shivering torrents through her frame. She moved against the hard body that was bending over hers, wanting to make contact with its power all along the length of hers. Somehow his arm was behind her, holding her so that she was firmly supported and free to think of nothing but what his mouth was doing. And of the movement of his body against her own. Raven was so vital, warm and real, and she wanted to touch his skin as she had last night. To feel it move beneath her fingers, a smooth sheath for the muscles underneath.

His mouth opened suddenly over hers, his tongue invading, hard and sure. As hard as the muscles she had just been imagining she was once again touching. As hard as the chest her breasts were crushed against by the power of his arm against her back. As hard as...

Catherine gasped a little under the shattering impact of the discovery that she was not the only one responding physically to what was happening between them—an occurrence so foreign to the arrangement to which he had scrupulously held in the long weeks of their marriage. This is what she had wanted, she now knew, but he had never before indicated that he had any interest in her body. As his was now clearly revealing that he did. She wondered why he had never before seemed to want to touch her.

I don't need a mistress, he had said so long ago. *What I need is a hostess.* The two roles had been clearly defined and separated.

So he already had a mistress. That, of course, was why he'd not shown Catherine his expertise at this art before. And expert he certainly was, she admitted bitterly. He had just forced her to forget what had happened yesterday in Amberton's apartment, and in doing so, he had left her trembling in his arms like a schoolgirl.

You're such a child, he'd told her. Apparently when it came to lovemaking, he'd been right. Or at least he'd reduced her to one. He was, she was forced to admit, far more experienced at this than she. Her mouth withdrew from the caressing touch of his tongue. She was embarrassed to remember how passionately hers had been matching the provocative movements of his—revealing, perhaps, in willingly following his instruction, how inexperienced she really was. The chaste kisses she'd allowed her beaux to steal on dark balconies and in the cunningly sheltered alcoves of a dozen ballrooms—kisses that she had thought so daring—had been nothing like this. Nothing to match what she had just shared with the man who was, and who was not yet, in any true sense of the word, her husband.

A business arrangement—that's all he had wanted from her. And she had practically thrown herself at his head. Raven had kissed her because she had made it obvious that she'd wanted him to. *Please,* she had begged, and he had accommodated her. In her embarrassed realization of what a fool she had just made of herself, she stepped back, removing herself from his embrace.

Raven let her go, but he stood watching her a moment. His high cheekbones were slightly flushed, the crystal eyes still lucidly shining in that dark face, and, Catherine was pleased to notice, his breathing was a trifle uneven.

"What's wrong?" he asked.

"I—I suppose I was remembering yesterday. What Gerald did," she said, grasping at any explanation he might believe, rather than the one that was really responsible for her retreat from what had been happening. From what she had been revealing about her feelings for him, feelings she knew he didn't share.

"Liar," he said, smiling at her.

"I don't know what you mean," she said, the conventional delay when one didn't have a response. Liar she certainly was. The memory of Gerald's assault had faded under the touch of Raven's lips, except as a contrast to how right this was as opposed to how wrong the other had been.

"I was afraid that bastard might have spoiled you for this. And then I was...delighted to find that I'd nothing to worry about. You aren't afraid of me."

"Of course not. You are my husband."

"Convenient," Raven said softly.

"I beg your pardon?"

"A convenient marriage. I believe that's the term you told me was used for our sort of arrangement."

Our sort of arrangement, her mind echoed bitterly. *The sort where you waltz off to Scotland while I sit at home thinking every hour about what you might be doing.* She wondered suddenly if he were going to Scotland at all. All these "business" trips ... Very *convenient* for visiting some discreet address somewhere. Like an idiot, she'd never thought to question his travel. She wondered now how many of those journeys had been undertaken not to examine some coal mine or foundry, but rather to visit his mistress. The mistress he'd acknowledged quite openly.

"Scotland, I believe you said?" Catherine questioned.

"Lancaster first, and then perhaps across the Border."

Manchester, she thought. Raven had very definitely told her Manchester before. *Damn him, I was right. This isn't a business trip. And I suppose the interlude this morning was simply a warm-up to what he has in mind for later in the day. Or night.*

She took another step backward, away from the warmth and the now-familiar fragrance of his body, which, despite the confirmation of what she suspected, was so appealing. Her knees were still trembling with the aftermath of his touch.

"Have a good trip," she said, unable to hide the trace of bitterness at her discovery.

Raven's head tilted slightly, questioning that tone, and a small crease she'd never noticed before appeared between the sweep of his dark brows.

"Thank you," he answered, his attitude outwardly as correct as hers. "No goodbye kiss for your husband?" he suggested.

"I think you've had your kiss."

"Do you?" he questioned, his lips quirking slightly at her primness. "And by the rules, husbands are limited to only one?"

"How many are lovers limited to?" she asked, her anger making her bold.

"I don't believe there's a limit to lovers' kisses. I think they're allowed as many as they are able to steal. Don't you think that's probably how it works?"

"I don't know, I assure you. I've never had a lover."

"Good," he said. "Let's try to keep it that way, shall we?"

"And if Amberton calls?" she asked tauntingly.

Raven was puzzled by her sudden shift in tactics. She had only a few minutes before been meltingly responsive in his arms.

"Lord Amberton won't call. On that you have my word. And do you know, Catherine, I don't believe that husbands are limited to one kiss, after all. And if in England they are, that should certainly be changed. By an act of Parliament if necessary."

Even as he was speaking, he caught her up again into his embrace, his right arm moving commandingly behind her back and lifting her to meet his descending lips. There was no hesitation in the contact of his mouth over hers as there had been before. He had been afraid that Gerald's attack might have made her reluctant to endure a man's embrace, but her willing response had given Raven ample reason to know that was not the case.

His tongue pushed into her mouth, which, almost against her will, opened eagerly. Her tongue met his, matching the caressing quality of its movements. She seemed to be unable to deny him anything he wanted. Because, she knew, mistress or not, she wanted this, too. And had wanted it rather desperately now for several weeks.

Catherine couldn't have said how long his embrace lasted. Every bit of strength she possessed seemed to be draining from her body by the hard, sweet union of Raven's mouth with hers. She found that her hands had lifted to rest on those massive shoulders, holding him, not wanting him to leave when she had only just discovered how much she enjoyed his lovemaking. Perhaps if she became more adept at this, as he certainly could teach her to be, then he wouldn't want to seek out his mistress again. Maybe he'd choose instead to stay here with her. Maybe.

A vow, his grandmother's voice whispered into Raven's consciousness. Freedom, he remembered. He had promised Catherine freedom from this. Freedom until she wanted him as he had always wanted her. Gradually the movement of his tongue against hers stilled.

His mouth began to lift away, and unwilling to let the kiss end, unwilling to let him leave, Catherine clung damply to his lips with hers. Raven touched his mouth gently against those clinging lips, once, and then again, before he finally broke the contact. He turned his head so that his cheek rested, warm and wonderfully close, against hers. She could feel the slight roughness of his skin against the softness of hers.

"Manchester," she whispered.

"What?" he questioned, turning his face so that his lips caressed her eyelids, which were still closed.

"You said Manchester before," she said. *Deny it*, she prayed. *Make me believe that you're not rushing off to some other woman.*

"Did I?"

"Manchester," she repeated, nodding slightly against the movement of his lips over her face. They had now begun trailing warmly down her slightly retroussé and very fashionable nose.

"I must have been thinking of something else," he whispered. He kissed the tip of her nose and then lifted his head enough to look down into her face.

She opened her eyes, to find the startlingly bright blue of his own set in the beautiful stark planes of his face. And the golden bronze of his skin. She could see the pulse of the vein in his temple, the sheen of midnight hair, still unfashionably long and pulled back from those strong features.

"Then it is Manchester?" she managed to ask. What did it matter? she wondered. She was wasting the last few precious minutes he'd be here, asking ridiculous questions. She had no right to censure his behavior. This was what they had agreed to. He had never hidden the fact that he had a mistress. Most men of her class did. She had grown up accepting that reality. Gentlemen were entitled to their ladybirds as long as they fulfilled all the responsibilities of their legal bonds. But she had been forced to admit this morning that she didn't want Raven to hold another woman as he had just held her. Or to kiss her. Ridiculously gothic, she supposed, but true.

"Does it matter?" he asked, smiling at her. "I have interests in both. I didn't mean to mislead you. As soon as my plans are finalized, I'll have Reynolds inform you."

"You could write me," she suggested softly. She had no pride left. Next she'd be begging him to let her go with him.

"That may not be possible," he said. His eyes were no longer smiling, and there was something serious in the quietness of his deep voice.

"I understand," she whispered. And again she retreated, stepping back from the too-dangerous nearness of his hard body.

"Probably not," Raven said, touching his lips lightly to her forehead.

She raised both hands suddenly, her fingers caressing the dark hair that swept back from his face. Smiling into his watching eyes, she pulled his head down to move her lips against one lean cheek, delighting in the slight roughness of his closely shaved skin. His flesh felt too hot under the brush of her cool lips. On fire, she realized suddenly. And then he lifted his head abruptly and stepped around her and through the open doorway at her back. She listened without moving to the click of his boot heels striking decisively against the marble floor of the hall. And the murmur of voices, his and Edwards. And finally, her heart sinking, she listened to the closing of the front door.

Chapter Eight

When Oliver Reynolds had received the hand-delivered communication from his wealthiest client, he'd wondered at the abrupt instructions it contained. Despite his wealth, John Raven had never before ordered him to do anything, and certainly not anything as bizarre as this. Not the legal aspect, of course. *That* Reynolds had unsuccessfully sought to bring to Mr. Raven's attention on at least two occasions during the last three months. No, it was rather the location the American had chosen for the consummation of the business that seemed so unusual. As his coach stopped before the shaded doorway, Reynolds again wondered at the motives behind Raven's suggestion that they meet at this out-of-the-way hostelry, situated less than ten miles from the capital.

Slowly descending the narrow steps the coachman lowered for him, the old man felt the cost of this ridiculous journey in his aching bones. He had taken a few days longer than absolutely necessary to prepare the documents he carried today because he had found himself stubbornly thinking that, as rich as John Raven was, he did not control Oliver Reynolds. The man of business was too old to be at the beck and call of every client requiring his undivided attention. To give the American credit, however, he had, after the first, sent no more demanding letters of instruction.

Leaning more heavily than usual on the walking stick he liked to consider simply a fashionable affectation left over from his youth, Reynolds entered the low doorway of the inn. The hostess, having judged the quality not only of his attire but also of the carriage that stood under the shadows of the ancient oak from which the White Oak Inn had taken its name, approached, wiping her hands on her apron, which crackled softly with the starch her girls had laundered into it. She smiled at the banker and then shot a glance over her shoulder at her husband.

"I'm Oliver Reynolds," the old man said, fighting to keep his shortness of breath from being obvious. He was too old to be traipsing about the countryside, even at the behest of so valuable a client as John Raven. And he thought he might tell the American that. "I believe Mr. Raven's expecting me."

"Oh, sir," the woman said, her nervousness apparent in the work-reddened fingers now twisting a fold of the crisp cotton. "I swear I didn't know what I should do. Although as to that, Mr. Raven's instructions was clear enough, but it don't seem Christian somehow to leave him all alone. I brought him the willow, leaves and bark, like he asked me, and I even offered to help with the brewing, but he said no. I imagine if you're a friend, you know what he's like, right enough. Set on having his own way, it seems to me."

"Indeed," the banker said, thinking that he could with good conscience agree to that assessment, though, of course, he certainly did not intend to discuss John Raven's idiosyncrasies with the innkeeper's wife. "If you would be so good, Mrs...?"

"Hawthorne, sir. I'm Mrs. Hawthorne and that's my man that keeps the public house."

"Then if you or your husband would be so good, Mrs. Hawthorne, to tell Mr. Raven I'm awaiting him in the parlor, I should be very grateful."

The silence that greeted his very reasonable suggestion stretched, and still the woman made no move to deliver his message. "He's upstairs, sir," she said instead, glancing again at her husband. "He insisted he needed a fireplace, although with this awful heat, you'd think... And then there was the rocks, although he paid well enough for the carrying up of those, and to be sure, I'm not the kind to be begrudging a guest things that make him comfortable.''

Especially a guest with as generous a hand as he knew John Raven to have, Reynolds thought cynically as Mrs. Hawthorne continued.

''And I *offered* to call the doctor, but he'd have none of that, so I don't really know what else I could have done,'' she finished apologetically. ''But, I swear, as I said to my husband, it don't somehow seem Christian to me, despite what he says—''

''The doctor?'' the banker repeated, his hand suddenly arrested in the act of wiping the perspiration from his brow. Definitely too old to be traipsing around the countryside, he'd been thinking again when the woman's explanation had finally penetrated. ''For what reason should you summon a physician, my good woman? If ever in my life I've seen a man less in need of the services of a sawbones, it's John Raven.''

She hesitated, the brown eyes rich with concern, and her fidgeting fingers found another fold. ''That's what he said when I suggested it three days ago, but if you could see him now, Mr. Reynolds, you'd understand. I swear, as I told the mister just this morning, that shoulder's swelled like a cow with the colic. And he just sits there with his eyes closed and those rocks steaming around him. It's enough to make a body think...I don't mind telling you, sir, that I don't know what to think. Heathen's what I call it, but then he's such a gentleman. There's no denying that, no matter what strange ideas about healing he's got in his head. It's just that...'' She paused, allowing the country shrewdness that had made her husband's business a success to show briefly in the dark eyes. ''It's just that deaths ain't *good* for an establishment, if you take my meaning. They ain't good for business. The doctor's what we need, I said to Mr. Hawthorne just this morning. And I've had a mind, Mr. Reynolds, to send for one, orders or no.''

The banker closed his mouth, which had fallen open, whether with the information just imparted or with the exertions of his descent from the carriage, he wasn't entirely certain.

"Upstairs," he repeated faintly. Rich or not, John Raven was proving to be a far-more-troublesome client than Oliver Reynolds had bargained for.

When Mrs. Hawthorne opened the door, steam wafted into the narrow hallway, curling whitely around the black serge of the banker's suit and wisping out of the way of the woman's determined entry. It was obvious she believed she'd found an ally in Mr. Reynolds.

A still figure was seated cross-legged before the blazing fire on the open hearth, where several dark rocks gleamed wetly, their sizzling moisture obviously responsible for the steam. As they watched, Raven's right hand slowly grasped a ladle that rested on the floor beside him and dipped it into the now empty china basin he'd taken from the washstand. When the metal rang sharply against the porcelain, the dark hand relaxed, releasing the ladle, which dropped again to the floor. The massive shoulders slumped and his head drooped, the black hair, loosened from its customary restraint, falling forward to hide his profile.

Oliver Reynolds walked the few steps that separated him from his client, and at the sound of his footsteps across the wooden floor, John Raven's head lifted, the fever-bright eyes blinking like an owl's as he tried to focus on the intruder. He realized only vaguely that this was what he had been waiting for, and the cracked lips opened to say the word he had imprinted on his brain, its normal intelligence seared by the heat of his illness.

"Will?" he asked hoarsely, and at Reynolds's nod, he finally allowed his lids to close in relief. There was something else he had to do, Raven knew. Something... He couldn't think. He had felt his mind slipping away into the steam. Something he had to do... for Catherine. And with her image, the task he'd been waiting to complete fluttered into the forefront of the darkness that was trying to rob him of the ability to think.

"Sign it," he whispered, but his eyes didn't open. At some level he was aware of the old man's trembling fingers touching his injured shoulder, but he couldn't really feel them against the familiar agony. That was something he had closed away four days ago, had locked outside of his consciousness and denied its ability to intrude on his prayers. Control of pain was one of the first lessons he had been taught, carefully instructed by the old woman, the ancient words whispering in his boy's mind like the drone of bees on a summer's day.

He had prayed to the All-Spirit, but the visions that had come, curling like the steam, had not been of strength and reassurance. He had defeated the pain, but the sickness that had entered his body through the hole Amberton had opened to the spirits would not be controlled. And there were, he had thought with regret, so many things he had wanted to finish.

He had allowed himself to hold her, to kiss her, knowing that if this time came, those memories would offer comfort. Catherine, he thought again, and knew he must have said it aloud when the old man spoke.

"I have it here," Mr. Reynolds said softly, but it seemed to take a long time before Raven was aware of the pen pressed into his right hand. He couldn't see the document, its inked lines wavering before him, and when the banker finally understood, he guided his hand until it was done. Raven had to trust the old man that the instructions he'd written out so carefully that morning, some morning, had been followed. His holdings in New York were to go to his family, and everything else was Catherine's. Everything... Raven allowed his eyes to drift closed over the fire that burned inside them. So hot. But it didn't matter because... He couldn't remember why it didn't matter, but he knew that whatever he had been waiting for was finished.

The massive figure tilted gently to the side, and once begun, the momentum carried his body downward like a ship listing in a storm. And by the time his cheek was resting against Mrs. Hawthorne's gleaming oaken floor, John Raven was no longer aware of the storm that still raged through his body.

* * *

It had taken the combined efforts of several men called up from the taproom below, but they had deposited the American in the inn's best bed, and Mrs. Hawthorne had, for modesty's sake, found a sheet to spread over the wide, bare chest. The soft buckskin breeches he was wearing seemed unrestrictive and so they left those alone. And they left the poultice with its infusion of willow leaves that Raven had placed over the entry wound.

The physician had arrived in short order, perhaps hastened by the generous fee Reynolds had sent as an inducement, and the banker had thankfully left his client in the competent hands of the physician and Mistress Hawthorne. It was almost two hours later when the doctor emerged, carefully refastening the cuffs he'd obviously rolled up to perform some service for his patient. The banker felt his stomach clench when he remembered the grossly distended flesh underneath the poultice. Resolutely, he blocked that image and watched the physician shrug into his frock coat.

"How is he?" Reynolds asked when the man seemed disinclined to share any evaluation of the American's condition.

"Lucky to be alive," the doctor said bluntly. He had not learned a fashionable bedside manner at the University of Edinburgh, which was surely why he preferred a rural practice, tending to the honest injuries of farmers and farriers, than a more profitable London one, soothing the imaginary vapors of delicate gentlemen and fainting females. "I lanced the wound and bled him. For today, that's all that anyone can do. Alone in the world, is he?" he asked casually.

"I beg your pardon?"

The physician glanced up, shrewd hazel eyes assessing the old man's puzzlement. "I assumed there's no one who gives a damn whether that man lives or dies, given the fact that he appears to be well on his way to the latter, alone and uncared for."

Reynolds swallowed uncomfortably, remembering the unnecessary delay his pride had demanded before his delivery of the papers John Raven had asked him to prepare.

"He has a wife," he said hesitantly. Catherine Montfort, he thought again. He couldn't imagine how the American had brought that off, but the marriage was legal enough. Reynolds had made certain of that before he'd drawn up the will. However, he couldn't picture a woman he knew to be the acknowledged toast of London and a diamond of the first water sitting in a second-rate country inn beside a dying man's bedside.

The doctor's eyebrow lifted slightly. "Indeed," he said softly, a world of meaning in the single word.

"She probably doesn't even know..." the banker began, and then hesitated, wondering if that were true.

"Well, if she expects to see her husband again—her living husband, I should say—then I suggest you tell her." With that brusque opinion delivered, the physician picked up his satchel and descended the steps.

Taking a deep breath, the old man turned back to the door of the bedroom where the American lay. The devastating sarcasm of the phrase echoed in his head. *Her living husband*. It seemed he had no choice, but he supposed he owed it to his client to inform him of what he intended. As quietly as possible, he opened the door and almost tiptoed to the side of the bed that Raven's massive frame filled. The injury had been rebandaged, the poultice discarded, and the American lay unmoving under the spread of sheet and counterpane, their smoothness disturbed only by his slow, too-shallow breathing. Mistress Hawthorne sat in a straight chair near the curtained window.

"Is he conscious?" Reynolds asked.

"I don't know. He never made a sound through the whole ordeal, which was ghastly enough, I promise you. I've never seen as much vileness pour out of a wound as when the sawbones opened that one. Enough poison to kill a normal man, I should have thought," she said softly, shivering at the memory.

"The doctor thinks I should send for his wife," the banker said, looking down at the man on the bed. The black hair was fanned against the whiteness of Mrs. Hawthorne's linen, the golden skin stretched too tightly over the bones beneath.

The blue eyes slowly opened, bloodshot and unfocused with the fever. "No," Raven said. He licked parched lips, trying to think what he could say to prevent that. He didn't want Catherine here. *Feeling maternal,* he had asked her mockingly. *He* was the protector. That was the way it was supposed to be. He didn't want her to see him like this, too weak, he knew, to pretend strength if she came. But also too weak, he was afraid, to prevent them bringing her here.

"I don't want her," he whispered finally, watching the old man's face waver through the mists above him. That was not what Raven had meant to say. He wanted her, of course, but not to see him this way—brought down by the bastard he'd promised would never bother her again. She would never believe he could protect her from the likes of Amberton if she saw him like this.

"But the doctor thinks..." Reynolds began, and then thought better of telling him that truth.

The cracked lips moved upward slightly. "Don't send for Catherine," Raven ordered, imbuing his voice with all the surety he could command. "I'm not going to die," he said, remembering the vow he'd made. The solemn, sacred promise that Catherine Montfort Raven would be his. That she would be his wife in every meaning of the word. He'd be damned if he'd die before he fulfilled that oath. "I promised," he finished, and then the clouded blue eyes were slowly hidden by the downward drift of his eyelids as unconsciousness claimed him.

He'd had his instructions and unwilling to go against orders again, knowing that if he'd only arrived two or three days earlier, his client might not now be lying at the edge of death, Oliver Reynolds nodded. And it was not until much later that he thought to wonder about the past tense.

* * *

Despite the supposed dearth of society in London at the end of summer, someone who was very determined could find endless engagements to occupy what otherwise might loom as empty hours. And Catherine Raven was very determined. Because when she was not riding or dancing or promenading through the park, shopping or chatting away the afternoon with old friends, she was remembering the morning of her husband's departure.

As he had promised, Raven had had Oliver Reynolds send her word of his itinerary. She supposed the banker received written communication from his employer, but if so, none of it was ever passed on to her—only the briefest note to the effect that Mr. Raven had asked him to convey the information that he was now in Lancaster or Glasgow or Edinburgh. And eventually the days stretched beyond the fortnight Raven had suggested he'd be gone. Far beyond, to three endless weeks, and well into the fourth.

By then, of course, she'd relived a thousand times that morning's encounter, remembering not only the kisses they'd shared, but the feel of his body against hers. Its fragrance. And then, unbidden, would come the frightening remembrance of the hot, dry heat of his face against hers. As hot as if he were fevered. As if his wound were already inflamed with the inevitable infection that followed any injury that broke the protective covering of the skin. After the realization had come to her that the warmth of his skin that morning was not normal, she had remembered, too, the abnormal brightness of his eyes. She'd noticed them, of course, but she'd not assigned the proper cause to their nearly luminescent glow. Not at first, in any case.

And so she deliberately filled every moment of her day with almost hectic activity. She had found that if she were not surrounded by the most entertaining and lively members of her set, those who were still in the city, she found herself picturing Raven's body twisting in pain on some strange bed, the shoulder she'd so ineptly bandaged agonizingly swollen.

Men died from the effects of wounds far less serious than the one he'd suffered because of her. He could be dead even now, she had realized, and she would have no way of knowing. She had heard nothing in the last week, not even the unsatisfactory travelogue that the banker had originally provided.

I could kill you, John Raven, she thought illogically, *for putting me through this. If only you were here, and I could see to it that you were being cared for. That you were receiving proper treatment. That you were eating the things that would keep you strong through a debilitating fever.* Whatever those things were. Surely Edwards would know what to feed an invalid. Or the cook would. Surely *someone* would know in this vast staff whose wages he paid while he himself lay somewhere, dying perhaps, with no one of his own to look after him.

Her hand trembled suddenly, spilling the wine she'd barely tasted. Edwards was there immediately, offering a cloth. She touched it unthinkingly to the slight dampness of her fingers, and then, unable to bear the direction of her thoughts any longer, she rose suddenly, dropping the cloth onto the table beside her untouched plate.

"Thank you, Edwards," she said.

This was one of the few times she'd dined at home since her husband had left. How different tonight had been from the evenings she'd spent with Raven, discussing a hundred topics, even his businesses. Anything he said or did, she thought in self-mockery, was interesting to her. As sitting alone at his table certainly was not. He had been gone long enough that the chairs he'd ordered removed the morning he'd left had been returned, recovered in an elaborately embroidered fabric that had very closely matched the pattern she'd originally chosen. Standing by the table, arrested suddenly by the memory of the dark stain that had covered the back of his chair that evening, she lowered her head, fighting tears.

"Is something wrong, madam?" Edwards asked in concern.

"No, nothing, thank you," she whispered. Embarrassed that she had given way to her feelings in front of the servants, Catherine turned and made her way out of the room and to the stairs that would lead to her chamber. And to another night that she would spend wondering where he was.

Sleep eluded her, as she had known it would. Sometime near dawn she slipped out of her bed and tiptoed, still in her night rail, down to the small room that served as Raven's office. She had done this before, sitting through the cold dark hours, her body curled into the chair behind his desk, somehow feeling closer to him here than in any other spot in the vast house in which he had spent so little of his time. Only here did he still seem real to her. And somehow present. And the hours she'd foolishly spent in his small domain this week had been the only comfort she'd found for her unreasoning fears.

The room was dark and silent. She stood a moment in the doorway, knowing that in less than an hour the servants would come upstairs to build up the fires in the kitchen stoves and to prepare breakfast. Just now the house was still deserted and quiet, and she had some minutes that she could stay here alone.

Raven was sitting in the darkness of his office when she entered, her body outlined by the dawn that was breaking through the tall windows of the salon across the hallway. She moved into the doorway, the material of her nightgown falling straight from its high waistline, the line of long, slender leg clearly revealed by its sheerness. She had left her hair unbound, and one dark red strand lay across her shoulder, resting smooth as a silk ribbon over her left breast.

He was unsure at first if he had conjured her here, if she were a phantom created by his desire. He had been savoring the familiarity of the small, dark room and envisioning Catherine sleeping above, unaware of the battle he had waged during the past month. Unaware of his illness, because he had never intended her to know. The suffering hero was not a role he relished, and he had known from her halting confession that she blamed herself for his injury. He knew her well enough now to know that Catherine would have felt guilty over the result of Amberton's attack. Guilt and probably pity, he'd acknowledged bitterly, had she seen him as he had been only two weeks ago. Neither of those was the emotion he wanted to arouse in his wife.

"Good morning," Raven said softly.

Catherine's heart leapt in response to the quiet voice that spoke out of the shadows. "My God," she whispered, her heartbeat slowing because she had recognized the speaker.

"I didn't mean to frighten you," he said.

"What are you doing here?"

"I had *thought* this is where I live. Or has that changed?"

"No," she said, slowly shaking her head.

Raven was alive. Alive and seated in his accustomed place behind his own desk. The gladness that sang through her veins over that realization was almost impossible to contain. She wanted to laugh out loud. To hug him. Hold him. Touch the dark, warm skin. To be reassured that he was truly all right.

"Nothing has changed," she said instead.

"And in my absence, Catherine, have you taken to wandering around the house in your nightgown like Lady Macbeth?" he asked.

She was very thankful for the teasing quality that she clearly heard in his deep voice. She'd been so afraid she would never hear him tease her again. "Sometimes. And have you taken to sitting in the dark, waiting to frighten visitors to death?"

"Sometimes," he echoed. "Although I can't ever remember having had a visitor at this hour. Is something wrong?"

"I was worried about you."

"About me? Why would you be worried about me?" he asked, forcing the amused note into his question.

"Because I hadn't heard from you."

"Surely Reynolds—"

"He would tell me where you were, but then you didn't come home when you had said you would. You've been gone a whole month, Raven. And this week I heard nothing. I thought you were sick, perhaps, or..." She paused, afraid somehow to confess the hours she'd spent worrying about him. "And even Mr. Reynolds's notes were so... He never told me *how* you were," she finished plaintively, knowing she was making a fool of herself.

"Why should he?" Raven asked simply. "I suppose he didn't realize you were worried. He had no way of knowing your imagination would suggest the delay in my return was because of some...danger," he suggested calmly.

She could see the quick gleam of very white teeth despite the shadows that surrounded him. He was laughing at her, she thought in sudden fury. "I didn't *imagine* the damage Gerald did to you," Catherine said hotly. She'd spent nearly a month in the worst sort of anxiety, and he was belittling her concern.

"Damage that Gerald..." Raven began, as if she'd mentioned some trifling mishap that had slipped his mind. "Surely, Catherine, you didn't think Amberton had inflicted any lasting injury. I told you it was nothing." He prayed the lie was more convincing than it sounded to his own ears.

"I *saw* what he did, Raven. And then the day you left..."

Suddenly, in the face of his denial, Catherine was no longer so certain of her interpretation of the events of that morning. She reviewed the evidence on which her anxiety had been built. His skin had been hot and dry, his eyes too bright, so she had taken that to mean that he was ill, his shoulder inflamed.

"What about the day I left?" Raven's question floated to her out of the shadows, as if he, too, were attempting to remember.

"Your skin was hot," she said, trying to convince herself that she hadn't made up all the carefully constructed clues to the terrifying scenario she'd been living with.

"That *is* one of the side effects of passion."

"Passion?" she repeated. At least, she thought bitterly, she hadn't been wrong about *that*.

"I've never denied that I have carnal needs," he reminded her. "I'm afraid it had simply been too long since I'd taken the opportunity to satisfy them." He hoped that in her innocence she wouldn't recognize the absurdity of that as an excuse for fever.

"Then what happened that morning..."

"My apologies, Catherine. You may put that lapse down to blood loss. And to too prolonged an abstinence. I hope you'll forgive me for kissing you without your permission. It won't happen again. I intend to take steps to guarantee that it doesn't." Raven hoped she couldn't see in the darkness the involuntary lift of his lips that promise invoked.

"Steps to prevent such *prolonged* abstinence?" she asked bitterly.

"Yes," he confirmed. It was a simple statement of fact. That was one of the decisions he'd made during the tiresome weeks of his recovery. Despite the promise of freedom he'd given to convince Catherine to wed him, he intended somehow to court and to win his own wife. To make her want him with the same fierce desire that moved through his body whenever he even thought of her. That was not against their contract. And it had been too prolonged an abstinence. Too damned prolonged.

"I see," she whispered.

No, my darling, you certainly don't see, Raven thought, *but you will. Soon, I promise you, you will.* Aloud he simply reminded her, "I *have* rendered my apology."

"Yes, you have," she agreed softly. How dare he apologize for kissing her? *Damn you, damn you, damn you,* she thought fiercely. *How can it have meant nothing to you?* And she wondered suddenly what his mistress was like. Was she beautiful? Witty and charming? *Damn you, John Raven,* she thought again.

"And what have you been doing in my absence? Besides imagining me ill?"

Again she believed she could hear his amusement.

"I've managed to entertain myself," she forced herself to answer, but the lie sounded brittle after the seriousness of their conversation. "London in the summer's not nearly so

dull as everyone pretends. I think it's become fashionable to
deplore the lack of society and adopt an air of ennui. Pretending boredom makes people believe you're accustomed
to far more exciting activities than the one you're engaged
in."

"You're probably right," he said.

Raven certainly sounded bored with what she was bab-
bling about, and she didn't blame him. "Did you just arrive?" she asked, trying to get back to some topic that made
sense. The meaningless chatter her cicisbei found so
charming apparently left her husband cold.

"I arrived in London last night," he said. "It was very
late, so I decided not to disturb the household."

"Where did you spend the night?" she asked without
thinking.

There was a small silence from the figure hidden in the
shadows on the other side of the desk. Raven certainly
couldn't tell her he had stood for hours in the darkness of
the street below, looking up at the window he knew to be
hers.

"I'm sorry. You needn't answer that," Catherine advised suddenly, realizing where he must have spent the night.

"I told you that you might ask me anything, and that I'd
never lie to you. Those rules have not changed."

"You don't have to explain. I'm quite capable of imagining that part of your itinerary on my own," she said
coldly.

"Forgive me, Catherine, if I'm wrong, but you seem
somewhat annoyed that I'm home. Shall I find some other
business to call me away? I promise not to interfere in
whatever flirtation you've undertaken to keep you entertained."

He wondered with sharp, cold jealousy if she *had* found
someone in the month he'd been fighting to live, desperately determined, despite his body's infuriating weakness,
to return to her. To fulfill his vow.

"Flirtation?" she repeated softly, thinking how different
the image called up by his choice of words was to the night-
mares she had been living with. "I haven't been engaged in

a *flirtation*." She could hear the bitterness in her voice and knew that Raven was astute enough to detect it, too.

"Then you *must* have been bored," he said teasingly.

"I thought you were ill. I have been imagining..." She paused, angry that she'd admitted what he'd accused her of.

"I instructed Reynolds to keep you informed. I'm sorry if you've been distressed. It was never my intent to worry you."

"Of course," she said. All her concern had been for naught. She'd thought he was dying, and instead he had been arranging for the satisfaction of the carnal needs he had never even bothered to hide. "I apologize for interrupting your solitude."

"You sound almost angry that I'm not lingering at death's door. I told you I'm accustomed to taking care of myself."

"Yes, of course," she said calmly, sure now that he was belittling her concern for him. She was beyond anger. As he'd reminded her, he had never given her a reason to believe he needed or wanted her. "I should have known that you'll never need anyone's care. Especially mine," she said.

She turned and left the office, and despite the fact that she'd managed to have the last word, it was not a very satisfying one. Raven was back and that, too, had turned out to be far less satisfying than she had been imagining.

Raven took a deep breath and then expelled it. He didn't seem to be very adept at courtship. Of course, he'd never before undertaken to make a woman love him. He knew far more about iron and steel, about coal and mining, and far too little about courting a woman like Catherine.

Despite the knowledge that he'd badly mishandled this morning's reunion, eventually he allowed a slight, controlled smile, still safely hidden by the surrounding darkness. She had worried about him. Sometime between the routs and the balls and the rides in Hyde Park with the elegant Reginalds and Geralds, she'd worried about her inconvenient husband. In spite of the fact that Raven had never wanted Catherine's concern, **would** have rejected it had she expressed it, there was something very satisfying about that thought.

It was another chip on his side of the table, added to the two that had given him hope through his illness: she was already his wife, and somewhere, an ocean away, a fragile, indomitable old woman was sending up powerful prayers on his behalf.

The odds are definitely not in your favor, Catherine, my darling, Raven thought, allowing his small smile to widen.

Chapter Nine

Catherine managed to avoid any prolonged contact with her husband for the next several days. Raven was apparently occupied catching up on the correspondence that had arrived in his absence, spending hours closed up in that confined office. *Her* social calendar was really quite full; she made sure of that.

She saw him once in the front hall. She had been on her way to a drum, and he had bowed to her as she passed him in the foyer, as if they had been the merest acquaintances. Again that small smile had played briefly over his lips, but at the spark of anger she couldn't quite prevent from leaping into her eyes, he had made an effort at controlling his amusement and had made his very proper bow. As if she were a stranger instead of his wife. She'd taken satisfaction in knowing that, arrayed as she'd been in a new and daringly cut gown of bronze satin, she had looked her best. The fury that had resulted from that encounter had carried her through the next day, righteously determined not even to think about her husband, who was, she thought, probably busy planning his next *convenient* visit to his mistress. Whoever she was.

Catherine listened to the gossip that flowed around her with a great deal more interest since Raven's return, knowing that if he *had* brought his demirep up to town, she'd be certain to hear of it. Someone would maliciously let it slip, but so far she had heard nothing and could only speculate

on Raven's taste in women. An activity she found herself
engaged in far too frequently for her own peace of mind.

Using Edwards as his messenger, Raven had asked her to
arrange another dinner party and had even suggested this
time some of those who should be invited. The invitations
had already gone out, and she was sitting at a small table
downstairs discussing the menu with the butler one morning, little more than a week after her husband's return, when
he entered the room.

Under the observant eye of her majordomo, she couldn't
retreat and was forced to endure the quick touch of Raven's lips against her forehead that he employed as his form
of greeting. She even managed to smile up into those crystalline eyes, which clearly revealed that their owner was well
aware of her true reaction to his almost paternal kiss. So
different, she thought with regret, from the last time he'd
kissed her.

She lowered her gaze to her list of instructions, trying to
hide the pain of that memory from his discerning eyes. He
greeted Edwards with his accustomed familiarity, and then,
unbelieving, she heard him dismiss the butler. Anticipation
tightened her stomach, and she fought to control her
breathing.

"I wanted to talk to you," he said. "I hope I haven't interrupted something that can't be finished at a later time."

"Perhaps you should have asked that *before* you sent
Edwards away," she said challengingly. She glanced up from
her pretended contemplation of her list, believing she had
her emotions well in hand.

"I'm sorry," Raven said. "Would you like for me to call
him back and postpone our discussion until later?"

"No," she admitted, deliberately directing her attention
again to her list. "It really doesn't matter. There's nothing
here that can't be dealt with later. I simply like to have everything organized and every eventuality planned for."

"No surprises," he suggested. She could hear the smile in
his voice, but knew that if she looked up, his face would be
controlled. "You don't like surprises."

She did glance up at that. "No, I don't suppose I do. Not about a dinner party. But you don't leave anything to chance, either. You don't seem to like surprises any better than I."

"I don't know about that," he said, and he did smile then. "After all, I married you."

"And I surprise you?"

"Almost constantly."

"Because we're from such different backgrounds."

"Perhaps you're right. I had begun to think, however, that it was because you are not what I had expected your particular background to produce. You're not the typical product of your class, Catherine."

"I don't understand," she said truthfully. "If I've failed in some way to live up to what you require, you have only to tell me." She could feel the blush creeping into her cheeks. She had not really expected his censure for her foolish actions concerning Amberton at this late date.

"You haven't failed my expectations in any way. On the contrary, you've far exceeded them."

"Then you're not angry with me?" she asked, daring to hope that what had happened because of her foolishness in allowing Gerald to trick her might finally be forgiven if not forgotten.

"No, I'm not angry. As a matter of fact, I had thought, since I've been back, that I had done something to make you angry, but I can't decide what it was."

Apologized for kissing me. Put it down to blood loss. Brought your mistress up to town. Ignored me. The true reasons for her anger ran fleetingly through her head, but she couldn't admit to any of those, so she was left at a loss, an unaccustomed loss for someone usually so quick-witted in awkward social situations. And this one was very awkward. What did a wife say to a husband she was madly in love with when he admitted that he would seek her embrace only if giddy from a loss of blood?

"Catherine?" Raven asked softly.

"I'm not angry," she lied. There was really nothing she could legitimately chide him with. He had followed the rules of their agreement, with one very memorable exception. She was the one who wanted this marriage to become something they'd never agreed to, something he'd never indicated he wanted. Her fingers touched the list she'd been discussing with Edwards before Raven had interrupted. This was the only role he wished her to play in his life. He had certainly denied her any other.

"I don't think you need be so concerned with this. The dinner is still several days away," he said, taking the list from her hand and putting it firmly to the side. He pulled out the chair across the small table from where she was sitting and sat down in it. Her eyes must have expressed her surprise, because he smiled at her.

"Play cards with me," he said.

"What?"

"Cards. Whatever you played with Amberton that night. Whatever game he beat you at."

"Piquet," she answered unthinkingly. And then she asked, shaking her head, "Why should we play cards?" It was the middle of the morning. She had a luncheon engagement that she wasn't even dressed for. And Raven always spent his mornings busily engaged with his business affairs. And now...

"Because you lost that night. And that loss resulted in an unpleasant situation for you. I don't intend for that to happen again. Not if I can help it. I told you I'm very good with numbers. I thought I might teach you a few tricks."

"An unpleasant situation for *me*?" she asked pointedly, thinking of what Gerald had done to Raven.

His lips tightened slightly at her reminder, but he admitted, "And for me, if you will."

"I didn't mean for you to be hurt," she said, meeting his eyes. It was the most honest thing she'd ever said to him.

"I know. That was my own stupidity. Edwards told me you really were quite concerned while I was away. I'm sorry Reynolds didn't do a better job of reassuring you."

"I told you to write," she whispered.

"Yes, you did. Is that why you're angry?"

"I'm not angry."

"Liar," he said, and she remembered the last time he'd accused her of that. Her eyes fell before the certainty in his, but he ignored her lie and began to deal out their hands very professionally onto the small table.

"You have to calculate your odds," he said. "Not only with the play, but with the discards. Especially with discards," he advised. "Show me your hand."

He put his fingers over hers, which had automatically picked up the cards from the pile before her. Again their callused warmth left her breathless, causing strange sensations to move uncomfortably, yet enticingly, through her lower body. As if, she thought in wonder, as if he were somehow touching her there.

As his patient instruction continued over the next half hour, she found herself watching his hands, so dark and beautiful. Graceful. And his mouth.

"Think, Catherine," he commanded, and suddenly she came back to reality, back from the image of his hands moving against her body with the same sure skill with which he touched the pasteboards scattered between them.

She glanced at her cards, trying to remember what he'd told her, trying desperately to do the calculations in her head. She was a very good card player normally, but she had always relied on her instincts and luck. The things he had told her, while she was still in some condition to listen, had made a great deal of sense. Raven was, as he had claimed, very good with numbers. Taking a deep breath, she selected what she hoped was the right discard for the situation he'd set out and put it on the table.

"Brilliant," he said.

She looked up to find him smiling at her.

"You really are a very fine player," he continued. "I can't imagine how you managed to let Amberton beat you."

"I was thinking about how angry you'd be if you discovered I'd gone upstairs with him," she said truthfully. "My mind wasn't on the game at all."

"Never play cards if you don't play to win. And that takes concentration as well as skill."

"I know," she said.

"And I would have had no right to be angry with you. We have an agreement."

"I know," she said again, but she was afraid the bitterness had shown through despite her ready agreement with what he'd said.

"And I'm not easily angered," he added.

"It's a good thing," she answered, finally smiling at him. "I must be a sore trial to your patience. Getting you stabbed and then having the nerve to worry about you. What inexplicable behavior from your wife." She knew she was challenging him.

"Inexplicable, perhaps, only to me," he offered softly. "I told you that I'm unaccustomed to anyone worrying about my well-being. I honestly didn't know how to react. I hope you'll forgive me for not dealing with your concern any better than I did the morning of my return."

"You made fun of me," she accused. "For worrying about you. And I thought I had just cause. I didn't have any way of knowing that you're indestructible." His laughter was quick and soft, and she felt her lips move upward in an answering smile.

"I didn't intend to make fun of you," he said, taking her hand. "I intended to reassure you that I was all right. I'm sorry it came out wrong."

His hand was warm and hard and incredibly strong, like the man himself. And feeling that strength, she again felt very foolish for worrying about him. He did seem indestructible.

"Will you forgive me for that, too?" he asked.

I'd forgive you almost anything, she thought, her eyes still on her small hand resting in that strong dark one. "Yes," she whispered.

Raven's fingers tightened briefly over hers, a quick squeeze, and then he released her. He rose from the table, and she looked up in surprise.

"Are you leaving?" she asked. She was a little disconcerted by how strong her sense of disappointment was.

"I have work to do," he said, smiling down at her. "Not all of us are persons of leisure in this household. Someone must make the money to pay for all that folderol you manage to purchase every month. Reynolds says we shall soon have to wheel in your bills in a barrow.''

Since she had spent almost nothing in the month he'd been away and very little since his return, she knew he was teasing her.

"Liar," she said in answer, and when his slight smile widened, she felt her heart turn over.

"Be careful or I'll become a slacker and let our fortunes go to rack and ruin. I'll spend the time I should be working playing cards with my wife or some such shocking activity.''

"Should I worry?" she challenged, smiling back at him.

"As you please, Catherine. I'll never chide you for that again. As a matter of fact..." he said, and then he paused, looking down into her eyes. And he was no longer smiling. "I found the idea that you'd worried about me quite pleasant. Far more pleasant than I could have imagined it might be.''

His tone was too serious for the discussion they'd been having, and she had no answer for what he'd just suggested. She finally began to breathe again, and then he reached down to touch her neck, his fingers moving slowly upward to a spot behind her ear. She had no idea what he was doing, but her head tilted automatically to lean against his hand. She wasn't even aware that her eyelids had dropped in response to his touch.

"Did you lose this, Catherine?" he asked. She opened her eyes as he removed his hand from her earlobe. "Your ear seems a strange place to keep something this valuable."

His fingers turned over as gracefully as a magician's, as if practicing some sleight-of-hand, to reveal on their outstretched tips a large blue gem. Its light hue was thrown into prominence by the dark gold of his skin. She blinked at the sudden, almost magical appearance of a stone that size. His hand, she was sure, had held nothing at all when he had first touched her.

"What in the world? Where did that come from?"

"Out of your ear?" Raven suggested helpfully.

"No," she denied, laughing. "That is certainly nothing I've ever seen before in my life."

He held it before her like an offering. The jewel caught the light in a strangely glowing way. Not like the glitter of a faceted stone. It was truly like nothing she'd ever seen before.

"Perhaps you should take a closer look. Just to be certain you don't recognize it," he said.

Catherine tore her gaze away from the pale depths of the gem to find the same compelling blue echoed in Raven's eyes, surrounded by their sweep of long dark lashes and his golden skin. Her breath caught and a blaze of some sensation, powerful and sensuous, moved through her stomach and then lower, searing deep and hot into areas of her body she'd never been so conscious of in her entire life. Intimate and seductive, the feeling burned and curled, and she wanted her husband in ways she'd never dreamed she could even think about a man. In response to her body's unbelievably physical reaction, she quickly glanced back at the stone resting on his fingers, trying to hide whatever might have been revealed in her eyes.

Her hand was very pale compared to the one she touched in order to pick up the gem he held out to her. To give her trembling fingers something to do, she lifted the stone to catch the light pouring in through the tall windows of the small salon and became aware for the first time of the pale streaks that marked the center of the orb she held. Like a star caught in the perfect blue of the sky that surrounded it.

"What is it?" she asked, her voice thready and breathless.

"It's called a star sapphire."

"I've never seen anything like it," she whispered, turning it back and forth in the sunlight.

"They're very rare. And, I think, very beautiful."

"Where did you find it?"

"In India. Kashmir. Beginner's luck, they told me."

Unable to resist, she glanced up and said teasingly, "I told you it was all a matter of luck."

He laughed, and she held out the stone to him. "It's very beautiful."

"I'm glad you like it," he answered politely, making no effort to take it from her. "I would have had it made up, but I wasn't sure whether you'd prefer a ring or a pendant."

"You're giving it to me?"

"Of course."

"But why? I don't understand. If you found it and it's very rare—"

Raven interrupted. "Perhaps it *is* all a matter of luck. Very rare," he repeated softly. "And I found it."

Aware that his words were intended to mean more than a simple repetition of hers, she closed her fingers suddenly around the stone.

"It's like your eyes," she said, unable to prevent the expression of the ridiculously romantic thought she'd had. Somehow the ease that had grown between them in the last few moments invited that very personal comment.

For a long time Raven made no response to what she had said, and eventually she felt a blush begin to creep into her cheeks. He was watching her with those beautiful eyes she'd just childishly remarked upon. *Like a lovesick schoolgirl,* she thought in disgust. But since he'd already admitted he thought her a child, she supposed it didn't matter how much more foolishly she behaved. Where Raven was concerned, she really had no pride left at all.

"Thank you," he said finally. When he turned and walked across the room, the Oriental carpet softening the sound of that decisive stride, Catherine closed her eyes. Finally, a reprieve from the intense examination his had just made. And when she opened them again, she also opened her hand and looked down into the depths of the priceless stone he'd just given her. He had presented it without any ceremony and with no fanciful words about his regard for her, it was true. He had, instead, plucked it from behind her ear like a conjurer at a fair. But he had given it to her.

And she thought again, looking down into its depths, that it really *was* very much like his eyes.

* * *

"But you can't believe that the workers are in favor of these innovations you're proposing as their salvation. You have only to look at the machine-smashing rampages of the Luddites," the Earl of Devon argued vehemently.

"Because they don't understand the machines' potential for improving their lives. They see them as taking jobs, not as—" Raven began to explain, only to be interrupted by Lord Elliot.

"Why shouldn't they? For most of them that has certainly proved to be the case. Jobs lost, families destroyed, land that could be in crop production used for factories."

"Surely you're not attempting to blame the lack of available farmland on the manufacturers? I should think you would more properly blame the greed of the landowners for that situation."

Her husband was treading on dangerous ground there, Catherine thought, since the gentlemen gathered around his dinner table were themselves large landowners.

"Enclosure, I suppose," scoffed Devon. "An old ogre."

"An old problem," Raven agreed. "One far more responsible for the dissolution of the family than the factories are. There they work together, I'm afraid, from the youngest to the eldest."

"Children?" Catherine asked. The ongoing debate had been waged with little contribution from the ladies. They had apparently decided this rehash of a favorite masculine subject would simply have to be endured.

"As soon as they are able to pick up lint from the floor in the textile mills," Raven answered, glancing at her.

Catherine had seldom taken an active part in these discussions, which were as lively, and often as heated, as those in Parliament, but she knew her dinner parties had become very popular because of them. No one seemed to mind what topics were introduced and threshed out over the exquisitely prepared courses her chef produced, the debates fueled by the flow of Edwards's carefully selected wines. She had been instructed by her husband to provide the best for those fortunate enough to be included on her guest lists these last few weeks, and she had done so unstintingly. And now an invitation to dine at the home of John Raven was one of the most sought after of the Little Season.

"It seems so cruel," she said, picturing such a childhood.

"Twelve- or fourteen-hour days. And the mines are far worse," her husband said.

"Mines?" repeated Lady Avondale. "Surely there are no children working in the mines."

"The smaller the better," Raven acknowledged. "The drifts are too narrow for the men. Women and children are employed to push the loosened coal up the inclines to the surface. And the owners prefer children because they can pay them less than a quarter of what an adult would make."

"But why would parents allow their children to go down into the mines?" Catherine asked, shuddering slightly as she pictured that dark, narrow tunnel Raven described.

"And if your choice were that or starvation for the entire family? What option do you believe you would have?"

"And your mines employ machines to do those jobs?" Catherine asked, almost forgetting the others listening to their exchange. As always, she was fascinated by the ideas her husband suggested.

"In several of the mines I own around Durham the coal is brought to the surface by machine."

"Then *you've* put workers out of their jobs," Devon pronounced, satisfied that he'd made his point.

"We've put *children* out of their jobs," Raven said patiently. "We've sent the children home."

"And the wages those children were bringing in? How have your workers endured that loss of income, Mr. Raven?" Lord Russell asked. There was simply interest in his question.

"Those particular mines are more productive than the ones around them—because of the machines, certainly. They're faster and they don't tire as the children do. And perhaps because the miners don't have to worry about their offspring. Because of that increased production, I've been able to raise wages."

"And I suppose your profits have remained as high?" Devon asked with sarcastic surety.

"No. To be honest, they've not," Raven acknowledged. "But they *have* been sufficient to allow me to undertake other innovations that will, in the near future, make profits even greater than they were before."

"That's well and good for a man of your resources, but there are owners who don't have the capital to bear the resulting loss of profit. What should they do?" Russell asked.

"Recognize that their ultimate success rests upon the efforts of their workers. On their workers' success."

"Bah," Devon said with disgust.

"Because the better paid they are, the stronger the workers are, the freer from disease, and the harder they're able to work. And the more interested they are in the success of what they're doing, in learning how to operate the machines that will eventually, I admit, take over some of the jobs. But by that time, the machines will also have allowed new mines to be dug, in seams that are now inaccessible. New foundries will be built to produce more and better iron. Iron rails and iron bridges will be built across England, gentlemen, and there will be a lot of manpower required to operate the machines that will build them."

"I'm not such a skeptic as Devon, Mr. Raven, but I must confess that I can see no practical application of the rails and the locomotives you're so set on," said Russell.

"They are already being used to take coal from the mines to the canals and to the rivers, and I personally intend to run rails from my mines all the way to the foundries."

"But why undertake that expense when the canals can transport your coal as easily, canals that are already in place?"

"Because the transport they offer is limited to the speed at which a horse can walk. And because of size differences, with a time-consuming transfer of cargo at the lock."

"And by rail?" Elliot asked, his fascination again evident.

Catherine was well accustomed to the spell Raven's conviction wove over his listeners. He'd shared his ideas with anyone who had professed the slightest interest. And to give the men of her class credit, more of them had been interested than she'd imagined before she'd seen the effect of Raven's words.

"Locomotives already exist that can run at over fifteen miles an hour. Compare that to the canals, gentlemen, and I think you'll see why I'm willing to go to the expense of building the rails to carry my coal and iron," Raven said.

"But you said the rails would spread all across England," Catherine reminded him. "Not just to carry coal?"

"To carry people. And anything else that needs to be transported quickly from one place to another."

"People? Even women?" she asked, smiling as if amused at the ridiculous idea of riding on a locomotive.

"I'll buy you a ticket on the first passenger run," her husband offered. "I assure you, you'll be perfectly safe."

"Perfectly safe? But how disappointing," she said, smiling at him. The tension that had grown with the intense discussion was released in the appreciative laughter that ran around the table.

Catherine took the opportunity their amusement offered to signal Edwards to replenish the gentlemen's glasses, and she found herself again watching her husband's hand caress the fine hollowware.

"We're behind times in implementing that idea in this country," Raven suggested after the laughter had died down.

"Behind?" Viscount Templeton commented. "I thought Stephenson invented the thing."

"Trevithick, Hedley, Stephenson. Englishmen, or Scots, Welsh. But if we're not careful it will be the Americans who make the quickest use of locomotives. And they have as many iron and coal deposits as we do here."

"They're ahead of us in employing the rails?" Elliot questioned.

"More than ten years ago an American, Colonel John Stevens, acquired a charter to build a railway across New Jersey," Raven answered, his eyes on his glass rather than on the questioner.

"And did he build it?" the viscount asked.

"He did not. Not because the technology was lacking, but because of a lack of money. He couldn't find enough backers willing to invest what was, I must admit, a great deal of money."

"If you thought it to be a great deal, I'm sure the rest of us should be staggered," Lady Avondale suggested with a touch of asperity.

Raven smiled at Lady Avondale, and at the laughter her comment had aroused, without a trace of discomfiture.

"Certainly more than one man could afford to bear," he agreed. "No matter the anticipated return. And that is perhaps where we have the Americans at a disadvantage."

"How so?" Lord Avondale questioned.

"Capital. *That* we have in abundance. And if enough people, gentlemen who can afford the investment, were convinced of the feasibility of rail transport, of its importance to the industrial development of Britain, and more importantly of the potential for gain it will offer them as investors..." Raven let the suggestion trail off.

Catherine knew that it was a compliment to his powers of persuasion that for several seconds no one spoke into the silence that fell. They were thinking about what he had said. And she knew that was all that he'd intended. For now, at least.

She glanced at him and found those remarkable blue eyes resting on her face. His lips moved ever so slightly in amusement at her expression. She had sat in on this same discussion, or one very like it, on several occasions, and no matter how many times he introduced these ideas, he always made believers of his listeners. Perhaps, she thought in fairness to her husband, because he himself believed so strongly in what he had just said. One dark, winged brow lifted, and knowing that was her signal, she rose.

"Ladies," she said, smiling openly across the table at her husband and then at the other gentlemen who were beginning to stand. "I believe we should leave the men to their port and their locomotives. I, for one, have heard all the steam I can bear for one evening."

Smiling slightly, her husband bowed to her, and amid the masculine laughter, Catherine swept the ladies out of the way of whatever else he might need to discuss with these very potential investors. This part of the evening was his business, and she was more than willing to leave him to it.

Chapter Ten

It was much later, as she sat before her dressing table, that Catherine decided she would finally share with Raven something she had been considering for weeks. The idea had grown more compelling with each dinner party at which she had listened to her husband's vision of the England he was sure would develop within the next few years, and finally she'd decided to act on it.

She knew Raven had been successful in finding men who were interested in supplying the capital he needed to begin the rail project, but not as many as he had hoped. He had acknowledged that disappointment to her on one of the few occasions their schedules had allowed them to dine together. And thinking of the little time she'd managed to spend with him in these last weeks, she sighed. It seemed nothing would come of the rapport they'd shared the morning he'd given her the sapphire.

She wore it often, always receiving admiring comments on the beauty of the stone, which she had had mounted as a pendant surrounded by diamonds. When she had come downstairs tonight, her husband's gaze had rested briefly on the sapphire as it lay just above the valley formed by the uplift of her breasts. His eyes had traced slowly over the skin exposed by the low neckline and had deliberately moved up to meet hers. There had been again something of the emotions of the morning he'd given her the jewel, and then he had turned to greet the first of their guests.

Catherine had long been accustomed to the adulation of the most eligible men of her world, and even Raven had seemed to find her decorative enough to be his hostess. But perhaps, she acknowledged disconsolately, it had really been only her position that had attracted him and nothing about her person. Looking at the woman reflected in the glass, she found herself wondering again, the most bitter of pastimes, about his mistress.

Knowing the futility of that train of thought, she rose decisively and found the silk wrapper her abigail had put out for her on the bed when she'd left. She drew it on and, without allowing herself time to reconsider, left the safe confines of her own room and walked the short distance to Raven's.

She lived in the same house with him. They had eaten dinner together surrounded by people who assumed that they were man and wife. They had even shared some brief moments of intimacy.

You may put that down to blood loss, my dear, Raven had told her, dismissing one of the most intimate of those memories. Catherine remembered also that he had sent her away the night she'd kissed him, the night she'd dressed his shoulder and had been allowed to touch the golden skin that shifted under her hands like warm velvet. But sometimes it seemed there was something in his eyes, something hidden in the lucid and open gaze, that made her wonder if he, too, spent sleepless nights remembering those moments.

She tapped lightly on the door to the small room he had selected as his own when he had chosen this house. She had expected to hear his voice, a spoken invitation to enter, but instead the door opened suddenly, and Raven was standing before her. He had taken off his coat and waistcoat, and his shirt was unbuttoned, revealing an expanse of golden chest and a tantalizing, mouth-drying glimpse of a flat, ridged stomach.

"Catherine?" he said, and she could hear his surprise.

"May I come in?" she asked.

The pause between her question and his answer was slight, but definite. She knew the terms of their agreement, and they didn't include midnight visits. And he had certainly never indicated that he wanted to modify those terms. She didn't understand why she kept putting herself in such a position that he would be forced to rebuff her.

"Of course," Raven said, moving away from the doorway and opening it to allow her passage. He had enough trouble keeping his hands off her during the somewhat formal moments they shared at dinner or at the theater. He wasn't sure his control was up to the challenge of entertaining his wife—his enticingly disrobed wife—in the intimate privacy of his own bedroom.

Catherine's eyes were drawn to Raven's disordered bed. The evening coat he'd removed had been tossed carelessly across the foot, and a glass of what appeared to be brandy stood on the small table beside it. A ledger lay facedown on the tumbled coverings, and from the arrangement of the pillows, she knew he must have been stretched out, studying it, when she'd knocked.

They stood facing each other for a moment, and she was again very conscious of the power of his body. She had to force her brain to dredge up the words that she had come to say.

"I'd like to invest in your railway," she said.

Some emotion disturbed the careful calm into which he had arranged his features while he'd waited for her revelation of why she'd come to his room in the middle of the night. And she realized only with that lapse of control what he must have been thinking when she showed up at his door.

"In my railway?" he repeated with a touch of disbelief.

"You *are* still seeking investors? That's why you were sounding out the men you invited here tonight?"

"If my tactics are that obvious, I had better rethink my plan of action," he agreed, amusement threading his admission.

"That obvious?" she repeated. "Obvious enough that even your *wife* knows what you're up to?"

"I didn't mean that as an insult," he protested, "but..."

"Your intent isn't obvious, I suppose, unless you've seen the same performance a number of times. As I have."

His laughter was quick and self-directed. "If *you* think it's a performance—" he began.

"Oh, I don't doubt you mean what you say. I'm here because I know you do. It's just that when you have the same discussion at every dinner, a discussion that leads to the same conclusion, it makes me believe it's by design. Eventually you'll find enough people interested that you won't need any more backers. And I wanted to ask you, before that happens, to let me in."

"You want to become one of my partners?"

"If you'll let me."

Again there was a pause, and finally, smiling, Raven indicated the chair he'd sat in as she'd bandaged his shoulder. "Then sit down, Catherine, and let's discuss business."

Always business, she thought with a trace of disappointment. But this was why she'd come.

When she was seated, Raven picked up the tumbler from the bedside table and arranged himself on the edge of the disheveled bed, waiting for her to begin.

"I have a trust. A rather...substantial trust. From my grandmother. It has just come under my control, and I thought I might use that money to invest in what you're doing."

"Have you mentioned this plan to your father?"

"I told him what I intend to do, of course. But it *is* my money, Raven."

"And how did the duke react?"

She smiled. "Do you remember the day you told him you intended to marry me, no matter what his feelings were?"

"Vividly," he said.

The scar that had marked his cheekbone had faded, but Catherine knew he would always carry that reminder of her father's fury.

"I think what you saw that day would be comparable. Except this time he threatened to disinherit me."

"Do you mean he hasn't already?" Raven asked.

She could hear his genuine surprise that what she had told him would be the inevitable result of their elopement had not come to pass. She knew then that Raven had never even checked on the status of her inheritance, that he truly was as unconcerned about the potential wealth she would bring to the marriage as he'd maintained he was at the beginning.

"And the duke suggested I had coerced you into investing your money in a very risky endeavor," Raven continued.

"But you're investing," she reminded him.

"*Not*, I hope, everything I have. Not if I can find enough men of vision. Enough men willing to form the partnership it will take to carry out a design of this magnitude."

"I'm simply suggesting that I become one of the partners. If the size of my trust is comparable to what you're asking others to invest," she said.

"It's not the amount of your investment that I object to. It's the idea of letting you risk everything that belongs to you personally in this scheme."

"What's so objectionable about that?"

"I can imagine your father told you. Probably in great detail," Raven suggested with a slight laugh. "If the railway venture fails, every aspect of my holdings will be affected. If that happens, your trust fund looms more important as insurance that you won't be left destitute if anything were to happen to me. If anything prevents my rebuilding."

"But you're not going to fail," she argued. "And I hardly think my father would allow me to wander the streets of London if you did. Or even if something happened to you. It seems there are too many disasters that would have to occur for me to be in any real danger of destitution."

"If I lose my investment—" he began.

"Then you'll start over. You'll make *more* money," she insisted. "I think you told me it's all a matter of numbers."

"And if something happens to me before I can accomplish this financial rebirth you're so sure I'll be able to bring off?"

"Do you have enemies I'm not aware of?" she asked, smiling. "You seem determined to make an early end."

"If I have enemies, I'm also unaware of them."

"You seem healthy. And not so *very* old," she teased.

"Thank you," he said sardonically, with a slight deepening of the indentations at the corners of his lips. "However, I think you should keep your trust fund, Catherine. If anything happens to me, you may need it. If it becomes mixed with my capital, or if you become one of the partners, everything you own will be taken to repay my debts if the rail venture fails. If anything happens to my businesses or to me personally—"

"I thought you were indestructible," she said. Raven was giving her the same advice her father had, but without the coldly sarcastic fury that characterized her father's every reaction to anything that involved her husband. Raven was as bent on protecting her as the duke, despite the fact that she was sure her husband could use the money she was offering.

"Only from the Ambertons of the world," he answered lightly. "To other dangers, I'm as vulnerable as the rest."

"You don't seem very vulnerable to me." Catherine was aware of the personal note that had crept into her voice. She didn't seem to be able to conduct a business discussion with Raven. Her emotions always interfered. As they were now.

"Or very aged?" he said, his lips lifting slightly with his amusement. "Thank you, Catherine, for that vote of confidence."

There was the briefest pause. She knew she should leave. She had made her request and had been given all the logical reasons why he wouldn't accept what she had offered. And this business meeting should be over. But she didn't want to go. His eyes were on his brandy and not on her. He didn't want her here, she supposed. He probably wanted to get back to the fascination of those endless numbers that the open ledger represented.

"And I still seem very young to you?" she asked instead, prolonging the bittersweet indulgence of spending time with him.

Raven glanced up at the seriousness of her question.

"I've not been forgiven for that remark, I take it?"

"No," she agreed, but she smiled at him.

"Perhaps young wasn't what I should have said. Innocent. Protected. And none of those are meant as criticisms. They are what every eighteen-year-old girl should be."

"Nineteen," she corrected.

"You should have told me. I've missed a birthday."

"You were away."

"And you were imagining..."

"That you were dying."

"And that you'd be a nineteen-year-old widow."

"A very wealthy nineteen-year-old widow," she said, her smile widening. At his soft laughter, she knew this was what she had wanted, what she had come for tonight—his attention. His teasing response. For whatever happened to his eyes when he relaxed enough to laugh. She had been so hungry for him. A hopeless case, she thought, mocking herself. I'm in love with my own husband and am flirting very openly with him.

"And since you're not a wealthy widow yet, what can I do to make up for my failure to recognize such a milestone?"

She shook her head. "I didn't tell you for that. I'm not angling for a birthday present. I only wanted you to know that I'm not *quite* so young as I was when you married me," she said.

"I told you that wasn't a criticism," he answered.

He was still relaxed, and not unwilling now, she thought, to allow their conversation to continue.

"What did you do with the children?" she asked.

"I beg your pardon? Have we lost our children?"

She laughed at the teasing quality of his question, knowing his quick mind would have easily followed her tangent. "From the mines. Where do they spend the hours when their parents are working?"

He glanced down at his glass and then, lifting it, drained the liquid it held. When he'd done that, he looked at her again, meeting her eyes. His were cleared of laughter.

"I opened schools. They go to school until their parents come home. I'm also phasing out the role of the women in the operation of my mines, and I can imagine what the Earl of Devon would say to that ridiculous practice."

"And you pay for the schools. And the teachers."

He nodded, waiting for her reaction. Her mockery, she supposed. No wonder he hadn't mentioned this tonight. She, too, could imagine what Devon would say. What almost any of those men who had dined here tonight would say to that confession.

"They'll think you're mad," she warned.

"Hopefully they won't ever find out."

"That they've invested money in the schemes of a madman?"

"Are you going to tell them?" he questioned, but she knew that he was again teasing her. He'd never have told her unless he believed that she wouldn't be as appalled as his partners.

"No, but if they find out, you may need my trust fund, after all. And what do you plan to do for an encore to this insanity?"

"I was thinking about requiring safety inspections."

"A shocking waste of money. You act as if you think miners should survive the experience," she answered, smiling at him.

"That *would* be a novel approach in Britain."

"Certainly too novel for the Earl of Devon, but I don't suppose he'll ever become one of your backers."

"He's in for seventy thousand pounds. You'd be surprised what the promise of profit will do to a man's scruples."

"I probably would at that," she agreed.

She rose, knowing that although she might want to stay, that didn't mean he was having the same response to her presence. "Thank you for listening to me. And please know that if you ever need Grandmother's money, I am more than willing to invest in your ventures."

"Thank you, Catherine," he said, standing also.

"Good night," she said, turning toward the doorway.

"Do you still ride in the mornings?"

"Most mornings," she answered, turning back to him and savoring the promising direction of that inquiry.

"Do you plan to ride tomorrow?"

"I hadn't thought. But I suppose so, weather permitting. Would you like to join me?"

"If you're willing to have company."

"You're more than welcome. Do you still have the black?"

"Driving the grooms wild. I really should exercise him."

"At seven," she said, naming an hour far earlier than she usually rode. She knew Raven to be an early riser.

"Sleeping in?" he inquired silkily.

"Six, but not a moment before or you may ride alone," she amended, slipping through the door.

Behind her she heard his laughter. She was still smiling when she reached her room and chose the most flattering of her habits. And still smiling when she turned down the lamp.

The fog swirled around the horses' hooves, slightly deadening the sound of their passage over the cobblestones. No one else, apparently, had taken advantage of the inviting crispness of the fall morning to ride, and it seemed they would have the park's meandering bridle paths to themselves. They spoke little, Raven's attention, despite his unquestioned skill as a horseman, demanded to control the black. He knew the blame for the stallion's ill manners lay at his door. A lack of opportunity on his part to ride him, and the grooms too afraid of his diabolical tricks and stratagems to exercise him properly.

"So they leave him alone," he had said to Catherine, "and then when I finally have a chance to ride, he makes clear his resentment of that neglect."

"Then you should try *this* time to give him enough of a gallop to calm his temper for a few days."

"Do I detect a challenge?" Raven asked, glancing up from the maneuvers the black was using as his own form of challenge.

"No, but like the black, I'm afraid I'm feeling rather restless. I think I'm as much in need of exercise as he. And we seem to have the park to ourselves this morning. It's the perfect opportunity to work off some excess energy.''

''Are you trying to tell me that the famous Catherine Raven, London's premier hostess and style setter, sometimes feels the need of excitement other than that provided by balls and parties?'' Raven mocked.

''I don't find *you* making trivial conversation with people who've never had a thought beyond what they should wear to the next rout or with whom they should share the next liaison.''

''I thought you enjoyed all that.''

''Enjoyed?'' she said in exasperation. ''Surely you can't believe that I *enjoy* all those empty exchanges.''

''Then why do it?''

''Because that was one of the requirements of our situation. I maintain our position in society...'' She stopped, not sure how to word the remainder of that thought.

''While I provide the money that allows you to do so. If you're unhappy, however, I suggest you refuse the invitations.''

''You need the contacts my mingling in society provides. Contacts with the men who dine at your table, for example. If I don't venture out to the entertainments they frequent, then they may accept other invitations for their presence at dinner.''

''I honestly thought you enjoyed moving within the ton. You grew up accustomed to that, after all. And I thought it was every Londoner's desire to be immersed in the kind of activities that you seem now to be dismissing as trivial and boring.''

''And you have *always* found them boring,'' she retorted. ''I notice you're continually too busy to accompany me.'' She couldn't help chiding him.

Raven took a moment to smooth his hand down the black's massive neck, trying to decide how to react to Catherine's complaint. The stallion's restiveness had not abated, and Raven was exerting very strict control. The horse was already beginning to sweat slightly with the canter he was being held to.

"I thought that's what you'd prefer," he said finally, glancing up from his pretended concentration on the stallion.

"What I'd prefer?" Catherine repeated in bewilderment. "Why should you think I would prefer to go out alone, forever forced to explain why my husband is again unable to accompany me? I assure you the excuses I've offered are quite threadbare."

"You should have told me," Raven said, thinking of the endless nights he'd spent working or reading, trying to block out images of Catherine gliding across some dance floor in the arms of her latest courtier. Fighting his growing hunger simply to be with her, to touch her, to hold her in his own arms. If only he had had a hint that she'd wanted him to accompany her.

He had been trying to give her time to know him, to understand the kind of man he was and, more importantly, to realize that she could trust him. To discover that he always kept his word. And now she was apparently confessing to the same longings that haunted the lonely hours of his own existence.

"When?" she asked, anger creeping into her voice. "I never see you. You spend more time..." She stopped the bitter words. She had no right to censure Raven because he was doing what she'd expected him to do when they had begun their marriage. Except she had never thought she'd feel about him the way she now did. That didn't mean his feelings about their situation had changed, simply because hers clearly had.

"I'm sorry," she said.

"Are you implying, Catherine, that you would like to spend more time with *me?*"

Leave it to Raven to cut to the heart of the matter. And, indeed, what else could he possibly read into that bitter avowal? She had just complained, far too obviously, that she didn't see enough of her own husband.

"I'm implying nothing more than I've been shut up in

drawing rooms and ballrooms too long. I'll race you, Raven. Like your black, I need a hard run.''

She heard him call her name, but she had already touched her heel to the mare, and responding to that permission and perhaps to the sharp, clear air of the fall morning, her horse had left the black behind. Catherine smiled when she heard the pounding of the stallion's hooves following her, knowing her husband had accepted her dare. A contest she would lose, of course, but she was willing to be bested. It was enough to feel the powerful muscles beneath her and the wind trying to tangle her hair.

The race was tight enough that she wondered if Raven had reined in to give her a chance, but glorying in the freedom of the run, she didn't care if he had. The exhilaration of the hard-fought contest was too strong to quibble over technicalities.

When she drew Storm up beside the still-anxious black, she was laughing. Raven had beaten her, but not by much, despite the superiority of his mount.

''If you had a better horse, I should be looking to my laurels,'' he declared as she approached. There was a touch of red in the golden skin over his high cheekbones, and a few strands of the gleaming ebony hair had escaped their confinement. He raised an ungloved hand to smooth them back into place.

Her throat tightened at the image of that dark hand smoothing over her breasts, as his eyes had done last night. She could almost feel the sensation, the abrasive brush of callused palm and the delight of hard fingertips caressing her exposed flesh. She looked down in confusion. God, she was mad for him, and other than throwing herself into his arms, she didn't know what she could do about it. A mental image of his disordered bed and gaping shirtfront made her close her eyes hard.

She lived in the same house with him, and every night he retired to that room. A room separated from hers by only a few feet, she realized suddenly. There was no reason not to retrace tonight the same journey she had made last night—with her quite legitimate excuse—for a very different purpose. No reason at all except her pride and her fear. He had invited her into his room last night. Somewhere, despite all the doubts and fears, she knew with sweet certainty that Raven wouldn't refuse if she offered herself to him.

"What's wrong?" Raven asked. Catherine had suddenly gone still, her eyes downcast and the laughing exhilaration from the race wiped away.

She waited a moment before she answered, at last raising her gaze to feast again on the darkly beautiful, almost forbidding features of the man she had first married and then fallen in love with. As she looked at his face, she felt tears prick hotly behind her eyes, although she didn't understand why she wanted to cry. He was just so...

"Catherine?" Raven said questioningly. "What's wrong?"

She tried to gather control, to think of anything that might explain this ridiculous lapse in her ability to think.

"My stirrup," she offered, her voice thready, the emotion too powerful to deny.

Raven swung down with the fluid grace that marked his every movement. She watched the muscles of his thighs bunch and shift under the tight, revealing knit of his fawn pantaloons. She found herself wondering what those hard muscles would feel like next to the softness of her thighs. Found herself wanting them there.

Raven's strong hands lifted her booted foot out of the stirrup and then he bent to check the buckles. "There doesn't seem to be—"

He was interrupted when the mare leapt straight upward, her body twisting in midair. By the time her hooves touched the ground, she was away, tearing across the park like a beast gone mad. Raven saw Catherine's automatic reaction—her body stretching low against the reaching neck of the racing animal. But he also saw in his mind's eye, his heart suddenly in his throat, the small booted foot he'd removed from the single stirrup.

Raven had been aware of the crack of sound that coincided with Storm's leap. But even as he had identified that unmistakable noise, he had pushed it to the back of his consciousness, throwing himself into the saddle to send the black on the most desperate race of his life, a race Raven knew he had already lost.

Chapter Eleven

As the mare flew from the clearing, Catherine fought to remain in the saddle and regain command. Storm, however, was totally panicked, and nothing Catherine did could abate her mount's terror. Hang on and let her run it out, she commanded her body, her years of experience fighting her own panic.

When she realized they were approaching the stream, she knew this would be the greatest danger to both horse and rider. The mare was exhausted, already winded from the race with the black, but in her blind frenzy, she was still uncontrollable. The stream loomed before them almost before Catherine had time to be afraid. She began desperately gathering the mare for the jump, trying to instill a confidence that, horsewoman that she was, she knew was beyond the trembling beast. Then they were in the air, soaring. The reaching forelegs came down short, slipping on the slime of the opposite bank.

With time suspended, Catherine was aware of every quivering stumble in Storm's desperate attempts to recover. But despite their combined best efforts to right the situation, she felt herself flying over the mare's neck. She turned, trying to roll into the fall, but it all happened too quickly to do much to prepare her body for its descent. Her shoulder took the brunt as she had intended, but her knee hit sharply against one of the rocks that lined the streambed and then she struck her head, and she didn't know anything else.

When she came to, it was to find Raven stooping beside her. His hands were moving over her rib cage with the same deliberate care he took in handling the crystal goblets at dinner. She couldn't prevent the image, nor her lips from lifting as she thought it. She tried to raise her head enough to see what he was doing, but her senses swam as soon as she moved.

"Lie still," Raven commanded softly, and because she really had no choice, she laid her head back against the bracken crushed by her fall and waited for her vision to clear. When she opened her eyes again, he was tracing down her right arm with the same gentleness he had used on her ribs and hips, but he was watching her face while his hands made their examination.

"I'm all right," she said. "This isn't the first time I've been thrown. The most embarrassing, perhaps, but not the first."

"Why the most embarrassing?" he asked, his voice relaxed.

"Because you were watching," she admitted. She closed her eyes and rested her head again on the damp ground. There was something very soothing about what he was doing. About the expertise of his hands. And the calmness of his voice.

"Everyone falls," he said. "If you ride long enough, you'll take your share of spills. Do you have any idea what set her off?" he questioned casually, forcing his tone to remain steady.

"I don't... She just..." Her voice faded because she had no answer for the horse's reaction, and it hurt to think.

His hands had deserted her, and she was aware that he'd shifted position, no longer beside her. He began rearranging the skirt of her habit, and she felt the cool air touch her bared legs. Despite the fact that he was her husband, she reacted to that invasion with a very conditioned response. Absurdly, she tried to sit up, but she never completed the attempt. Raven was again beside her, holding her securely against the hard warmth of his body, when the mists cleared yet again.

"You seem determined to lose consciousness. I promise to be gentle, but I need to see if anything's broken."

"Nothing's broken," she said, leaning into his strength.

"There's blood on your skirt."

"My knee," she whispered. Her cheek was resting against the muscles of his chest. Like the child he'd called her, she felt most secure enclosed in his embrace.

"I need to see to it," he said. "I'm going to help you lie down again, and this time, Catherine, you damn well stay there. There is a place for modesty, and there is also a place for common sense. You're too intelligent to fight my taking care of you because of what would be false modesty in this situation."

"Because you're my *husband?*" she suggested, reminding him how far from reality that was.

"Because you're hurt," Raven said simply, and he gently lowered her back to the loam to continue his examination.

Incredibly, despite the throbbing in her head and her aching shoulder, she began to enjoy his touch. Raven's hands moved impersonally, but she couldn't help reacting to the warmth of his palms firmly tracing the line of bone upward from her ankles to her thighs. She gasped when he manipulated her right knee, and at her response the blue eyes lifted to meet hers. He smiled at her, and although the tears had gathered, unwanted, in her own eyes, she managed a rather tremulous smile in return.

"I think this needs a more professional inspection than I'm qualified to give," he said, finally rearranging her skirt to cover her legs. He allowed his hand to rest lightly on her thigh, its contact intended to be reassuring.

"Storm?" she asked, remembering her mare's stumbling landing.

"She's fine. She didn't go down."

"Thank God," Catherine said. She held out her gloved hand to him, but instead of taking it to help her sit up, he stooped beside her, placing his arm beneath her shoulders and lifting. She was allowed to lean against him again until the world stopped spinning. Finally, with fingers that still shook, she began to unfasten her veil, removing the small, jaunty hat she'd donned with such high spirits that morning. The autumn air felt refreshing against her brow, and she even thought about how unbecomingly disarrayed her hair would be, and then disregarded that concern as foolish, given the situation.

Raven's left hand lifted to touch her temple. His fingertips brushed over the thin skin, and she knew by the resulting pain that there was a bruise there. When his fingertips came away covered in blood, she felt her stomach clench despite her determination not to behave any more childishly than she had already. She knew she'd be very sorry tomorrow for this day's misadventure.

"You'd better help me mount," she said, gathering her resolve for the effort it would take to stand.

"Surely you don't think—" he began.

"You're horseman enough to know that's the best way. The sooner the better. There's nothing serious among my injuries. My pride's far more damaged than my body, I promise you."

"That may be true, but it doesn't mean you're riding home."

"And what do you suggest?" she asked, smiling. They were still alone in the park and probably would be for another hour or more. "It's by far the easiest way."

"Easiest for whom?" Raven asked, answering her smile. "Cast steel you may be, Mrs. Raven, but you're not indestructible."

"I suppose you're the only one who may lay claim to that."

He said nothing for a moment, and she turned her head so that she could see his face. He was looking down at her as she rested very comfortably against his massive chest. There was something in his expression she couldn't read. "What's wrong?" she asked, touching his lean cheek with her gloved hand.

"I think I'm beginning to understand what you went through when you believed..." She could feel the deep breath he took.

"That you were ill?" she suggested, at his continued silence.

"Come on," he said, refusing to answer her. He was still fighting the terror he'd experienced watching that terrible fall, helpless, pushing the black to his limits, and all the while knowing he would be too late. "However pleasant this may be, I think I should get you home."

"Pleasant?" she repeated, wondering, but her question was forgotten as he lifted her easily in his arms. She quickly stifled her small cry as he slipped his arm under her knees.

"Sorry, my darling," he said softly. "I won't hurt you again, I promise."

Shocked into silence by the unexpected endearment, she found herself relaxing. Raven carried her along the streambed despite the terrain and then across the footbridge that spanned it.

"Raven?" she said as he strode through the deserted park.

"Am I hurting you?" he asked, glancing down to smile at her.

"No, of course not. It's not so bad. A little sore."

"I can imagine it is," he said.

"I wondered if you intend to carry me all the way home."

"If necessary. But I believe we'll meet someone who'll be willing to take us up once we reach the street."

"And the horses?"

"Eating their heads off at the king's expense. They'll probably get colic and have to be put down. I may do it myself."

"Why?" she asked, smiling, knowing it was an idle threat.

"You need a steadier mount," he said simply. He knew it hadn't been the mare's fault she'd been hurt, but if he forgave the roan's panic, then that left only himself to blame. To blame for it all. He had been unable to push the black fast enough to reach Catherine in time. Raven couldn't bear the thought that he was responsible for hurting her.

"I don't know what happened to Storm. She's usually the most dependable of mounts. I promise to maintain a firmer control the next time."

"Can I trust you to keep that promise?" he asked.

"Have I ever broken a promise to you?"

"Have you ever made one?" Raven asked lightly, looking down again into her face. His mouth was arranged in its customary forbidding line, but there was something very tender in his eyes.

"Only one," she whispered, remembering their simple vows.

He was still looking down at her with that enigmatic tenderness when a familiar voice hailed them from the street.

"Mr. Raven!" Lord Avondale's greeting was rich with genuine concern. "I say, is there something wrong?"

"My wife's been thrown. I wonder if I might impose upon you to take us up and drive us home."

"Of course. Only too glad. Shall I help you to..."

The offer was made ridiculous by Raven's ease in mounting the steps of the high phaeton, despite his burden.

"Mrs. Raven," said Avondale, nodding at her. Catherine knew she was blushing at having to face anyone in this embarrassing situation. Raven seemed immune to discomfiture. He acted as if he daily carried his wife through the streets of London.

When they reached the town house, Raven carried her upstairs, carefully placing her on the chaise longue in her bedroom. He left her to the care of her abigail and one of the maids, who removed her boots and, the operation painful in the extreme, her coat and stock and then finally the skirt of her habit. It seemed that Dr. Stevenson arrived in only a matter of minutes.

He confirmed her own claim that nothing was broken, but he was of the opinion that she'd severely bruised her knee as well as gashed it against the stone. Her shoulder was aching abominably by this time, but she didn't mention that to the doctor. The headache she'd been vaguely aware of in the park was beginning to throb with increasing violence.

"Laudanum to help you rest," the doctor said after he'd bathed her forehead and dressed her knee. He measured the dose in a glass of water, ignoring her protest that she really didn't need the drug. Despite its popularity as a nerve soother, Catherine had never liked its effects. But because she had grown up doing everything this prominent London practitioner instructed her to do, she drank the medicine under his demanding eye.

"And now I suppose I should let your husband know that you're really all right. A love match, I believe your father told me. And I should judge by Mr. Raven's concern that the duke's assessment was correct."

He pinched her cheek as if she were five years old, but since she had endured that exact treatment since she *was* five, she smiled at him and watched him walk out her bedroom door.

A love match, she thought in amusement, already beginning to feel the effects of the drug he'd given her drifting over her senses. She wondered what Raven had said to him to make him believe that. And then she remembered that it had been her father, surprisingly, who had originally offered that opinion. A rather astonishing revelation, she thought, closing her eyes.

She heard the door later, but it was almost too much trouble to respond. Her head had stopped pounding, and if she didn't move, she could forget the stiff knee and bruised shoulder.

"Catherine?" Raven said softly.

She opened her eyes, turning her head carefully to find that he was again stooping beside her so that his eyes were on a level with hers.

"Hello," she whispered, and she lifted her left hand to touch his cheek as she had in the park.

He caught her fingers in his and, bringing them to his lips, pressed the smallest kiss against them. "How are you feeling?"

"I told you nothing was broken," she said, closing her eyes against the disturbing sunlight that was pouring into the tall windows of her room.

"And I was delighted to have that information confirmed by a disinterested observer."

"How are the horses?"

"I sent Jem for them. I hope they've been abducted by highwaymen, but he'll probably find them just where we left them, waiting patiently for someone to come for them."

"Horses are really not very intelligent," she agreed.

"Then neither are we who trust ourselves to them."

She opened her eyes again to see his expression. Smiling at what she found in his face, she tried to shake her head. She gasped at the sudden stab of pain that resulted.

"I didn't mean to disturb you. I'll come back tomorrow—"

"Don't go." Against her will, in response to the drug's pull, she felt her eyes fill with tears. "Please don't go."

"Catherine," Raven said, brushing his thumb lightly across her wet lashes. He wondered if, despite the doctor's assurances, she might be more seriously injured than they thought. He had never seen Catherine cry. Except over the pitiful, shivering donkey he'd helped her rescue the day he'd met her.

"Don't go," she whispered again. She was shamelessly begging her husband not to leave, but she really didn't seem to be able to stop the words. "Stay with me, Raven, at least for a while," she added with a small catch in her voice. A watering pot, she thought in disgust, but she couldn't prevent the hot tears that continued to seep from under her lashes.

"Catherine," he said again. "Don't cry. I think you'll be more comfortable completely undressed and in bed. I'll get your maid, and then I'll come back and sit with you until you fall asleep." He stood up in preparation to carry out those actions.

"No," she protested, her fingers tightening their hold on his. He had called her a child, and she was certainly acting like one. With the greatest effort of will, she forced her hand to relax its desperate grip, but she couldn't seem to release him. "I'm sorry," she said. "I know you have things to do. Business to see to that is far more important—"

His soft laughter interrupted. "Guilt, Catherine? If I let you rest, then I'm once more the villainous husband who spends more time with his businesses than with his very beautiful wife?"

"Do you think I'm beautiful?" She forced her heavy lids open again to assess the truth of his answer.

"You surely don't need my affirmation of your beauty added to that of every eligible—and ineligible—man in London. Fishing for compliments?"

"Of course. Or I shan't have any. Not from my husband, at any rate." By the strongest effort of will, she took her hand completely away from his, curling her fingers under her chin. But her wide eyes didn't leave his face.

Smiling again, Raven shook his head. "Shameless," he said. "There's no weapon you won't use to get your own way. Let me get you into something you'll be able to rest in more comfortably."

"All right," she whispered. Still caught in the unthinking lethargy of the drug, she didn't realize that Raven had only intended, of course, to call her maid. Catherine began to unfasten the buttons of the soft lawn shirt she'd worn under her habit. Her hand didn't obey the intention of her brain very well, however, and in frustration, she felt the hated tears begin. She looked up to find Raven's gaze fastened on her trembling fingers, which had managed the top buttons, but were struggling with the one that lay just over the valley between her breasts.

"Raven," she begged softly.

His eyes, shimmering with some emotion she didn't understand—one she'd never been allowed to see before in their depths—lifted to hers.

Considering what she'd suggested in the park about spending time with him, Raven wondered if she could mean... Slowly he denied that incredible possibility. Catherine was hurt. No longer the elegant sophisticate he'd enticed to marry him, she was as vulnerable now as an injured child. What kind of bastard would he be to take advantage of this situation, no matter how long he'd waited? Banishing the desire that had already begun to smolder deep in his body at whatever he had seen in the tear-misted eyes, he took over the task she was unable to perform.

Catherine marveled again at his fingers' dexterity and gentleness, despite their size. "Your hands are too large...." she began. For these absurdly small buttons, she intended to add, but somehow the thought didn't reach her lips.

He glanced up from what he was doing, the firm line of his lips straightening even further. "I can't help my size, Catherine. I'm sorry you find it distasteful."

"I don't find your size distasteful. Why would you say that?" she whispered.

"Sit up," he directed, instead of answering her question, his hand supporting her shoulders firmly.

He slipped the sleeve of the shirt off her left arm and then very carefully off the discolored right shoulder. His eyes examined the injury and then moved over the swell of her breasts, exposed by the low, ribboned neckline of her chemise. Again his body reacted, becoming painfully hard and tight. He wanted to press his mouth into the shadowed recess between those ivory globes.

Catherine saw his lips whiten under the pressure suddenly exerted to prevent that response, and then the breath he took before he deliberately lifted his gaze to her face.

"Put your arm around my neck," he forced himself to say impersonally, bending to lift her. He carried her as he had in the park and laid her on the high bed, where the covers had already been turned back. Too inviting. Too intimate.

She had controlled her reaction to the pressure on her injured knee by biting her lip, determined not to let any sound escape this time. She closed her eyes against the pain in her head. He had put her down as carefully as if she, too, were made of Venetian glass, one arm remaining behind her back to support her until he'd arranged the pillows to serve that same purpose.

Finally it was over, and she was in control enough to open her eyes and face him without any tears, tears he had accused her of employing to get her own way. And there was, of course, a great deal of truth in that assertion, but she would never have resorted to that stratagem to hold him if it were not for the uninhibiting effects of the laudanum.

"Would you pull the draperies, please?" she asked.

She watched him stride across the chamber, his masculinity out of place in its decidedly feminine atmosphere. He swept the draperies across the window, effectively shutting out the strong light and leaving the room in a dim, artificial twilight.

When he had done as she'd asked, he returned to stand looking down on her. She hadn't bothered to pull the sheet up. Since he had helped her undress, it seemed that in struggling to cover her body now she would certainly be guilty of the false modesty he'd accused her of. She lay very still, hoping the throbbing in her head would ease as it had before.

"Thank you," she said finally, thinking that perhaps he was waiting for permission to leave. After all, she had begged him to stay. She would explain that it was all the effects of the drug sapping her willpower, but now it was too much trouble. She'd tell him later, when she felt better. When everything was not so difficult and confusing. Later, she thought, the last conscious thought she would have for several hours.

"Just where you told me it would be, Mr. Raven," the groom said, running his hand over the mare's rump. The furrow he had been instructed to look for was raw and ugly, cutting across the gleaming hide of the horse.

"That old bastard," Raven said under his breath, feeling again the horror he'd felt as he'd watched the mare racing away from him. This fear was from the realization of the tragedy that might have happened.

"But why anyone would shoot at her ladyship—begging you pardon, sir—at Mrs. Raven, I can't imagine." Jem knew that was the title his mistress preferred. She had made that clear to the staff.

Shaking off the remembrance of his helplessness this morning, Raven met Jem's serious brown eyes. "They weren't shooting at her," he said softly. To test the truth of what he already knew, he aligned his body in the same position in which he had been standing after he'd dismounted. The bullet that had cut the long gouge in the horse's rump would have passed directly through his body had he not bent to adjust his wife's stirrup. The marksman had definitely not intended the mare—or Catherine—to be his target.

I'll see you in hell.... Catherine's father had threatened. *Damned fortune hunter!* The words had been echoing in Raven's brain for several hours now, ever since he'd put together this morning's attempt at murder with the proposal Catherine had made to her father about giving her trust fund to her husband. And having made that connection, John Raven knew with certainty who wanted him dead. Montfort had already tried to kill Henning for that same reason. *He'd shoot you, or hire someone to do it,* Catherine herself had told him.

Deliberately he pushed away the circling memories.

"See to the mare, will you, Jem. And keep your mouth shut. There's no need to worry Mrs. Raven." Turning, Raven stepped out of the stall and disappeared into the shadowed stable.

Behind him, in the pleasant dimness of the hay-scented enclosure, the groom ran a soothing palm over the mare's flank. Jem shook his head, a slow movement full of regret. He'd grown to like the tall American he had come to work for when his mistress had married. But as he had warned John Raven from the beginning, it didn't pay to cross the Duke of Montfort. Especially where his only daughter was concerned.

"Catherine."

Raven's voice seemed to come from a great distance away, but she had no doubt who was calling her. She forced open her eyes, finding the artificial gloom he'd created this morning had been replaced by the genuine darkness of evening.

"Catherine," Raven said again, and she turned her head to find him standing beside the bed. He had discarded his coat and was dressed only in a white shirt and pale blue-and-silver striped waistcoat above cream pantaloons. Surprisingly, his hair had not been pulled back into the neat queue in which he always wore it. It was loose, its slightly curling midnight blackness long enough to touch below his shoulders. She was fascinated by the transformation. Its surrounding frame softened the harsh planes of his face. She had always imagined Raven's hair would be straight and coarse, but its appearance tonight seemed to contradict that. She had a sudden impulse to run her fingers through the dark strands to confirm her impression.

"I thought it was time you woke up. I brought you something that will be more beneficial than what the doctor gave you."

"Almost anything would be better..." she began, and then stopped, embarrassed because she could vaguely remember clinging to Raven's hand, begging him to stay with her. "What is it?" she asked instead, attempting to sit up, only to feel her head swim.

"Be still," he ordered sharply, putting the cup he'd been holding on her night table. As he had this morning, he slipped his arm behind her back and held her until he could arrange the pillows to offer more support for her shoulders.

He picked up the cup to bring it to her lips, but even when her hand fastened around it, he didn't remove his. Instead he held it steady, her cool fingers trembling over his warm ones, allowing her to drink some of the acrid liquid the cup held.

"It's my grandmother's recipe," he said, and she heard but didn't understand the amusement in his deep voice. "Willow tea. It will help your head."

"How did you know my head hurts?"

"Because I've been thrown my share of times."

"Somehow I find that hard to believe."

"I told you. If you ride enough..."

Once again he raised the cup, resting its rim against her lips. "Finish it," he commanded.

"I seem to be very trusting," she said, sipping the bitter concoction. "I've never heard of tea made from trees. Maybe you're trying to poison me. Are you tired of your clinging wife already?" Because she was terribly afraid he *had* found her tiresome today, with her tears and her demands, she raised her eyes to search his.

"How could I be tired of my wife? Since she thinks I spend so little time with her," Raven said, his lips lifting slightly.

"I suppose I deserve that. You have my apologies for that remark. You may put it down to blood loss, my dear," she said, echoing his words to her on the morning he'd kissed her.

"And I haven't yet been forgiven for that, either, I see."

"No," she admitted. Why deny the obvious? She had just demonstrated that his words that day had made an impression.

"Unforgiven for the kiss or for the excuse?" he asked.

"I enjoyed the kiss," she whispered. Apparently all the effects of the drug had not disappeared as she'd thought. She couldn't believe she had told him that.

"Did you, Catherine?"

Wordlessly she nodded.

He replaced the cup on the table and sat down beside her on the bed. She looked up to find the blue eyes studying hers. He took both her hands in one of his large ones and held them a moment. Raven was so close she could smell him. Could feel the heat from his body. If she raised her hand, she could discover if his hair was as soft as it appeared to be. Fighting that impulse, she lowered her eyes from the contemplation of his face. She had already revealed so much today of what she felt. Feelings that she had successfully hidden until now.

"May I take it you would like to try it again sometime?" he asked.

Slowly she nodded, knowing how true that was and wondering if he might kiss her now.

"And our contract?" he asked very softly. "What should we do about our agreement, Catherine?"

"Begin again," she suggested, raising her eyes to meet his, daring to hope that that was what he, too, wanted.

"With new rules?"

"Without rules," she said, holding her breath.

"Are you suggesting that we might have a *real* marriage?"

"I know you think I'm very young."

"I think you're very beautiful. Especially now," Raven said. He touched her chin, and she turned her head, rubbing it against his fingers. "But I also think you're very vulnerable. And I'd hate to have you decide later that I'd taken advantage of that vulnerability. We could discuss this when you're stronger."

He wondered where he had found the strength to suggest that. *A vow, Raven,* his grandmother's whisper reminded him. Catherine seemed so fragile now—incredibly beautiful, but exquisitely fragile, in need of his care and protection. Not his lovemaking.

"You think I suggested that in a moment of weakness?" she asked, wondering if she would ever find the courage to tell him how long she'd thought about that possibility.

He raised his hand to touch with one knuckle the bruised temple, the evidence of her fall a livid contrast to the clear, translucent paleness of her skin. "A blow to the head can cause all sorts of complications," Raven said softly.

Such as making me fall in love? she thought. How he could fail to know what she felt? Or perhaps he *did* know. Perhaps . . .

"Catherine?" Raven said questioningly.

But suddenly she saw nothing of what was occurring here in her bedroom, remembered nothing of the closeness they'd shared during the last twenty-four hours. Instead she was recalling the careless phrase he had thrown at her before their marriage, as an enticement to marry him. No wonder he'd put her off with that ridiculous excuse! He didn't want her in that way. He had told her that. *I don't need a mistress.*

"What's wrong? Your head?"

She could hear the concern, undeniable in Raven's voice.

"It's nothing..." Her voice trailed off, the lump in the back of her throat growing too large to speak around.

"Are you going to cry again?" he asked, using his thumb to wipe away the single tear that was sliding down her cheek.

Swallowing, she shook her head. The resulting jolt of pain loosened a small, involuntary, sobbing breath. She put her hand up to her temple, closing her eyes. She felt Raven's hand close warmly over hers.

"Catherine?"

"I'm sorry. It's nothing. Just silly tears. I don't know why I can't seem to stop crying. I never cry. I despise women who weep," she said disjointedly, turning her head slightly to move it out of contact with his hand.

"I don't think anyone would deny your right to a few tears. And no one will ever know."

"*I'll* know that I'm turning into a disgusting watering pot. Please forgive me. And now if you'll excuse me, I believe I'll try to sleep again. I think your grandmother's tea has helped. Thank you, Raven."

He said nothing for a moment, his eyes again studying her carefully arranged features. Catherine was glad she was accustomed to hiding her true feelings. If nothing else, her experiences in society had taught her to school her face to reveal nothing more than what she intended it should.

"And our discussion?" he asked finally. She seemed to be backing away from the suggestion she'd made. Perhaps he'd been right. Too much emotion. Or the drug. The blow to her head.

"I think you're right. Perhaps we'd be wise to postpone any decisions until I'm feeling a bit stronger."

His lips tightened involuntarily, but Raven allowed nothing else of what he was feeling to show. He had promised her freedom, and by virtue of their marriage vows she was entitled also to his care. *In sickness and in health.* The rest could wait, as he had waited. Always it would be Catherine's decision to at last give *him* freedom. To free him from the constraint of his vow.

Catherine couldn't tell whether Raven was hiding a smile or was angered at her about-face. If only she knew what he was really feeling! But that always-controlled expression gave away as little as she hoped hers was now.

"Of course," Raven said, standing to follow her suggestion. "Sleep well, Catherine."

He bent and touched his lips to the darkened, abraded skin over her temple. There was no pain occasioned by the gentle movement of his mouth, but for some reason she felt hot moisture begin to sting her eyes again.

"Thank you, Raven," she whispered, closing her lids to hide that ridiculous reaction.

She was aware that he stood for a long heartbeat by the bed, but she never reopened her eyes to look at him. Finally she heard his footsteps cross the room and the sound of the door opening and then closing behind him.

Chapter Twelve

Catherine didn't fall asleep for quite a while after Raven left. She'd already slept too long. The pain in her head subsided and eventually the urge to cry had faded.

Lying in the still darkness of her bedroom, she had come to realize that the next step was really up to her husband. She had offered herself to him like the lovesick schoolroom miss he surely thought her to be, and now he would have to decide whether he wanted to fall in with the suggestion she'd made.

They had both known that eventually intimacy would have to find its place in their marriage. He had never denied that he would want an heir. And that was, of course, the major responsibility of every wife—to perpetuate the family line. Catherine's own mother had been guilt ridden by her failure to produce a son who survived infancy, and her father had been forced to lavish all his attention on Catherine, his only child. She wondered suddenly if her father had had a mistress during his marriage, especially during the long last years of her mother's illness.

Catherine wished there was someone she could talk to. She had a deep longing for her mother, dead now four years. There was no one to ask what a wife—a wife who had discovered she was very much in love with her husband—did when confronted by the painful reality that he had a mistress. Another woman who shared his attentions and perhaps even his affections. Who already shared, as Catherine had not, his physical responses.

Her thinking was no clearer with the light of dawn which she watched first brighten her window and then creep slowly across the polished wood to bring to life the rich colors of the oriental carpet. She would have to face Raven again this morning, she thought, remembering the painful images of his body in another woman's embrace, images that had played in her consciousness throughout the night, waking and sleeping. She was not, as were the other women of her class, sophisticated enough to dismiss the emotions aroused by those mental pictures.

She was, however, in control enough to speak pleasantly to the maid who brought her morning tea. She smiled against the rim of her cup at the remembrance of Raven's kindness yesterday. Kind and comforting to children, she thought, the smile fading.

"They said you were awake," Raven said from the doorway.

She glanced up at the sound of his voice and felt again the heat of pure physical reaction. The navy coat deepened the blue of his eyes. His hair was again neatly confined, emphasizing the hard, very masculine contours of his face, the high, white cravat a startling contrast to the bronze of his skin.

"May I come in?" he asked politely.

"Of course," she said, setting her cup on the night table.

He stood at the end of the bed and placed his hands over the curving footboard, studying her face in the morning light. "Feeling better?"

"Much better, thank you," she said.

The russet eyes met his with their usual serenity, the small chin courageously raised. He had spent half the night praying that he would find Catherine recovered, again poised and in command. And the other half practicing what he wanted to say to her.

His lips moved slightly, and again she found herself wondering what he was thinking.

"Well enough to finish our discussion?" he asked, and this time his smile tilted the corners of his mouth.

"If you'd like," she said, knowing that she really wasn't sure what she could say. She had thought she would have more time to plan for this encounter, but she should have known better. Raven would always come straight to the point.

"I'd like it very much."

"You want to discuss—" she began, only to be interrupted.

"The provisions outlined in our original contract."

She couldn't prevent her own quick, almost resigned smile at that wording. *Contract,* she thought, shaking her head.

"Forgive me," he said, accurately reading the cause of her amusement. "I know I speak in the language of the business world. I'm not by nature given to flights of poetry, but I know, Catherine, that what we discussed yesterday..." He paused, and for the first time since she'd known him, he seemed unsure. "I know that there was nothing businesslike about what happened between us yesterday."

So apparently he, too, had felt some of the emotions generated by their intimacy. Or at least he had been aware of what she was feeling. "No," she agreed.

"I promised to give you the opportunity to rethink what you suggested. When you weren't feeling the effects of your fall."

"The complications of my fall?" she said softly, smiling.

He didn't answer her smile or even her comment, but what he did say made her breath falter and her heartbeat begin to race.

"But I hope that you won't want to reconsider. Even if the idea developed in a moment of weakness."

"*You* hope? Are you saying that *you* want our marriage to become..." She paused, unsure why discussing the ideas she herself had introduced yesterday should be so difficult this morning. There was no shock of injury to hide behind. No drugs. No dim lighting to soften the reality of what she had asked him for.

"A real marriage. That was the term suggested last night."

His eyes were resting with calm attention on her face. *You may ask me anything,* he'd promised long ago. And what she wanted to ask him now would certainly strain the boundaries of that.

"And your mistress?" she asked, schooling her features and forcing her eyes to meet his without any trace of discomfiture.

"My...mistress?" Raven repeated hesitantly, as if he'd never heard the word before.

"You told me when you made your proposal that you needed only a hostess. That you already had a mistress."

He glanced down at his hands, still resting on the wooden foot rail. She watched, as he seemed to be doing, his fingers tighten and then relax against the unyielding wood. Straightening, he removed his hands and clasped them behind his back. When he looked at her again, she would have sworn there was amusement in the blue eyes. But his mouth was set in a line that was even straighter than his normal austere expression.

He's going to tell me that he loves her too well to give her up. Or that I knew the rules when we began this. That I have no right to ask, Catherine thought. The painful possibilities ran through her mind and a sudden sickness began to coil in the pit of her empty stomach. She wished she hadn't drunk the tea.

"When I told you that," he said, "there *was* someone." He paused, but his eyes didn't falter from hers. "Not perhaps what the word *mistress* implies in your world, but someone who..."

The pause was painful for her, but finding her courage, she completed his confession. "Satisfied your physical needs."

She expected nothing less than his agreement.

"It was not a relationship of long standing. But not, I would hope, as cold-blooded as you suggest."

"I'm sorry," she said, feeling a touch of anger at that. "I didn't mean to insult you."

"However that relationship might have been defined," he said, speaking as calmly as before, "it ended with our marriage. I was raised in a very traditional society, Catherine, and my values are different, perhaps, from those of your world.''

"Ended?" She wondered why he bothered to make that claim. It certainly didn't fit with what he'd suggested before.

"'Forsaking all others.' I told you I *always* honor the terms of my contracts."

"But you told me..." She stopped, trying to remember exactly what he *had* said that dark dawn in his office. "You said you'd kissed me because of too prolonged an abstinence."

"Very prolonged," he agreed.

"You suggested you'd taken steps to rectify that situation."

"I had. I had married you. And I was hoping our marriage would, eventually, *rectify* a great many situations." His lips were curving again in his slight smile.

"Are you trying to tell me that you intended all along—"

"To make you my wife? In every sense of the word? Of course. I thought you understood that. I simply wanted to give you time to grow accustomed to the idea. And to me. And then yesterday..." Raven paused again, taking a deep breath. This was the hardest part. "Yesterday," he began again, "you led me to believe that's also what you wanted. That you were ready to modify our contract. Or did I misunderstand you last night?"

"You don't have a mistress?" she asked again, to be sure she'd not misunderstood him.

"No," he acknowledged.

She thought of the hours she'd spent visualizing the kind of woman Raven would want. And she realized suddenly that the kind of woman Raven wanted was, apparently, herself.

"And you want our marriage to become..." She found her voice unaccountably trembling over the simple question.

"Very much," he said, saving her the trouble of finishing. "I believe the question is if that's really what you want."

It seemed that every obstacle to what *she* wanted had miraculously disappeared. All she had to do was say yes—a far simpler decision than the one she'd made six months ago when she'd agreed to become his wife. Then he had offered her freedom. And what he was offering now was, she supposed, a kind of bondage—the creation of physical ties that she knew, even as inexperienced as she was, could never be broken lightly. The most intimate bondage on earth.

"Yes," she said, and unbelievingly, felt the ready tears of yesterday well again in her eyes. "Oh, damnation," she said in disgust, "I can't do anything but cry." She found the corner of the sheet and used it to wipe away the moisture. She found herself hoping that he'd take her in his arms. When she looked up, Raven was watching her with the same tenderness that had transformed his harsh features when he'd carried her from the park.

"Don't tempt me, Catherine," he warned softly. His hands were once again curved around the footboard, his fingertips white with the pressure he was exerting.

"Tempt you to what?" she asked, sniffing.

"To give you something to do besides weep," he said, and as she had when he'd entered her room, she felt the sheer physical response to what was in his dark face sweep through her body, causing a very peculiar sensation in the depths of her belly. Or, she realized, not exactly in her belly. Lower. Fluttering inside. Moving. Aching. As if he were touching her there with those graceful, skillful fingers that had impersonally examined her body yesterday. She remembered the callused strength of them moving over her skin, and she shivered slightly.

"Exactly," he said, watching her. "You have the most beautiful eyes," he added unexpectedly. "Like the beech leaves we rode under yesterday. Russet and touched with mist."

"Thank you," she said, sniffing again. She watched his smile begin. She could imagine how ridiculous she looked.

Eyes red from weeping, a scrape over her temple, a bruised
shoulder, wearing yesterday's chemise, which she'd slept in.
And she couldn't begin to imagine what her hair was like.
No wonder he was amused. She pressed her lips together
tightly, trying to gather her dignity, and then she was forced
to sniff again or be further humiliated by having her nose
run.

"Will you promise to miss me while I'm gone?" Raven
asked, and the worry she'd had about her appearance flew
from her mind.

"Gone?" she repeated blankly.

"I have a meeting. Here, exactly a week from tomorrow.
With the men who have committed to become partners in
the railway. And I have to complete *my* part of our contract. I've already invested substantially in the land across
which the rails will be laid, but I have to hire the men who
will forge and lay them. And the engineers who build locomotives. And none of that, I regret to say, can be done from
London."

"You're leaving," she said, finally understanding that he
really intended to walk out after what they'd just decided.

"And by the time I return, you should be over most of
the...complications of your fall. Not, I hope, all of them,"
he said, smiling at her. "I think it would be wise to postpone the...renegotiation of our contract until then. Since
I have to meet my responsibilities to the men I've convinced to risk joining me in the rail venture, it seems the best
solution to go ahead with my journey immediately. However difficult that may be."

"Why difficult?" He had said she might ask him anything.

"Because I'm finding it very hard to keep my hands off
you."

"And you think that's necessary?"

"I think that would be best for you."

"Because you still think I'm a child," she said, hurt by his
unexpected decision to leave just when everything between
them had seemed to be moving in a very promising direction.

"If I'd thought you were a child, I'd never have married you."

"But you did marry me. And you seem to be suggesting... I don't know what you're suggesting, except that you're leaving."

"I'm suggesting that when I make you my wife, I don't want to worry about a bruised shoulder and a cut knee. Or a headache." For some reason, his lips quirked gently at the last item. "I'd like to be able to concentrate on making the consummation of our marriage as pleasurable as possible for you."

"And you're afraid it won't be... pleasurable?" she asked, wondering why he thought she wouldn't like having him make love to her. She knew enough to have some idea of what was involved. It had never sounded pleasant to her before, that was true, but the thought of Raven touching her with those hands she'd always admired, hands that she knew to be as graceful as she'd imagined them to be, made the prospect appealing. Extremely exciting.

"Forgive me, Catherine, and believe me, it has nothing to do with your age—with the difference in our ages—but you are..."

"Inexperienced?" she supplied, at his hesitation.

"Yes," he said.

"I'm sorry," she offered, the words falling on top of his.

"Delightfully inexperienced."

"Delightfully?" she repeated. "Then you don't mind."

"I'd want to kill any man who touched you before you belonged to me. The hardest thing I've ever done in my life was manage *not* to kill Amberton. I think he was aware of the struggle I was waging. That's probably why he stabbed me. He read murder in my eyes."

"Because he had... touched me?"

Raven hesitated a moment before he answered. There had, of course, been far more involved in his attack on Amberton, but Catherine didn't need to know what the viscount had suggested. Finally he said simply, "And because I hadn't."

"But you'd wanted to?"

"Since I'd met you. Since I saw you defending that donkey."

"Why didn't you tell me that?"

He smiled in self-mockery. "Because I was afraid you'd run like the hounds of hell were after you. I knew I was nothing like the men you admired."

She tried to remember the men she'd admired before she'd met Raven. No one was memorable enough among her previous suitors to offer the smallest challenge to his dominance of her senses now.

"I thought my only hope was to negotiate a contract you couldn't refuse, to give you what you seemed to desire most, to agree to whatever terms I thought you'd accept, and then gradually try to make you think about me in a different way."

"And how long were you prepared to wait for that to happen?" she asked, fascinated by his revelations. They were far more courageous, she supposed, than hers had been yesterday.

"As long as it took. The only problem was that I'd promised not to interfere in your flirtations. And I couldn't even bear to watch you waltz with someone else. I didn't want anyone else's arms around you but mine."

"Is that why you played cards at Aunt Agatha's?"

"Neither set of my ancestors was noted for tolerance where their women and other men were involved. Nor am I. I played cards as an alternative to playing the jealous husband."

"May I congratulate you on your skill," she said, smiling.

"At cards?"

"At deception."

"You never suspected?"

"No," she said, shaking her head. "Quite the reverse."

"You thought I was enamored of my mistress," he teased.

"And that you enjoyed discussing business more than conducting even a business relationship with your wife."

"And now you know that you were wrong. On both counts."

"I know what you've told me."

"Are you doubting my word, Catherine?"

"Which words? The words about undertaking a journey on the day that..." She paused uncertainly.

"We've finally admitted our feelings."

"Must you go, Raven?" she asked, fighting the urge to cry.

"I should have left yesterday. It's what I intended."

"Until I was thrown."

"And, of course, I couldn't leave until I knew you were all right. And you are all right, Catherine. Bruised and battered, but beautifully all right. I need to leave today if I'm to complete the arrangements that must be presented as a fait accompli to the investors. Since you need time to recuperate, it seemed best to get this journey out of the way while you do so."

"And I'm supposed to be the understanding wife and smilingly bid you goodbye."

"I had hoped that you would." His eyes were on her face, his small smile still touching that firm mouth.

"Goodbye, Raven. I hope you have a very pleasant journey," she said, raising her chin slightly. And then she smiled at him, slowly and deliberately, a small upward tilt of her lips that she knew to be very becoming and very provocative. She'd practiced it often enough before her glass.

"That's a good child," he said, teasing her.

"I'm not—" she began.

"A child," he acknowledged. "And I think I might have time to verify the truth of that before I go."

"I thought you were going to wait until your return to..." She paused, and her eyes fell to where her fingers were twisting the ribbon that fastened the low neck of her chemise.

"A week seems, suddenly, a very long time."

"I believe you told me husbands are allowed one kiss."

"A rule that hardly seems to apply in our situation."

She glanced up to find that he was no longer at the foot of the bed, but was standing beside her.

"Our situation?" she questioned. His eyes, looking down into hers, were again starred like the sapphire he'd given her.

"Lovers," he reminded her softly, "are allowed as many as they can steal. Don't you remember anything I've taught you, Catherine? Shall I be forced to begin all over again?"

She was once more mesmerized by him, by the powerful body, his voice, the piercing crystal eyes. And his beautiful hands.

Her fingers had played with the narrow satin ribbon until the bow had loosened. Now her hand stilled under the spell he was weaving. He placed his palm over her fingers. With his forefinger he stroked the hollow at the base of her throat. She swallowed suddenly, feeling the soft pressure of his touch against that movement. The long dark finger began to slide slowly down her chest and into the rift between her breasts. He carried her hand down with him, out of his way, so the opening at the top of her chemise, which the ribbon had once secured, was now unobstructed. With his thumb he pushed the material away from the swell of her breast. His eyes never left hers, compelling her to allow this. And she had no strength, in the face of his, with which to deny him. She lay against the propped pillows, acquiescent and more than willing for him to touch her.

He eased down to sit beside her on the bed, his thumb continuing the slow rhythm it had begun, smoothing over the soft, milk white skin of her breast. She knew he could feel her heartbeat, running too rapidly, like a frightened hart, just under the heel of his hand. And her breathing, uneven, coming in shuddering inhalations. And he was barely touching her.

His fingers slipped under her breast and lifted gently. Her eyes closed with the impact of the sensations moving through her. He held the heavy globe a moment, his thumb never stopping its now-familiar stroke, from the darker valley up onto the curving ivory swell and back. His fingers began to spread out under the weight of her breast, to glide upward until the callused edge of his forefinger was under her nipple. And then over it, sliding across with a sensuous abrasion that sent sensations shuddering through her stomach and between her legs, which moved involuntarily, loosening, waiting for what, she didn't know. Wanting.

And then he allowed his fingers to catch her nipple between them. She gasped softly, her eyes flying open to find his. Reassuring. Steadying. Telling her without words that this was what she had waited for so long. So long when she hadn't known what she'd wanted. Only Raven.

She waited still, and when his fingers moved again, pressing the small, sensitive nub between their strength, her eyes closed and her hips writhed uncontrollably. Pushing into the bed, seeking. Still innocent of what they sought.

His hand shifted, the hard palm again cupping under her breast and lifting it. His fingers pushed the soft cotton of her chemise away, the air suddenly shocking against the dark warmth his hand had given her skin. She felt his breath—hot and moist, tantalizing—a second before she realized what he intended. His lips touched where his fingers had been, enclosing the peak that had grown taut and aching under their relentless demand. That demand was now replaced by the caress of his mouth, soft and sweet. Wet and hot. Moving over her nipple. Pulling. A dark embrace. Lifting her skin into his mouth. Suckling gently.

And all the nerve endings nature had so generously supplied in that place responded, acting according to divine design. A spectacularly emotive reaction. Building and tearing down. All the barriers destroyed. All the preconceptions rearranged by the reality of what it meant to have Raven's mouth on her body.

As she moved, her hips arching again without her conscious volition, she never once remembered Amberton's touch. There could be no parallel between what had happened then and what was now taking place under the exquisite command of Raven's lovemaking. Her lips breathed his name, a sighing surrender. Her fingers tangled in the blackness of his hair, finding it as silken as it had appeared last night, loose then, unrestricted as she wanted it now to be.

At the sounds that began in her throat, torn, almost, from lips that had opened at the first contact of his mouth over the reaching peak of her breast, he allowed his teeth to close very gently over the rose nipple. Teasing. Then his tongue's caress replaced that nearly painful tension, circling, pushing back and forth across the hard tip.

She couldn't breathe. There was no more air left in the universe. Their universe. No one else had ever inhabited this world or ever would. His teeth grazed her flesh again, biting softly this time. Nibbling on the edge of pain. She was aware of the heat building between her legs, burning and yet so wet. Needing.

The feel of his mouth was primitive, dark and elemental. And somehow elegant, like what happened to her body when she danced or rode. The movements awakening something inside that demanded a response, just as his lips were demanding. And her body was trying to respond, moving against the bed, lifting as if to find his. As if to meld her softness into that hard strength.

"Raven," she begged, because she didn't know anything else now but him. There was nothing in her experience to help her. He had taken her far beyond what was familiar and into a realm that was unexplored. And she was lost without his guidance.

At something in those whispered syllables, at what was very obviously a plea, Raven responded. The pressure of his mouth and teeth eased until he was holding her only with his lips. And then, lifting his head slightly, he released the distended nipple. The sudden breath of cool air against the moist skin that his mouth had been warming was harshly invasive, another almost-painful sensation. She whimpered at the loss of his touch. At that pleading sound, his lips caressed the peak he'd so lovingly created and then deserted. Caressed as gently as he'd kissed her nose the last time he'd deserted her.

He eased away from her body, sitting up to look down into her face, which was softened with passion as it had never been before. She no longer cared that he could read what she was feeling. And, of course, she couldn't have hidden what he'd done to her even if she *had* desired any longer to keep her emotions hidden. But she didn't. She was his and she had no will to hide her feelings from him ever again.

"I told you," he said. "Very rare."

She couldn't speak. Not yet. It was too new, whatever bond he'd forged between the masculine beauty of his body and the small, seeking softness of hers. And so she lay, watching him. Drained. Exhausted by emotion. And he'd only touched her.

"You, Mrs. Raven, are indeed very rare."

Her smile was not practiced. She was too far beyond the boundaries of flirtation. Too far into a place she'd never before entered to be able to command her features.

"Why?" she whispered. She raised her hand to touch the single strand of dark hair that had escaped confinement. It was as soft as before and as enticing to her trembling fingers. She wanted to loosen the ribbon that held the rest and feel its curling length run like silk threads through her hands.

"Because little girls aren't supposed to react like that," he said, answering her smile. She didn't resent, this time, the suggestion that she was very young. She felt very young, especially when confronted with his obvious experience.

"And how are little girls supposed to react?"

"Shocked?" he suggested softly, his smile widening into small creases that broke the hard plane of his lean cheeks.

She shook her head.

"No?" he asked, his fingers rearranging the edges of the chemise and, graceful despite their size, retying the small ribbon.

"I like your hands," she said.

He looked up from his task, and his soft laughter was very pleasant. She felt her mouth responding with a smile, answering his laugh just as her body had answered his caress. So in tune to his every movement.

"I thought you said they were too big."

"No," she whispered. "I like you big."

Raven's amusement deepened, suddenly breaking through his normal control. He laughed, full and rich, and without self-consciousness, revealing very white teeth against the golden skin. Although she wasn't entirely sure what had caused that response, she laughed with him. Because she belonged to him.

"I hope so, my sweet darling," he said finally, the laughter still lurking in the lucid depths of his sapphire eyes. "Dear God, I certainly hope so."

"Goodbye, Raven," she said bravely, exactly as she had before in response to his request. *Before,* she thought, shivering. "I hope you have a very pleasant journey."

"And I wonder if you know how impossible that's just become. How impossible you've made the likelihood of that."

"No," she said.

"Will you try to stay out of trouble while I'm gone? No more card games with lecherous bastards and no water hazards?"

He took her fingers and brought them to his lips, his eyes meeting hers as he allowed his tongue to trace over the fine porcelain skin on the back of her hand. She followed the movement with her eyes, remembering the previous journey of his tongue over her breast, as he had, of course, intended.

"Recuperating." She forced the word through dry lips.

"What?" he asked, dropping a small kiss between each finger.

She swallowed, trying to find the breath to answer him. The sensations in her lower body were beginning again. Simply because he was touching her hand, she realized with wonder.

"I'm going to be recuperating," she said, fighting the urge to tighten her fingers over his, to try to hold him to her. God, she didn't want him to leave, now that she had just discovered how very much she desired him.

"Good," he said softly, placing her hand carefully against the sheet. "And I'm going to be remembering. Miss me," he said, and she wasn't sure if it was a question or a command.

"I miss you already," she whispered truthfully. She missed his touch. The feel of his mouth against her skin.

"Close your eyes," he commanded. Willingly she obeyed. She felt his weight leave the bed, and then unexpectedly and very gently, as if she really were as fragile as the Venetian goblets downstairs, he kissed her forehead.

And the hated tears were already welling when the door closed behind him.

Chapter Thirteen

"But if you think that Mrs. Raven—" the groom began.

"I don't think Mrs. Raven's in any danger. I'd never undertake this journey if that were the case," Raven explained patiently. "The doctor has ordered at least a week's recuperation, which should preclude any activities outside the house. If she does venture out before I return, I want you with her. And I don't think she's in danger." Raven wondered for whom he'd made that repeated assurance. He knew, however, that *he* had been the target of the attack, and the farther away from Catherine he was, the safer she should be.

"But Mr. Raven—"

"Don't let her out of your sight, Jem. I'll be back on Sunday. I'm trusting you with the most precious thing I possess," Raven said, placing his hand on the shoulder of Catherine's groom. "Don't let me down."

Jem nodded, his eyes meeting his master's in perfect understanding, and Raven's lips relaxed into a softer alignment. This man would protect Catherine with his life.

Intellectually, Raven might know for whom that bullet had been meant, and that the last thing the old man would want was to hurt his daughter. Whatever estrangement might have been caused by her marriage, Catherine was still the Duke of Monfort's only child. Raven would never leave if he believed his wife's safety was threatened, but to be certain . . .

"One stop," he instructed the coachman as he mounted the narrow steps of the carriage that would carry him north. His hand touched the fine line of the scar on his high cheekbone. He imagined his welcome this time would be even colder than when he'd last visited that elegant town house. And as he remembered, it had been remarkably unwelcoming then.

Montfort's butler recognized him. Raven could see the same fear reflected in the man's eyes that had been there before. Especially when the American pushed open the door of the Mayfair mansion, despite the servant's resistance.

"But his grace isn't expecting—" Hartford began.

"He damn well should be," Raven said, easily breaking away from the trembling hand attempting to grip his arm. He threw open doors until he found the duke, seated at a rosewood desk.

The old man looked up from whatever had been occupying his attention, lifting the gold lorgnette he had been using and focusing its glass on the massive figure of his son-in-law. If he was surprised by this invasion of his office, that emotion was not evident in the expression with which he regarded the American.

"I'm going to assume you have a reason for being here," Montfort said.

"You may be certain, your grace, that I'd never put myself in the position of having to be civil to you without reason."

"Civil?" the duke taunted softly at Raven's tone. One white eyebrow climbed cynically. "But perhaps our standards are different," he suggested with more than a trace of condescension.

"Very different," Raven agreed, his words as mocking as his father-in-law's. "*I've* never ordered anyone shot in the back."

"Indeed," Montfort said, his lips twitching in amusement. "I'm very relieved by that confidence. If, however, that is the extent of the information you desire to impart..." Pausing, he waved one bejeweled hand at the stack of documents on his desk.

"I'll fight you or your hirelings any time you wish, your grace," Raven said, anger building at the dismissal, "but if you ever hurt my wife again, I'll gut you like the animal you are."

The boredom in the midnight eyes remained a fraction of a second before the import in his words reached the sharp brain behind them. Something shifted in their glittering depths, and Montfort repeated, his voice no longer taunting, "*Hurt* your wife?"

"Your assassin missed, as I'm sure he informed you. What he didn't tell you, I suppose, is that his ball grazed Catherine's mare, which as a result bolted with her."

There was a long silence. Montfort said finally, his eyes never wavering from the cold fury in Raven's, "And my daughter?"

"Catherine was thrown."

There was another long, silent heartbeat. Raven could hear his own, pulsing too quickly, frightened as well as furious at the renewed images of what might have happened.

"I assume you intend to tell me the outcome," Montfort suggested. He had lowered the lorgnette, the thin, elegant fingers of both hands playing with it restlessly, so that Raven periodically caught glimpses of gold. Unbidden, the surety came again that the old man had never meant to hurt Catherine.

"Bruises," Raven admitted, watching the white fingers pause suddenly. The duke's mouth tightened, and then he set the quizzing glass on the desk. When the midnight eyes glanced up from under those intimidating brows, they were again politely amused.

"How fortunate," he said. "If you are unable to protect my daughter, Mr. Raven, perhaps it might be better if you allowed—"

Raven didn't bother to listen to whatever suggestion the old man was about to make. "I'll protect Catherine from the devil himself," he promised softly. And then remembering what Jem had told him, he released his own lips from the rigid line in which they'd been set. The Devil Duke, the groom had called the old man. How bloody apt.

"Don't hurt my wife again," Raven said. "I'm warning you."

He turned on his heel and started across the room. The butler was standing in the open door of the duke's study, backed by four burly footmen. Raven met the majordomo's eyes with nothing but contempt in the cold blue ice of his own. The servant's glance flicked to his master, and at whatever silent communication passed between them, the butler stepped out of Raven's way, sending footmen scattering behind him. For a moment Raven allowed his amusement to show before he strode across the wide foyer.

As he reached for the front door, it opened before him, and for the first time in months Raven found himself confronting the Viscount Amberton, the sartorial elegance of the bottle green morning coat he was wearing almost matching the duke's. Birds of a feather, Raven thought, his lips moving at the mental image of two strutting male peacocks. Still smiling, he bowed slightly to the English aristocrat, who had stepped back with the same alacrity just exhibited by his grace's servants.

"Don't worry, Amberton. I'm not going to hurt you," Raven promised, amusement again allowed to tinge that assured voice.

The viscount's blue eyes met his, revealing in their depths an emotion Raven identified correctly as unadulterated hatred.

"Family business?" Amberton asked, recovering his aplomb, his own mockery very clear at the idea that the coal merchant and the English duke might have any other business in common.

"Exactly," Raven agreed calmly. Nodding, he stepped around the viscount and into the clean sunshine of the London street.

When the door closed behind the American, Amberton's lips whitened and a small muscle twitched beside his mouth. Realizing finally that the servants were watching, the viscount strolled across the foyer with his usual languid grace and entered, unannounced, the office where the duke sat.

Montfort had been tapping the lorgnette he held lightly against his cheek. The dark eyes came up at the nobleman's entrance. "Tell me, Amberton," his grace said, "do you know anyone for hire with, shall we say, a disposition to violence?"

Raven closed his eyes and rested his head against the leather of the carriage seat, exhausted by what he'd accomplished in the short time he'd been in the north. He had spent the last four days pretending interest during endless meetings, and additional hours at night writing out the terms that had been agreed to in contracts to be signed the following day. In the dim quietness of his lonely rooms, in which he seldom had the opportunity to rest his head against the pillow of the undisturbed bed, the memories of a very different bed intruded.

Catherine. He savored again the unexpected responses she'd made to his touch, welcoming his hands and even his mouth against the soft, smooth fragrance of that porcelain skin. Raven's body would harden against his will, against all his determined intent, torturing him with the promise of what awaited his return.

And even here in the confines of the coach, bound finally for London, he could feel that painful reaction to the unending fantasies he had of making Catherine his. Of finally being allowed to show her what he felt, what he *had* felt since the day he had first looked up into those russet eyes misted with unshed tears. Exactly as they had been the morning he'd left.

As his heritage had compelled him, he had honored the vow he'd made to Catherine so long ago, when they had begun this inconvenient *mariage de convenance*. And now, finally, he would honor, too, the promise he had made only to himself.

The noise that shattered the intensity of his memories was as recognizable as it had been the morning in Hyde Park. Harsh commands and then shots, sharp and clear, dis-

turbed the cold upland air. His orders to Tom, however, had
been explicit. John Raven was no one's fool, and he'd
known that another attempt to put an end to his life and,
therefore, to his unsuitable marriage, might be made on this
journey. The mate to the pistol that was now held compe-
tently in Raven's right hand had been given to the coachman in anticipation of just such a challenge. And Tom had
been told to drive on, no matter what.

The coach swayed more strongly, the tiring horses prodded with the whip to outrace the men who were trying to
stop them. Raven wondered if this assault had been that
carefully planned—the site well isolated and yet near the
next post station to ensure the team's fatigue. And remembering the shrewd mind behind those midnight eyes, he
knew that nothing had been left to chance.

The road was dangerously narrow, the coach rocketing
between the sweep of wind-gnarled trees on one side and a
rock-strewn drop on the other. Raven fired methodically,
exposing himself briefly at the window as he squeezed off his
careful shots, then retreated inside to reload, his hands automatically performing the necessary procedure. He could
hear their pursuers, shouting to one another and their occasional shots. He never knew which of those had the desired effect, but Tom would, of course, have presented a
stark target for the following riders, his body silhouetted
against the leaden sky of the north country.

The horses plunged onward, now without the familiar
guidance of experienced hands on their reins. Legs trembled from exhaustion and panic, and eventually there came
the fatal stumble, throwing off the steady cadence that had
sustained the chase. The break in rhythm began to unravel
the confidence of that precise team that had strained in
unison for miles. Dangerously out of synchronization now,
the horses faltered, allowing the carriage to careen too close
to the hillside along which the roadway had been cut. The
outside leader lost its footing in the rubble, struggling fran-
tically to regain its stride, but it was too late. The rear wheel
of the coach rounded the curve well off the road. It col-
lided with one of the boulders that edged the decline and

splintered, ending any prospect that the horses might, in their exhaustion, have slowed enough to allow the man inside, waiting his chance, to attempt the hazardous climb to the empty box.

Instead, pulled by the resulting tilt of the damaged vehicle, the outside pair first and then the entire team were dragged over the edge with the heavy coach, onto the rocks below. At the initial impact with the boulder, Raven had braced his body in the protected space between the facing seats. The fall seemed to take an eternity, the vehicle rolling end over end to the bottom of the decline. Eventually the shattered carriage came to rest, one wheel still spinning drunkenly, the traces attached to the carnage of broken and dying horses.

Raven was not aware when the crushed door was forced open by his pursuers, who had willingly made the treacherous climb down the rock face. After all, they had been very well paid to make sure the American never reached London. Very well paid indeed.

The long hours of Saturday trudged by without any sign of Raven's arrival. Despite her determination to react with calmness, Catherine had started, her heart in her throat, at every sound of carriage wheels in the street. She stayed up very late waiting, not even bothering to offer an excuse for her behavior to Edwards, who unobtrusively kept watch over her vigil. When she had finally surrendered to her disappointment to begin the long climb upstairs, the butler himself had lighted her way and had bid her good-night with an almost paternal kindness.

Sunday was an endless succession of hours that she spent going through the motions of living. Foolishly, that night the tears came again. She remembered her anxiety the last time Raven had been away, but then there had been some excuse for her behavior. This was sheer lovesickness. She wanted Raven here, teasing her, his blue eyes glinting with hidden laughter and the stern line of his beautiful mouth controlled. Until it touched her and left her uncontrolled. Lost without his guidance.

* * *

The boot that prodded Raven's ribs was not gentle, but compared to the other sensations his body had endured in the last hours, not particularly brutal. The journey up the incline, and then the endless ride draped across the back of the rough-gaited cob they'd thrown him over, hands and feet tied, dangling like an ill-arranged pack of tinker's wares, had been far worse.

He had drifted in and out of consciousness, pain almost defeating his ability to plan, to think, to care anymore what happened. All he wanted was to stop the agony. His will to endure, trained and instilled from childhood, had been lost with the cataclysm in his skull. Only by focusing on the one image that remained, untouched by what was happening to his unprotesting body, could he retain a desire to survive. Catherine. Again he allowed her picture to superimpose the agony in his mind, to block it. He had made a vow, and had been so close to fulfilling it. So near that he could feel her slenderness beneath his driving body, arching upward into—

"Time to wake up," a voice said, interrupting that fantasy.

He was lying on the ground, with rocks embedded in the muscles of his back. He forced open the one eyelid that still functioned, and watched the wavering outline of a man appear between him and the graying sky of twilight. Hours must have passed since the coach had crashed.

"Why?" he whispered, the one syllable all he could manage.

"Because someone don't like you very well," the disembodied voice affirmed. "And he's willing to pay to have you disappear."

"I'll give you ten times—" Raven began, the offer cut off by his captor's laugh.

"He said you'd try that, but honor among thieves, you know. I have a contract. And, I understand, you ain't got that much money anymore. All your ready gone in some worthless scheme to build a railway." Again the laugh jarred in Raven's skull. "Some folks'll believe anything," the man said mockingly.

"What are you going to do?" Raven asked. It was almost idle curiosity. Trussed like a dressed fowl, there wasn't much he could do to prevent whatever they intended.

"I'm going to make you disappear, Mr. Raven. And I thought of the perfect way—a way that gives a little justice to men like me. You want to put miners out of their jobs, I hear. To use machines in your mines, and let the folks that have always worked them starve to death, along with their babes."

"That's not true," Raven said, anger imbuing his voice with strength. They didn't understand. No one understood the potential of the machines to ease human suffering.

"You ever been in a coal mine, Mr. Nabob? Ever had coal dust ground into your skin so it don't wash off no matter how hard you try? I thought you might like a taste of what a mine's like."

Raven swallowed the sudden fear, fought its control. He was beginning to win the battle to think, to fight the lethargy left by his injuries, but if they threw him down a shaft...

"You can cooperate or we can throw you in. I don't have no stomach for killing a man all tied up. Not quite sporting, it seems to me. But eventually, time will accomplish the same end. It ain't a real mine, just a test hole. And if it rains, you'll have some time. A few days to think about the miners you've put out of work, their starving families. There may even be some water down there from the last rain. Uncomfortable being cold and wet, but I don't imagine you'll mind after a while. Get him up," the man ordered, and rough hands callously accommodated him. Someone fitted a loop of rope around the toes of Raven's boots and then put the trailing hemp into his hands.

"Hold on now, Mr. Raven," the one who had done all the talking commanded. "Let's see how you like the dark."

Three of them picked him up, swinging his body over the edge of the pit. Raven was afraid suddenly that they wouldn't be able to hold the rope with the pull of his weight, but when they began to slowly lower him into the increasing blackness, he wondered why he had worried about living through the descent. Wouldn't it be better to die quickly, to fall to death rather than to starve, prolonging the torment of dying, alone and in the darkness?

The rope was released suddenly and he dropped a short distance, his boots striking the ground first and then his knees banging painfully onto the damp, unyielding hardness. His hands, tied palm to palm, automatically broke the rest of his fall. He felt the remaining rope drop over his back and shoulders.

"Goodbye, Mr. Raven," the voice said from a very long way above his head. Despairing, he closed his eyes, and before him, again, was the image of Catherine as he had left her that morning, her lips parted slightly and her eyes, wide and dark, locked onto his as he touched her.

You made a vow, his grandmother's voice echoed inside his head. *And you must keep your promise, my dark and beautiful Raven. All your promises.*

He rolled slowly onto his back, and despairing, watched the light fade from the sky far above his head and the stars gradually replace the dusky dimness of twilight with true night.

"But the situation is extremely critical, Mrs. Raven. I must impress upon you—" Oliver Reynolds argued, wondering why he had believed it might be beneficial to visit his client's wife.

Since the disastrous meeting with the investors this morning, a meeting at which John Raven had failed to appear, the banker had tried to decide upon the best course of action. He had, he supposed, been a fool to allow the bank to become involved in a scheme this speculative. Visions of the profits that would accrue if the American nabob succeeded had blinded him to the risk. That and the character of the man himself.

It had been in remembering John Raven's character that he had made his call, uninvited and unannounced, on Catherine Montfort Raven. A last hope. A desperate gamble for information. Information which he now knew she didn't possess.

"What's *critical*, Mr. Reynolds, is the fact that my husband seems to have disappeared. And you're far more concerned with protecting your investment than with determining what might have happened to him," Catherine retorted angrily.

"*His* investment as well. I assure you, Mrs. Raven—"

"Have you sent out inquiries? Do you have people looking for my husband?" she interrupted again to ask.

"I hadn't..." Reynolds began, and then paused, wondering if he dared tell her what had been suggested today as a reason for her husband's disappearance. Montfort's daughter, he thought again. That devious old bastard. And judging by the steel in the girl's voice, she had inherited some of the old man's temper. "No," he finished simply, meeting the steady brown eyes.

"And why not? If you're so concerned about Raven's—"

"It was suggested Mr. Raven might not *wish* to be found."

The movement of the slender fingers tearing at the lace edging of her handkerchief was arrested. She waited a moment, the mind behind those remarkable eyes obviously also owing something to her father.

"Suggested?" Catherine finally asked, her voice controlled.

"By one of the investors."

"But why? Why would Raven want to disappear?" she asked, thinking of the morning he'd left. Of the promise that had been in the flame of those blue eyes. She shook her head. Her lips lifted slightly, knowing how ridiculous that was.

"Mr. Raven carried with him to the north a rather large sum of money. Other such sums have, in the past weeks, supposedly been used to secure the land and to make the necessary—"

"*Supposedly?*" Montfort's daughter repeated coldly.

Oliver Reynolds could feel the perspiration beginning to dew his forehead. He removed his own handkerchief and dabbed at the moisture before he answered, "Your husband's accounts are dangerously low, depleted, he said, to finance the venture. The investors, however, whose moneys are also involved, are not so certain of that situation. It was suggested,'' he said again, thinking how to word what could only be an insult, ''that Mr. Raven's disappearance at this juncture is too... coincidental.''

''Implying Raven has absconded with the investors' money?''

''I am simply repeating what was said. This morning. At a very important meeting your husband failed to attend.''

''And what did these partners suggest you do about it?'' she asked bitterly. She could hear the anger building in her own voice, but was pleased to believe that the old man was unaware of it. How dare they accuse Raven of stealing their damned money?

''They want an accounting of your husband's remaining holdings. They're demanding to be repaid.''

''But you said Raven's funds were tied up in the land he's bought, in the contracts he's made for the railway. If they pull out now...'' She was beginning to realize the extent of that potential disaster. No wonder the banker was so upset. ''Then it's over. It collapses. And Raven loses everything,'' she breathed aloud. This was what he had warned her about. Everything he owned would be taken to pay off his partners.

''Exactly,'' Reynolds agreed, relieved that she'd arrived at that point on her own. He wiped his face again and then stuffed the cloth back into his pocket. ''I thought he might have told you... something of his intentions.''

''His intentions to steal from men I lured to my dinner table so they could be fleeced?'' the girl asked, her lips again curved in a small, knowing smile. ''No, Mr. Reynolds, I assure you my husband didn't impart anything of that plan to me. What he did tell me, and what you may be very sure is the truth, is that he intended to return to London on Sunday. And since he has not yet arrived, I can also assure you that something has happened to him. And I intend to discover what it is.''

''But how will you—''

"I'm going to do what you should have already done. First I'm going to send out search parties. And then I'm going to consult my father. I imagine he'll want a list of the investors. If you would be so good as to provide one?"

Thinking about handing the Duke of Montfort a list of the gentlemen who had only this morning been screaming for John Raven's head on a platter sent a tremor through the banker. He was too old for this, he thought with despair. "Your father?" he repeated, just to make certain he'd not misunderstood.

"The Duke of Montfort," Catherine said, smiling at him. It was the provocative one she'd practiced so often at her mirror. "After all," she assured the old man, "this is a family matter."

When Oliver Reynolds finally stood on the stoop of John Raven's town house, he again wiped his brow. At least it was no longer his problem alone, he thought. Montfort's daughter had been extremely efficient, once informed of the situation. As businesslike as her husband when it came to making decisions. And that was surprising in itself, given her age and her class. Women of her circle were supposed to be highly decorative and nothing else.

What the banker had found even more surprising than her intellect was Catherine Raven's unshakable faith in her husband's intentions. Everyone in London might be convinced of the American's duplicity, but his wife's calm amusement that John Raven could have planned anything remotely dishonest was the most reassuring thing the banker had heard today.

Now, however, he must prepare the information she had requested for her father. The Devil Duke himself, the old man thought again, remembering all the stories. A bad man to cross, they said, and Reynolds couldn't imagine Montfort being willing to bail out a son-in-law not of his choosing. The gossipmongers had been quite specific about that. The Viscount Amberton had been the horse the duke had been backing, and the banker could imagine what his grace had felt about his daughter's runaway marriage.

There had been something else, Reynolds remembered, following that train of thought. Some rumor about Amberton. Something financial, he believed. He couldn't remember exactly what those whispers had concerned, but it would come to him, he knew. He never forgot anything dealing with money.

"Excuse me, sir." A voice interrupted his effort to remember.

Cap in hand, Jem had stood respectfully waiting for the old man to notice him. It seemed to him that someone should know what had happened, now that Mr. Raven had disappeared. The responsibility the groom had been given for Mrs. Raven's safety loomed as a task beyond his ability, especially with the master missing.

"You *are* Mr. Raven's man of business, aren't you?" Jem asked, hoping he was doing the right thing.

The old man nodded, wondering what kind of household the American had put together, where a schoolroom chit gave orders about business and the grooms addressed callers.

"Then there's something, sir, I think you should know. Something that happened before Mr. Raven left London," Jem said, "and some right disturbing things I've noticed since."

The groom's relief, now that he had made the decision to unburden himself, hurried the careful recitation he had planned. And eventually he found it very gratifying that he had such an avid listener.

Chapter Fourteen

Catherine watched her father scan the list Oliver Reynolds had prepared. She already knew the names it contained. Devon, Cumberland and Avondale. Russell and Elliot. Templeton and the Earl of Surrey. Even the Duke of Exeter. There were one or two she didn't know very well, but all were friends of her father's.

Because of that friendship, they had come to her home to meet her husband. And now that Raven had failed to keep his appointment with them, it appeared he had intended to cheat them all along. She understood the men of her class well enough to know that whatever plans her husband had had to involve these gentlemen in future projects would now be doomed.

"You must be joking," her father said, his thin lips curled in a very self-satisfied smile. In spite of the fact that she loved him, Catherine felt the urge to wipe the smirk off his face with the flat of her hand. She had been forced to deal with this business while almost frantic with worry about Raven. And she knew that her father was enjoying very much the idea that he had been right about John Raven and she had, again, been quite wrong.

"Why should I guarantee an extremely risky scheme concocted by your husband to divest some of my more gullible acquaintances of their money? Surely you know me better than that, Catherine. Just because he's managed to take you and these idiots—"

"Raven hasn't taken any one in. He offered them an opportunity to become partners in an investment that promises a very high rate of return. He himself has invested far more than any of the others. Probably more than all of them combined."

"You may convey my thanks for that opportunity to Mr. Raven, my dear, at the same time you convey my regrets. My funds are all tied up in legitimate and quite practical ventures. And now if you'll excuse me..." He raised one brow.

"No, I won't excuse you. I need your help," she said angrily. "Why else do you imagine I would give you the chance to gloat as you're doing? And I must tell you, it's most unbecoming."

They had always struck sparks off one another. Too strong willed and too much alike to deal easily together, they had been bound by the fact that neither had anyone else. And she realized for the first time that in her case it was no longer true.

"Forgive me, but I still don't intend to invest. You must have known that when you came. I'm surprised at you, Catherine."

"I had no choice," she admitted.

She knew she would have to tell him the truth and throw herself on his mercies. He was, after all, her father. And no matter how strongly he'd threatened her with his displeasure in the past, his anger had never withstood their mutual affection. He needed her, she knew, as much as she needed him. And loved him, she admitted. She hadn't stopped to think what her marriage and their estrangement would mean to him before today, and she had been shocked by the changes these few months had wrought. He was an old man, and he looked his age. Stubborn and proud as always, but older than she'd ever realized before.

"No choice?" he questioned, his black eyes studying her.

"Raven went north to finish the arrangements for the rail system before last Monday's meeting. He intended to return on Sunday, but...he hasn't yet come home." She refused to put into words the reality; that he had disappeared. "And now the partners are demanding to be repaid, but with the expenditures he's already laid out for the land and the rails, the contracts he's already signed..." She hesitated, but was forced by the situation to admit the rest. "Even if Reynolds sells what he can and uses my trust fund, there won't be enough capital available to repay the investors. If they pull out now, the entire venture will collapse, and Raven will lose everything. Unless you convince them that Raven's railroad is still a sound investment, and..." She paused before she finally found the courage to suggest, "And that you're standing behind your son-in-law."

"What do you imagine has happened to your husband, Catherine?" her father asked, his eyes still on her face.

"I don't know. I can't imagine. It's so... But I know something's happened to him. He promised..." Her voice faltered, but again she forced herself to continue. "I've hired people to look. To follow the route he took, but so far there's no word. I don't know what else to do," she admitted. That admission was very painful. An admission of her failure.

"Let me arrange a divorce," the duke suggested softly.

"A divorce?" she gasped, unable to believe that was his response to her plea. "I don't want a divorce. Why would you believe that I want a divorce?"

"It seems apparent to me you've been deserted, my dear."

"I haven't been deserted. That you could suggest such a thing shows how little you understand. Raven would never..." Knowing the futility of continuing that line of argument, she shook her head. What could she say about their evolving relationship that would make the duke as certain as she that her husband had not voluntarily walked away from their marriage? "Raven always honors his contracts," she ventured finally, knowing as she said it that words would never convince her father.

"I would imagine Elliot and the rest are finding little comfort in that claim," he suggested cynically.

"Then they don't know him as well as I do," Catherine said, meeting his eyes with conviction in the depths of hers.

"Not, perhaps, in the biblical sense," her father agreed, his thin lips moving slightly. "Admit it, my dear. You've simply made another mistake. Whatever you've done, however outrageously you've acted in the past, you've always been just this certain that you were right. And clearly, again, you were wrong. But because I'm your father, I am willing to help you. More than willing, if you'll allow yourself to be guided by me.''

"To divorce my husband? To make a more suitable match? With someone like Amberton, I suppose," she said bitterly, remembering the announcement to the *Post* and the viscount's subsequent actions. But given Raven's disappearance, it would be hard to persuade her father he was the one who had been wrong.

"I haven't heard much from Lord Amberton. At least not since their confrontation. Broke his arm, you know."

"Raven?" Catherine asked, fascinated. She couldn't imagine how her father could possibly know about that incident, but she wasn't surprised to find out that Raven had hurt the viscount, given Gerald's actions that day. "No, as a matter of fact, I didn't know. But I'm not surprised. He stabbed Raven. With a sword. And Raven wasn't armed."

"Apparently to deal with the viscount, he didn't need to be," the duke said, the trace of amusement still in his voice. "What happened? Did you lead Amberton on to make your husband jealous? Lead him on enough that it became a blood feud?"

He knew her too well, Catherine thought. He knew her recklessness would have had something to do with the incident.

"Gerald objected to my marriage to Raven. He had expected I'd marry him. You had led him to believe I would, and that such a union would have your blessing."

"I thought you liked Amberton."

"I didn't want to *marry* him. Especially..." She remembered Gerald's actions at the dance, and how he'd treated her in his apartment. And how he'd stabbed Raven, who hadn't been armed.

"Especially after you met the coal merchant and fell in love," her father finished for her.

"No," Catherine admitted, smiling at him for the first time. "Our marriage, in the beginning, was a business arrangement."

"And now?" he asked softly.

"And now..." She hesitated, remembering. "Now it is something very different. I don't know what's happened to Raven, but I do know that he hasn't disappeared by choice. He wouldn't do that."

"What do you want from me?" Montfort asked.

"Help me find Raven. And until we do, protect his investment by agreeing to come into the partnership."

Raven forced his body up from the cold dampness of the stone floor. He knew as he moved that it had been a mistake to allow the brief respite. His swollen knees and the cramping muscles of his thighs had convinced him that a few moments of precious rest would enable him to go back to the task he had stoically accepted as the only way out, the only hope that he might escape. Now, however, he knew what a serious mistake that pause had been.

He had believed his hands had lost all feeling. Had feared it. In the back of his mind had stirred the horror that the condition might be permanent, but he'd pushed the possibility away, realizing that even if that were true, he had no other choice. Not if he intended to fulfill the vow he'd made.

He had finally found, inching carefully on his knees around the pit into which he'd been lowered, a small, rough outcropping. He had then spent hours, still on his knees, working the rope against the sharp edge of rock.

And now, with the first renewed abrasion, he was forced to acknowledge that there was still a great deal of sensation in those damaged hands. Swollen far more grotesquely than his knees, bleeding and raw with their continual contact against the rock face he was using to sever the ropes that bound him, they still, definitely, had feeling. The edge of rock that seemed to have so little effect on the hemp had abraded the flesh of his hands extremely well. There was only one position in which they would fit over the narrow outcropping and allow it to make contact with the rope—at

least, now that the rock had removed a great deal of flesh
from his hands.

He closed his eyes, pushing the pain again toward the
small dark circle he began to create inside his head, to be
swallowed and lost in the darkness. The fakirs in India could
do this—destroy their consciousness of sensations that
should be too painful for human flesh to bear. As his
grandmother's people had been trained to do. Raven tried
to remember the lessons she had taught him so long ago.
Tried to close off the unending agony of forcing his muti-
lated hands over and over against the rock.

He allowed the sibilant whispers of the old woman's voice
to circle in his mind, fighting the pain and fear. He could
destroy his hands, will his mind to allow that destruction, in
spite of screaming nerves and raw flesh, but he had no control over the rope. No control over how long it would take
its strands to fray and part. No control. Only prayer. And a
remembered vow.

Catherine's father had proved a valuable ally during the
days following Raven's disappearance. The shattered coach
had been found by the searchers, and Tom's body brought
home, but there had been no trace of the American in or
near the wreckage. The duke expanded the search Catherine had begun, sending his agents to areas far from the route
Raven had taken.

Although she believed she had held up remarkably well
under the pressure, Catherine was beginning to fear they
wouldn't find him. Indestructible, she constantly reminded
herself. Raven was indestructible, but she came to dread the
entrance of one of the servants and felt an almost euphoric
relief when the interruption turned out to have been caused
by some household question.

She had racked her brain for any explanation for Raven's disappearance, other than the one everyone else believed. She had found herself remembering the fight with
Amberton and her husband's subsequent disappearance.
Gerald's attack had been done in fear, a reaction to Raven's anger; one might even argue that Gerald had acted in

self-defense. She imagined that a furious John Raven would certainly produce terror in most men. Amberton was physically no match for her husband. When she suggested to her father the possibility that Raven's disappearance might somehow be laid at Gerald's door, he was reassuring.

"We have no reason to believe Amberton harbors any ill will against your husband. They both suffered from their encounter. Gerald has been peacefully tending to his own affairs. I can't think of any reason to connect the viscount with this business."

"And *I* can't forget the cowardly way he stabbed Raven when he was unarmed. That alone speaks to the character of the man."

"The man I intended you to marry?" her father reminded her.

Her lips lifted in a small, twisted smile, but she didn't reproach him. She was surprised when he went on.

"My apologies, Catherine. I was mistaken in that intent."

It was unusual for the Duke of Montfort to admit to being wrong about anything, but owning that he'd erred about a matter of such importance was almost unheard of.

"Thank you," Catherine said. "I hope..." She paused, thinking that all she had hoped might now never come to pass.

"What is it, my dear?" the duke asked, and at the kindness in his tone, she felt her eyes burn with tears, which were nearer the surface with each passing day. Resolutely, she had not allowed herself to shed them. Except in the dark loneliness of her bedroom, the last place she had seen Raven.

"I just thought that I would like you to know Raven. I would like very much for the two of you to be friends."

"We may never be friends, Catherine," Montfort replied, his tone amused. "Not given our past relationship."

She had a brief mental image of his raised hand bringing her crop down across Raven's face and knew he was right.

"But," he continued, "if we are successful in locating your husband, I will attempt to make amends for my previous behavior."

It was quite a concession for a man as proudly stubborn as His Grace, the Duke of Montfort, and Catherine was well aware of what an about-face it represented.

"Thank you," she said again. "I would like that. I'd like for you to know Raven as I do." And then realizing what her father believed about her relationship with her husband—a relationship that had not yet become conjugal—she amended, smiling at him, "Not, of course, in the biblical sense."

The staggering figure blended with the shadowed twilight that had crept over the back garden of the Mayfair mansion. There was no stealth employed in the approach, so that the Duke of Montfort's hireling had been aware of the man who transversed the alley behind the town house since he'd appeared on the edge of John Raven's property. His grace had employed the watcher to be alert to just such an event as was unfolding. As the intruder left the shadows to cross the broad expanse of lawn, which would give him access to the vulnerable doors at the back of the house, the duke's man moved silently into position behind him.

John Raven paused before the completion of this endless journey, a journey that had begun at the bottom of the hellhole the old duke had intended to be his tomb. He looked up at the welcoming glow from the windows of his London town house, feeling his throat close with emotions he had forced himself to hold at bay until now. He had won, and he stood at last on the threshold of his own home. He blocked from his mind the toll he'd paid for that escape. Blue eyes lifted to find the windows he knew were Catherine's, and finally he allowed himself to imagine what she might be doing in that room as he stood below.

The point of the knife biting into his back was totally unexpected. He was a fool, Raven suddenly realized, to think that Montfort would not have planned for the possibility of his reappearance—would not have prepared for *every* eventuality. Panic clawed in his belly at the thought that he might have come so far, might have given up so much, only to now be denied.

No, damn it, you old bastard. Not when I've come so close, Raven swore. As that resolve formed, his body automatically began the graceful series of moves he had been taught during his years in the Orient. A downward twist accompanied the hammering blow of his elbow into the gut of the man behind him. Knowing he had already exceeded the limits of his strength, Raven also knew that if he did not succeed in his first attack, this would be a fight he would ultimately lose.

The remembrance of the old man's insults flashed into his head. *Your stench offends me,* Montfort had taunted. And so the two kicks with which Raven disarmed and then felled his assailant were fueled more by the idea of how satisfying it would be to assault his elegant father-in-law than by any anger against the duke's hireling. Gasping, Raven watched as the man dropped, but his opponent had already been forgotten. *Your time will come, Montfort,* he found himself thinking instead.

Threatened now only by his own exhaustion, Raven leaned against the wall of the coach house, watching his attacker for any sign of returning life and wondering what he thought he could do if the man did revive. But when a hand reached out of the growing darkness and touched his arm, Raven reacted to the new assault with the same unthinking skills he'd used to free himself before. Sweeping his attacker's legs out from under him, Raven threw him to the ground, even as a belated recognition swam to the surface of his mind.

Jem lay on the smooth lawn, looking up at him as if he belonged in Bedlam. "Mr. Raven," the groom whispered, his voice full of concern.

"Get that man up, Jem," Raven ordered, making no effort to hide his condition, but not acknowledging the anxiety he had heard underlying the groom's shock. "I have something I need to ask him." The henchman's answer would only be confirmation of what Raven already knew, but made now before a witness.

Unquestioning, from astonishment or from force of habit, the groom obeyed, pulling the man Raven had downed to his feet. Raven stepped behind his attacker and, using the advantage of his height, positioned his forearm around the man's throat, exerting as much upward force as he could without snapping his neck.

"Who hired you?" he asked.

"Go to hell," the man gasped through a windpipe he expected to collapse like rotten fruit under the pressure. In answer to that foolhardy bravado, his head was suddenly jerked upward, so that he strained on his toes, desperate for relief. He'd seen enough public hangings to know what was happening—his face darkening, tongue protruding as he fought for air.

"I'm sure they know you there. *And* your master. I want you to tell me his name, and this is your last chance," Raven warned.

Something must have broken through to the thug, so hardened by violence and deprivation he had believed he had no fear of death. Suddenly confronted by someone who promised it with such quiet conviction, he found he very much wanted to live.

"Montfort," he acknowledged, and felt the blessed air trickle through his bruised throat.

"Get out," Raven ordered, releasing the pressure he'd been maintaining with the last of his strength. And more than willing to obey, the man disappeared into the shadows. Startled by the unexpected command, the groom darted after him, realizing almost immediately that he had no chance of finding his quarry in the gathering darkness. Giving up, Jem returned, to find his master leaning, eyes closed in the sunken sockets, against the wall.

"You shouldn't 'a let him go, Mr. Raven. We should have—"

"He'll report to the old man."

"You want *him* to tell Montfort you're back?" Jem asked, puzzled by that idea.

The blue eyes opened, full of amusement. "Someone will have to. Let him bear the brunt of his grace's displeasure. I should think that would be punishment enough for his role in all this."

"Displeasure?" Jem echoed. "But—"

"Get Edwards," Raven said, allowing his eyelids to fall again. Slowly the aching muscles of the legs that had carried him so far gave way to the weakness he had fought, and finally the abused knees bent. As the groom watched, the massive body folded as gracefully as a lady's fan, and John Raven slid down to lie on the comforting grass of his own back garden.

Catherine could never remember exactly what Jem told her, but by the time she arrived in the garden, her knees were trembling uncontrollably. The fear engendered by whatever the groom had said wasn't lessened by the sight of Edwards bending over the figure that lay collapsed on the lawn.

She was kneeling by her husband's side in a heartbeat. Edwards had slipped one of the maids' cloaks, a makeshift pillow, under his head. Raven's lashes were resting against the parchment gray of his skin; she had never before realized how long and thick they were. His hollowed cheeks were stubbled with a heavy beard and his lips were cracked and slightly parted.

"Raven," she whispered, touching his temple with her hand.

His lashes flickered, as if responding to her voice with the greatest effort, and then finally his lids lifted, revealing the heartbreakingly beautiful blue eyes trying to focus on her face.

"Catherine?" he breathed, and as she watched, the lids again begin to drift downward.

"What's happened, my darling?" she whispered. Glancing up, she found Edwards's eyes reflecting the same anxiety she felt.

"I tried so hard to reach you," Raven whispered, his voice faltering. She had to lean close to hear him. "I can't..."

His lids fell, hiding the unfocused paleness of his eyes.

"No," Catherine said. Her hands framed his face, turning his head. She could feel the thrust of cheekbone, too prominent beneath the gray-tinged skin. "No, damn it.

Don't you dare die on me, John Raven. Don't you dare,''
she ordered in terror.

The lids lifted again, and this time there was something
behind the dazed irises that he eventually succeeded in focusing on her features. Something that she recognized, with
shocked relief, as amusement. He met her eyes. His lips began to move upward into the curve that passed for Raven's
version of a smile.

"Not dying," he said, his voice slightly stronger than before. "I didn't come all this way to die. I promise you that,
Catherine." His voice faded again, and the heavy lids
dropped to cover the blue. But she believed him. Her
shoulders heaved once, and then she gathered her courage,
wiping at her tears with fingers that still trembled slightly.

"Get a doctor," she ordered.

"I've already taken the liberty of dispatching one of the
footmen for him, Mrs. Raven," Edwards assured her.

She looked up to find a circle of faces surrounding them,
the servants in various stages of dress and undress.

"We have to get him upstairs," she said, trying to think.

"May I suggest, madam, it might not be wise to move Mr.
Raven until we know the extent of his injuries," the butler
said.

"Of course," Catherine agreed, realizing the logic of that.
"Thank you, Edwards."

"You are very welcome, madam," the butler said. "And
if I might also suggest . . ."

"What is it?" Catherine asked, glancing up.

"With your permission, I should like to send the staff
about their business. It really would be best, Mrs. Raven."

"Yes, of course," Catherine agreed, knowing that there
would already be a wealth of gossip from tonight.

She turned her attention again to Raven's crumpled body,
barely hearing Edwards's efficient marshaling of his staff
back to their quarters or on various duties to prepare for the
master's care. For the first time she began to take in the details of Raven's appearance. He was wearing trousers and
boots. His own, she decided, although considering the
gathering darkness and their begrimed and tattered condi-

tion, she couldn't be completely sure. But at least they fit. As the filthy garment that partially covered his broad chest and massive shoulders did not. It gaped in several places, revealing many shadowed bruises and abrasions on his upper body.

Again fighting tears, Catherine looked up into the eyes of Jem, who had come to kneel on the opposite side of her husband's sprawled body.

"It's his hands that's hurt the most. I tried to take his hand to help him up, but he cried out." Dark with concern, the groom's eyes looked into hers. "What do you suppose he's done to them?" he asked, trying to imagine, as was Catherine, what sort of injury could make a man like John Raven cry out.

"I don't know. But the doctor will be here soon. He'll see to everything. Raven promised me he wouldn't die," Catherine whispered, her voice breaking slightly. And then, forced by an incredible act of will, she finished the thought she'd been holding on to. "And he always keeps his promises."

It seemed that the doctor's examination took an eternity. He had finally given permission for Raven to be carried upstairs, and then he disappeared into the master bedroom for another eternity.

Catherine paced the hall outside the closed door, fighting for control. Finally the door opened and Dr. Stevenson emerged.

"A dreadful business," he said, shaking his head. "Dreadful to think something like this could happen in England. I don't know what this country is coming to. Damned ruffians. I swear it's not safe to go out of doors anymore without an armed escort. And that's exactly what I told Mr. Raven."

"How is he?" Catherine asked, less concerned about what had happened than about the consequences for Raven's well-being.

"Nothing that a few days of rest and good nursing won't cure," he said.

Catherine closed her eyes in a brief prayer of thanksgiving.

"I've left laudanum. He'll not sleep with those hands. They're by far the worst. But even so, I believe there'll be no permanent impairment. Damned lucky at that. I beg your pardon, my dear, but it's the most bizarre tale I've ever heard. And Catherine..." He paused as he began to make his way down the curving grand staircase.

"Yes?" she said, turning back from the door it seemed she had finally been given permission to open.

"See that he takes the laudanum. Despite his denials, he's in a great deal of pain. Never seen anything like it. Self-inflicted. Says something about the determination of the man, although I'm not sure exactly what."

The doctor's voice faded with his descent. Catherine took a deep breath and, without knocking, opened the door to the bedroom.

Chapter Fifteen

The light was very low, and it took a few seconds for her eyes to adjust. Gradually she was able to make out Raven's form. His face was turned toward the door, the long lashes fanned over the shadows that surrounded his eyes like bruises. She could smell the pleasant aroma of the soap he always used. Someone—Edwards or his valet—had used that same soap tonight to bathe and shave him. She stood a moment looking at him, savoring the fact that she was finally able to do so, despite his obviously battered condition. At last, unable to resist the urge to reassure herself that he was truly all right, she brushed her fingers against the midnight blackness that swept back from his forehead.

"John," she whispered, willing him to respond to that entreaty. She needed to hear him speak to her, and then she'd be able to believe Stevenson's assurances.

His lashes rested against his cheeks, unmoving, but his mouth began to curve. "If you've taken to calling me John, I must be in worse shape than your sawbones admitted," he said.

She felt her own lips tremble upward in relief. If her husband could tease her, he must, as the doctor had tried to assure her, not be seriously injured.

"Raven," she amended, and was rewarded by the slow opening of his eyes. The starred sapphire gleam seemed unchanged.

"That's better," Raven said. "But you're crying. I thought you despised women who weep."

"And I thought you liked to comfort them."

"You have me at a disadvantage. I can't even hold you."

"It's all right," she whispered, stroking the dark hair.

"Give me a few days."

"As many as you like."

"What I'd like..." he began, and then he deliberately banished that thought, realizing the impossibility of doing what he'd *like*, what he'd dreamed about for months, given the state of his hands. "Damn," he said softly, closing his eyes again.

"Shall I get the laudanum? Dr. Stevenson said that you'd—"

"I don't need Stevenson's drugs. I need you. I've needed you so long."

"And I'm here," she said. "So there's nothing—"

His eyes opened again, the self-mockery clearly revealed in their depths. "I want you here, Catherine. Make no mistake. But that's not *exactly* what I meant."

"Oh," she said, suddenly understanding. Color flamed into her cheeks, but she leaned down to put her lips against his forehead. "Do you want to..." She hesitated, having no idea what to suggest in response to that unexpected confession. Her thinking had not yet made the adjustment from fear that Raven was dying to a remembrance of the passion that had flared between them. As his obviously had.

"Bloody bastards," he said softly. He shifted his body carefully, easing toward the center of the bed. She heard the small intake of breath occasioned by that movement. "Sit down," he ordered. "If I can't hold you, at least I can look at you."

She sat on the very edge of the bed, moving as carefully as he had, unwilling to add to his discomfort. He raised his hand to touch her neck, the thick bandaging making the usually graceful strength misshapen, alien. In unthinking response, she touched the thick linen strips that had been wound professionally around his palm and over the back of his hand. Only the tips of his fingers emerged from their cocooning protection. Putting her fingers carefully under the bare tips of his, she brought them gently to her mouth, placing a small kiss on each. Still supporting his hand, with pressure only against the fingertips, she glanced up to smile at him.

"As long as you're safe," she said, "the rest can wait."

"I *have* waited. Too bloody long," he said. "Thinking. Imagining. The whole time I was in that hole, I was thinking about you. And about how long I'd waited, wanting you. About what a fool I'd been to walk out that morning. I should have stayed here to look after you until you were well. And then I should have made love to you. Really, finally, made you mine. Instead—" He stopped abruptly and removed his hand.

"And instead you went to build a railroad," she accused, but she let him see her smile. "Business," she finished, shaking her head, "always business."

"I'm sorry," he said.

"And while you were away, you realized that business wasn't as important to you as I was?"

"You've always been more important—"

She laughed suddenly, too glad to have him back to even pretend to be angry. "I never believed I'd play second fiddle to a coal mine. Or to a locomotive. I really don't know why I'm willing to put up with it."

"Because you know how much I love you. Or at least I hope you do," he suggested softly.

"And how should I know that? Because you've kissed me? Twice in the six months we've been married?"

"But you have to admit, they both were very satisfactory kisses. Confess, Catherine."

"Very satisfactory. When do you suppose we might try for a third?" she whispered. Her hand had again found the sweep of dark hair, damp from the ablutions his servants had arranged, in order to return their master to a state more in keeping with his wealth.

"There's nothing wrong with my mouth," Raven said, his eyes locked with hers. "It's only my hands. I can't hold you, my darling, but if you want a kiss..." he suggested, his lips curving upward again.

As she had downstairs, she allowed her palms to frame his face. Too thin, she thought again, wondering what had happened to return Raven to her in this condition. She was too glad he was here to bother him with questions. They could come later. Now was the time to simply relish that he was once more with her, teasing her. Demanding, both emotionally and physically.

She lowered her head until her mouth met his. As if the intervening days had never interrupted what had happened between them, when her tongue met the hot caress of his the reaction was as strong as it had been before. Her lips cherished his, trying to tell him all the fears of the last weeks, the joy at having him here again. She deepened the kiss, hungry for whatever fulfillment they could find in clinging mouths and melding tongues. She wanted so much more now, as she knew he did. She wanted his lips on her body, commanding, teaching, urging her response. His hands caressing, the sensations building inside her. And instead, she remembered the bandages. Raven, she thought bitterly, what have they done to you?

"Bloody bastards," she said, softly echoing his invective when the kiss ended. She raised her head to find the blue gaze shimmering with emotion. She knew his frustration was as great as her own. And there was no need to tempt him with what couldn't be accomplished tonight. She had seen the marks on his ribs and stomach—livid bruises and scrapes. She didn't want to cause him any more pain. And she wasn't a child. She could wait.

"Not very ladylike, my lady," he said.

"Jem called me that tonight."

"*My* lady," Raven whispered. "And you always will be."

"Very confident, Mr. Raven. I'll have you know my father offered to arrange a divorce should I desire a husband less prone to extended journeys. He seemed to feel I'd been deserted."

Raven had pushed the thought of her father to the back of his mind. He hadn't wanted to deal with that. He didn't want to imagine what the knowledge that it had been Catherine's father who had arranged for his "journey" would do to their relationship.

"And what did you tell him?" he asked finally.

"That we had a contract. And you never break a contract."

He laughed softly, the sound tinged with bitterness. "You must be the only person in London who believes that."

"I don't understand."

"I missed the meeting. With the partners. They're not likely to forgive me."

"It's all right. My father took care of it."

The laughter faded from the blue eyes, and he was very still. Suddenly the inclusion of her father into Raven's project didn't seem the painless solution she'd thought. Catherine had believed that appealing to her father, groveling before him to beg his help, had been the most difficult thing she'd ever done. But faced now with the question in her husband's eyes, she wasn't sure that was true. Including her father into Raven's investment no longer seemed so minor nor so wise, now that her husband was back.

Her gaze moved to the small white scar that marred his cheekbone and rested there uncomfortably while she tried to think. She didn't know why this had become so difficult. She had done what she had to do to prevent Raven's losing an incredible amount of money, losing everything. And after all, her father was simply another investor. Why should Raven care whose money saved his railway? Again the image of the crop descending on his dark face intruded.

"Why?" Raven asked, almost to himself, remembering the fate the old man had arranged. Why had the duke gone in on the investment? Because Catherine had asked him? Raven knew Montfort would have had less altruistic reasons for that action.

"The other investors were reassured by my father coming in," Catherine said. "That's the only way..." She paused, hating to tell him that they had lost faith in Raven himself. She glanced up to find the blue eyes resting on her face, their color shading to ice. He didn't attempt to touch her now. His bandaged hands rested quietly against the sheet that concealed the bruised ribs. A coldness was beginning to grow in her stomach to match the coldness in his face. So she forced herself to finish it. "They would stay, hold to their financial commitments in the project, only if he agreed to join the partnership."

"And he guaranteed the investment? Out of the goodness of his heart, I suppose?"

She flinched mentally from the ice in his tone. "Of course. He *is* my father, your father-in-law. And it was the only way. They were demanding to be repaid, and Reynolds said there weren't enough assets to manage that. The project would have collapsed."

"And so your father intervened?"

"Yes," she said. Why did she suddenly feel guilty? Raven should be thanking them. They had between them saved the rail system, and he should be grateful. But she knew he wasn't.

"Because he believed so strongly in the railway?"

"Because he's my father. And I asked him."

"I see," Raven said softly.

"There was no other way," she argued.

"How do you know that?"

"They were demanding their money."

"They know my reputation. They were involved in the first place because they want to make money. And they believed that I would. That the railway would."

"You weren't here," she said, suddenly angry at his continued condemnation. She had thought that what she had done had been clever. Mr. Reynolds had been pleased at the duke's intervention. Grateful. Catherine had thought that Raven would be proud of her, and instead he seemed bitter that her father had agreed to help.

"Not because I chose *not* to be here. And in light of what's taken place in my absence, I'm beginning to understand..." Raven paused, thinking that now it all made sense. The old man had arranged not only his death, but to take over a venture that anyone as astute as the duke would surely realize would eventually be highly profitable. That sly old bastard. *Catherine's father,* Raven reminded himself, wondering if the old man's scheming had left any hope for this marriage.

"What?" she asked, when he didn't finish the thought.

His eyes held hers for a long moment, wondering if he should tell her what he suspected about Montfort's motives and his role in his disappearance. But finally Raven simply shook his head. "It doesn't matter," he said, his expression closed.

Catherine recognized that something was very wrong, but she didn't understand why he was so furious. All she knew was that the closeness that had been growing between them was broken. Raven had become again the controlled stranger she had married.

"It matters to me," she said angrily. There should be nothing between them but joy that he'd returned from whatever ordeal he'd undergone, and instead there was this cold bitterness. "You promised that I might ask you anything and you'd tell me the truth. We have a *contract* to that effect. So I want to know, Raven. What do you think you understand? Just what are you suggesting has taken place in your absence?"

Raven said nothing for so long she began to believe he intended to break that particular vow, but finally the blue eyes met hers. "I'm wondering exactly what role your father played in my abduction," he said quietly.

The shock of what he'd said held her speechless a moment. "My father?" she repeated finally, incredulous at what he seemed to be suggesting. "What the hell does that mean?"

"It means that he would have gotten his way."

"His way about what? What are you talking about? Damn you, John Raven, you tell me just what you're accusing my father of."

"Of attempting to rid himself of a highly inconvenient son-in-law, whom he believed was a stain on his family's honor. Of getting back into his daughter's good graces. And even of taking control of a venture that's bound to make him a great deal of money. All in one fell swoop. Very neatly done, Catherine. You have to admire his boldness. Only I'm afraid I put a spoke in the cogs of that particular machination. I wasn't supposed to return. I was supposed to die in that bloody shaft, a singularly unpleasant death. Starvation or drowning, depending on the duration of the next rain. I promise you he'll be extremely annoyed that I've shown up here tonight.''

''Are you suggesting that my *father* tried to kill you? In order to take over the railway? My God, you must be insane.''

''Complications from a head injury?'' he mocked. ''No, Catherine. It all fits.''

''It's ridiculous! And you must know that. My father would never do something like that.''

''Pardon me if I doubt the duke's goodwill. But I have no reason to believe that, as he openly told me, he wouldn't like to see me in hell. He made his feelings about both my stench and my unsuitability to be his daughter's husband very clear that day.''

''He was angry. Enraged. But for you to suggest... How can you possibly believe that? He's my *father*,'' she argued, desperate to make him realize how ridiculous that suggestion was.

''And he again has you eating out of his hand. Well-tamed to that bit, Lady Montfort. As you always were.''

''I don't intend to listen to you blacken my father's character any further. You should be very grateful to him for saving your project, and instead—''

''Pardon me for not kissing his feet. Perhaps when I've recovered from what his hirelings did I'll be able to react more calmly, but for now, my dear, if you'll forgive me—''

''No, I certainly won't forgive you. This entire conversation is unforgivable. But I'll be glad to leave you alone so you can think about how stupid this is. My father hasn't tried to hurt you, Raven. I'll see you again when you come to apologize for that suggestion, and not before.''

She had risen sometime in the midst of their argument and it didn't take her long to cross the expanse between the bed and the open door to her room, which she slammed angrily behind her.

By the time she had changed into her nightgown, she knew she had reacted childishly. With anger instead of logic and calmness. He had no reason to trust her father's goodwill. She herself had told Raven that the duke had tried to arrange for their divorce while he was missing, suffering deprivations and injuries, the extent of which he had not yet shared with her. And it would be natural for Raven to doubt the duke's motives, given the events of their one meeting. Instead of trying to convince her husband rationally that what he had suggested could not possibly be true, she'd railed at him and demanded apologies. She had acted like a shrew and not at all like a loving wife.

"You're right," Raven said softly.

She looked up in surprise, as if her regret had somehow conjured him up. He was standing in the connecting doorway between their rooms, wearing only a pair of cotton drawers, which made his masculinity far more obvious than even the tight pantaloons had done. The bandaged hands hung loosely, slightly curved, at his sides. He was clearly waiting for her response, but instead of managing to formulate any answer, she found her eyes irresistibly drawn to the front of his body.

"I couldn't manage my trousers," he said, his tone revealing a trace of amusement at her fascination with his near nudity. "I promise you I tried. And I'm sorry."

She glanced up to find his eyes no longer rimmed with ice. "Sorry for not putting on your trousers?" she asked, the teasing light in her eyes matching the returning warmth in his.

"And for accusing your father of trying to murder me."

Raven was sorry he had told her that. Whatever he knew about the duke's plotting, it wasn't fair to expect Catherine to accept those ideas about her own father. And Raven had no proof to offer her. Nothing tangible.

"He didn't. He wouldn't do that. And I think he has even begun to accept the idea of having you as a son-in-law. He told Dr. Stevenson we'd made a love match."

"Do you think he could possibly be right?" Raven asked.

"Yes," she whispered.

"We didn't act very much like it tonight."

"I know. I was just about to come and tell you I'm sorry."

"Were you, Catherine? I'm glad."

"And I'm glad you're home. And safe. But you haven't told me what happened," she said. "While you were gone."

Raven shifted his weight to lean against the frame of the door. He glanced down at his hands, unconsciously lifting them, holding them up as if examining damage he could no longer see.

"I told you I was used to taking care of myself. Apparently I wasn't as apt at that as I believed."

"Not indestructible," she suggested.

He looked up, letting his hands drop. "Not entirely."

"I'd really like to hear the story, if it's not too painful."

"It's not the story that's painful," he confessed, smiling.

"What did they do to your hands?" she asked, although she found she preferred not to know. Eventually she would have to be told what had happened during those weeks he was missing, and the injuries to his hands were sure to be a major part of the story.

"To my hands?" he said, sounding surprised. "*They* did nothing. Beyond tying them."

"But... then why... I don't understand."

Raven looked down again, his hands making that almost involuntary turn, palms up, as he remembered what he himself had done to them. The only way to get home. And now, instead of what he'd envisioned... He took a breath, but still he didn't explain.

"Raven?" she said.

He didn't respond in any way.

"Are you all right?" she asked, worrying again.

"Of course," he said, his head still lowered.

She waited, as unmoving as he was.

"Except..." She watched him take another deep inhalation. "Except tired. And still a little..."

"A little?" she prodded carefully, watching him.

"Could we continue this conversation next door, Catherine?"

"In your room?"

"You're perfectly safe," Raven said, looking up suddenly, the laughter back in the blue eyes, despite their tiredness. Despite the dark shadows and sunken cheeks she'd almost forgotten when faced with the obvious strength of his body.

"I doubt it," she said, but she rose and walked past him toward the bed he'd left to make the apology she'd demanded.

Moving with more assurance than she felt, Catherine threw back the counterpane and straightened the bed until it lay smooth and inviting. She plumped the pillows hard, a very small cloud of feathers flying out to surround her. When she had completed the task she had never before performed in her life, she turned back to find him standing in the open doorway watching her.

Neither of them moved for what seemed an eternity as the feathers drifted slowly back down to settle on the bed. She blew one away from her nose, and the corners of Raven's mouth began to tilt. She knew he was trying to control his amusement at her attempted housekeeping, and that he was about to lose the battle. She sent him a rueful smile.

"Come on, Mr. Raven," she invited, patting the mattress. She lifted the edge of her gown and climbed up onto the high bed. She sat on one side, her legs crossed like a red Indian at his campfire, leaving more than half of the wide expanse for Raven to stretch out on. "Come to bed."

"You don't know how long I've waited to hear you say that," he said softly. He began to walk, more slowly than she had ever seen him move. A trifle unsteadily, he maneuvered his body onto the edge. Using his elbows, he levered his big frame entirely onto the bed and lay back, his wide shoulders propped against the pillows she'd stacked against the headboard.

For some reason she was very disconcerted by the look those sapphire eyes were now directing at her, their color darkened and intensified by the dimness.

"Come here," he suggested.

"I don't want to hurt you."

"You're not going to hurt me, Catherine. Come here."

Raven stretched his right arm along the top of the pillows, creating a space for her body to fit next to the powerful solidness of his. It took her less than a second to respond to that repeated invitation. She doubted the scramble with which she transversed the small distance between them was graceful, but she really didn't care. And from the strength with which Raven's arm enclosed her, neither did he.

He pulled her to him, the muscles of his chest hard against the unconfined softness of her breasts. His mouth roamed over the loosened auburn tendrils at her temple and then across her forehead. Her fingers pressed into his warm, golden skin, moving languidly across the breadth of his shoulder and upper arm. Finally she was again where she wanted to be.

"I missed you," he whispered softly, lips against her brow.

"I missed you, too. And Raven?"

"Hmm?"

"I worried about you."

"Did you?"

"I know you think that's ridiculous."

"Maybe not. There were a few hours I spent worrying, too. I'd thought I wasn't ever going to be allowed to do this."

"This?" she asked, brushing a light kiss over his lips.

"Hold you. Make love to you. Make love to my wife."

"Don't think about that. You don't have to tell me what happened. Not if you don't want to."

"Nothing happened that's to my credit. I allowed myself to be taken captive, tied up and left to die. Not a very attractive list of accomplishments."

She heard the derision in his voice. "And you don't know who did it?"

"They tried to stop the coach, but I had ordered the coachman not to slow down for anything." Raven didn't tell her about the attempt on his life in the park, which had prompted that precaution. "I used the pistol I always carry, but there were too many of them. They shot Tom, and then the carriage went over the edge of the road and onto the rocks below."

The quiet voice paused, and his lips again touched her hair. She lifted her hand to his cheek, but she didn't try to look up to read whatever was in his face. To see if it matched what she could hear in the deep voice. Her face rested still against the bare skin of his chest, listening to the steady rhythm of his heartbeat. She knew he'd finish the story in his own time. He would face the memories, the bitterness of being taken. The humiliation of whatever they'd done to him. Raven wasn't a coward, and so she knew he'd tell her. Eventually.

"I didn't think then to wonder why they didn't shoot me, too." Again he paused. Her fingers, finding the fall of dark hair, were gently combing through its silken softness. It was dry now and curling against his shoulders. "I suppose I was too disoriented by the accident. They had tied me up before I regained consciousness, and then they took me to the shaft." He drew in a breath, but his quiet voice continued, his calm tone never varying. "They seemed to think it was poetic justice."

"Why?" she whispered.

"Someone had led them to believe I was putting miners out of their jobs by employing machinery in my mines. The same logic the Luddites used to stir up their riots."

"You take care of your workers. That's so unfair."

"I don't think they were concerned about fairness."

"Maybe they really believed that. At least it offers an alternative..." She couldn't bring herself to repeat the accusation he'd made against her father.

Raven didn't have the heart to deny her that possibility, especially not with the warmth of her small body pressed closely along the length of his for the first time. They would deal with all the painful realities later. Not tonight. He didn't want to think of anything tonight but holding Catherine.

"How did you get away?"

"They'd left me tied, hand and foot, at the bottom of that hole. I realized I had to first get my hands untied."

She waited again, her fingers caressing, as he paused, letting him tell it without prodding him with questions.

"There didn't seem to be anything to use against the ropes. There was nothing down there except the walls and floor—no discarded tools. Nothing. I'd probably inched my way around the shaft a dozen times before I found it—a narrow little outcropping, a couple of feet off the floor, the stone rough edged. I began to rub the rope against it, trying to abrade it enough that I could break it."

"And you did."

"Eventually," he agreed. There was another long silence before he added softly, "They make damn fine rope in this country, Catherine."

"That's how you hurt your hands?"

"I thought the bonds were shrinking because they were so wet with blood, but my hands were swelling and finally I lost feeling in them. I suppose that was good. At that point. But it made the climbing a nightmare."

"You *climbed* out of the mine?"

"It was only a shaft. A test hole. It was like climbing up a chimney—feet and elbows, like the sweeps. It was wider, of course, and if I weren't as tall as I am, I'd never have done it. And they'd left me my boots. I guess they thought it wouldn't matter. They never expected me to walk anywhere."

"They *knew* you were alive? When they left you there?" she asked, horror coloring her voice.

"I'm sorry. I should never have told you this. We should concentrate on the here and now. A very pleasant here and now that I was afraid might never happen."

"I want to know. I *need* to know. And Raven, I'm not a child. Did they leave you there, knowing you were alive?"

"They tied me up, Catherine. You don't worry about dead men walking out of the grave you've dug for them."

She shivered suddenly at the fate they'd intended for him. She found it hard to believe that anyone could treat another person with such inhumanity. But then, as Raven had told her, she had been very protected from the realities of human misery the world contained.

His arm tightened comfortingly around her shoulders.

"It's all right," he said softly. "It's over."

"Once you were out, how did you get home?"

She felt his laugh lift the solid muscles of his chest.

"I'd thought that would be the easy part. After I'd finished the climb. After I reached the outside. But I had no idea where I was. The hole they'd lowered me into was part of a site that had long been abandoned. There were no cottages nearby. I hadn't eaten in days. At that point, I had no way of knowing how many days. My only thought was to get back here as quickly as I could. But even when I eventually stumbled on a village that offered some semblance of civilization, no one wanted to help. And considering the way I looked, I guess I understand their reluctance. I tried to convince them that if they'd arrange for my transportation to London, they'd be amply rewarded. You can imagine their reaction.

"So I ran. And then walked. As long as I could. I stole food and someone's shirt. Eventually a carter took me up. By then I was afraid all the effort was going to be wasted because I was going to die by the road. I still don't know why he stopped. But he saved my life. He gave me water and something to eat, and then he brought me to the outskirts of the city."

"We'll have to find him," she said, thinking how grateful she was. Human kindness given without hope of reward. It had returned Raven to her, and despite the horror of what his attackers had planned for him, he was safe and holding her.

"I don't know his name or anything about him. But you're right. We'll find him."

They said nothing for a long time. By now the great house was totally silent, even the excitement over the master's return and the doctor's visit fading as the tired servants sought their own beds and well-deserved rest. Catherine could hear the tall hall clock and Raven's heartbeat and nothing else in the peaceful stillness of the London night.

Eventually she felt her husband's breathing even into a regular rhythm and she knew he was asleep. She thought briefly about returning to her own room in order to allow him to rest undisturbed, but the arm that enclosed her was strangely compelling, even loosened and relaxed in sleep. She closed her eyes and lay in the darkness, and before she slept, she thankfully acknowledged the divine intervention she'd so fervently prayed for in the days he'd been gone for sending Raven back to her.

Chapter Sixteen

When Catherine awoke the next day, she was alone. She closed her eyes again, savoring the fragrance of Raven's body, his scent caught in the sheets of the bed they had shared, surrounding her as his arms had enclosed her last night. She wondered briefly where he was, and then acknowledged with amused resignation that he was probably in that small office downstairs, again overseeing the business empire she had guarded until his return. She and her father. Remembering the duke's kindness, she wondered how her husband could possibly believe—

"Mr. Raven thought you might like breakfast in bed, madam."

Catherine opened her eyes to find Edwards holding a tray on which a teapot and cup reposed along with a covered silver dish. Raven was again issuing orders to the staff.

"Thank you, Edwards, but just the tea, I think. I'll have luncheon downstairs with Mr. Raven."

"I believe Mr. Raven's in his office. And he's eaten. Shall I tell him you wish to see him?"

"No," Catherine said, still smiling. "Don't bother him."

She needed to let her father know about Raven's return. She remembered again Raven's bitterness last night and his accusation. The duke needed some warning that the emotion John Raven entertained about his investment wasn't gratitude.

"Thank you, Edwards," she said aloud. "If you would, return in half an hour, please. I'll have a letter to be delivered to my father."

"I'd be delighted, Mrs. Raven."

When the door closed behind the butler, Catherine rose and, putting on her wrapper, sat down at her secretary to compose the difficult letter she knew she must write.

The afternoon seemed endless to Catherine as she waited for Raven to rejoin her. The door to his office remained securely closed. She knew that because she made several otherwise unnecessary trips downstairs to check. She'd see him at dinner, she assured herself more than once when he didn't reappear. Raven would surely join her at dinner. Her thoughts went back to the early months of her marriage, those private moments at the huge table and the daylong anticipation of being with Raven the only comforts that had sustained her then—as they must now.

The hours crept by, but she forced herself to work her way through the pile of invitations that had accumulated, unopened and unanswered, during Raven's absence. Her hands trembled suddenly if she allowed any of the images to form in her head—Raven standing in the doorway last night, or his mouth against her breast on the morning he'd left. Her body reacted to that last memory, the sweet, hot ache of desire tormenting her.

She entered the dining room that night with that same fluttering anticipation. It had taken her an hour to decide on the gold satin gown, which seemed to create answering highlights in the upswept auburn hair and to give a glow like candlelight to the clarity of her skin. The mirror in her bedroom had been complimentary, and she entered the room with the same provocative smile she had practiced before its reassuring reflection.

She allowed Edwards to seat her, never questioning that Raven would join her. He always informed her when he was going to be absent from the dinner table, and today she'd received no such message. It was probably taking longer than he'd anticipated to dress, given his injuries. It was not until the first course was served that she realized something was wrong. She turned to Edwards, standing silently behind her chair.

"Mr. Raven—" she began, only to be interrupted.

"Mr. Raven has dined, madam," the butler said simply, but there was something—some unexpressed thought—behind the impenetrable calmness.

"He's already dined?" she repeated, all the pleasant expectancy collapsing. "Here?" she asked.

"In the kitchen," Edwards affirmed. For some reason, a dark flush was beginning to stain his cheeks.

The answer she sought should not come from her majordomo, Catherine realized in embarrassment. Whatever had compelled Raven to desert his own table would be better explained by the man himself. Not waiting for Edwards's help, she pushed back the heavy chair in which she was sitting and rose, leaving her napkin and the untouched food. She didn't notice the small smile Edwards allowed before he directed removal of the first course.

Catherine walked purposefully to the room where her husband had been sequestered most of the day. The office was as dark as the morning she'd made this same journey, clad only in her night rail, to find Raven in the chair behind the desk. The master suite that connected to hers was also empty, the counterpane stretched smoothly over the huge bed. There had been no preparations for occupation of this chamber tonight. Which meant, of course...

Without allowing herself to think about the possibility that Raven might not welcome her intrusion, she retraced her steps down the upstairs hallway to the door of the small chamber in which, until last night, he had slept since before their marriage. She listened briefly at the door and then, knocking softly, she entered without waiting for permission.

The two men occupying the room looked up in surprise. The valet had just removed his master's waistcoat. He stood behind Raven, frozen by the shock of her unexpected entrance.

"Thank you, Browning. That will be all," she said, holding her husband's eyes, daring him to countermand her dismissal.

The valet looked quickly to his employer, and never glancing at him, Raven nodded, his gaze unmoving from Catherine's face.

She was made aware that the valet had left by the click of the latch. They were alone, but still the silence stretched.

"Did you come to ask me something, Catherine?" Raven inquired. She had come here the night before she was thrown. Before their agreement to rethink the contract they had made for this most inconvenient marriage of convenience. Before he'd left on the journey from which he'd almost not returned.

"No," she said. "I didn't come to ask you anything."

"Then . . . ?" Raven allowed the question to trail off.

"I have been waiting to be with you all day. At dinner, if you couldn't break away from business before. And then at the table, Edwards said you'd eaten. I had so looked forward to having dinner with you, Raven." She broke off that confession, fighting childish tears of disappointment.

"I ate in the kitchen," he said.

"Why? Why didn't you tell me? I could have joined you."

"No," Raven said simply. The firm line of his lips tightened, but he didn't explain. His eyes fell, and his hands began a small upward movement, the palms turning. Suddenly the gesture was halted and the bandaged hands were allowed to slowly return to his side, but his eyes didn't lift to her face.

"I don't understand," she said, but she knew something was wrong.

"Someone had to help me," he admitted softly. He had hated the dependence. Hated every mouthful Edwards fed him, the butler's features carefully arranged in the mask of the perfect servant. But Raven would have hated even more to have Catherine watching. To see him helpless as a child.

Of course! Catherine thought. What a fool she had been not to have realized all the restrictions those damaged hands

would impose. But she should have been the one. It wasn't
fair that someone else had been allowed to help Raven.

"Who?" she asked, fighting jealousy. "Who helped
you?"

Raven's eyes came up at whatever was in her tone.

"Edwards, of course. I think he felt it was his province."
The small, controlled smile that was uniquely Raven's
touched the line of his lips.

"It was *my* province," she said bitterly. "*My* place, and
you denied me that right. And what about after dinner,
Raven?"

"Forgive me—" he began, but she cut him off.

"You're still avoiding me. And I can't imagine why.
Given what you said last night."

She paused, waiting for him to deny what she'd suggested. "Raven?" she said softly.

There was no response.

"What's wrong?" she asked. "It's not that you don't
want me here. You told me last night..."

He looked up at her hesitation, reading in her breathless
whisper the sudden fear that she might be wrong. That he
might have changed his mind.

"I want you," he said, his features still perfectly controlled, the stern line of his mouth now giving nothing away.

"Then why...?" she began. "Why are you here instead
of in the room we shared last night?"

"Last night," he echoed. He shook his head slightly.
"Forgive me, Catherine, but I don't believe..." She saw the
depth of the breath he took. "Last night I was exhausted,
and our sleeping together then was possible. But tonight..." Slowly his eyes met hers. "I don't think I can *sleep*
with you tonight, my darling."

"I don't understand," she said. What was different about
tonight? He had held her last night, curled into the solid
warmth of his body, held her as if he never wanted to let her
go.

Correctly interpreting her unhappiness, Raven knew he
would have to explain. Despite the painfulness of that confession, he would have to tell Catherine why he had come

here and not to the bedroom where last night he had finally been allowed to touch the woman who had haunted his dreams since the first day he had looked into her eyes.

"Because tonight I want far more than to hold you," he admitted softly. "And because that's not possible."

"Why?" Catherine asked, trying to comprehend.

Again a brief smile slanted the hard mouth, holding no trace of amusement. This time Raven deliberately lifted his damaged hands, held them out between them, palms up, as if they explained everything.

"Because of these," he said, looking down on the bandages, fighting the bitterness and frustration. Abruptly he turned and walked to the bed, its smoothness marred by the stacked pillows.

"You'll let Edwards help you. And your valet," she said to the expanse of broad shoulders, "but not me."

He turned at the pain she had just revealed, that had trembled in the strained confession. His eyes were full of regret at hurting her.

"I can help you," she argued, unable to prevent the entreaty that echoed clearly in her tone.

"Not with this. Not given our situation," he said.

"I don't understand. You could tell me what to do...."

He glanced up at that suggestion, his lips moving quickly in involuntary amusement.

He was laughing at her ignorance, Catherine thought. And against her will, the hot tears burned. She blinked to control them, but it was a battle she was destined to lose. She despised women who wept, but he could reduce her to tears with a smile.

"Catherine," he said gently, comfortingly.

"Tell me why!" she demanded, swallowing against the building lump. Despite what he had said, he didn't want her. *I don't need a mistress,* an echo in her heart taunted bitterly, but she knew now that there was no other woman. Raven didn't lie. He didn't lie! She closed her eyes tightly, fighting for control.

And felt his lips on her forehead, warm and sweet. "There's so much I want to show you. Things I've wanted to teach you since the beginning—'' He broke off that thought, but his mouth touched against her eyelid, caressing, even as he continued. "All those long months I watched you. And I wanted you. Meeting you in the hallway on your way out to dance with some other man. Or to ride. And I thought only about making love to you. Slowly. Touching you. Teaching you to *want* my touch. Wanting to show you all my hands could tell you about what I feel. And now…''

He rested his chin briefly against the top of her head. And then he stepped back, the spell he had woven deliberately broken.

"Raven?'' she whispered, the word as full of pain as his broken confession had been.

"I can't. Don't you understand? If we had been lovers… If I had taken you before… If you weren't—''

"If I weren't so inexperienced?'' she finished bitterly.

"I don't want to hurt you. You don't deserve a clumsy lover. I don't intend that for you. And so… we wait.''

"And if I don't want to wait?'' she challenged. She had to show him none of this mattered. He wanted her. All she had to do was convince him that what they both wanted was possible.

She closed the small distance he had created between them. He watched unmoving as her fingers lifted to the front of his shirt. She held his eyes, smoldering blue flames, as she began to unfasten the buttons. Finally she tugged the material out of his trousers to complete the task she'd undertaken.

She took a step backward to look at him. The soft cotton hung loosely from the massive shoulders. The ridged stomach and the deeply muscled chest were exposed by the opening she'd created, so totally masculine that something inside her shifted, aching with the realization of the difference between the hard strength of his dark body and the soft, pale weakness of hers.

Tentatively, she lifted her hand and, using one finger, touched the hollow at the base of the wide brown column of his throat. His skin was warm beneath the coolness of hers.

She smiled at him, but the careful alignment of his features didn't change. He was waiting. Watching her.

She let her finger slide downward, following the line of bone that divided the swell of muscle on either side, barely exposed by the opened shirt. Down to the concavity below his rib cage; down the channel that bisected his flat stomach. Gently into the small cave of his naval, her nail touching into the center and then downward again. Fascinated by the dark hair her fingers encountered at the top of the trousers that rode low on his hips. Having reached that barrier, she pulled her finger across the band that blocked its descent. To the right and then slowly back to the left.

His breath trembled suddenly, sighing through nostrils that were slightly distended. Encouraged by the evidence that what she had instinctively done had had some effect, Catherine slipped both hands into the gaping front of his shirt, moving them, palms flattened, to his sides. And then upward, skimming ribs and iron-hard bands of muscle, to the dark nubs of nipples that she could feel but couldn't see. She turned her hands, allowing her fingers to capture the hard peaks between them, and the breath Raven took then was a gasp, his body jerking under her fingers.

But he hadn't asked her to stop. And the shuddering breathing she could feel vibrating under the smooth, golden skin she was touching was exciting, revealing a power she hadn't realized she could have over this strong body. Her hands smoothed upward, finding the line of collarbone, following its rim outward to the knot of bone at the top of his shoulders. She opened her hands, lifting, thumbs up, until they caught the material of his shirt and peeled the edges open and then down, pushing it off his upper arms so that his chest and shoulders were exposed. Skin—golden velvet that she had touched once before—stretched over muscle and sinew, sleek and tawny like the hide of a great cat, warm and smooth under her fingers.

At his small, quick inhalation, she looked up into his face.

A tiny nerve jumped at the corner of his mouth, but his lids had fallen, hiding his eyes. Her palms skimmed down the outside of his arms, thumbs pausing to caress the sensitive skin inside his elbows, but his shirt was in her way. She unbuttoned one cuff and eased the sleeve over the bandaged hand. And then the other, allowing the lawn garment to fall, discarded, to the floor.

"Catherine," he whispered, a plea.

"Do you want me to stop?" she asked, not really worried any longer that he might deny her. Might deny them both.

"No," he said hoarsely, surrendering. "Don't stop."

Smiling, she bent her head, and as he had the day he had introduced her to passion, she touched her lips to the small nipple rimmed with brown against the surrounding bronze. Again his body jerked. Reacting. His hand came up to find the back of her head, cupping gently to strengthen the contact between them.

She nibbled, teeth delicately teasing, her tongue at the same time tasting the dark warmth. She suckled, pulling the hard nub, lifting even the brown ring that surrounded it into her mouth.

His hand found her shoulder, and he asked, his voice ragged with the unevenness of his breathing, "Do you have any idea what you're doing to me?"

She slowly lifted her mouth away from his chest. Looking down, she could see the moisture her tongue had left on his nipple glinting softly in the candlelight.

"Tell me," she commanded, using her thumb to wipe away the trace of dampness that was almost too intimate to contemplate. He flinched at the movement of her finger across the hardened nub.

"Damn bloody bastards," he whispered. He rested his forehead against the top of her head, his eyes still closed.

"Tell me what to do," she suggested.

He hesitated so long she thought he intended to deny them both the release they so desperately needed. Whatever happened between them, whatever awkwardness was inevitable, she knew they could wait no longer. They belonged to one another. And only the joining of bodies remained, necessary to complete the joining of spirits that had already taken place.

"Tell me," she urged. She turned her hand and slid her palm downward toward the barrier she'd hesitated to force before. This time she pushed her fingers between the slim, hard belly and the material of his trousers. She could again feel the coarseness of the dark hair under their sensitive tips, and then the unfamiliar contours of his body. Almost involuntarily, it seemed, he pressed into her touch, arching upward into her hand. Wanting her. She hoped that desire would be strong enough to overcome whatever reluctance he felt about making love to her.

Please want me enough, she prayed silently. Her fingers slipped farther downward, exploring, entreating.

"Catherine," he breathed against her hair.

"Tell me what to do," she whispered.

"They fasten at the sides. There's a flap. To close the front. Help me, Catherine," he begged softly.

"Of course," she said, her fingers quickly moving to unravel the mysteries of masculine attire. "Of course I'll help you, my beautiful Raven. You had only to ask."

When she had tugged the tight trousers down, kneeling to slip them off his feet, she found herself grateful that the valet had already undertaken the job of removing the Hessians. She glanced up to find the sapphire eyes considering her, watching her exactly as Aunt Agatha's tabbies regarded the sparrows they stalked, safely separated by the glass of the windows.

"And the rest," he suggested. She hesitated, realizing the incongruity of his near nudity compared to her fully dressed primness. She was afraid that if she allowed him to sense her reluctance, he'd again retreat behind the excuse of his hands.

Reaching up blindly, she stripped the knit undergarment down the slim hips and over the muscles of long thighs and calves. As he had with the trousers, he stepped out of it at her guidance, the tips of his fingers pressed into her shoulder for balance. She found herself nervously smoothing both garments across her lap with hands that shook. She was afraid to look up, and she was certain he must know what she was feeling.

"Catherine," Raven said softly, a command.

Steeling herself, she raised her eyes, slowly skimming upward from broad, bare feet, finely made, to ankles and shapely calves, and then to his knees, the right one slightly bent with his stance. Bravely her gaze moved to the deeply delineated muscles of his thigh and finally higher. Her heart rocketed into her stomach at the evidence of how much he wanted her. And then she forced her eyes away, upward to meet his. She expected amusement at her obvious fascination with his masculinity. She had known, of course, from a childhood spent on her father's country estate, what to expect, but until faced with the startling reality of Raven's body, she had not known how very little she understood. She should be frightened by his sheer size, she supposed. But this was Raven. And she could never be afraid of Raven.

She smiled at him, a small, trembling, upward slant of her lips. And suddenly it was all right. Nothing mattered but that she was with him, and she knew he'd care for her with the same protective tenderness he'd always shown. When his lips lifted in response to her smile, she felt none of the resentment his amusement had always caused. Not even when the teasing note in his question lightened the tension that had been between them.

"Do you think you might join me?" he suggested.

Wordless with the intensity of anticipation, she nodded. Awkwardly she rose from her knees, still holding his clothing.

"Drop them," he said, and at what was in his face, she obeyed, letting the garments fall to the bare wood of the floor.

She stood before him, fully dressed, holding her eyes on his by sheer force of will. Hers wanted to move downward, to touch again that compelling, essential difference between his body and hers. She began to struggle with the buttons and laces of her dress, as clumsy as if her hands were impeded by the bandages that wound his. Fingers trembling, she knew she was making a fool of herself. Too young. Too unfamiliar with this. And too obviously disconcerted by his blatant masculinity.

When she had finally managed the business of gown and slippers and petticoat and was clad only in the thin chemise, she looked up, trying to assess his patience with a process that had seemed to her both endless and endlessly embarrassing. Whatever she had expected Raven's expression to reveal, it was not the emotion that marked the harsh planes of his face. They were very still, but the skin had been stretched by his ordeal too tightly over the bones to hide what he was feeling. And what he was feeling, what was reflected in the shadowed eyes and the stern line of his mouth, was not impatience with her clumsiness or annoyance at her lack of experience. It was desire. Even in her innocence she was left with no doubt that he wanted her, that he found her body enticing and her hesitancy provocative rather than annoying.

"You are so beautiful," he said.

Well used to compliments on her truly remarkable beauty, accustomed to the adulation of the best-looking men of her exclusive circle since childhood, she found herself tongue-tied at the simple avowal. The poised and sophisticated society hostess, unable to formulate any reply, shook her head mutely.

"Take down your hair," he commanded, still watching her with those crystal eyes.

Her hands lifted to remove the pins that held the elaborate chignon. Unthinking, she saved the hairpins as she removed them, holding them in one palm until she had loosened the entire mass. Running the fingers of her other hand through the heavy strands, she let the perfumed cloud of rich red-brown fall over her shoulders, the vibrancy of its color a contrast to the maidenly whiteness of her chemise and the cream of her skin.

Raven said nothing in response to her obedience. He offered no other suggestion, so the stillness again echoed between them. Frightened, finally, that he had once more decided this was a mistake, she opened her hand and allowed the hairpins to cascade to the floor, a few of them landing on the small pile of masculine garments and some bouncing across the wooden boards.

She found the ribbon that laced the bodice of the chemise, and as she had before, she loosened it, quickly sliding her thumb under the narrow, crisscrossing satin. With the release of tension on the fabric that covered her breasts, she slipped the straps off her shoulders, guided the soft material to her waist and then, bending, pushed it down her hips. The garment puddled over small, arched feet. She resisted the urge to cross her arms over her breasts in that primitive gesture of femininity. Instead she bravely raised her head, finding his eyes still lowered, having followed the drop of the last of her clothing.

His eyes traveled upward, as slowly as hers had done. Up the smooth, slim length of leg his callused palms had once traced, exactly as his gaze was doing now. Over the width of very feminine hips and the slender shaft of her waist. To the high breasts, rose tipped and peaking in the cool air of the small, shadowed chamber. Touched and softened by the lamplight.

"So beautiful," he said again.

At that invitation, she took a step out of the pool of white at her feet. And then another. His arms opened, inviting. She moved against his body as if she had always belonged there, and when he enclosed her in his strength, she knew that she had. She wondered why she had been embarrassed before, why she'd hesitated in enjoying the incredibly sensuous sensation of her bare skin against the warmth of his. Every inch of that muscled body fitted hers, as if it had been made to meld into her smoothness.

Her hands found his shoulders and, as if reading her mind, he moved the hardness of his chest teasingly against the tips of her breasts. Some inarticulate sigh escaped with the rightness of that abrasive contact and with her pleasure in the contrast of his body to hers. While she was still savoring that, he bent his knees and then arched upward, so that the heavy masculinity that had so fascinated her made a tentative union with her body. She was the one who gasped at that, shocked by the feel of Raven's virility in such intimate proximity. But when he eased back, afraid he'd frightened her, her hips instinctively moved with him, to repeat and prolong the contact he'd briefly allowed.

"Yes," he said softly. "Very rare."

Ignoring the awkwardness of his hands, he lifted her, as easily as he had in Hyde Park, and deposited her on the bed. He stood a moment looking at her, blue eyes shadowed in the low lamplight.

Smiling now at what was in his face, she lifted her hand and ran the back of her knuckles along the length of his arousal. His eyes closed, and again that shuddering breath shook his body.

"Come to bed, Mr. Raven," she invited. And this time there was no doubt of what she intended.

And now, long after she'd whispered that suggestion into the darkness, Catherine Raven woke to the weight of her husband's leg resting over her thighs. Her body was pale cream against the golden ruddiness of his, Raven's massive frame, work hardened, a contrast to the slimness of hers. Yet they were one, no longer joined, perhaps, in sexual passion. They had slipped, unaware, into the relaxed intimacy of lovers, familiar and uninhibited.

Catherine's toes traced slowly the long, hair-roughened muscle of Raven's calf. Eyes still closed, she moved carefully, turning her body more snugly into the inviting warmth of his. She was aware of, and ignored, the slight soreness between her legs. The pain of Raven's entry had been negated by his determination to pleasure her exactly as he'd promised. And this small, telltale evidence of her lost virginity was not something to regret, but a memory to cherish. To hold to her heart as she had held Raven's body, its strength controlled and dominated by his desire for the enclosing frailness of hers.

She realized he was still asleep, the strong features vulnerable as she'd never before seen them. She resisted the urge to touch his lips, parted with the soft exhalations and inhalations of his breathing. She was afraid she'd wake him, and despite the fact that he had, being Raven, made no reference to the suffering he'd undergone during his abduction, she remembered that there had been injuries beyond the damaged hands.

Her fingers wanted to caress him, to feel again his responsive reaction to their touch, but they were forced to wait. She allowed them to move over her own breast, lightly tracing across the rose nipple, remembering the touch of his lips.

Denied the use of his hands, Raven had employed what tools his expertise allowed. His warm mouth drifting with sure experience over and then into all the small, provoking contours and silken crevices of her body. His tongue darting quickly to explore, to touch, to suggest. And then returning, hot and sensuously slow, stroking and building. Heating to flame the tinder that was her body.

She had known the first time he'd touched her that her responses to his lovemaking pleased him. And that they were apparently unusual in a woman uninitiated into these arts. Tonight he had again made obvious his delight in that so easily evoked responsiveness. She lifted her head to look down with remembered pleasure at the intimate position they shared.

Their bodies, still entwined, lying among the stained sheets of the high bed, were clearly marked with the evidence of their first joining. Suddenly embarrassed by that realization, Catherine began to move carefully out of Raven's embrace, only to feel the muscles of that confining leg tighten over hers, his knee squeezing downward, effectively holding her prisoner.

"What's wrong?" he asked, his lips lazily caressing her temple. "Are you trying to leave me already?"

She knew by the teasing tone of the question that he certainly didn't understand her sudden discomfort.

"I just thought I should..." Somehow she couldn't find the words to finish that embarrassing confession.

"You should what?"

His mouth moved, slightly opened, along her cheekbone and down the slender slope of her nose, finally stopping over hers. His tongue dipped inside and then retreated, to trace slowly around the outline of her lips. When she didn't answer his soft question, Raven propped himself on one elbow to look down into her face.

"What's wrong?" he asked, studying her features.

Her eyes fell, and she shook her head. Despite all they had shared as he'd made love to her, despite the fact that he had worshipped delicately but thoroughly at each of the shrines to Eros nature had erected in its design of her body, she was hesitant to confess that she wanted to get up to wash off the embarrassing evidence that she had given him her virginity.

"I told you that you could ask me anything," Raven reminded her, still smiling. "Or tell me. What's wrong?"

"I thought I should clean up," Catherine whispered, feeling the heat moving under the translucent skin of her cheeks.

"You're getting up to clean the room?" Raven asked, amused. He turned to survey the clothing scattered in shadowed mounds across the gleam of the polished wood.

"No," she admitted. Her eyes again found the dark smears, so obvious she wondered why he didn't understand.

There was a long silence. Finally, his gaze followed hers, his lips lifting in understanding. "Catherine?" he said softly.

She looked up, to find the planes of Raven's face highlighted by the lamplight, the hollows darkened with mystery. Only his eyes were readable, and in them she found the same enigmatic tenderness with which he had always regarded her innocence.

"To my grandmother's people the first blood is holy, as sacred as baptism. And the honor of cleaning your body should be mine."

He said nothing else, although she waited another eternity. She was fascinated by his concept of something she had felt could only be an embarrassment.

"The honor?" she repeated finally.

"The first act of caring for a wife," he said. "The promise of eternal protection."

She felt again the quick burn of tears at the images he'd drawn in the soft dimness of this English bedroom, so far removed from those who had devised that ritual.

"Your grandmother's *people?*" she whispered, suddenly wondering at the strange phrasing.

"They called themselves The People," he said, smiling down at her puzzlement. "My grandmother is Indian."

"Raven," she said, thinking aloud, finally understanding so much. "That's... Indian?"

"My father took her clan name. It was a matriarchal society. Since she and my grandfather were never married except by tribal ceremony, my father had no right to call himself MacLeod."

"And so you became John Raven."

"By choice," he explained softly. "The old man, my grandfather, wanted me to be John MacLeod. But like my father, I chose to retain the ties to the other part of my heritage. My mother's family were also Scots. They had come to America as indentured servants. My mother fell in love with my father too quickly to worry about his background. She thought, as you did, that Raven was simply his name. Until she met my grandmother."

Catherine could hear the love and humor in his tone. An often repeated and beloved family story, she imagined, the inevitable confrontation between two different ways of life.

"I never even thought to wonder," she said, touching again the bronze skin of his shoulder. That heritage explained so much. The dark, angular beauty of Raven's features. Even, perhaps, the way he wore his hair, deliberately clinging to his American ancestry in the face of the fashions of London society.

"And your eyes?" she asked, running her thumb across the black brow, arched like a raven's wing, above the piercing blue.

"My inheritance from the Scots side of my family tree."

Slowly the corners of her lips began to lift at the thought of His Grace, the Duke of Montfort, acknowledging an Indian half-breed as his son-in-law. "I don't think we should tell my father until *after* the grandsons have appeared. I'm not sure he's quite ready for that revelation.''

Raven didn't answer, knowing, as she could not, how far from acceptance Montfort's feelings for him were. Instead he lowered his mouth to nuzzle softly along the underside of her jaw and then over the slim column of her throat. His lips found, eventually, the small peak of her breast, and he began to tease gently until he caught the hardened bud between his strong, white teeth. He pulled, his eyes laughing into hers at the whimpering response that escaped her lips.

''Could you...'' she began, and then paused, unsure of how to ask. ''I mean could we... Would it be possible to...''

With a laugh, he released his captive. ''I believe that might be arranged. Given that my wife is again willing to help.''

''Of course,'' she said softly, feeling, despite the soreness, sweet anticipation at the thought of all the ways he had touched her last night, in spite of his inability to use his hands.

''And this time...'' Raven said, rolling onto his back.

Surprised, she lifted herself on her elbow to look into his face.

''This time,'' he whispered, cupping that bandaged hand on the back of her tangled hair, ''you do most of the work, my lady.''

She still didn't understand until he told her, in whispered phrases, what he intended. Because there was no barrier to his entry and because she had always enjoyed controlling her own affairs, the experience proved even more satisfying than before.

And when it was over, she lay limply against the massive body beneath her, feeling each breath he took, harsh and deep and then easing, slowing, until they both were still and still one.

''I love you, Catherine,'' he said, whispering the words into the darkness. But she heard them most clearly in the ear that lay on his broad chest.

''I love you, too, John Raven.'' She touched her tongue to the small dark bud of his nipple. ''Every inch of you.''

"Are you measuring me, Catherine?"

"No, but I told you I liked you big. And you laughed," she teased, remembering.

He laughed again, the intimate noise vibrating under her cheek.

"Always happy to oblige a lady." As he said the strange American expression, he arched his hips under hers ever so slightly, so that she realized what he was suggesting.

"Raven?" she whispered in wonder.

"We are taught endurance," he said softly, lifting once more. "And patience," he whispered, his body arching into hers, slowly advancing and then retreating. "But I've waited for you a long time, Catherine. A very long time through this most inconvenient of marriages. And tonight..." The movement of his hips was stronger now, thrusting upward, so that her nails tightened into the red-gold skin of his shoulders with the growing, sweetly shattering sensations moving through her body.

"I thought Indians were also taught silence," she suggested daringly, raising her upper body away from his. But she was smiling down into the gleam of starred sapphire eyes as she said it. And slowly she again began to move above him. Helping him, as he had taught her.

Chapter Seventeen

His grandmother's voice whispered from the darkness. He was again in the shaft, stretching far above him into the starred sky, matching its blackness. He could feel the rock's abrasion against the unyielding rope and the too-yielding flesh of his hands. To fight the pain, he filled his mind again with the images that had sustained him there, their promise overlain now with the perfection of fulfillment. With the remembrance of Catherine's body arching in trembling response beneath his, he fought his way out of the net of the dream.

Bothered by the clarity of the nightmare, Raven sat up in the wide expanse of the bed. The relaxed form of his wife lay beside him, still secure in the comfortable, protected world he had promised her. But underneath the quietness of the London night, Raven could sense something moving, dark and evil. Something that should not be in this place was here, in his home.

An Englishman feeling that same cold breath of dread against the back of his neck might have denied the premonition, given in to a practical man's disregard of any hint of the supernatural and put a pillow over his head to return to sleep. Or turned again to the welcoming embrace of the woman who slept beside him. John Raven was not far enough removed from a society in which heeding such warnings meant the difference between life and death. There was this time no snap of breaking twig, no whisper of undergrowth, no sudden silence of the night birds—nothing that he could point to as significant. But still the hair all over his body was rising in the age-old precursor of danger.

He glanced at Catherine's small form, and the line of his lips softened, but he did not allow himself to think of touching her to wakefulness. Spoken or unspoken, his vows had included the promise of protection, and that was what he must concentrate on now, rather than the panting sweetness of her responses.

He pushed off the sheet, slipping out of bed silently to stand naked on the oriental rug. On broad, bare feet he crossed the room to the small chest he had not opened since his arrival in England. The memories it held were too emotionally weakening for a man so far from all that he held dear, so far from home. But now this was his home—the small, hesitantly guiding fingers, the gasping reaction to his touch, the fragrance of Catherine's skin trembling under his....

He pulled his mind away from the seduction of those memories and with the tips of his fingers released the simple catch on the box. He knew he could manage none of his London clothes. He thought, however, that the softness of the buckskin tunic and breeches his grandmother had made for him so long ago would allow him to pull them on, despite his ruined hands.

He didn't let himself consider what he intended to do if the danger was as real as his prescience warned. He had fought Montfort's man in the garden without using his hands. Whatever the duke had planned this time Raven was more than willing to face. He was tired, however, of dealing with his father-in-law's henchmen. Despite what it would do to Catherine, he knew the day of their personal confrontation could not be put off much longer.

Slipping his arms into the sleeves, he allowed the tunic to fall over his head, fitting his body as smoothly as it had when the old woman had given it to him. It covered the massive shoulders without a wrinkle, the finely tanned skin tightening over his flat belly and then ending in a fringed edge that touched against the muscles of his powerful thighs. The breeches took him more time, but finally they

were secured on the slim hips, fitting loosely over his legs.
The laces made the moccasins impossible, he knew, and so
he left them in the bottom of the chest.

He stepped back to the bed, almost hidden in the shadows. Only moonlight illuminated the chamber now. Using
the tip of the finger that protruded farthest from the bandage, he touched the curve of Catherine's hip. She didn't
stir, and not knowing what threat he might face downstairs, Raven didn't wake her. He stood a moment in the
darkness, looking down on her, barely able to see her in the
dimness of the bedroom, remembering. And then he disappeared into the blackness of the hallway.

He glided like fog, ghostlike, across the grounds of the
London town house, blending into the darkened contours
of broken light and patterned shade. Hidden by the shift-
ing moonlight and the drifting shadows cast by floating
clouds. Noiseless and patient, Raven examined the mansion's environs, using eyes that had been trained from
childhood to make use of whatever light the night allowed.
And he found nothing. No threat to the woman who slept
above.

Some instinct guided him to the expanse of glass that
backed the main salon. His senses still screaming alarm, he
reentered the house through one of those tall Palladian
windows. He knew his entry had been noiseless, but the man
seated in one of the chairs Catherine had chosen to compliment the soaring dimensions of the room seemed remarkably unsurprised by his presence. There was no betraying
start of the graceful hand.

His Grace, the Duke of Montfort, allowed his glass to
complete the journey it had begun to his thin lips. He
sipped, and then savored the excellence of his son-in-law's
brandy.

"Come in," he invited softly.

"Since it *is* my home," Raven agreed, stepping down
from the low sill onto the gleaming oak of the floor.

"Would you care for a warming draught against the
night's chill?" Montfort asked, lifting his own glass in in-

vitation. The crystal caught a moonbeam and flickered briefly in the dimness.

"Thank you, no," he replied, his tone as polite as the duke's.

With his long, graceful stride Raven moved halfway across the salon, to where he could see the old man clearly. He was dressed in full evening dress, its elegance and cut in keeping with the current mode. The size of the diamond in his cravat and the scattered fobs, however, proclaimed that the duke belonged to a generation whose tastes had formed before Brummel's strictures had forbidden such evidence of wealth.

"You wanted to see me," Raven suggested, waiting. The next move was Montfort's, and apparently he had come here to make it.

"Not particularly," the old man answered, smiling.

"Then why are you here?"

"Unfinished business?" Montfort mocked, one brow arching.

"No hirelings?" Raven asked, his tone as sardonic.

"I didn't think I'd need them. Not to eliminate vermin."

Raven's lips involuntarily tightened at the insult, but he controlled any other reaction. It was no shock that Montfort hated him, the old man had been open about that from the beginning. The only surprising thing was that the duke himself was here tonight. But, Raven acknowledged with some satisfaction, his hirelings had proved less than dependable, so apparently the old bastard had decided to take things into his own elegant hands.

At that thought, Raven's eyes found the frail white fingers and found them once again gently caressing the object they held. Not, this time, the gold lorgnette. A pistol appeared fleetingly under the restless movement of the duke's exquisitely jeweled hands. Raven's gaze lifted to meet the dark, unfathomable gleam of Montfort's eyes.

"Because I'm not good enough for your daughter?" he asked.

"No one ever was. All they wanted was the money, like the bastard who tricked her before. Making her think he loved her, and that I'd accept the match. Fortune hunters. Bloodsuckers.''

''So you tried to kill him. When you caught them.''

''Catherine told you the story?'' The duke sounded surprised.

''No,'' Raven admitted. ''It was my lord Amberton who shared that particular...gossip.'' He remembered the viscount's suggested ending to the escapade, an ending that he knew now, without any shadow of doubt, had been a lie.

''What did he tell you about my daughter?'' Montfort asked. His tone had changed subtly, the mockery erased.

''Whatever he...suggested, I promise you he paid for.''

''Is that why you broke his arm?''

''Yes,'' Raven said, his lips lifting in remembrance of how satisfying that encounter had been, despite its cost.

''Not because he stabbed you, then.''

The blue eyes refocused on the duke's face. ''How did you know that?'' Raven asked.

''I've made it my business to know all about you, Mr. Raven. I thought I had a vested interest in acquiring that knowledge.''

''Because of Catherine.''

''Yes.''

''And then you decided to get rid of me.''

The old man didn't speak for a moment, the movement of his hands on the pistol again drawing Raven's attention.

''To free Catherine and allow her to marry someone more suitable,'' Raven continued.

''That was my original intent,'' Montfort agreed.

''Rather ineptly handled. I'm surprised at you, your grace. That's not your reputation.''

''It's so difficult to get good help these days,'' the old man murmured, smiling slightly.

''And if Catherine doesn't want another husband?'' Raven asked, moving closer to the chair where his father-in-law sat.

''I've always believed I know more about what Catherine requires for happiness than she. She's innocent of the evil that walks the world, still inclined to romance rather than reality."

"Making her a widow is your idea of an introduction to reality?" Raven asked mockingly, as he took another step closer to the chair. "Have you asked your daughter what she wants?"

"I believe I know."

"Amberton," Raven suggested.

"Amberton made himself very agreeable, always a willing and acceptable escort for Catherine. A friend and companion to me."

"But there's one problem. She's not in love with Amberton."

"In our society being 'in love' is not generally considered a requirement for a successful marriage."

"A marriage of convenience," Raven suggested, smiling. Just as he had promised Catherine. When all along his intentions had been quite different.

"As was yours. At least, in the beginning," the duke said.

Raven was beginning to register the surprising fact that the Duke of Montfort possessed that information about his daughter's marriage, and then he watched as the pistol in the frail white hand began to track upward toward his body. He was not close enough to rush Montfort before he could fire, not close enough to dislodge the weapon with a kick. He could see the muzzle, a dark eye, move unerringly toward his heart.

"*Now,* Mr. Raven," the duke ordered.

Reacting to that command, a threat that was also a warning, Raven dived sideways, throwing his body in a controlled roll across the salon, even as the echoing report shattered the quiet.

The movement that brought Raven to a crouching stance, hidden in the most deeply shadowed corner of the room, was simply a continuation of that which had taken him out of the path of the duke's bullet. Adrenaline pouring into his bloodstream, his big body poised for whatever threat the duke would offer now, Raven waited, the blue gaze fastened on the small, satisfied smile that touched the thin lips of Catherine's father. The light caught the enormous ruby the duke wore on his right hand as he laid the smoking gun on the small table beside his chair.

"It's very gratifying to find that one hasn't lost all one's skills to age," Monfort said musingly, his hand now caressing the smooth translucence of the glass that held his brandy. The ball that had shattered the filial of the chair in which the old man sat had come within an inch of his head. There were small splinters of dark wood caught in the shining white hair.

Taking a deep breath, Raven's gaze followed the duke's across the wide expanse of the room to the same window through which he had entered earlier. The sprawled body of the Viscount Amberton rested half inside and half out. The fingers of his outstretched arm were locked around the dueling pistol that lay on the edge of the oriental rug. Even in the shadowed dimness, the gleam of blond hair was unmistakable in the moonlight which spilled from the sweep of glass behind the body. It touched also the still-open, rapidly glazing eyes of the English aristocrat.

"Amberton," Raven whispered.

"Of course," the duke confirmed. "He had far more reason to want you dead than I. I'm surprised you failed to realize that."

"Because I broke his arm?" Raven questioned, his eyes coming back to Montfort's reactive smile.

"Because you took from him everything he had worked so hard to acquire. Catherine. Her trust fund. And eventually, of course he believed, the control of my wealth at my death. When you married Catherine, all of that disappeared from his reach. He had spent years insuring that those things would be his. I always did think he was a trifle toadying. However, one becomes too accustomed to that. Until I met you, I'd almost forgotten what it was like to encounter someone unintimidated by my money and position. It was rather refreshing," the duke admitted.

"Refreshing," Raven repeated, finally remembering to breathe. Amberton and not the old man. And he realized the echo he had heard when the duke fired had not been an echo

at all. It had been the viscount's shot, aimed at his own un-
protected back.

"Damned coward," Montfort said, his gaze again on the
dead aristocrat he had once chosen as his son-in-law. "I
knew when Catherine told me he'd stabbed an unarmed man
that he would never do. And then when Reynolds explained the financial situation—"

"The rail project?" Raven asked, trying to follow.

"Amberton's situation," the duke said impatiently. "He
was dead broke. Had been living on his mortgages for years.
And then when we signed the marriage agreements, he'd
taken out an additional, rather substantial loan from the
moneylenders, secured solely by my signature on those
documents. Only—"

"The marriage never occurred because Catherine
eloped."

"And Amberton was left with no prospects and too many
wasted years. Apparently, the situation embittered him
enough that he became...unbalanced, which led to his repeated attempts to kill you. He thought that if he got rid of
you, things would return to the way they had been before.
The way they *should* be. He would become my son-in-law."

"And Catherine's husband," Raven said, thinking of that
bastard's hands and mouth again profaning his wife's body.
He blocked the image from his mind with the greatest effort of will, wondering what would have happened had he
not escaped from the shaft.

He suddenly remembered the man who had greeted him
in his own garden on his return. Montfort's henchman.

"Then why did I find your hireling on my grounds?" he
asked.

"I told you if you couldn't protect my daughter, I
would."

"He was here to guard Catherine?"

"Of course. I employ a large number of people, and I use
them however I see fit. To guard this house. To spy on Amberton. That's how I knew what he intended tonight. I pay
quite well for information. Amberton would have liked to
hire another assassin, but unfortunately he was out of

funds. His creditors were closing in, the threat of Newgate very real, and there was nothing he could do. Except, perhaps, take revenge on the man who was responsible.''

''I thought you were the one hiring assassins,'' Raven said.

''Why should I want you dead, Mr. Raven? I believe that Catherine...'' The duke hesitated, always hating to admit an error. ''I think Catherine has grown to like you,'' he finished finally, but he had the grace to blush at Raven's laugh.

''I believe you might be right, your grace.''

''And your marriage is no longer a business arrangement.''

''Catherine said you wanted to arrange a divorce.''

''That was before she told me what she felt. My first consideration has always been Catherine's happiness.''

''I'll take care of her,'' Raven promised. ''I always—''

''Keep your contracts,'' the old man finished for him. ''So I've been told. And since I believe Catherine is waiting upstairs...'' He smiled.

''What about Amberton?'' Raven asked, his eyes moving back to the man who had tried on at least three occasions to kill him. As he had come here tonight to do. Raven could feel no regret for Amberton's death, but there would be the necessary cleaning up, explanations to the authorities as to why the viscount's body had been found in his home and who had fired the fatal shot.

''A wedding present?'' the old man suggested. ''I owe you one, I believe. I think I have enough influence to handle the explanations. And if not, I certainly have enough money.''

Hard blue eyes met the fathomless dark ones. Their gazes held, and slowly the blue ones softened and the stern line of Raven's lips relaxed enough to move into a controlled smile.

''Thank you,'' he said, and watched the graceful incline of the erect white head. ''And now, if you'll excuse me...''

''Of course. Pressing business, I suppose...which will be less pressing shortly, I imagine.'' The duke's lips twitched quickly and then were still. He lifted his lorgnette to survey the figure of the man who stood, relaxed and unintimidated as always, before him. Montfort's gaze drifted over the supple skins that had been used to fashion the long tunic Raven wore over the matching leggings.

"Remind me, Raven," he said, "*not* to ask your tailor's name, a gentleman whose acquaintance I prefer not to make."

Raven laughed suddenly, the straight white teeth a surprise in the bronze face. "Do you know, your grace," he said, still smiling, "I believe you're mistaken. I think you would enjoy meeting my... tailor. You and she are, I think, two of a kind."

The duke's head tilted slightly, questioning the comment. But Raven had already turned, his long strides carrying him swiftly away from the old man's presence. He crossed the salon, and when he had left the room where his father-in-law continued to sip his brandy, he began to move with greater speed.

By the time he reached the grand, curving staircase, he bounded upward, taking the stairs two at a time, his mind no longer occupied by images of the stiffening body or even by the old brigand he'd found sitting at ease in his salon, but on the woman that he'd left sleeping above when he'd dressed and set out on his mission tonight. Only on Catherine.

She was lying as he had left her, in the center of the vast bed. The width of mattress that stretched on either side of her slightly curled figure emphasized her smallness.

His throat closed with emotion as he stood looking down on her. He had wanted her from the first time he had seen her in the noisy London street. And he wanted her still. He could feel desire for her welcoming embrace move painfully through his groin. He would never tire of touching her. Of holding her, possessing her and being possessed by her.

And eventually there would be far more: the intimacy of the mind, shared stories, laughing remembrances of growing up. Separated in experience by the vast differences between the worlds into which each had been born, they would begin to bridge the gulf between them by talking, by sharing memories. Lying in this bed, night after night, they would begin again to find the ease of companionship of those long-ago private dinners, which he had been surprised to discover Catherine seemed to relish as much as he. Those quiet meals had provided the hope he had lived on during those empty months. And now here, again, they could talk—long conversations interrupted by lovemaking, unhurried and relaxed. Or shatteringly urgent.

My wife, he thought, with the same amazement that had sometimes possessed him as he looked across the dinner table lined with high-ranking guests and watched her insure the success of the evening for everyone present without seeming to exert herself in the slightest. He remembered the innocence she had revealed about her own body and about the mysteries of his, mysteries that she was rapidly unraveling. Child and woman. Assured and then so charmingly uncertain. Sweetly and seriously questioning. She hadn't minded his delighted laughter last night when a query caught him off guard. She had laughed with him, pounding a small, ineffectual fist against his chest. Until, laughing, he'd pulled her to him, carrying her down into the softness of the mattress to hold her captive beneath his body.

Raven struggled awkwardly out of the tunic. Its fall to the floor was followed eventually by the trousers, until finally he stood nude once again, looking down on the small sleeper. He placed one bandaged hand gently over the smoothness of her upper leg, against the pale perfection of her body.

At his touch she moved, turning so that she could look up at him sleepily. She put her warm, soft hand over his forearm, avoiding the bandage. Remembering and caring.

"You're so cold," she said. "Come back to bed." But her eyes closed again even as she made the suggestion.

Raven lay down beside her, his hand still resting on her thigh. She eased her body back into his.

"Did you have to get up?" she questioned.

He didn't answer, and because it was such a pointless question, she let it go, cuddling into the hard strength behind her, preparing to return to sleep.

But the bandaged hand began to move upward, drifting over her hip bone. Her eyes opened in the darkness, and she waited. The abrasive cloth that swathed his palm brushed slowly over the small mound of her belly and then slipped lower, his bare fingertips edging nearer the hidden area between her legs. Unthinkingly she parted her thighs, her bones suddenly molten at the simple promise of Raven's touch. She eased onto her back so she could look at him. He was propped on his left elbow, his chest elevated above her, his damaged hand still making its slow and inexorable journey. She closed her eyes suddenly, her breath released in a soft gasp as he stopped that movement and began another. As he touched her with one finger, his hard mouth lowered to her throat. Her hands found either side of his head, tangling in the long dark hair, holding his mouth captive against her body. His lips moved against the tip of her breast. Almost with that same motion, he suckled, pulling strongly, and her hips arched into the compelling movement of his finger.

"Raven," she said, her own fingers tightening in his hair. He bit gently and then withdrew slightly. His tongue circled the pearled nipple, and then he suckled again. Harder. Already her breathing was heavy, her lungs gasping, seeking enough air. His mouth deserted her breast and found her lips. He thrust his tongue against hers, blocking the small moaning noises she hadn't even been aware she was making. She had forgotten to think why his skin was so cold, moving over the warmth of hers. She didn't wonder anymore where he had been. She couldn't think of anything but the demands he was making on her body. He could make her mindless in seconds. If he were not Raven, she would be frightened by how easily he could control her responses. Frightened by what he could make her feel.

His mouth left hers and returned to her breast, pulling and teasing. Wet and hot and hard. His tongue against her body. Demanding. Giving what she wanted. And what she knew he wanted.

He stirred in the darkness, his mouth again removed from the aching contact with her breast. She wanted him there, and she wondered why he was deserting her. And then, with his shift over her, she knew. His face was against her hair.

She could hear his harsh breathing beside her ear, and he was no longer touching her. Instead she felt him slip into the wanting moisture he had coaxed from her. At the heavy sensation of his body filling hers, she moaned again.

He held his weight off her slenderness with his elbows. She could feel the movement of his knees against her legs and the shattering entry and retreat of his body, into and then almost out of hers. To the edge of no return. Slowly retreating, and then the sure, hard invasion. Rocking her. The hammering intensity of the sensations surging upward through her body. Wave after wave of force, building in a power that she could not deny, even had she wanted to. And then she exploded, her body arching under his, almost faint with what she felt.

This was not, of course, the first time he had carried her here. But before, he had stopped, easing the pressure and letting her rest with the ebbing tide of sensation. Now he continued, allowing no rest, no luxury of release while he had waited, patient with her pleasure, waiting for her to rejoin him in fulfilling his own need. This time the demand was relentless, and she felt the sensations begin again. Her fingers tightened into his back, nails biting as the surging peak built yet again. So quickly this time. Her body bucked under the power of his, but she was too small to force him to stop. And when the sensations began to grow again in the center of her body, she knew she didn't want him to stop. She thought she might really lose consciousness she was so lost in sheer physical response.

When the explosion of release came this time, she cried out, lifting again and again at the relentless, inexorable demand his body was making. She heard the echo of her own wordless ecstasy somewhere inside her mind, but she was unaware enough of its reality to be surprised when Raven's voice whispered, "Shh, my darling. Your father will hear."

She couldn't imagine why Raven thought her father would hear her. Or why he cared. Or thought she would. To make him stop talking to her and concentrate on what her body wanted, she bit into the damp skin of the broad shoulder that was against her mouth. Bit hard. And was re-

warded by the pulsing thrust of Raven's body into hers.
Deep, so deep. And again.

She cupped her palms over the hard muscles of the driving buttocks, feeling them contract with each movement.
Her nails dug, urging him inside, pulling him to her. Wanting him. She felt the shuddering explosion everywhere. Inside her. Under her hands. His body slamming downward into her stomach. Bone beating into bone. Hard and exciting. She heard the harsh, guttural shout of his release, and thought fleetingly of what he had said about her father. And then finding, in the midst of his spiraling emotion, her own release, she thought about nothing at all. Not for a long time.

Again they lay entwined, exhausted. Drained. They were learning each other. How to trigger the most intense passions, the deepest responses. If there were no longer mysteries, there were still surprises, as this had been. Not in the fulfillment, but in the degree. In the profoundness.

They were still joined. Raven had rolled over, pulling her on top of his still-heaving body as soon as he could think about some reasoned movement. Protecting her from his size. Careful of her comfort even at the height of his surrender.

"Cold," she whispered, her lips moving against the dampness of his skin.

He held her shivering slimness against his heat. He was so warm now. He felt so good against her trembling body. So strong and secure, keeping her safe. Her lips lifted at the thought of any threat defying Raven's strength. When she was a child, her father had protected her. And now Raven did. She wondered idly if there were any other woman in London as fortunate as she. He had promised her freedom, so long ago. And he had kept that promise. But she knew now that what she had believed to be freedom was so incomplete. Now she was complete. Free to belong to Raven. Free to confess that belonging.

"I love you," she whispered.

He said nothing. Only his lips moved to answer that acknowledgment of his power over her. Power he never used to control her. For, of course, she could exercise a like control over him. Bondage.

For a man born to a freedom few in this confined society could understand, a freedom of open vistas, unpeopled and unexplored, Raven had recognized long before she had the intimate bonds of marriage. Had recognized them and still had sought them. And would never regret giving himself into her hands.

Turning into his body, she moved to guide him, offering help. He relished the feel of small fingers willingly handling his body in the most intimate of ways. He whispered something then, phrases strangely sibilant, their softness lost as his mouth brushed across her temple to find her eyelid.

"What did you say?" she asked, her hands still moving against him.

"A vow," he whispered in English. "The marriage vow."

"I think you're a little late for wedding vows," she said, laughing. "I believe we took care of that legality in Scotland."

"There are legalities," he said, his lips over hers, "and then there are marriages."

"I don't understand."

"*Marriages* are forever, vows or no vows. Didn't you know?"

"I do now," she agreed, lifting to match his movements.

"I love you, Catherine Montfort MacLeod Raven," he whispered.

Smiling, she once more gave herself willingly into the sweet bondage of Raven's love.

Epilogue

One year later

The scarred fingers suddenly unclenched their grip on the crystal tumbler. Finally, from the floor above, the soft wail of a newborn had drifted down. Raven closed his eyes in a quick prayer of thanksgiving, and then realized that the birth of the child did not guarantee the safety of the mother, which was for him, of course, the more important consideration.

"Congratulations," the Duke of Montfort said, raising his glass in salute. "It seems that Catherine has finally made you a father."

"I have to know she's all right," Raven said, putting the brandy down and standing. Surely now he would be allowed into the sanctum of the bedroom. He had been banished, first by Stevenson, when the fashionable London practitioner had given them no hope of the safe delivery of the too-large infant or the survival of the slender mother who struggled so valiantly to give birth, and then by the stern but loving command of the old woman he had at last gone to for help.

His grandmother's unexpected arrival at the door of the Mayfair mansion a week ago had been a shock. Although Raven had urged his family in America to join him in London, now that he knew this would be his home, he had never dreamed that the matriarch of that beloved clan would be the one to undertake the hazards of the incredibly long journey.

Catherine, uncomfortably in the last stages of her pregnancy, had made a charming effort to be the welcoming hostess, but the old woman's unfathomable black eyes had simply watched her, studying her every move. As if she were evaluating her suitability to be Raven's wife, a worried Catherine had confessed privately to her husband.

As Raven bounded up the stairs, he met his grandmother halfway down, the child held securely in her arms.

"You have a son, my Raven. A strong and beautiful son." She pulled back the swaddling to reveal the baby, the tiny head covered with the same black hair as his father. After glancing at the small, perfect face of his son, Raven's eyes came back to his grandmother's.

"Catherine?" he asked.

The wrinkled features softened, the dark eyes smiling into the sapphire blue. "I delivered *you,* John Raven, and you were bigger even than this one. I would not let anything happen to your Catherine."

Raven took a deep breath, the first real breath, it seemed, in the long hours he had been waiting. He knew that the old woman would never have given him that assurance unless it was true. The long, still-elegant fingers of Raven's scarred hand reached out to caress the head of the babe. He dropped a kiss on the child's forehead, and then his gaze moved to the top of the stairs.

"Go," his grandmother said. "She has been asking for you."

"Thank you," Raven whispered, and they both knew that it was not gratitude for that permission. It was acknowledgment that she had again been the one who had protected John Raven and those who belonged to him.

"You chose well, my Raven," she said. "A woman worthy of what you are. Worthy to bear your children."

"I think, perhaps, I had some . . . help," he suggested.

The old woman's thin lips moved, the enigmatic smile very much like Raven's own. "A small intervention," she agreed. "For your own good, of course."

"Would you do one other thing for me?" Raven asked. "Catherine's father is downstairs. Would you show him the baby?"

The dark eyes held his for a moment, again evaluating. "I will show this English lord what fine sons the Raven clan makes," she said. "And you will go and hold the brave girl who waits for you."

The room was shadowed. The draperies had been drawn to allow Catherine to sleep, but the russet eyes opened as soon as he knelt beside the bed.

"Have you seen him?" Catherine asked, her voice hoarse with exhaustion.

"He's perfect," Raven said. He bent to touch his lips against the sweat-dampened curls at her temple. "Although I had hoped he might have the wisdom to take after his mother..."

"Perfect," she whispered, denying the idea that anyone could be disappointed in a child so much like her beautiful Raven.

"I hope your father will think so. I asked my grandmother to take the baby down. I thought it was time they met."

She wondered what her father would make of the old woman, and then, her lips tilting, she thought about how much she would have liked to see that particular meeting.

"She was so kind to me, Raven. I was afraid that she'd be disappointed you'd married me, but... I don't think that's true. It was like having my own mother here. And unlike Dr. Stevenson, she didn't make me afraid. Suddenly, I knew that I could trust her to see to it that everything would be all right."

"You don't have to worry about her approval. After all, Catherine, she chose you," he said.

The question was in her eyes, but despite her desire to understand, her mind had begun to drift. Everything was

perfect. The baby. And Raven was here. She'd ask him what
he meant when she woke up, when she wasn't so tired.

The Duke of Montfort lifted the gold lorgnette to survey
from head to foot the strange figure which had entered the
formal salon where he and his son-in-law had awaited
Catherine's delivery. Despite the woman's obvious age, her
braided hair was as long and as dark as Raven's. The eyes
were different, of course, almost black in the seamed face,
but as unintimidated, despite his deliberate attempt to in-
timidate, as his son-in-law's.

"This is your grandson," she said, holding out the baby
for his inspection. "Born of the clans Raven and Mac-
Leod."

One of the duke's white brows arched, and then he said
simply, employing a tone reserved for those whose conduct
approached familiarity, "Indeed."

The calm black eyes met his, and she moved across the
room to stand before him. Because she had known that the
girl would need her help, she had this morning donned the
white ceremonial dress, made of the finest doeskin and
decorated with beading that had required hours of careful
work, so that she might be properly attired for the important events of this day. And she was too old and far too wise
to be impressed by this Englishman's title or his posturing.

Finally the duke glanced down at the child. Despite his
intent to allow nothing of his emotions to be revealed, he
touched the small fingers very gently with the tip of the glass
he held.

"You may hold him," the old woman offered.

Montfort raised his gaze to her, desire to do just that
warring with his arrogant pride.

"He will be the comfort of your old age," she said very
softly, looking into his eyes. "The son you never had. And
like his father, he will be a builder. The new has come home
to the old. New blood—rich and powerful—to blend forever with the strength of yours."

The soft syllables had slipped into a smooth singsong, almost mesmerizing Montfort with the force of their conviction, and their power held him speechless for a moment.

"Indeed," he said finally, fighting to keep the customary sarcasm in place, despite the emotional pull of that promise.

A small enigmatic movement of the thin lips was the only answer she made, still holding the child out between them.

The duke gestured her dismissal with a quick upward movement of the lorgnette. She still watched him a moment, and then she inclined her head with all the dignity of her own royal line. She turned, carrying the babe she intended to instruct as she had instructed his father. This man could choose, as he wished or no, to be part of that circle. When she reached the door, the duke's voice stopped her.

"And the clan Montfort," he offered. A challenge which they both recognized.

She turned back and looked at the English aristocrat whose blood also flowed in this baby's veins. "Raven and MacLeod," she said again, and then she added. "*And* the clan Montfort."

The old man smiled and, picking up his glass from the table, raised it in silent salute to the mingled heritage of the child she held. And to the future.

* * * * *

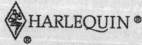

Bestselling

author

Ruth Langan

presents
Book III of her exciting Jewels of Texas series

JADE

When the town preacher meets the town madam,
the little town of Hanging Tree, Texas, will
never be the same

The Jewels of Texas—four sisters as wild and vibrant as
the untamed land they're fighting to protect.

DIAMOND February 1996	PEARL August 1996
JADE February 1997	RUBY October 1997

Heartbreak RANCH

Four generations of independent women...
Four heartwarming, romantic stories of the West...
Four incredible authors...

Fern Michaels
Jill Marie Landis
Dorsey Kelley
Chelley Kitzmiller

Saddle up with Heartbreak Ranch, an outstanding
Western collection that will take you on a whirlwind
trip through four generations and the exciting,
romantic adventures of four strong women who
have inherited the ranch from Bella Duprey,
famed Barbary Coast madam.

Available in March,
wherever Harlequin books are sold.

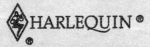

HARLEQUIN ®

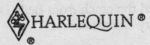

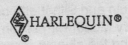

Not The Same Old Story!

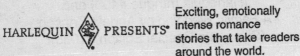 Exciting, emotionally
intense romance
stories that take readers
around the world.

 Vibrant stories of
captivating women
and irresistible men
experiencing the magic
of falling in love!

 Bold and adventurous—
Temptation is strong women,
bad boys, great sex!

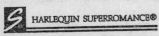 Provocative, passionate,
contemporary stories that
celebrate life and love.

 Romantic adventure
where anything is
possible and where
dreams come true.

 Heart-stopping, suspenseful
adventures that combine the
best of romance and mystery.

LOVE & LAUGHTER™ Entertaining and fun, humorous
and romantic—stories that
capture the lighter side of love.